W. Russell

Eccentric Personages

memoirs of the lives and actions of remarable characters

W. Russell

Eccentric Personages
memoirs of the lives and actions of remarable characters

ISBN/EAN: 9783337091408

Printed in Europe, USA, Canada, Australia, Japan

Cover: Foto ©Andreas Hilbeck / pixelio.de

More available books at **www.hansebooks.com**

ECCENTRIC PERSONAGES

MEMOIRS OF THE LIVES AND ACTIONS OF REMARKABLE CHARACTERS

Including

BEAU BRUMMELL, BEAU NASH, DANIEL DEFOE, DEAN SWIFT, CAPTAIN MORRIS, J. M. W. TURNER, CHEVALIER D'EON, ETC., ETC.

W. RUSSELL, LL.D.

LONDON

EDWARD AVERY

GREEK STREET, SOHO

CONTENTS.

ECCENTRIC PERSONAGES.

MONSIEUR LE DOCTEUR DEVINE.

In the street of Saint Jacques, Havre de Grâce, Normandy, and nearly opposite the fine church of Notre Dame, dwelt Antoine Tricard, a boot-and-shoemaker in a respectable way of business. He had been twice married; his second wife, " une belle Allemande"—German women of the middle class are rarely beautiful, by the way—had a son by a previous marriage—Eugène Devine. This union took place in 1742, Eugène being then about five years old; a precocious boy, singularly so, he is reported to have been. Remarkably impressionable too; any striking circumstance was indelibly photographed upon his sensitive mind. He was an artist of promise, and might possibly, had not an accident led him to embrace the medical profession, have become an eminent painter. When about twenty years of age, Madame d'Estrées was condemned to be executed at Rouen for the murder of her husband. M. Tricard went with the young Devine to witness the terrible spectacle. Madame d'Estrées was a young woman of rare beauty, who had married a rich man thrice her own age, under parental compulsion—the family Marin, her maiden name, being at the time, if not absolutely poor, in pressing difficulties. M. Marin was a grocer at Havre de Grâce. The Tricards visited at the grocer's, and Eugène Devine appears to have early conceived a boyish passion for the beautiful girl, who was about two years older than he,

B

knowing at the same time she was attached and affianced to Edouard Cazo, the son of a herbalist established in the Rue de Paris. The wealth of Monsieur d'Estrées, a farmer-general of king's taxes, was too potent an influence to be resisted by the grievously-embarrassed M. Marin; and at his stern command Joséphine Marin was sacrificed in marriage to the rich merchant. In less than two months afterwards, M. d'Estrées was seized with sudden and fatal illness immediately after taking his breakfast; M. Portalis, an eminent physician of Rouen, near which city M. d'Estrées resided, was quickly in attendance, but medical aid was useless. The farmer-general had been poisoned, and was dying in great agony. He could only ejaculate with much difficulty, and a word or syllable at a time, in answer to M. Portalis, "*Ma femme—ma femme m'a empoisonné—le café—le café.*" (My wife—my wife has poisoned me—the coffee—the coffee) —and died with the last word upon his lips. The wife, who passionately protested her innocence, was immediately arrested and taken to prison. A long inquiry into all the circumstances of the case ensued. The main facts established were, that a subtle tasteless poison had been mixed with the coffee of which M. d'Estrées had partaken—Madame d'Estrées, as was her custom, had previously breakfasted—the coffee was prepared in the kitchen, but of course Madame d'Estrées, who was in the breakfast-room where it was served two or three minutes before her husband came down-stairs, and left it immediately he did, which she was also proved to be in the habit of doing, had full opportunity of mixing the poison with the coffee. It was also proved that Edouard Cazo had been seen prowling about near M. d'Estrées' residence for several days previous to that on which M. d'Estrées was murdered. No one had, however, seen him and Madame d'Estrées together. The only person in the farmer-general's establishment who had been seen with him, and that more than once, was Fanchette Le Blanc, a personal attendant of Madame d'Estrées, whom she had brought with her from Havre de Grâce. Fanchette Le

Blanc was a fine-looking, fine-eyed girl, the daughter of
a Havre tradesman, who not long before had been reduced in circumstances. Before that, her family had
visited upon equal terms those of MM. Marin and Cazo.
It also came out that Fanchette Le Blanc and Edouard
Cazo had been intimate in a lover sense with each other.
It was Fanchette Le Blanc who carried up M. d'Estrées'
breakfast. These circumstances were not, however, supposed at the time to have any significance with regard
to the guilt or innocence of Madame d'Estrées, except
by one person—Eugène Devine. The young man had
chanced to save the life of Monsieur Courtrai, a surgeon
in excellent practice at Havre de Grâce. Devine had
been to Harfleur upon some business for his stepfather,
Monsieur Tricard. M. Courtrai was there, in compliance with a pressing message from the Prince de la Tour
d'Auvergne, an ancestor, I suppose, of the present French
ambassador at the English court, who in passing through
Harfleur had met with an accident, and having no confidence in the medical skill of the place, sent for M.
Courtrai. His difficult professional duty successfully
performed, for which service the Prince felt very grateful, M. Courtrai, extremely anxious to get back to Havre,
and no decked vessel being for the moment procurable,
and it being fine summer weather, embarked in a large
open boat, which was laden with fowls and other provisions for the Havre market. Devine also took passage
in the boat. Suddenly, when they were about half way
from Harfleur to Havre, a white squall arose. A "white
squall" is a furious wind which gives no token of its approach by dark gathering clouds, and the coming on of
which can only be discerned by watchful, experienced
mariners. It is usually brief as violent. The white
squall struck the sails of the boat or barge with such
force that it instantly capsised; and the crew, four men,
M. Courtrai, and Eugène Devine were of course precipi-
tated into the boiling sea. The crew disappeared at
once, and were not seen again. Devine swam like a
cork, and was a powerfully-framed young man, though

less than sixteen years old. M. Courtrai had been a tolerable swimmer in his youth, but the weight of seventy years pressed him down, and he was sinking when the youth Devine struck out to his assistance, attracted by the surgeon's cry of mortal agony. He was just in time to clutch the collar of the drowning man's coat. The barge, which, as I have said, had turned over, had already drifted, driven by the fierce wind and strong current, to a considerable distance. By dint of great exertion, however, he contrived to reach it and drag himself and M. Courtrai on to its upturned bottom. Fortunately, the squall was a very brief one : the rapid tide of the channel quickly runs down the heaviest sea when the wind has abated, and there was soon no danger of being washed off the boat, incapable as M. Courtrai was of holding on by his own efforts. After about two hours of anxiety and exposure they were rescued by a fishing-smack, and conveyed in safety to Havre de Grâce.

M. Courtrai felt grateful for the service rendered him by Eugène Devine, and finding moreover that the young man was possessed of singular intelligence, he sent him to the Ecole de Médecine, Paris, where he made such rapid progress as to call forth the highest encomiums of the professors, who predicted for him a brilliant future.

That dazzling prospect was suddenly overcast. A letter from M. Tricard told of the death of M. d'Estrées, the frightful accusation brought against his widow, her arrest, and the generally-entertained opinion that she would be capitally convicted.

The studies pursued by Eugène Devine with so much ardour and success immediately lost all their charm. " I could think," he said, in his minute diary, " only of Joséphine Marin. If I read, her image gleamed from the page; and so morbidly excited did my brain become, that I sat for hours absorbed, horrified by a mentally-pictured panorama, in which all the incidents of the terrible affair, past and in all probability to come, passed before me,—the death of D'Estrées—the declaration of the dying man—rash, unfounded, I had not the slightest doubt. Did I not know Joséphine?—the guileless candour of her nature—the spotless purity of her life? But rash, unfounded, that declaration would not, I felt, be the less fatal to Joséphine. The gloomy mental procession moved on. I saw Joséphine in her dark prison-cell, bowed down, sobbing with agony—her face white as stone, and yet palely lustrous with the light of a conscious innocence. Then passed before me the trial—the scowling audience; I heard the judges pronounce sentence—sentence of death; and at the last dreadful scene of all pictured to my excited imagination, I several times lost my senses—fainted!

"Could I—even I—poor, uninfluential as I was, do nothing for that beautiful unfortunate? I was conscious of possessing an analysing, critical intellect. Might I not, by diligent inquiry on the spot, discover some clue to the real murderer, who I was sure, positive as of my own life, was *not* Madame d'Estrées? It was quite useless to affect attention to study. My thoughts were far away. I was a favourite with the principal of the college, Dr. Cabanis. I may almost venture to say that, notwithstanding the great disparity of years, I was his friend. I spoke with him about Madame d'Estrées, or by the name my heart knew her—Joséphine Marin. He was the father of *the* Cabanis, friend of Turgot, Mirabeau, and Condorcet, but a man very different from his distinguished son. He had sympathy with sentimentalism, with human weakness; he heard me with patient kindness, but his logical mind remained, I need hardly say, totally unaffected by my passionate assertions of Madame d'Estrées' innocence, grounded solely upon my estimate of her character before her compelled marriage with a man old enough to be her grandfather, and whom she did not affect to esteem, much less to love. The accusing words uttered by the poisoned man were, I could see, conclusive proof with him of the wife's guilt. Still, pity for me, and the possibility—the very faint possibility that by personal persistent investigation I might be able to elicit some fact or facts which might throw doubt upon the young wife's criminality, induced him to give me three months' leave of absence, and a letter of introduction to M. Portalis, the eminent physician who had attended the Sieur d'Estrées in his last moments. MM. Portalis and Cabanis had been fellow-pupils.

"Arrived at Rouen, I waited without delay upon M. Portalis. He could tell me nothing more than I had read in M. Tricard's letter. I inquired the nature of the poison which had been taken by M. d'Estrées. 'Ha!' said M. Portalis, 'that is the circumstance—the nature of the poison—which has caused me to doubt for a moment of the wife's criminality. It is that well known to the profession as *poudre de succession*. Its sale, its manufacture even, is prohibited under rigorous penalties, and I myself do not know where it could be procured. Like almost all poisons, it is said to be a potent remedy in certain cases.' 'I know—I know,' said I. 'Only in Paris *could* it be obtained, and there only of one—perhaps two persons—at a heavy price, and by some one in whom the vendor could repose implicit confidence. How should Madame d'Estrées, a young countrywoman, country girl, have any knowledge of such a deadly drug, much less know of whom to purchase it in Paris, if indeed she has ever been there?' 'The difficulty is obvious,' said M. Portalis; 'but Madame d'Estrées has been to Paris, and made a long stay there with her husband, who in those days supplied her with any amount of money she asked for. Her motive for getting rid of her husband is very clear. He was very jealous of his beautiful young wife—whether for good cause or not I cannot say; bitter quarrels took place, and M. d'Estrées, a man of iron will, told her in the hearing of several persons that he should completely change the disposition of his wealth—bequeath her only a bare subsistence, whereas he had formally executed, during the first week of the *lune de miel*, a notarial deed which would have entitled her at his death to every thing he might die possessed of. Had he told her, which is the fact,' added M. Portalis, 'that he *had* actually destroyed the first deed and executed another in the sense of his threat, *poudre de succession* would not have been mixed with the unfortunate fermier-général's café. She expected to be deprived of the 'succession;' and being unaware that she had been legally so deprived, resolved to be swift and deadly. She was swift and deadly.' 'Pardon, Monsieur Portalis; and I beg you to excuse the freedom with which so youug a man as I presume to address you. My conviction of Madame d'Estrées' innocence is as firm, as unalterable as yours is of her guilt.' 'Parbleu!' replied he, with a half-cynical smile; 'but there is this difference, my young friend, that your conviction has no other foundation than the illusions of boyish sentiment, whilst mine is based upon the inexorable logic of facts.' 'Presumed facts, permit me to observe, monsieur. And there is one point which occurs to me, which seems to deny completely the always improbable supposition that Madame d'Estrées purchased the *poudre de succession*, so called, in Paris. She was with her husband in Paris, you say, during the first part of the honeymoon, when he adored her, and had no mistrust of her. Was it at such a time, I would ask, that the newly-wedded wife would devise means, and face terrible risks to obtain them, for destroying the indulgent husband's life at some distant period—a life which in the course of nature could not long endure?' 'That is plausible, young man, very plausible. Error is often plausible—more frequently so, perhaps, than strict truth. The devil very soon effects a lodgment in the heart, and whispers his suggestions in the brain of a young, beautiful woman who is fettered by the marriage chain to an aged man whom she loathes. But this is vain talk, M. Devine. The fate of Madame d'Estrées will be decided by the Court of Criminal Justice, not guided by your conviction or mine. If, however, there is any real service I can render you in this sad affair, I will willingly do so.' I reflected a few moments, and said quickly, 'Yes, monsieur; I very, very much desire to see Madame d'Estrées. Could you obtain me an order to be admitted to a private interview with her in the prison?' Monsieur le Médecin paused. Such orders were difficult of obtainment. He, however, promised to speak to the magistrate who alone had power to grant such permission, and if I called the next day, he would tell me the result. I thanked M. Portalis, bowed, and withdrew.

"I was so restless, so perturbed, that, contenting myself with a glass of wine and a biscuit for dinner, I took my way to the deceased M. d'Estrées' domicile. I wished to speak with Mademoiselle Le Blanc, whom I had known in Havre de Grâce.

"As it happened, she was upon the point of leaving the house as I approached it. Our eyes met; she started; a visible terror shook her frame, and her face paled to the hue of marble. What might be the meaning of that? Fanchette Le Blanc re-entered the hall, and sank down half fainting upon a seat. 'How!' said I to Mademoiselle Le Blanc; 'does the sight of an old acquaintance alarm, terrify you?' 'No—no,' she said, recovering herself by a strong effort. 'What folly to suppose such a thing! Seeing you brought suddenly to mind the dreadful tragedy in which poor Madame d'Estrées is involved. Of course,' she added, with a glimmer in her glowing eyes, which I could but doubtfully interpret—'of course, I long since knew how much you adored—I mean, felt interested in her welfare.' 'You knew the truth, Mademoiselle Le Blanc. Who, indeed, would not feel a profound interest in so charming, so amiable, so pure and innocent a being, and now especially?' The glimmer in the fierce eyes brightened to a vivid flash, and her lip curled with a mocking expression, as she exclaimed, 'Innocent—innocent! Well, I hope so. But youthful lovers seldom see stains or defects in their idol.' 'That is not language, pardon me, mademoiselle, to address to Eugène Devine at such a time. Has M. Edouard Cazo,' I asked abruptly, 'seen Madame d'Estrées since her arrest—interested himself for her?' 'Oh, no!' was the reply, in as abrupt a tone as mine, whilst her eyes flamed, her cheeks flushed with what bore the expression of exultant scorn,—'oh, no—assuredly not!' 'Yet he was seen lurking about the place several days before the catastrophe occurred.' 'That is exact,' said Le Blanc, the hot colour in her cheeks fading again. 'He did not speak with Madame d'Estrées, I understand?' 'I did not see him speak with her.' 'He came and spoke with you, Mademoiselle Le Blanc?' '*Eh bien!*—yes. You are very inquisitive, M. Devine,' retorted the demoiselle, colouring again. 'Have you any serious question to ask me?' she added. 'If not, I must make you my adieu; I have business in Rouen.' 'I will not detain you, Mademoiselle Le Blanc. Stay one moment. Edouard Cazo's father is a skilful—a very skilful herbalist. Do you think it possible that he may know the secret of making the vegetable poison called *poudre de succession*, and have——' Before I could finish the sentence, Fanchette Le Blanc, who had risen, fell back into the seat, and fainted outright. There was a carafe of water on a table in the hall, and I soon restored her to consciousness. Another woman-servant appeared before I could again address her, and both entered the house together.

" ' This is all very dark,' I murmured to myself as I walked towards Rouen. 'I strongly suspect Fanchette Le Blanc and Edouard Cazo are the poisoners of M. d'Estrées.' Knowing or believing that the murdered gentleman had disposed of his wealth in favour of his wife, and imagining that he, Cazo, had the same hold of her affections as previous to her marriage, he might have prevailed upon Le Blanc, for a large promised reward, to administer the *poudre de succession;* Le Blanc having probably informed him that no time should be lost. The affair had no doubt been blundered. *Poudre de succession* should be administered in such small doses that the victim at first merely feels *malaise*, a sensation of uneasiness, and gradually sinks about the seventh, eighth, or ninth day, according to the strength of his stamina; whereas such an overdose had been given that D'Estrées died almost immediately, and in great agony. It might possibly have happened that during the entrance into, or approach of some one to, the room where the operation

was going on, all the terrible powder was tipped in at
once, in order that it should not be seen in her hauds.
This, of course, was mere conjecture, but the words and
manner of Le Blanc gave it a strong colour of likelihood.
Time proved that I had not quite hit upon the truth, but
very near to it. I determined, however, and wisely, to
give no hint of my suspicions, except to the Avocats
whom M. Courtrai and M. Tricard would enable me to
engage in defence of the accused. I already knew that
Madame d'Estrées was without means of paying Messieurs les Avocats.

"M. Portalis was successful. When I waited upon
him on the following day, he placed in my hand a written
order to the governor of Rouen jail, to see Madame d'Estrées, accused of the murder of her husband; the interview to be for half-an-hour, and private; and I was warned
that the application would not be again acceded to.

"A terrible interview! My imagination in the pano-
ramic vision I have described had not deceived me.
There she sat in the gloomy cell, bowed down with
agony—the shadow of an inexpressible despair on her
white, beautiful face, yet illumined or rather arrayed in
conscious innocence. Her father had been some months
dead; she was an orphan, and believed herself abandoned
by God and man. Unhappy Joséphine! She threw herself into my arms with a spasmodic, passionate cry of joy.
'Help me, Eugène! save—save me from the terrible doom
with which they threaten me! I am innocent, Eugène;
indeed, indeed I am!'

"A flood of fire—a hurricane of tears and flame swept
through me at that agitating moment. I thought I
should have fainted—to hold her in my arms, who had
been the angel of my boyhood—to hear her express a
fearful hope that I might save her, abandoned as she
was by the whole world—I, Eugène, which name, speaking to me, had never before passed her lips! It was the
supreme moment of my life! When we had sufficiently
calmed down, I questioned her tenderly as to all the circumstances connected with the accusation. She could

tell me nothing I did not know. She knew nothing, I found, of the peculiar nature of the poison. I needed no assurance of that. I pointedly mentioned the names of Edouard Cazo and Fanchette Le Blanc—that they had been seen together near M. d'Estrées' house. Joséphine glanced at me with sudden, eager scru''ny, as if my words gave form and colour to some thought, some vague surmise which had arisen in her mind. It was so. 'Eugène,' she said, again Eugène! speaking in a low shaking voice, 'I cannot help thinking that those two persons are guilty of the murder of M. d'Estrées!' Asking her the reasons of her belief that they were the culprits, she could give no other than that such was her impression. That Cazo, whom she as much disliked and despised, and for sufficient reasons, as she had once liked him, had sent her a a note requesting a meeting with her. This note was brought to her by Le Blanc. It was immediately torn in pieces before her face, and the girl was told that her master should be made acquainted with her unpardonable insolence in making herself the bearer of such a request to his wife. 'The girl's face darkened as I spoke, and her eyes flamed with rage. I at once gave her notice to quit, but was finally persuaded to promise not to inform M. d'Estrées, at least not for the present, of the criminal indiscretion she had been guilty of, if she did not repeat it.'

"The precious half-hour had terminated. I was compelled to quit the persecuted, unhappy Joséphine. She was not more unhappy than myself.

"I called once more on M. Portalis to assure him of my conviction of the accused's innocence: as, however, I had no proof, no legal proof, the physician remained firmly incredulous. I mentioned having called at M. d'Estrées' house, and that I had seen Mademoiselle Le Blanc; but I did not allude to what had passed between us. 'A demoiselle of spirit,' said M. Portalis, 'is Le Blanc, and a handsome one too. Poor d'Estrées, a man of extravagant caprices as regards le beau sexe, must have taken a strong fancy to her, for he has left by the instrument which superseded that made in favour of his wife, forty thousand livres *tournois* to Mademoiselle Le Blanc.'

" ' Forty thousand livres *tournois* (about eighteen hundred pounds sterling)—forty thousand livres *tournois* to Mademoiselle Le Blanc, which bequest a man so capricious might have at any moment revoked! Ha! light begins to break from the black, lowering clouds. And Le Blanc knew of this large bequest ?' ' Possibly; but there is no proof that she did. Such a man as D'Estrées would be likely enough to tell her that he had made her a handsome provision.' ' Certainly he would. And it was Fanchette Le Blanc who served the poisoned coffee. Light breaks, I say again.' ' Error— illusion, young man! you are blinded by sentimental enthusiasm. The possible culpability of Mademoiselle Le Blanc has not escaped the attention of authority. A rigorous inquiry has been instituted, and the report, for various cogent reasons, acquitted her of the slightest complicity with Madame d'Estrées. In fact, Le Blanc and her mistress were on bad terms, Madame d'Estrées having given her peremptory notice to leave her service.' ' It is very well, Monsieur Portalis; but I repeat, light breaks—is hourly becoming brighter, clearer. *Nous verrons.* I start in an hour for Havre, and thanking you for your kindness, I take my leave. I salute you, Monsieur Portalis.'

" M. Tricard and M. Courtrai were quite willing to furnish me with sufficient money to engage an Avoué and two provincially-celebrated Avocats to defend Madame d'Estrées; but both were firmly persuaded of her guilt. Nothing could weaken this conviction—nothing that I could *say.* And this rooted prejudice against Joséphine, if it could not be eradicated, would destroy a hope which I had not ceased to cherish—that in the last resort, when all other hope had vanished, M. Courtrai would invoke the aid of Le Prince de la Tour d'Auvergne, who was all-powerful at court, to at least save the unfortunate lady from the last dread penalty of the law! M. Courtrai would not lift a finger to save a convicted murderess of whose guilt he felt no doubt. That set me thinking: we shall see with what result.

"The trial in the Hall of Justice, Rouen, would not commence in less than two months. In my restless mood of mind, I was constantly going backwards and forwards from Rouen to Havre, from Havre to Rouen. It was something to look upon the prison where Joséphine was confined, to stroll through the grounds where she had often strolled. I was always *romanesque:* eccentric was the word applied to me by the commonplace humdrums of society. That absurdest, vainest of eccentrics, De Genlis, had the impertinence to call me in one of her trashy books *Un drôle de génie.* But *bavardage* is out of place in this page—a dark, terrible one—over which a mist of blood seems to hang. Whilst haunting the grounds round about the deceased Monsieur d'Estrées' mansion, I frequently amused myself by sketching the most striking scenes. This desultory occupation proved of great after-service.

"I certainly did, whilst *battant le pavé* at Rouen, a very silly thing, which no staid, sensible youth, unless he had been madly in love—and staid, sensible youths never are, according to my experience, madly in love— would have dreamed of doing. I chanced to hear in a café where I was dining that one of the turnkeys of the Rouen prison had been taken suddenly ill, and that some trustworthy person was immediately required to take his place. Hey! presto! I was off in an instant; hurried to a fripier's (second-hand clothes-shop), purchased such apparel as I thought suitable; waited upon the Avoué who was engaged for the defence of Madame d'Estrées, asked him to give me a certificate of respectability and trustworthiness under his own well-known signature. He readily complied. M. Portalis did the same. Of course I did not mention for what purpose I required such documents; but I do not remember—I made no note in my diary—what excuse I made for requiring them. With these documents in my pocket, and suitably attired, I presented myself to the governor of the jail. A turn-key was urgently required. I seemed a suitable person enough, though rather too young. I was engaged, and signed an agreement for one month, during which time I should not be permitted egress from the prison, that being a rigorous stipulation with all the subordinate officials. I was distinctly informed that the sentinels at the gate would no more hesitate to put a ball or a bullet through me, should I attempt to leave the place, than if I were a regular prisoner. I was duly shown to those gentlemen, in order that they might recognise me, and should it be desirable to do so, instantly act upon that knowledge. The motive for this stringent regulation was to prevent any clandestine correspondence being carried on, through the medium of the officials, between the prisoners and their friends outside. Keys duly numbered were given to me, and when the time came to lock up for the night, I should be shown the different cells.

"'How is that?' said I to a brother official who was instructing me in my duties, and helping to dispose of a flagon of wine, the cost of which, according to usage, I, a new hand, defrayed. 'How is that, my friend? I always understood prisoners were confined under lock all day and night.'

"'*Parbleu!* That is correct of prisoners under detention for crime, but not as to debtors. This is the debtor department of the prison. Quite a separate building is that where criminals are confined.'

"Good heavens! I was as hot as fire in a moment, from the crown of my head to the sole of my foot. What an ass I had made of myself!

"'Well, but the two buildings communicate with each other, I suppose?' said I.

"'*Pas du tout.* Not at all. They are, I tell you, separate buildings. It is impossible to pass from one to the other without first going into the street—quite impossible. To your health, comrade, once more. You don't look well.'

"No wonder that I didn't look well. I was completely bouleversé—turned up and down, inside out. What the devil! was I to be shut up in that dismal place, without a chance of seeing or speaking with Madame d'Estrécs, for a whole month, unable to communicate with her even through the Avoué (attorney)? It was dreadful—desolating—the end of the world! I should go mad! I reflected for a few moments as well as the hot tumult in my brain permitted.

"'Maître Jean Dubois,' said I, 'you are right in saying I don't look well. It is impossible that I should. I am very ill. The close, dank atmosphere of this place has already produced a terrible effect upon me. Should I remain, it will kill me. I must speak with the governor. It is vexing to be obliged to give up so good—at least, so promising a place; but life, you know, before all!'

"'*Parbleu!* But listen, my friend: whether you live or die here, you must remain till the term for which you have engaged—one month, six months, twelve months—has expired. The doctor will attend you. Certainly, if you die, and Monsieur le Médecin certifies you are really dead, your friends, if they bring a coffin, may have your body. Yes, I think that indulgence is allowed—I am sure of it. And, *mon enfant*, it is well to remember, as you are retained for one month—you said one month? Yes. Well, remember that really means two months. You must give a month's notice of your desire to throw up the place, before the expiration of the stipulated month, and then, if your services are needed, they won't let you off. *Mon ami!*' added the veteran, 'taking service here is much like taking service in the army. It is an easy life for a strong active fellow like you, but very, very difficult to get out of. *A la santé, mon cher.* We'll have another flagon. I could tell you a good story,' continued Dubois, 'of one of us who shammed mortal illness in order to get out. There was a wealthy merchant confined here. He had great transactions—had been arrested unexpectedly, and there were papers in his house that

would have gravely compromised him. No letters are
allowed to pass out of prison; but all that are sent are
received and opened. Well, Joseph Marceau was prevailed upon to assist the merchant out of his alarming
difficulty. Marceau feigned, as I have said, dangerous
illness, and feigned so well that an order was given to
carry him home in a litter. This was done. Marceau
saw the merchant's wife, gave her a list of the compro-
mising papers, which were of course immediately destroyed. That done, the merchant had nothing to fear,
and was soon afterwards liberated. Marceau, who was
very poor before, took the Poisson d'Or tavern in the
Rue d'Arc. This raised suspicion; an inquiry took
place, and, though the affair was by some means hushed
up, enough transpired to cause the issue of an edict that
no subordinate prison official in France should leave
until the expiration of the term agreed upon, and notice
of a month beyond that. And they do not engage married men; old soldiers are preferred,' &c. &c. The gar-
rulous old man talked and drank on uninterrupted by
me. The situation in which I, with the heedlessness
of a schoolboy, had placed myself, confounded, appalled
me. The thought of being caged in that gloomy dun-
geon for two months was maddening. Madame d'Estrées
would believe I, like the rest of the world, had abandoned
her. And there was a considerable sum of money at my
lodgings wherewith to pay Messieurs les Avocats, who
would certainly not plead for Joséphine if not previously
paid. And I could communicate with no one, as I was
told, not even with M. Portalis. *Sacré-é-é!—nom de—
nom de Dieu!* 'Bah!' I reflected, recovering myself, 'this
must be an invention of that old farceur Dubois. I will
see the governor at once.' I feigned sudden illness, and
asked that, if not better in the morning, I might be allowed to go into the town of Rouen for an hour, half-an-
hour, to consult a physician who understood the malady
which afflicted me. The governor, a grim, good-natured
veteran, smiled, and said it was simply impossible to com-
ply with the request. I should have well considered be-

fore accepting the post. The prison regulations were, he admitted, absurdly strict; but they could not be relaxed under any circumstances. No communication could be permitted with the outside world by the subordinate custodians of the prisoners. 'Well, Monsieur le Colonel, will you send a note, an open note, to M. Portalis?' No, he dare not do so. 'A verbal message, then?' 'No; it is impossible to know what occult meaning may be conveyed in seemingly the simplest message. There are state prisoners just now in the Rouen jail, and it is important that no possible communication shall be had with them. It is true they are on the criminal side, but Messieurs les Autorités at Paris have, in their ignorance of the building, prescribed the same rules for the custodians of debtors as for men or women accused of crime. That is their affair; mine is to obey the instructions sent to me. There is nothing to be said, young man; no one obliged you to come here. As to your illness, if it be real, you can have no better advice than that of the resident physician, M. Bourdon. Now leave me; I am busy.'

"Hundred thousand devils! this was the climax! I had not previously believed that such insane regulations could really be in force. I afterwards knew the reason why such ridiculous orders had been sent from Paris. That, however, is a subject upon which I do not care to touch, even in my private journal.

"But, good heavens! what was to be done? How get away from those accursed walls? For three miserable days and nights I pondered that question of questions; but no solution came to me. On the fourth day a bright idea struck me: Madame Chiron, who was emphatically the governor's governor, had a dog, delicately white, with a glossy black tail, black head, and brilliant eyes; the paws of the animal were also black. I am not a connoisseur in dogs, and do not know whether such a curiously-coloured dog is rare or valuable. Enough for me that madame's affections appeared to be centred in the little beast. That set me thinking. I must state that, having shown my knowledge of medicine, I had free access to M. Bourdon's laboratory, and saved him labour in compounding medicaments for the prisoners.

"Madame's pet-dog is taken very ill, refuses food— will not touch the most delicate viands—droops, pines— will, it is evident, if some remedy be not found, die. Dr. Bourdon is summoned. He prescribes. The remedy is of no avail. That was my affair. Madame is in despair. The dog gets worse and worse. Madame, in such a state of distraction as a tender mother would be if a dear child was dying, hurriedly enters the laboratory. I meant to have sought her had she not come. Fleurette is no better —worse—and can nothing be done? ' Where is Bourdon —the unskilful fool?' she added, ragefully. ' He will be here presently. Will madame permit me to remark that neither M. Bourdon nor myself, though I have studied in an Ecole de Médecine, understands the maladies of dogs? The charming Fleurette—beautiful Fleurette—will certainly die if the proper remedy be not promptly applied.'

"' Well, and the proper remedy! You say you are not acquainted with it?'

"' That is quite true, madame. I recognise in Fleurette the same symptoms which I saw in another dog, which did not, however, die. I will give madame the proof. To-morrow, or perhaps not till next day, Fleurette's legs will be paralysed. And then the remedy must be prompt. It is, however, certain to be effectual.'

"' What remedy, I ask again?' said madame, with passion.

"' I have already said that I myself am not acquainted with the remedy, but I know where to find the man who could cure Fleurette in five minutes. That is to say, I would undertake to find him in, say, three or four hours.'

"Madame, who was a shrewd woman, looked at me sharply, suspiciously. I sustained her scrutiny very well, and she left the laboratory, bidding me tell Dr. Bourdon that she wished to see him immediately.

"At about four o'clock the next day madame sent for

me. She was alone and in tears. Fleurette's legs *were* paralysed, stiff, cold. 'See, see,' exclaimed the lady, with extravagant passion, 'the electuary which, by that fool Bourdon's directions, you administered, has done poor Fleurette no good. It is as you said it would be—her beautiful legs *are* paralysed. And you are sure that a certain remedy may be obtained?' 'Quite certain, madame. But there is not a moment to spare. It may, as I said, be three or four hours before I can find the individual who possesses the secret.' 'Three or four hours! Fleurette will live till then?' 'No doubt of it, madame.' 'You will return with the medicine yourself?' 'Undoubtedly, madame, at my best speed. I answer for Fleurette's perfect cure.' 'You do! I will confide in you then. My husband is absent. Follow me; I will let you out by the private door. Allons! I must risk something to save Fleurette. When you return,' said madame, as she softly unclosed a private gate—'when you return, pull three times—each stroke about a minute apart—at this bell. I shall be at hand. Now go, quick.' I *did* go quick—ran to my lodgings, discarded my turnkey habiliments, and was myself again. I was not, however, ungrateful to Madame Chiron. I, that had administered the bane, knew the antidote, and a phial containing it was delivered in less than three hours at the private gate, accompanied by a note from me, stating that I could not, for peculiar reasons, return to the prison, but had sent the potion for Fleurette, which speedily administered, would restore her to perfect health, as if by magic. It did restore her, and the affair was allowed to pass *sub silentio*.

"There were several letters awaiting me at the hotel, amongst them one from my *beau-père* Tricard. It contained a startling piece of news. Édouard Cazo was married to Fanchette Le Blanc, who had received a fortune of forty thousand francs. Cazo, so enriched, was about to give up the herbalist business, and embark in some other, which would give more scope to his ambition. Ho! ho!

"Joséphine d'Estrées was convicted of the murder of her husband—a conviction due, in some measure, although the dying declaration of Monsieur d'Estrées would perhaps have sufficed, to the calculated malignity of Cazo and his wife. Cazo could never have loved Joséphine. His was a nature utterly incapable of love in its exalted sense, its purifying influences, its self-sacrifice — a sensuous passion merely—straw on fire. How eagerly I watched them both during that terrible trial—noted the facial index of their cruel hearts, their fear-haunted consciences! Glancing from them to the pale, tremulous features, the suffused eyes gemmed by anguish to a more touching beauty, of Madame d'Estrées, it seemed to me that I was before the tribunal of a Rhadamanthus, where fiends were pleading for the condemnation of an angel.

"Guilty! Sentence of death! I am lost. A universe has crumbled at my feet, and I remember nothing more till the morrow of that dreadful day. My friends Tricard and Courtrai were present when I awoke from that trance of despair; but, attentively perusing their faces as soon as I was able to do so, I read no hope there.

"They believed Joséphine to be guilty—that she had committed a brutal, unnatural murder, in order that her husband, by whom she had been treated with the most deferential kindness, should have no time to alter the testament made in her favour. 'Un assassinat inexpiable,' said M. Courtrai; 'and thy obstinacy in persisting she is innocent, is to me only another proof that, with all thy capacities, there is something flighty; something flawed in thy intellect.' 'You will at least, M. Courtrai, give me a letter to the Prince de la Tour d'Auvergne, asking him to intercede with the king—to intercede, I mean, for the saving of Madame d'Estrées' life?' 'I would not,' was his pitiless reply, 'move a finger to save the murderess from the just doom pronounced upon her. Certainly not.' 'An appeal has been lodged, I suppose?' 'Oh, yes; but it will avail nothing. The righteous sentence will be carried out.' 'The *righteous* sentence! But never mind, I pass that. If you, M.

Courtrai, can be morally convinced that Madame d'Estrées is an innocent woman, you will appeal to the Prince de la Tour d'Auvergne?' 'Yes, with the greatest pleasure. But the thing is impossible. Thou art a dreamer of dreams with regard to that beautiful serpent.' 'We shall see, monsieur—we shall see.'

"The appeal could not be judged in less than three months. I had plenty of time. M. Cabanis prolonged my leave of absence, and I set to work with energy. The idea was germane to that which an English dramatist, I have since heard, embodied in a play called *Hamlet*, but differently carried out. Ever since I can remember, I possessed a talent for taking likenesses of persons, and not only of persons, but of scenery—fields, trees, men, women, the living and the dumb world. Those sketches were not models of painting, very far from that. But they presented the man, the woman, the trees, the fields, vividly before you. He who had seen could not fail to recognise them at a glance.

"M. Courtrai was somewhat intimately acquainted with Edouard Cazo. He had known, respected his father, and had attended him during his lingering last illness gratuitously. He also liked the new Madame Cazo— thought her a worthy woman. He was a man of skill in his profession, of great skill, and well-informed generally, but he had no faculty of vision to see through human masks. I had, and still have; and in the case of Madame d'Estrées, love, pity, rage, added strength to that peculiar power. I was as sure, after I had seen and heard them give evidence at Rouen against the accused, that they were the murderers of Monsieur d'Estrées, as I was of my own life.

"At last I was ready for the decisive experiment. I had painted with my best skill four tableaux. Never have I achieved such success as a painter. The *ange gardien* of Joséphine must have guided my pencil. The four paintings are now in the possession of M. Courtrai's nephew. The first showed Edouard Cazo and Fanchette Le Blanc conversing eagerly with each other at a spot near Monsieur d'Estrées' mansion, where I had ascertained they had more than once met. He was handing to her a small packet. The dark light of meditated murder gleamed gloomily in the eyes of both. The next sketch reproduced a small apartment in M. d'Estrées' mansion, contiguous to that in which that gentleman took breakfast. It was in that room a garçon in the establishment handed Le Blanc the tray upon which was the cafetière with various comestibles. This was proved at the trial. I felt sure it was there the *poudre de succession* had been mixed with the coffee. Madame d'Estrées was in the breakfast *salon*, the door of which she might have opened at any moment to bid the waiting-woman bring in her master's breakfast. The painting represented Le Blanc in the act of pouring the powder into the cafetière with her shaking hand—her fierce, averted, straining eyes fixed the while intently upon the door The accessories were faithfully done. I had taken a sketch of the apartment and furniture. The cafetière itself was reproduced with exactness. The third tableau supposed that the real culprits had been discovered; the scene was the High Court of Rouen, but instead of Madame d'Estrées, Edouard Cazo and his wife were upon ' *le banc des accusés* ' (the bench where prisoners seat themselves when not under course of being 'questioned' by the magistrate)—Edouard Cazo and his wife. The witness—the denouncing witness giving her testimony was Madame d'Estrées, and into her face I threw all the force, the expression, which I was capable of depicting. She was a beautiful embodied Nemesis, as with flashing eyes and outstretched hand she pointed to the trembling prisoners. The last tableau represented M. and Madame Cazo in the charrette on the way to execution. Ah! that painting occupied longer than all the other three. The brush often and often fell from my hands, as with sudden sickness at heart and a hot flush in my face I bethought me that those two vile figures, were Truth the artist, would be paiuted out, and in their stead would stand the pale, martyred angel of my life—Joséphine!

"It was finished at last. The paintings were carried from my bed-chamber, where no one had been permitted to see them, to the principal *salon*. They were hung together in a row, a green silk curtain with rings running upon a stout wire before.

"M. Courtrai and M. Bourdon humoured the caprice, yet smiled sadly at my folly. 'As thou wilt,' said the patron, 'but it will end in nothing' (*cela aboutira en rien*).

"Monsieur Courtrai would, however, do his part in the *petite comédie de circonstance*, and mark, closely mark the demeanour, the countenances of Monsieur and Madame Cazo.

"Monsieur and Madame Cazo were invited to dine at Bellevue, the private residence on the côte of M. Courtrai. It was a great honour, and the Cazos accepted the invitation with eagerness—delight.

"The dinner was capital—the *convives* in excellent spirits. There were only present Monsieur and Madame Courtrai, their widowed amiable daughter Madame Bonjean, author of *La Fille Sage* (The Wise Girl), Monsieur, Madame and Alphonse Tricard, myself, and the two Cazos.

"Madame Bonjean, who was in the secret of our little plot, was hopeful of it. She had long known Madame d'Estrées, and spite of the general concurrence of public opinion in the judgment of the Rouen court, could not believe her guilty of the murder of her husband. I was charmed with Madame Bonjean.

"The dinner is over—the dessert accomplished. M. Courtrai invites his guests to view his pictures. We all rose. There were some excellent works of art, Dutch chiefly, which all admired.

"'I have four pictures concealed by this curtain,' said

M. Courtrai, with marked emphasis, addressing the two Cazos, aud looking fixedly at them. Madame Bonjean, who had only returned to Havre a week previously, had helped to shake his conviction of Madame d'Estrées' guilt—'I have four pictures concealed by this curtain, which are more than pictures. They reveal both the past and the future. Look, Monsieur and Madame Cazo.'

"A wild, bubbling scream broke from Madame Cazo's lips. She fainted, and would have fallen to the ground had not Madame Bonjean caught at and upheld her. As for Edouard Cazo, he was transfixed with terror as if confronted by a new Gorgon, and I noticed that his fascinated glance was riveted. by the fourth picture — the going to execution in the charrette, surrounded by a hooting multitude. He was as white as paper, and large beads of perspiration stood out upon his forehead.

"'Leave my house, Monsieur and Madame Cazo!' said M. Courtrai, in his sternest accents. 'I had not thought to entertain assassins. Begone!'

"The guilty pair left without a word, not daring even to lift their eyes. The terrible secret which haunted their lives, and, in the shadowy shape of the murdered man, pursued them during day, and crept with them at night to bed, whispering, suggesting horrible fantasies, was known to others. One unseen had looked upon their deeds. That charrette with its two occupants would never pass from their memory till the world itself did.

"'Eugène,' said M. Courtrai, 'thou art right, I am convinced. But no legal proof is supplied by what we have just seen. I shall, however, speak of it to the Prince de la Tour d'Auvergne, and set off for Paris in the morning. There must be no delay, my poor Eugène, for the appeal I knew this morning has been rejected, and the sentence—the unjust sentence—will be executed this day week. There, don't you faint away. I shall be successful, depend upon it, in saving Madame d'Estrées' life. More than that I dare not hope for. Now take a glass of eau médicinale and go to bed, or you will be seriously ill.'

"The day of doom had dawned. Monsieur Tricard and I, who had arrived in Rouen the previous evening, were early up. Need I say that I had not slept since the departure of M. Courtrai for Paris? Yet, early as we were, the Rouen folk were astir as early, and groups of countrymen and women were streaming into the city, brutally eager to obtain a near view of the 'spectacle' appointed to take place at ten precisely. We had not heard from M. Courtrai since he left for Paris, and I walked in the shadow of a gigantic despair. Through M. Portalis we made a vehement application to the authorities to delay carrying out the sentence for a few hours. The request was granted; the time changed from ten to two o'clock, greatly to the chagrin of the sight-seers from the country. Their indignation rose to fever-heat as, soon after ten o'clock, the clear bright sky became overcast, the clouds grew black and dense, and soon the rain poured down heavily, and with every sign of continuance for some hours at least.

"I had not been able to obtain an interview with Madame d'Estrées since her condemnation. Only a priest could be allowed to see her. Père Duchesne was a worthy, warm-hearted man. He sympathised with me in my terrible distress, and readily charged himself with a note to the unfortunate, by which she would know that it was through no coldness or want of effort on my part that I did not personally see and endeavour to support her in the afflictive days through which she was passing. 'It is as well, perhaps, my young friend, that you have not been permitted to see Madame d'Estrées. It would but torture you and intensify her despair. She is completely *abattue*, prostrated with terror. She is deaf to religious consolation, not for want of piety, but because her mind is overwhelmed, paralysed with horror. She has never for one moment doubted your sincerity, your devotedness. I have never had a duty so painful to perform. I can only weep with—pray for her.'

"One o'clock has struck; the rain still pours down in torrents; but the crowd around the scaffold—sanguinary brutes—does not diminish. As for me, there is not only rage in my heart, but blasphemy in my brain. I doubt the goodness, the justice of God. There could be no omnipotent, merciful Father, if such a crime as the legal murder of that innocent woman took place. What a frightful fascination the black scaffold, the hideous apparatus of death, exerts over me! I cannot wrench my eyes away. Joséphine—the imputed crime being the murder of a husband—is to be broken on the wheel. Horrible! a thousand times horrible! Yet I cannot leave the spot, though passionately urged by the good Tricard, with tears in his eyes, to go away. No, I must see out the terrific tragedy, should the last act drive me mad.

*   *   *   *   *

"A ferocious shout in the distance, rapidly increasing in multitudinous volume as the charrette slowly approaches the scaffold. The priest is kneeling therein over the doomed woman, who is crouching in terror at the bottom of the cart. The mob can only catch sight of the white, coarse, penitential dress of the victim. This enrages them. They have come to gloat upon the murderess, and refuse to have the entertainment curtailed. ' *Debout! debout, assassin!*' (Up, up, assassin!) they shout. That demand of devils produces no effect. A numerous armed force is present, and the multitude are powerless. *   *   *   *   They lift Joséphine out of the charrette, and bear her up the steps of the scaffold. She is insensible from terror. Better so, infinitely better.

"Hark! There is another shout from the south entrance into Rouen; carriage-wheels moving rapidly can presently be heard; the officials on the scaffold look eagerly in that direction, and the terrible preparations are suspended. In a few minutes the carriage comes full in sight. M. Courtrai, whom I instantly recognise, occupies it, with an officer in uniform; both gesticulate violently; the officer waves a sheet of parchment, M. Courtrai a white handkerchief. They are shouting, but their voices cannot be heard for several minutes. At last, the words ' Grâce! grâce!. Sa majesté lui fait grâce!' are heard. A howl of rage arises from the multitude, who stop and are endeavouring to overturn the carriage in their ferocious madness, when the mounted arquebusiers force their way through the crowd, and rescue M. Courtrai and the officer. The officer in command takes the parchment, speaks a few words to the occupants of the carriage, aud rides swiftly back towards the scaffold. I became cold as stone while this was going on—rigid as death—I see and hear, but as if in a dream; not with my bodily eyes and ears. I saw the executioner unbind and give up Joséphine to the care of the priest and two civil functionaries who had helped her to mount the steps to the scaffold, and who now prepared to assist her back to the charrette amidst a storm of wolfish execrations from the disappointed populace. I hear, see no more. As when sentence was pronounced, I recover intelligent consciousness—the certainty that I am not dreaming—but to lose that recovered consciousness, and am borne safely out of the crowd by the good Tricard. M. Courtrai had not only obtained, through the good offices of the Prince de la Tour d'Auvergne, remission of the capital sentence upon Madame d'Estrées, but that instead of being confined for life in the Bagne at Brest or Toulon, which was the usual secondary punishment awarded in such case, she should be transferred to the prison La Force, Paris. That was a great, unusual favour; and but that De la Tour d'Auvergne was at last brought to believe in the innocence, or more correctly to doubt the guilt of madame, he would not have persisted till that relaxation of punishment was granted. It was simply seclusion, consequently, to which Madame d'Estrées was finally condemned; and at La Force she could be supplied with such modest luxuries as her friends would be disposed to supply her with."

Two days after the narrow escape of the unfortunate lady from a cruel death, Eugène Devine and the Père

Duchesne entered the room in the hotel where M. Tricard impatiently awaited his step-son, he being anxious to leave without delay for Le Havre. M. Courtrai had left the same evening he arrived at Rouen from Paris.

Eugène was evidently much excited—very pleasurably so. Father Duchesne was also agitated, but uneasy.

"Give me your blessing, cher papa!" exclaimed Devine—"your blessing and felicitations. I am married!"

"What art thou talking of, Eugène? Married! Thou art either jesting or mad."

"Neither, Père Tricard. Father Duchesne married me to Joséphine d'Estrées, widow, in the prison about half-an-hour since. Madame Devine is now on the road to Paris."

"It is true, Monsieur Tricard," said the Rev. Duchesne; "I have been prevailed upon to confer the sacrament of marriage upon Joséphine d'Estrées and Eugène Devine. There is no law of the Church which forbade my doing so. That which prevailed with me was, first, the conviction I had acquired of the lady's innocence; secondly, the devoted affection felt for her by Eugène, who is a virile man in intellect, if not in years; lastly, because it will give him a right to see her once in each month, in the presence, it is true, of one or more of the prison officials, and minister to her needs. He will also have the right, if he sees fit, and reliable evidence of their guilt can be obtained, of prosecuting certain persons at Le Havre, who, since the incident of the four tableaux, neither you nor M. Courtrai doubts are the real assassins of Monsieur d'Estrées."

"Well," said M. Tricard, "I doubt the prudence of such a proceeding; but it being an accomplished fact, I shall take no step to annul the ceremony—and I only could do so. Do you return to Havre, Eugène?" he added with a grave smile, "or does your body follow your soul to Paris?"

"It is of the first necessity," said Eugène, "that I resume my studies without further loss of time."

"Precisely; I knew that would be your answer. Well, then, we have simply to dine and depart our several ways."

Devine completed his brilliant studies at the Ecole de Médecine, and in due time received a diploma. Nothing meanwhile had been discovered that promised to remove the stigma of guilt from his wife, pining her life away in prison—the only ray of light which penetrated its cheerless gloom being the visit, once a month, of her true, faithful husband, for a few minutes only, and always in the presence of a third party. Still, even that made sunshine in the dismal place. As for M. le Docteur Devine, the one sole object of life was to free his beloved wife from prison, restore her to society. A terribly up-hill game to fight. The odds against success were as one thousand to zero.

Messieurs Courtrai and Tricard both died in the same year, when Devine was in his 27th year, and Madame Devine had been incarcerated eight years. Le Sieur Courtrai bequeathed his protégé thirty thousand francs, Monsieur Tricard five thousand. These bequests fell in opportunely. Devine had made an important start in life. He had taken a house, or portion of a house, on account of its cheapness, in an unfavourable locality. His clientèle, when his patron and stepfather died, was consequently a very scanty one; would barely have sufficed, without the bountiful aid of M. Courtrai, to keep body and soul together.

Much reflecting upon this condition of things, and knowing that in the utterly corrupt, rotten French Court of the period, the only talisman which could burst open the dungeon-doors where his adored wife was slowly dying—languishing to death—was gold—gold in heaps; Eugène Devine, one of the most skilful physicians that ever lived, young as he was, determined to re-begin the world as a charlatan. Quack, we should say. "I had tried the legitimate, and should have starved; so I betook myself to the illegitimate! It was an inspiration,

without which mine would have been an utterly defeated
life. The world is mostly composed of fools. My experience was young, but it had grasped that truth and held
it firmly. I bought a carriage, had it painted in gayest
colours; the coachman wore a coat half scarlet, half yel
low. Two couriers, habited in like manner, preceded th
carriage, which traversed the principal thoroughfares of
Paris at a slow pace, befitting the solemnity of the high
mission intrusted to the gentleman seated within, whom
his heralds (the aforesaid couriers) proclaimed to have
been miraculously gifted with the power of indefinitely
prolonging human life—was possessed of the true Elixir
Vitæ, of which the 'Pilule Divine' was an indispensable
preparative. 'Pilule Divine' (Divine Pill)—the second
letter so formed that in a Court of Justice, as afterwards
happened, I could say that it was Devine's Pill.

"The Pilule Divine, as every body knows, had an immense, an extraordinary success. Yes, and it was a very
excellent pill. I had very early detected the legitimate
charlatanry of the profession, and convinced myself that
certain simple medicaments would, in nine cases out of
ten, have a beneficial effect. The result confirmed my
judgment. Gold flowed in upon me in a torrent—the
shower of Danae was nothing to it. I tried to utilise
that gold in the only way for which it was precious in
my eyes—the liberation of my wife from that accursed
prison. I did not succeed—was always victimised. One
Jezebel, whom I knew to have intimate relations with
the king, robbed me of ten thousand francs upon the
solemn promise that before noon on the morrow the
king's pardon for Joséphine Devine, otherwise D'Estrées,
should be sent to La Force. Bah! I was swindled! and,
veritable ass that I must have been, deserved to be swindled.

"The next year the *petite vérole* (small-pox), of which
Louis the Fifteenth subsequently died, broke out with
great virulence in Paris. I had had opportunities of
studying the disease, and had satisfied myself that the
ordinary medical treatment was wholly wrong. Instead

of shutting up the patient in a close room, and stifling him or her with blankets, and reducing the system, I opened the windows, gave free access to the air, and administered stimulants enabling the sufferer to throw out the disease. This was the real secret of my great success; but the 'Pilule Divine' had all the credit of the cures. I cannot think there was any crime in that pretence. No one would have believed in fresh air, light covering, ordinary stimulants; but all did in the 'Pilule Divine,' and hundreds of lives were saved. My fame resounded throughout Paris.

"Early one morning I was summoned to Le Petit Trianon, Versailles. The all-powerful Du Barry had sent for me. Her mulatto *protégé* had sickened, it was feared, of the small-pox. My heart leapt up at the message. A great hope sprang to life within me. I hurried off with the messenger, saw the mulatto, and that he was really seized with the *petite vérole*, but, I judged, of a mild type. I looked grave, but expressed confidence, nevertheless, that the 'Pilule Divine' would conquer the disease.

"I was quite aware, with all Paris, of the attachment of the beautiful Du Barry for the young African, and I carelessly asked if that lady had been in the room. Yes, once, before the nature of the malady was suspected. And madame wished to see me before I left. That was enough.

"I think the Du Barry was the loveliest creature I have ever seen. I did not wonder that the sensuous king was her slave—that La France, as she used to call the French monarch, did her bidding as a slave would. 'Well, what is the disorder?' she asked. '*La petite vérole*, madame; and of a very virulent type.' '*Grand Dieu!* he will die, then?' 'No, I can save him; at least, I believe that to do so is within my power.' I looked keenly at the beautiful creature. 'Will madame,' said I, softly, 'permit me to feel her pulse, to see her tongue?' The Du Barry turned deathly pale, and trembled in every limb. She complied with my request. I assumed my gravest look. 'It is surely impossible that madame has entered the infected room?' I said. 'Yes; once—once only,' she almost screamed. 'You do not mean, you cannot mean, that I—I—have caught the—the——' She could not finish the sentence. 'No question, madame, that you have caught the infection.' This was true. 'It is false,' she shrieked, springing upon her feet; 'it must, it shall be false!' She stamped her beautiful foot with rage and terror. 'It is true, madame; but I can save you.' 'Ah, yes, my life, perhaps; but the disfigurement—you cannot save me from that.' And the Du Barry sank down upon the gilded canapé in an agony of distress. 'Yes, I will undertake that not the faintest blemish shall mar madame's dazzling beauty; but I must insist upon conditions.' 'Conditions?—what conditions? Gold? You may have whatever sum you please to name.' 'Not gold, madame. The condition is simply this:—That madame gives me a written memorandum, promising that if I save her life, her face and person from disfigurement, and the life of her servant, she will obtain the king's full pardon for my wife—my innocent wife—imprisoned in La Force!' 'I know—I know. I have heard that history. I give you my word,' the Du Barry added, 'that if you fulfil your promise, Madame Devine shall receive the king's pardon.' 'Excuse me, madame, I must have the promise in writing, or I decline to act. The happiness of my life equally with your own is at stake. This is a great chance which God has vouchsafed to me. I will not cast it away. I further pledge myself that it shall never be known, that no whisper shall go forth upon the subject to the gay world, which, whilst crouching at madame's feet, are eating their hearts away with envy of her marvellous beauty, her supreme influence.'

"This was perhaps *maladroit* on my part. Madame du Barry had been saturated with compliments upon her beauty, by persons whose adulation was worth courting; that of a pill-manufacturer, though the pill was a *divine* one, she considered a gross impertinence! Her glorious

eyes told me that. Still, Death—the Shadow of Death—
is the master of the world. She believed that I, perhaps
alone of all the doctors in Paris, could certainly shield
her from, exorcise the horrible phantom. She glared at
me like a beautiful panther at bay; but I feared not her
spring. Madame du Barry would have done, promised,
given anything rather than it should be surmised she
was or had been infected by such a loathsome malady as
the *petite vérole*. A ridiculous notion was prevalent at
the time that the disease, though it was subdued, if not
a visible trace of the attack was to be seen, had nevertheless tainted, vitiated the blood for ever with malignant
scrofula, which, sooner or later, might break out in other
forms. 'You feel no doubt that I am infected with that
dreadful disease, and that you are certain of being able
to save me from death and disfigurement?' 'There is
not the slightest doubt, madame, that you are infected
by the disease; and that I can save you, not only from
death, but from the least disfigurement.' 'I consent to
the condition. There are writing materials: draw up the
memorandum yourself.' I did so. Madame signed, and
placed it in my hand. 'Now, Monsieur Devine,' said she,
'let us quite understand each other. I shall seclude
myself till the danger is past. How long may that be?'
'Ten days at most.' 'Ten days. Fortunately the king
has left for the provinces, and will not return in less
than a fortnight. *Revenons.* I was about to say that I
shall write a note to his majesty, place it in a sealed
packet to be delivered to him immediately after my
death. It will consign you to the Bastille for life.
More than that: should I be disfigured, I shall still
have sufficient influence to inflict upon you and Madame Devine the same doom; and be quite assured I
will in the case supposed exert that influence. On the
contrary—if you fulfil your promise, I will keep honourable word with you. Madame Devine shall receive the
king's plenary pardon, and I will besides promote your
interest in every way within my power.' 'Madame, I
joyfully agree. But there is no time to be lost. You

must immediately take my magic pill and other medicaments which I constantly carry about me, according to
the directions labelled thereon. Have you a discreet,
trustworthy female domestic?' 'Yes.' 'I must see her
then, and give her a few plain, simple instructions, which
must on no account be neglected; and it will be best to
give out that madame is suffering from a slight attack
of fever.' This suggestion was approved. Madame la
Comtesse added that, if possible to be done, she was
desirous to conceal the nature of the malady even from
the trustworthy female attendant. It was of such paramount importance to obtain the written promise of the
all-powerful favourite, that I should not have hesitated
at any assertion, however audacious it might be; and I
boldly replied that I had little doubt my remedies would
so act as to render it quite possible to prevent the attendant from suspecting the real state of the case. At last
all was arranged, and I left Le Petit Trianon floating
upon the wings of an inexpressible ecstasy ('*flottant sur
les ailes d'une extase inexprimable*')"—a bewildering meta-
phor of the eccentric doctor's, and attributable, we may
benevolently conclude, to the exaltation of his brain when,
on reaching his domicile, he wrote it down in his journal.

Fortune favoured, as the fickle goddess often does,
the brave and bold. Madame du Barry had gone through
the different phases of the terrible disease, and was completely convalescent several days before the king's return
to Paris. But two pustules had appeared; one on the
nape of madame's neck, the other on the great toe of
her left foot. Her brilliant beauty was undimmed. She
was grateful to Monsieur le Docteur Devine—presented
him with a large sum of money, and assured him again
that his wife should be pardoned, liberated within twenty-
four hours after the king's return. The mulatto also recovered. It seems reasonable to conclude that the "charlatan" doctor, so called, was really much in advance of
the medical profession of the day in his treatment of *la
petite vérole* and other blood-diseases. Monsieur le Docteur Devine thus continues his journal :—

"My heart is torn with impatience. It is forty-eight hours since the king alighted at the Tuileries; and Madame du Barry promised that within twenty-four hours my wife should be set free. What am I to think? Can it be possible that his majesty has not visited Le Petit Trianon?—that some new favourite has thrust Madame du Barry from her throne, usurped her place in the king's affection? That would be terrible—fatal! But no—impossible! * * * * Joy! Ecstasy! I hold a note—three precious lines, which dazzle me. They are now gold, now vermilion, the blue of summer skies. 'The royal pardon for your wife has been sealed, and an order sent to the governor of La Force to liberate Madame Devine. You had better present yourself at the prison without delay. Your wife awaits you. The written promise must be returned to me by a sure hand.'

"There was no signature to this precious note, and the hand was a disguised one. Bagatelle! The great purpose was accomplished. In a few minutes my beloved Joséphine would be in my arms, recovered to free life, to love, to happiness! I give Philip just ten minutes to be ready with my coach! *Bon garçon!* he has done it even in less time. *Je sors.*"

Madame Devine, trembling in every limb, faint, bewildered, dizzy with the suddenness of so great a change, was given into the charge of her husband, lifted into his carriage, and driven off to a charming *séjour* in the environs of Paris, which he had rented since his interview with Madame du Barry, and named L'Elysée.

"Seen in the sunlight of revealing day, how pale, how worn, how mournfully sad was that sweet face, that wasted form! Was I too late? Could it be that she, so young, guileless, beautiful, was sinking into the tomb in the *fraîche matinée*—the young morning of her life! I feared so, and the fever of that fear excited in my brain, whilst she was still insensible, a veritable access, paroxysm of insanity, violent but brief—tears relieved me. In a few hours I had satisfied myself that although the springs of life were weakened in Joséphine, she was suffering under no organic disease. Quiet, care, the tenderness of a lavish love, with scientific ministrant· agencies, would bring back the roses to her pale cheeks, roundness to her shrunken form. This was my prayer—my hope. The prayer was accepted, the hope realised. Joséphine's health was rapidly restored. At the end of three years she was the mother of two beauteous buds of promise, herself still as fresh and fragrant a flower as any that flourished in the king's parterre.

"In the mean while, during those three years of delicious life, I had played my part in the world with success. Madame la Comtesse du Barry pushed my fortunes: the 'pilule divine' was sought after by the highest classes; esteemed to be a universal panacea! And, as I have said before, it was a good pill,—a really good pill. I changed my variegated liveries every month—the bizarre display always going on crescendo. Paris, valetudinarian Paris, was at my feet. All that greatly amused Joséphine, and enriched me. Vive le charlatanisme! Yet I was not a charlatan—far from it. I was a more, much more, scientific adept in pathology than the solemn humdrum fools who affected to laugh and sneer, and in reality were bursting with envy at my success.

"The brightest prospects fade, grow dim. The heavens are overcast; the sunlight disappears, and the gay, laughing landscape—gay, laughing but a short time since —is sombre; the gorgeous hues of the trees and flowers become neutral, gray with a tendency to black. This is every one's experience. It was mine in a moral sense. My success could not be forgiven by the faculty of medicine. Their calumnies gradually produced an impression. The falling off in the demand for the 'pilule divine' was rapid, continuous. One or two, perhaps five or six, cases terminating fatally—which fatal result all the physicians in Paris could not have averted or postponed—helped to swell the strong current of prejudice setting in against me. I had soared to the sun like the lark, and had got my wings singed; but there was a charming, well-lined, sweetly companioned nest upon the earth, into which I could quietly drop down and pass my days in peace,—peace hallowed by the consciousness of duty done—after an odd fashion, it may be admitted—but duty done, nevertheless, and illumined by the purple light of a pure, constant love.

"'*Bien aimée*,' said I, addressing Joséphine one calm balmy evening in summer, as I sat beside her in the veranda of L'Elysée; '*Bien aimée*, I have made money enough. I—you and I are rich. I have resolved to abandon, with your consent, this feverish life of Paris——'

"Joséphine interrupted me with a cry, a sob of joy. 'Ah! my husband, that is my desire, my hope.'

"'And, Joséphine, I should wish to settle at Le Havre de Grâce, your birthplace, beloved.'

"'Eugène, you have read my soul.'

"'There we can watch the Cazos, and I have a firm confidence that in good time we may elicit proof, irrefragable proof, of your perfect innocence, now only known to God and me. What say you?'

"'Nothing but God bless you, Eugène; God bless you!'

"We had lived upon the charming côte which overlooks Havre de Grâce, in quiet, retired style, for some four or five years; two additional children had been born to us, when Monsieur le Curé of Notre Dame called at our house, and asked to speak with me in private.

"'Monsieur Devine,' said the venerable priest, 'you are, I know, acquainted with—at least you know—Monsieur and Madame Cazo, of the Rue de Paris.'

"'Cazo the grocer, whose father was a clever herbalist? Yes.'

"'Madame Cazo is dead. She died miserably about four hours since. Some live ember in the charcoal chaufferette under her feet set fire to her dress. She was dreadfully burned. There was no hope of life from the first. I was sent for. The physical torture of the wretched

woman was nothing compared with the soul-agony by
which she was convulsed—maddened. During an inter-
val of comparative calm, she solemnly enjoined me to
say to Dr. Devine, to his wife, to all the world, that it
was she, Madame Cazo, then Fanchette Le Blanc, who
poisoned M. d'Estrées—that Madame d'Estrées was innocent of the deed as an unborn babe. I have not failed to
communicate that avowal of the dying woman to the
authorities, by which means it will have general pub-
licity, though that may be of no legal value.'

" ' Of not the slightest legal value, but its moral value
to me, to mine, is immense. Those words vouched to
have been uttered by the dying woman by a witness of
unimpeachable character will go far to dissipate the
shadow in which my wife, our children, have been so long
encompassed. Did the repentant woman say who it was
that furnished her with the poison, with the *poudre de
succession?'*

" ' Yes. But it was said under the seal of confession.
That dread secret cannot be divulged. Still I have a
right to proclaim aloud the innocency of Madame Devine,
to declare that *I know* she is innocent.'

" '*Remerciments—mille remerciments*—thanks—a thousand thanks, reverend father. Possibly we may yet be
vouchsafed such legal proof of my wife's innocence as will
compel the High Court of Rouen to rescind the judgment
upon Madame d'Estrées.'

" ' I have little doubt of it. Trust in God, in *His*
mercy. That is a staff that will never fail you.'

" My Paris reputation had both preceded and followed
me to Havre de Grâce. Though I had given up practice,
I from time to time gave advice, always gratuitously,
under special circumstances. I was held to be an oracle
in cases of *petite vérole.*

" One evening, soon after we had dined, an assistant
to M. Massieu, a physician, called at the house, and desired to immediately speak with me.

" He was the bearer of a message of intense interest

to me from Massieu. Cazo and his only child, a daughter, the very apple of his eye, had been stricken down by small-pox. Informed that he must abandon all hope of life, that nothing could be done for either him or his child Fanchette, he, refusing to die, insisted that M. le Docteur Devine should be sent for. If he required a fée of ten thousand francs, it would not be refused.

"I hastened with the assistant to the Rue de Paris—not, God knows, to receive a heavy fee, but in the hope that some confession might be made by Cazo, which would effectually and for ever clear the character of my wife.

"Edouard Cazo was dying. He was past cure—past hope; but with his daughter the disease had taken a favourable turn. She would live—of that I was quite sure. The change denoting that the disorder was killed, the plague stayed, was not observed by M. Massieu. He had had less experience than I. M. Massieu honestly believed, and was honestly telling Cazo, when I entered the room, that he and his daughter would be in their graves before twelve hours had passed. We bury the dead quickly out of our sight in France, especially in such cases.

"There was a world of agony, of terror, of despair in the look which Edouard Cazo fixed upon me. I passed from him to the daughter; then turning towards the doomed felon, I said, 'Nothing can save *you*. But I can, will save your child, if you will confess before an officer of the municipality that it was you who furnished Fanchette Le Blanc with the *poudre de succession* with which she poisoned M. d'Estrées. The confession must be a formal one, regularly attested.'

"There was a mighty struggle in the dark mind of Edouard Cazo. Rage, hatred of me, of me and my, by comparison, triumphant life, which he was required to make yet more triumphant, and love, intense, absorbing love—the fallen angels no doubt retained some hues of the Paradise they had lost—swayed his struggling spirit by turns. Love conquered. He consented to make the confession. The proper functionary, much against his will, attended; the instrument was formally drawn up, signed; and an hour afterwards Edouard Cazo was a loathsome corpse. The daughter recovered."

The High Court of Rouen finally rescinded the judgment and sentence pronounced upon Madame Devine, *ci-devant* Madame d'Estrées, and condemned the representative of Edouard Cazo to pay all the costs of the investigation from first to last. M. le Docteur Devine refused to take advantage of the judgment of the court in that regard. Mademoiselle Cazo was not mulcted in a single franc.

After this, nothing worth transcribing is reported of M. le Docteur Devine, except that he resumed the harlequin attire which, for business purposes, he had assumed in Paris, and laboured assiduously to revive the reputation of his " pilule divine"—not with any marked success.

When Louis the Fifteenth sickened of small-pox, of which disease he died, Madame du Barry—who, in losing the king, would lose all—despatched messengers to summon Devine to his majesty's assistance. Unfortunately, the charlatan physician had but a few days previously had his thigh broken by the falling across it of a tree which he was assisting to fell. He could not move—be moved. The king died; and to the day of his own death M. le Docteur Devine persisted in explaining to all who would listen to him, that but for the sudden falling of that tree, Louis the Fifteenth would have been saved— the crown might not have devolved upon the head of Louis the Sixteenth till he was able to sustain the splendid burthen—and monarchy would have endured another thousand years in France.

That there was some fissure, some flaw, in M. le Docteur Devine's brain can scarcely be denied; yet he was a clever, skilful physician, one of the tenderest of husbands and fathers, and emphatically a good man. His eccentricity was healthily developed; it harmed no one, and enriched himself and his. Madame Devine died two days before her husband. She was not apparently ill—

physically ill—when she expired in his arms. The blow was mortal. He refused to be comforted. Nor would he move from the chair where he was seated when he last pressed her dying form to his bosom. He would not have the coffin-lid screwed down, and his gaze continued to be fixed upon the dead face till his eyes had lost their speculation, till he himself was dead. He was so found by the attendants. M. le Docteur Devine died possessed of, for France, great wealth. His two surviving children, Madame Joséphine Ouvrard and Madame Estelle Bontemps, were amply provided for; and he left funds for the endowment of a Maison-Dieu at Ingouville, near Havre.

SIR ANDREW SELLWOOD, KNIGHT.

THE word 'eccentric' applied to human character, I hardly
need say, usually means one whose bent of mind prompts
him or her to overleap or break through the conventional
barriers which hedge-in the different classes of society—
to escape at any risk from the beaten highways of life.
These are frequently persons of powerful, if flawed, intellects; and to some of them the world owes much.   In
some instances they are justly entitled to be called the
pioneers of society: though they themselves, in their
devious gropings, often stumble into inglorious, forgotten
graves, they leave footprints on the sands of time, which,
followed by more wary walkers, lead to great results.
Of this truth I have to sketch some striking illustrations.

The story of Andrew Sellwood, Esquire, "soldier, artist, mechanician," is somewhat obscure.   Notices, frag-
mentary notices of him are scattered here and there in
the meagre chronicles of the county (Northampton) in
which he was born, for the most part lived, and at a
comparatively early age died.   Still, those brief notices
fit together, and enable me to depict his chequered career
with a oneness—considered in its totality, and allowance
being made for certain gaps and obscure passages—which
will give the reader a tolerable correct idea of "Crazy
Andrew Sellwood."

Sir Andrew Sellwood, Knight, was born in the parish
of Blakenley, in Northamptonshire, and was the son, or
the reputed son, of a shoemaker, Jacob Sellwood.   The
year of his birth was 1620—the year, by the way, when
the Pilgrim Fathers sailed from Southampton, in the

Mayflower, for the Promised Land. An enterprise which Andrew Sellwood would have abominated from the bottom of his heart, had he been of age to abominate any thing; his ruling passion, strong in death, having been loyalty —chiefly, I apprehend, because he believed himself to be a natural son of the Duke of Buckingham (Steenie)—the Duke of Buckingham who was slain at Portsmouth by Felton. Jacob Sellwood's wife—Andrew's mother—was a very handsome woman, and much younger than her husband. She was the granddaughter of one John Fothergill, a gentleman of local celebrity and good estate, who had the folly to join the northern insurrection provoked by Henry the Eighth's forcible suppression of the monasteries, and got hanged for his pious zeal, in plentiful companionship, at York. From that time the family appears to have rapidly declined in circumstances. Fothergill's only son espoused a damsel of low degree, the sole issue of which marriage was Margaret Fothergill, the mother of Sir Andrew Fothergill, Knight—a gay-spirited damsel, who for some three or four years resided in London with an ancient female relative of her grandfather's as a sort of humble companion. . . . It were needless to mark, even if accuracy were attainable, the degrees of degradation by which Margaret Fothergill fell so low that she was content to marry Jacob Sellwood, who, with some money she brought him as dower, set up as a master shoemaker in a humble way in his native county. Her son Andrew was born six weeks after the marriage. The husband seems to have been a good-natured, industrious clod, who lived in great awe of his wife.

Mrs. Margaret Sellwood died when her son was in his fifteenth year. She had taught him to read and write "as well as any clerk in the county." When dying, the mother's last words were, "Never forget, Andrew, that you are a born gentleman."

The strangely-tempered urchin had, in a certain sense, long since forgotten, though I suppose he had often been admonished to that effect, that he was a born

gentleman. He was always skylarking, as the phrase is
—robbing orchards—puddling in ponds, and altogether
grievously misconducting himself. There were flashes,
nevertheless, revelative of a high and generous, if erratic,
disposition. Take, for example, his rescue of Peg Twyn-
ham, a reputed witch, which has been quoted. "Old
Peg"—a half-crazed beldame, who gained a scanty, precarious livelihood by fortune-telling—had earned the
gratitude of the lad by fishing him out of a river when,
being an indifferent swimmer, he had got out of his depth
and was in danger of drowning. He did not forget that
supreme service. A murrain had spread amongst the
cattle in the neighbourhood, and the superstitious fools
of the place believed that old Peg had bewitched them.
She was consequently to be lynched after the old English
fashion of dealing with witches—*videlicet*, tying their
hands and feet together, and throwing them into a sufficiently deep pond or river. If she swam, there could
be no doubt she was a witch, and summary execution
followed. If she sank, the result, as regarded the poor
wretch herself, was generally the same, but there was a
moral acquittal. The clamour consequent on the seizure
of old Peg caught the ear of Andrew Sellwood, who,
seizing one of his father's sharp shoe-knives, hurried to
the rescue, and dealt about him vigorously, "wounding,
though not mortally, five of the ringleaders. Upon the
God-speed of the business, some gentlemen of the Northampton Hunt came up, by whom the riot was quelled,
and the old woman and Andrew Sellwood saved from the
rage of the mob."

Before his mother's death, and encouraged by her, she
being a skilled musician upon the "virginals," Andrew
Sellwood, who had "a turn for mechanics and harmony,"
completed after a fashion what seems to have been a rude
sort of barrel-organ. This he obtained permission to exhibit before the family of Sir Ralph Brisbane. The instrument, whatever it was, did not obtain the approbation
of Sir Ralph. Andrew Sellwood's pretension to be an
inventor of musical instruments was rudely mocked at,

except by the baronet's third daughter, Lucy—"a young and beautiful. girl, to see whom was to look into the face of an angel." Lucy Brisbane spoke a few kind words, which words photographed upon his sensitive boy-heart by the light of her rare beauty, became the scripture of his soul, the illumination, or, more correctly perhaps, the *ignis fatuus* of his life.

The immediate consequence of the youth's failure in the musical-instrument manufacturing line was that he ran away from a home made desolate to him by the death of his mother, and more repulsive still by the insistence of the father, that since his supposed skill in organ-building had proved to be a delusion, he should stick to shoe-making. "Old Peg" lent or gave Andrew sufficient money to pay his way to London, and in about a month after his departure from Northampton, Andrew Sellwood was serving as cabin-boy or powder-monkey on board the Garland—one of Admiral Sir William Monson's fleet, des-patched to frustrate or break a combination which was forming between the French and Dutch navies. It was in a chance encounter, during a tempest, of the Garland with the Jungfrau, a ship of superior force, that the ex-ploit occurred which, first reported to Prince Maurice, and by him to Prince Rupert, obtained for Andrew the command of "a Colour of horse" in the last-named Prince's famous cavalry. During the aforesaid chance engage-ment, the two ships forged together, in sailor-phrase. The Dutch boarded. During the desperate fight on deck, Andrew Sellwood, cabin-boy or powder-monkey, had mounted, certainly not in discharge of his routine duties, to the main-yard. The boarders were led by a celebrated captain—at least he was afterwards celebrated for his conduct in the great fights between Admirals Blake and Tromp. The boarders, I have said, were led by a celebrated captain; his name, Van Spyck, or Spycke. He was the life, the soul of the assailing party, and the struggle was going against the English, when Master Au-drew Sellwood, nicely judging his opportunity, literally "dropped down" upon the Dutch captain; that is to say

having no fire-arm with which to kill Van Spycke, it occurred to him that his own body would be pretty nearly
as effective as a cannon-ball. The consequence was, that
the fighting Dutchman suddenly found himself in the
condition of Sinbad the Sailor, the difference being, that
instead of an old man of the sea, it was a young sea-
monkey that bestrid his shoulders, and by the shock of
the collision prostrated him face foremost on the deck.
Captain Van Spycke was sorely bruised, and made prisoner. Curiously enough, the termination of the battle
is not set forth. I conclude it was a drawn fight; that
the greatest portion of the Dutch boarders got back to
their Jungfrau, and that the ships parted unpleasant
company.

The next notice I find of Andrew Sellwood is that
he was in command of " a Colour of horse" in Rupert's
cavalry, and fought in the action or skirmish at Chal-
grove, where John Hampden gave up his pure great life.
At the assault upon Donnington Castle by Earl Man-
chester, the Parliamentary General, he so distinguished
himself that Charles I. created him a Knight upon the
actual field of battle. He was severely wounded in the
last encounter, and ever afterwards limped in his gait.
Disqualified for active service, he necessarily left the
army.

About that time, I imagine, though the dates are
rarely given, Sir Andrew Sellwood was informed that the
relative with whom his mother lived in her youth had
died and bequeathed to him her whole property, landed
estate and money, amounting, in capital value, to the
enormous sum, in those days, of fifty odd thousand
pounds.

Sir Andrew Sellwood, Knight, would not have been
an exemplar chosen by me of eccentric character had he,
having come into immediate unmolested possession of his
aged relative's large legacy, set up a private establish-

ment, and married sensibly, having first erased from his brain all trivial fond records anent one Lucy Brisbane, whom he had never heard of since he ran off to sea, and who, no question, had long ceased to have the faintest recollection of the shoemaker's son who had essayed to manufacture a new-fangled instrument, and failed to accomplish his task.

Sir Andrew Sellwood, Knight, decided upon a very different course. He must have, one would think, lost count of time, and thought not of the havoc which Time works amidst the best-laid schemes of mice and men, to say nothing of the certain evanishment of Youth's fantastic dreams.

The image of Lucy Brisbane was fresh as ever in his memory. He imagined, and not without some reason, that fifty odd thousand pounds—equivalent to two hundred thousand pounds, at least, in these days—would atone for his limping gait and ignoble birth. The old shoemaker had been dead and buried some years.

Sir Andrew went to Northampton *incognito*,—I mean that he put off his rank,—and reappeared amongst such old friends as had not fallen into the sunless land, as Andrew Sellwood, the runaway son of Jacob Sellwood, the shoemaker, and not greatly improved in his worldly circumstances, besides having been lamed. His purpose was, of course, to ascertain how the land lay.

Lucy Brisbane had been married to Sir Arthur Fuller from about the time when he, Andrew Sellwood, dropped down upon Captain Van Spycke from the mainyard of the Garland. It was a marriage of affection; but Sir Arthur, through loss of estate brought about by the civil war, he being on the Royalist side, had become, people said, cankered in temper, dissipated, giving way more and more to excess, and would, people with wisely-wagging heads prognosticated, soon bring himself and family to utter ruin.

It chanced, too, that he was just then in want of a groom. Andrew Sellwood at once determined upon the absurdly romantic step of tendering for the place. He was engaged; and for fourteen years, incredible as the story seems, Sir Andrew Sellwood, his knighthood, his wealth unguessed of, remained in the service of the family.

At least he himself believed, or affected to believe, that he was known only by the Lady Lucy and her husband as Andrew Sellwood, the son of the shoemaker. I doubt this. It is *not* credible. The lady must have wilfully shut her eyes—affected blindness. Whence could she suppose those large sums of money came which always arrived so opportunely when her husband, of whom, spite of his follies, she appeared to have been exceedingly fond, was pressed with debt? Sir Andrew, who, by the way, was soon advanced from the post of groom to that of butler, prided himself upon the clever expedients by which he sought to conceal the source from which such fairy treasures so opportunely flowed. But he deceived himself; closed his eyes at noonday and said it was dark. "Crazed Andrew" was happy to so think. There is reason to believe that a sabre-wound on the skull which he received from one of Cromwell's troopers had irreparably damaged his intellect, though the illusion took but one direction; he being perfectly sane in all things except when the Lady Lucy was concerned. Like Hamlet, he was only mad west-nor'-west.

The Lady Lucy's husband had once been an enthusiastic and very serviceable Royalist; but finding himself —as did thousands of others—neglected at the Restoration, flung aside like a shelled peascod, he became involved in the plots of factions who, from various motives, sought the destruction of the Stuart dynasty. As every body knows, there was no end of "plaats," real or imaginary, during the reign of Charles II.

Finally, the reckless man had so gravely committed himself, that a warrant was issued for his apprehension upon the charge of high treason.

Conviction was certain; escape seemed impossible. Captain Aymard and his soldiers surrounded the mansion, and presently a thundering summons at the barred outer door demanded admittance in the king's name. The game was up. The inculpated rebel, who had not the faintest notion, it would appear, that he was suspected of complicity with traitors, was in the house; and there was but one hiding-hole—a recess in which fugitive priests were in the preceding reign hidden, not always successfully, from the hunters. The Lady Lucy was in a state of distraction closely bordering upon insanity. She sought—vehemently sought—counsel of the butler, Andrew Sellwood. This circumstance confirms the impression made upon me by the narrative that the Lady Lucy was perfectly conscious, though she may never have admitted the fact distinctly, even to herself, that she had a devoted *cavalier servente* in Sir Andrew Sellwood.

Sir Andrew Sellwood did not fail her. A few words between him and the Lady Lucy sufficed.

There was a hot search through the mansion as soon as Captain Aymard had forced an entrance, without successful result for some time; but as it was well known that the proclaimed rebel was there, the king's officer declared, and he meant to keep his word, that he would pull the house down sooner than permit the traitor to escape.

"Can I speak with you, captain, a few words in private?" asked a serving-man.

"Certainly; step aside. What have you to say?"

"If I showed you where the man you want lies concealed, would the promised reward be paid to me?"

"Yes; I pledge you my word it shall be paid to you, and without delay."

"Follow, then, with a file of soldiers. You will not betray me to the Lady Lucy?" added the butler, who was no other than the "traitor" himself. "I would remain in her service."

"Do not suppose for a moment I would do such a thing. Lead on."

"Here," said the pretended butler, in a whisper, and

pointing to a panel in the wainscoting, "here is the priest's-hole. You will find your man there. I will be gone."

The captain did find his man there. At least he thought he did, neither he nor one of his soldiers ever having seen the person he was in search of. Not the shadow of a doubt was entertained that they had got the right man in the right place.

The rebel baronet was arraigned at the Old Bailey. There was a great crowd, and Justice Scroggs presided. A great drama—a solemn tragedy was about to be enacted. Error! It was a farce, to be concluded in one scene.

A distinguished personage who sat on the Bench with the Chief Justice, and was present to hear the trial, started up the moment the prisoner was placed in the dock, and exclaimed aloud, "Why, God be gracious to us! the prisoner is my valiant friend and comrade, Sir Andrew Sellwood, knighted on the field by my royal uncle himself. What mockery is this?"

The speaker was Prince Rupert! There was great commotion, of course. Sir Andrew, spite of the prince's urgent entreaties, he himself offering to be bail in any amount for his appearance, was remanded to prison. When it was known that the real delinquent had escaped to France with his wife, with a large amount of coin supplied by Sir Andrew, that self-sacrificed gentleman was tried and convicted of misprision of treason, and condemned to imprisonment for life. He died in fetters. The following is his brief obituary, extracted from a newspaper—the *Public Ledger :* " Sir Andrew Sellwood, Knight, died yesterday in the governor's apartments, Newgate. The curious revelations which came out upon his trial are still fresh in the public memory. He was a good, gallant, but singularly eccentric gentleman. He was no doubt crazed by love—an early love ; a very rare instance."

BEAU BRUMMELL.

IT is a solemn truth that every death-bed is the final scene of a great tragedy, though the death be a beggar's, the bed one of straw. Yet to the human imagination the supreme catastrophe is magnified in its impressive terror when the miserable death strikingly contrasts with the glittering life, as, for example, in the instance of his splendid Grace of Buckingham, who expired

> " In the worst inn's worst bed,
> Where tawdry yellow strove with dirty red;"

and—a modern illustration—the tinsel life of Beau Brummell fading into the darkness of death in the hospital of the Good Saviour, Caen, France.

The perverted, lost life of the famous Beau Brummell dates from the 7th June 1778. He was one of three children—two boys and a girl. The father of George Bryan Brummell was secretary to Lord North, of disastrous memory. The noble lord's administration, however unfortunate for his country, was greatly beneficial to Brummell senior, who was able, by wise thriftiness, to save upwards of sixty thousand pounds, which, at his death, when the future Beau was but sixteen years of age, was bequeathed in equal portions to his children.

Beau Brummell received a fair education, and was a student at Eton when his father died. He exhibited very early much cunning perception, and seems to have foreseen the Georgian Era which was soon to dawn, when taste in tailoring would be a more potent introduction to " high society" than fame in arts, arms, or learning. He was, besides, well fitted by nature to be a distinguished clothes-peg. His face was not so handsome

as the late Count d'Orsay's; but his elegant figure would
show-off a tailor's skill. as well as could that doubtful
nobleman, or Prince Florizel—Mr. Thackeray's Prince
Florizel—afterwards George IV.   George Brummell had
one virtue in perfection—that of cleanliness in person
and apparel.   Lord Byron, who knew him well, has said,
with respect to his dress, that it was only remarkable for
its exquisite propriety.   The noble lord himself belonged
to the now happily obsolete class of " dandies."   Young
Brummell's general character whilst at Eton was that of
" a clever idle boy."   He had some humour too—good-
natured humour.   One trifling anecdote is sufficient proof
of this.   A bargee having in some way offended the Eton
students, was seized by a number of the exasperated lads,
and was about being hurled from the bridge over the
Thames into the river, when George Brummell interposed
in perhaps the only manner that, during the excitement
of the moment, would have been successful.   "My good
fellows," he exclaimed, "don't; the man is in a high
state of perspiration, and would be sure to catch cold."
The droll way in which this was said tickled the boys.
They burst into laughter, and the alarmed bargee was
set at liberty, with a solemn warning not to offend again.

From Eton George Bryan Brummell went to Oxford,
and was entered at Oriel College.   Previous, however, to
leaving Eton, he had attracted, by the " exquisite propriety" of his dress, the favourable notice of the Prince
of Wales, who had seen him on the terrace at Windsor.
That favourable notice, which the young man plumed
himself upon as about the highest honour that could be
conferred upon a human being, was unquestionably the
great calamity of his life—the unbarring of a door which
led by a primrose path for a considerable distance, presently with abundance of nettles and thorns, towards the
end, whence there was no turning back, to the abyss of
shame and ruin.

At Eton young Brummell was smitten with the ex-
ceeding loveliness of a youthful damsel, the niece of
Colonel Brewster, a retired officer in the service of the

East India Company. The young lady had perhaps not been strictly educated, her uncle, by whom she was adopted as a daughter, not having long returned from India. George Brummell would appear to have been as much in love as such an incarnation of vanity and conceit could be; but was suddenly disenchanted. "How is it that you are never seen now with Colonel Brewster's niece?" asked one of his companions. "Don't speak of it, there's a good fellow," rejoined young Brummell with a shudder; "she asked for soup twice."

At Oriel George Brummell was remarkable chiefly for breaking the college rules, and assiduous tuft-hunting. He was a devout believer in the doctrine enforced by Mr. Thackeray in one of his lectures at the Marylebone Institute—"Cultivate the society of your betters, young men." By betters, meaning persons of the highest reachable social position, possessed of present wealth and distinction, and in some cases glorified by the gleam of stars and garters shining in the distance. He entered himself as a competitor for the Newdegate Prize, and, though diligently "coached," was unsuccessful—not a result to be surprised at.

His failure was more than compensated by the gift of a cornetcy in the Tenth Hussars, then commanded by the Prince of Wales, who had so admired the eccentric exquisite on the terrace at Windsor. The notion of making George Brummell a soldier! He rode pretty well; yet but for one fortunate circumstance would never have recognised his company when the regiment was paraded: one of the non-commissioned officers had a remarkably large blue nose—red and blue, more correctly —and of very brilliant tints. That nose was Brummell's beacon. "My good fellow," said he, offering the man a handful of silver—"my good fellow, take care to keep up that illumination; it's worth the cornetcy to me."

His inefficiency as a soldier did not, however, prevent his rapid advancement. He was gazetted captain on the 1st of June 1796, through favour of Prince Florizel, with whom he continued to be a great favourite. He was also the " soul of the mess"—a very earthly, mundane soul, the coarse quality of which no coating of varnish could conceal from moderately discerning eyes. Still the *protégé* of a prince, and that prince the colonel of the regiment, would necessarily be a pet of the dandy officers of the aristocratic Tenth, especially as Brummell claimed to be the direct descendant of a line of illustrious ancestry, dating from the Conquest. The endorsement of Prince Florizel sufficed to make current this claim to an illustrious, as distinguished, I suppose, from a noble descent.

The remark attributed, I fancy wrongly, to the Chancellor Oxenstiern, of Sweden, who, alluding to some flagrant instances in question, exclaimed, ".See with what little wisdom the world is governed!" might, with perfect appositeness, be paraphrased into " See with what slender wit the world of fashion may, under certain circumstances, be amused, delighted, entranced! Before what a poor humanity all that glittering, pretentious throng will bow down in wondering admiration!"

The very best witticisms recorded as the utterances of George Brummell, in his time "the glass of fashion and the mould of form," and with which he set the mess-table of the gallant Tenth in a roar, were sorry stuff. He had a slight cold, and being asked how he caught it, said, "I went to Pietri's Hotel, and was shown' into a room where there was a damp stranger." This sally convulsed the officers of the gallant Tenth. Again—this was after he obtained his captaincy—" Why, Captain Brummell, you surely are not off with charming Lady M——." " An ounce of civet, good apothecary," replied the incipient beau, who had probably read elegant extracts from Shakespeare—" an ounce of civet, good apothecary. I positively saw her eating cabbage!" . " But surely you, Captain Brummell, sometimes eat vegetables?" said a somewhat gruff old major. " Yes, yes, major ; yes, I once ate a pea."

Having attained his majority, and come into possession of his inheritance, 30,000*l.* or thereabouts, the principal having augmented during his minority, and there moreover being ugly rumours afloat that even the Tenth Hussars might be ordered upon foreign service, George Brummell, who had a constitutional objection to expose himself to the action of that villanous saltpetre which ought never to have been digged out of the bowels of the harmless earth, sold his commission and retired from the service.

George Brummell at once determined to cultivate "a life of pleasure"—Sybarite, Epicurean pleasure; therein being at one with his patron the Prince of Wales. That flowery path to ruin was gaily trod. Mr. Brummell took a house in Chesterfield Street, furnished it in exquisite style, and forthwith devoted himself to the cultivation of society in "high life," and the best mode of tying white neckerchiefs. He succeeded in both those grand objects of ambition to his heart's content. "I can stand," he boasted, "in the pit at the opera, and beckon to Lovain (Duke of Argyll) on one side, and to Villiers (Lord Jersey) on the other, and see them come to me." Fortunate Brummagem Beau Brummell! But the tie and set of the white neckerchief was his America of discovery. The how and the why disturbed the peace and exercised the ingenuity of the whole fashionable world. Vainly was he importuned to disclose the wonderful secret. The oracle remained persistently dumb. Not even to the Prince would he shed a ray of light upon that sacred mystery. It was only when hurriedly leaving England to avoid a debtor's prison, that he vouchsafed to enlighten "high life" through the medium of his friend Lord Alvanley. "Starch is your man," he wrote with a pencil, directing the scrawl to that nobleman. The Lord Alvanley was delighted, and gave in after-years substantial proofs of his gratitude for so signal a favour. The *beau monde* participated in the enthusiasm of Alvanley at the solution of the grand secret. Such were your gods, O Israel! And these Brummels, peers, princes, were contemporaries with the men who wrestled down the giant wars which for a quarter of a century had convulsed Europe.

That Beau Brummell was the rage amongst the upper ten thousand is indisputable. No dinner, no ball, no assembly was held to be complete if he were absent. Very careful was he to preserve his exclusiveness. He recognised the peerage, but no other class of society, and like another Regency-George-the-Fourth impostor, John Wilson Croker, affected to be ignorant that there was such a locality as Russell Square "within the confines of civilisation."

Once, when remonstrated with by the wealthy father of a young man whom he, Brummell, had helped to "pluck" at cards, he said, "Upon my honour, sir, I did much for your son. I once gave him my arm all the way from White's to Walters'. Think of that, sir!"

Brummell, as I have said, had some humour of a weak eau-de-cologne kind. He condescended to accept an invitation to dine with a rich young man whose acquaintance he had made in a gaming-house. The young gentleman called upon him about half-an-hour before the time that dinner would be served to remind the Beau of his promise. In the mean time Brummell had received an invitation from Lady Jersey; and just as the rich nobody was speaking with Brummell, her ladyship's carriage stopped at the door to convey the distinguished dandy to her residence. "Well," said the plebeian acquaintance, "I see you will not honour me with your company to dinner this evening. Lady Jersey's claim is of course paramount. As my house lies in the direction of her ladyship's, I will ride with you part of the way." "Good God!" exclaimed Brummell, "ride with me! But perhaps you mean to get up *behind*." By the bye, one of the Beau's notions was that a sedan chair "was the only vehicle for a gentleman."

One Mr. Snodgrass, a F.R.S. and grave philosopher, happened to attract the notice of Brummell. The name offended the Beau, and he would ring the bell, and knock at the door about midnight, when there was no one up but the philosophic student himself. The window of the venerable man's study was thrown open, the venerable head thrust forth, and an angry demand screamed forth in pantaloon treble to know the meaning of such knocking and ringing at that dead waste and middle of the night. "*Is* your name Snodgrass?" asked the mellifluous bland voice of Brummell. "*Is* your name Snodgrass?" "Yes, it is—what then?" "Only, my dear fellow, that it is an extremely vulgar name. Snodgrass is decidedly vulgar." "You be ——"—we need not print the participle past—was the reply, as the wiudow was slammed down. The torment was fitfully repeated, till at last Mr. Snodgrass found himself obliged to appeal to the authorities, and Beau Brummell received an emphatic warning that such conduct would incur ignominious punishment. The Beau kissed the rod, and no more disturbed the philosopher's peace. This incident suggested the once popular farce of *Monsieur Tonson*.

Once Brummell was induced to accept an invitation to dine from a wealthy alderman, having first, however, obtained the civic dignitary's promise " not to tell." The dinner was served, and Brummell, who had made himself waited for a considerable time, at last arrived. There was a baron of beef on the table. " Good heavens!" he exclaimed, glancing at the table; " Good heavens—Ox!" and vanished.

The familiar terms upon which he stood with the so-called great men of the realm will be sufficiently illustrated by one or two anecdotes.

He was walking with the Duke of Bedford along Pall Mall, when his Grace asked him if he liked the cut of his coat—an improvisation of the Duke's tailor. Beau Brummell examined critically the ducal coat, and the survey finished, said, with an air and accent of deep compassion: " My dear Bedford, *do* you call this thing a coat?"

Again, being on a visit at Belvoir Castle, the seat of the Duke of Rutland, where a numerous company was assembled, and feeling somewhat indisposed, he left, at an early hour for him. Suddenly sounding a powerful alarm or fire-bell, which at once arrested the flying feet of the dancers,—" I beg your pardon, ladies and gentle-men," said the Beau, from the gallery which overlooked the *salon de danse;* "I beg your pardon, ladies and gen-tlemen, but there is no hot water in my room."

There have been various versions of the origin of the Beau's quarrel with the Prince Regent. The accepted story was that Brummell, having dined at Carlton House, and being desirous of tasting some wine of a celebrated vintage, said, "Wales, ring the bell;" whereupon the Prince did ring the bell, and to the answering servant said, "Order Mr. Brummell's carriage." The same story, or something like it, used to be told of Thomas Moore and the Regent. Brummell always denied that he had so misbehaved himself. According to the Beau's own version, his disagreement with the Prince was entirely owing to the marriage of his Royal Highness with Mrs. Fitzherbert. He had in some way offended that lady, and the "night crow," all powerful for a time, placed her veto against his admission to Carlton House. The Prince deeply resented Brummell's behaviour towards or con-cerning Mrs. Fitzherbert; and fop, fribble as he was, George IV. was a good hater. He never forgave. Brum-mell used to show his resentment in his own small way. Once after the final rupture with the Regent, the Beau, riding through Bond Street with Lord Sefton, met the Prince, who was taking an airing in a carriage. Seeing Sefton, the carriage was stopped. The prince and peer exchanged some commonplace courtesies. Sefton pre-sently rejoined Brummell. "Who is our fat friend in the carriage?" he asked, affecting not to have recognised the Prince. This sort of thing used to be thought very witty, cruelly sarcastic!

In the mean time the Beau's thirty thousand pounds are rapidly diminishing, becoming fine—very fine by de-grees and beautifully less. At last all is gone, and Bean Brummell's exquisite neckties will not appease the cla-mour of his furious creditors.

One incident in the eccentric life of this gay glitter-ing human moth should be mentioned before I follow

him into exile, and show what this "observed of all
observers" was when the paint and plumes were stripped
off. If not a vain boast, which is most likely, it speaks,
in perhaps a dubious sense, to his credit. The Beau was
on a visit to Earl H——. It was understood that his stay
would be a long one. Three or four days only had passed
when Brummell, brusquely presenting himself, said to
his lordship : "My lord, I must leave at once. I cannot
stop here." "Why, in Heaven's name?" "I am in love
with her ladyship, your wife." "The devil you are! But
never mind that. A passing fancy. Nothing more. Her
ladyship is not in love with *you*." "Well, your lordship,
I am afraid her ladyship does incline to be in love with
me." Brummell left immediately.

Alderman Coombe, an extensive brewer—Beau Brummell will be most faithfully depicted by these stray anecdotes—Alderman Coombe, an extensive brewer, had lost
a considerable sum of money to the Beau, who with
hilarious impudence said, whilst pocketing his winnings,
"All right, Alderman Coombe; in future I shall never
drink any porter but yours." "I wish," retorted the
angry alderman, "that every other scoundrel in London
would say the same, and keep his word." In this passage of arms between the Beau and the Brewer, the latter
had certainly the best of it.

At last all was gone: the pet of high society, the inventor of unapproachable neckties, was cleaned out. He
must make himself scarce as quickly as might be; but in
order to pass over the strait which divides Dover from
Calais funds were required. There were half-a-dozen exe-
cutions in his house, and no money could consequently
be obtained by sale or by hypothecating or pawning of
furniture, plate, &c. In this extremity, George Bryan
Brummell sent a note to one of his friends, a Mr. Scrope
Davis. I subjoin the note and the reply:

"May 16, 1816.

"MY DEAR SCROPE,—Lend me two hundred pounds.
The banks are shut, and all my money is in the Three

per Cents.   It shall be repaid to-morrow morning.—
Yours, G. B."

Mr. Scrope Davis to G. B.

"MY DEAR GEORGE,—It is very unfortunate, but all
my funds are in the Three per Cents.—Yours truly,
SCROPE DAVIS."

Brummell must have been more successful in other
quarters, as he certainly raised funds enough to enable
him to reach Calais, and support himself there till he
could organise a method of levying black-mail on his
titled English friends, upon whose charitable alms Beau
Brummell, the star of fashion, was thenceforth content
to exist.

The habits of this eccentric gentleman clung to him
through life.   He was as preposterously exclusive when
a fugitive from his creditors, and living upon the charity
of his former acquaintances, as in the days of his ephe-
meral prosperity.   He took up his quarters at a Calais
hotel, where he lived in very comfortable style for seventeen years.   His correspondence and the occasional visits
of great people imposed upon the French tradesmen, who
believed that he was suffering under a temporary eclipse
only, and would again shine out resplendently, a bright
particular star in the aristocratic galaxy of England.
The French are an acute people, but they have strange
notions with regard to England and English society.
For example, they believe the Lord Mayor of London to
be a potentate second only in dignity and power to the
monarch of Great Britain.

It is not at all surprising that they should have believed in Brummell.   The Duchess of York, a very amiable lady, sent him not only money, but a table-cover
worked with her own hands.   This steadfast friendship
of her Royal Highness seems to show that, after all, the
vain coxcomb must have had something good in him.
Lord Sefton moreover paid him a visit; so did Wellesley
Pole, and Prince Puckler Muskau, the Prussian noble-

man who once made a small splutter in the literary
line.

Let us pass swiftly over the decline and fall of this
once celebrated gentleman. His debts in Calais rapidly
accumulated. His English friends, generous as many of
them were, could not supply his extravagances; and when
George IV. passed through Calais on a visit to Hanover,
and did not send for *ce célèbre* Brummell, the faith of the
French in the great man sank to zero as quickly as did
that of Justice Shallow in Sir John Falstaff, when Henry
V. (in the play) publicly rebuked and cast him off.
Brummell was refused credit, and a prison was not ob-
scurely hinted at. Driven to desperation, he applied to
the Duke of York to procure for him, through his influence with the Ministry, a Government appointment.
The application was successful, and on the 10th of September 1830 Beau Brummell was appointed English
Consul at Caen, at a salary of four hundred pounds per
annum.

Landed at last, one would think, safe out of Fortune's reach. Not at all. His debts followed; his fool-
ish habits clung to him to the last; till at length the
only person whom he could rely upon to befriend him
was Mr. Armstrong, a grocer established in Caen. "My
dear Armstrong," he wrote one day, "lend me seventy
francs to pay my washerwoman." Yet the man who
wrote that note would not "honour" with his presence
any assemblage at which people in the remotest degree
connected with commerce were to be met with!

Beau Brummell had been Consul but about two years
when he appears to have been smitten with positive
lunacy. He memorialised Lord Palmerston, then Foreign Secretary, to the effect that there was no necessity
for a British Consul at Caen. He appears to have imagined that if he gave up the Caen Consulship he would
certainly obtain a more lucrative one—in sunny Italy,
he hoped. Lord Palmerston took the unfortunate Beau
at his word—abolished the Caen Consulship, presented
Mr. George Bryan Brummell with a *solatium* of two hun-

dred pounds, but gave no hint of the recipient obtaining any other appointment. This was the climax. No sooner were the arms of England taken down from the front of his house, than his French creditors determined at once to arrest his no longer inviolable person. This was done with a great deal of unnecessary display and circumstance; and poor Brummell was carried off to jail. A very weak creature the pet of courtly circles proved when subjected to the pressure of misfortune. He could do nothing to help himself; continued to weep and wail, and pour forth bitter complaints that his dinner was not regularly served—that his washerwoman did not get up his white cravats so well as she had formerly! At last, the grocer, Armstrong, who appears to have been actuated by a real sympathy for the broken-down Beau, proposed that he himself should go to England and personally solicit—being, of course, furnished with proper credentials—the help of Mr. Brummell's rich friends. This was done. Armstrong's mission was so far successful that sufficient funds were obtained to release Brummell from jail. But the Beau's future was bleak and dreary as ever. The end was near at hand. The intellect, such as it was, gave way; and it was determined by Mr. Armstrong and other friends to obtain him an asylum in the hospital of "Le Bon Sauveur." This charitable design was carried out; and George Bryan Brummell, screaming with idiotic terror, for he fancied he was about to be again shut up in jail, was conveyed to the convent or hospital. There he died, and was buried. The sad lesson which this life teaches needs no interpretation. He who runs may read its mournful significance.

LADY HESTER STANHOPE.

She surely must be a singularly eccentric woman who, born in almost the highest rank of the upper ten thousand, and who before she was out of her teens was possessed of great political influence, chose, whilst still young, to cast in her lot with semi-civilised inhabitants of Asia, and who, though not in the slightest degree influenced by genuine religious feeling, cherished visions, and died dreaming of a sacerdotal empire in the East—of a throne to be shared with the Messiah in Jerusalem!

Lady Hester Stanhope was the eldest of three daughters—Hester, Griselda, Lucy. They were the children of Charles Earl Stanhope, by his first wife the sister of William Pitt, the great Minister.

Charles Earl Stanhope was himself a singularly eccentric personage, and, one cannot help thinking, of flawed intellect. Himself a peer of the realm, he professed profound contempt for hereditary rank, and, as a tangible proof of the reality of his convictions, ordered the erasure of the armorial bearings from his coach-panel! A whimsical gentleman in other respects: he slept, Lady Hester reports, under the weight of a dozen blankets; and when he rose, squatted down on the floor, and ate his breakfast of tea and dry bread. The noble peer, not satisfied with having painted out the armorial insignia of his coach-panels, sold the carriages. The second Lady Stanhope was indignant at this development of aristocratic democracy. Precocious Lady Hester devised a plan to shame her father out of his plebeian propensities. She got a pair of stilts, and stumped down a muddy road where the Earl would be sure to see her.

"I say, little girl," said his lordship, "what have you been doing? Where was it I saw you going upon that pair of—the—the devil knows what—eh, little girl?" To which Lady Hester replied, that as the Earl had sold his carriage, it seemed to her that the best mode of getting through the mud was by the help of stilts. The practical lesson thus taught had its effect upon the Earl, who promised to restore the carriage, "but no more ar-morial bearings."

There must have been an hereditary craze in the noble family of the Stanhopes, but the disease manifested itself in divers forms. The Lady Hester, for example, gloried in being an aristocrat of the purest, most exalted blood and breeding—one conclusive proof that there was no particle of common clay in her composition being "that her instep was so high that a kitten could walk under the sole of her foot."

Education, in the true sense of the term, she had none; neither had her sisters. After the death of her mother, who died whilst she was still young, the ladies were consigned to the jurisdiction of their grandmother, the Dowager Lady Stanhope, who employed French and Swiss governesses. Their most important duty was to squeeze the Ladies Hester, Griselda, and Lucy into symmetrical shape by back-boards. "How I did hate those wretches!" Lady Hester often exclaimed in after-years. "They would have squeezed me, had it been possible to do so, into the size of a tiny miss;" and—inconceivable misappreciation of the infallible sign of distinguished lineage—positively endeavoured to flatten down the sole of her foot, "which a kitten could walk under." One reason for her ladyship's lofty dislike of the British people was, that as a nation they are deficient in the pedal arch—a flat-soled generation, of whom no great and noble achievement could be hoped for.

Mr. Pitt, her uncle, invited her to reside with him permanently, and preside over his household. Lady Hester at once accepted the offer, and continued with the great minister till his death. Lady Hester had a sovereign contempt for books, especially books of history, which the instinctive genius of a lady possessed of such a high instep instructed her were all lies. She was not, however, incredulous of biographic sketches of her charming self. " Men who were no fools declared that I might well be proud of the alabaster whiteness of my neck, rivalling that of any pearl-necklace, of my cheeks' fine contour, rounding off so beautifully that the exquisite Brummell exclaimed, ' For Heaven's sake, take off those earrings, that we may see what is beneath them.' " The chivalrous sailor Sir Sidney Smith's admiration was, if we may believe her ladyship, more enthusiastic still. He is said to have thus described her *entrée* into the society of the *grand monde* assembled at Mr. Pitt's mansion. " You entered the room in your pale skirt, exciting our admiration by your magnificent and majestic figure. The roses and lilies were blended in your face, and the ineffable smiles of your countenance diffused happiness around you." The Lady Hester must, one would suppose, have anticipated Captain Cuttle's advice to make an immediate note of any thing thought worthy of preservation by the hearer. The same with the following passage, uttered by no less a personage than his Majesty George the Third: " You have not reason, Mr. Pitt, to be proud that you are a minister, for there have been many before, and will be many after you; but you have reason to be proud of your niece, Lady Hester, who unites every thing that is great and good in man or woman." And yet this lady, who comprised in her own person all that is great and good in man or woman, was, according to her own candid confession, " a mischievous mimic, as fierce and proud as the devil."

A very precocious damsel, too, was the Lady Hester Stanhope in other respects. The Dowager Lady Stanhope had given strict orders to the French and Swiss governesses to keep the young ladies in ignorance of all things improper for young ladies to know. Lady Hester, though only sixteen summers had passed over her head,

F

"quickly knew and remembered every thing." She nevertheless admired, or affected to admire, delicacy of manners, and speaks approvingly of Earl Grey, then a young man. She dropped one of her garters at the trial of Warren Hastings, and the earl, knowing whose it was, handed it to a female attendant who served tea and coffee in the lobby.

Lady Hester Stanhope not only reigned supreme in Mr. Pitt's establishment, but had a potential voice in the disposal of the minister's patronage. Of marriage, which the young lady early knew to be all "star," she appears to have thought but little, "though there were men who would have gone through fire and water for me." "She had determined to be the wife of no one less clever than herself." Mr. Pitt, hearing her express that resolution, exclaimed, "Then you will never marry. There is no such man."

Her ladyship further reports that Mr. Pitt once remarked, "That it would be quite useless trying to conceal any thing from me; for if I wished to cheat the devil, I should succeed in so doing." Quite true, complacently added the youthful Lady Hester.

Mr. Pitt died, and, as by a *coup de théâtre*, the brilliant scene in which the Lady Hester had so long shone supreme at once disappeared. The obsequious crowds of courtiers, who had been so proud to sun themselves in her smiles when the haughty damsel condescended to bestow them, made the sudden discovery that the delightful *brusquerie* of speech, the charming frankness which they had so greatly admired, was, in reality, hoydenish impertinence; her contempt of conventionalism, which, whilst Mr. Pitt was living and in office, they had supposed to indicate a great original genius, to be, after all, mere vulgar rudeness, and indicative only of the revolt of a coarse-minded girl-woman against the decencies of polished society.

Queen Hester's reign was over—the diadem reft from her brow. She removed to a splendid residence in Mon-

tague Square; but nobody that was any body visited her
there.   She next tried rustication at a cottage in Wales.
That did not at all harmonise with her ladyship's soaring, transcendental visions; and she finally resolved to
abandon England, and seek a home either in the mysterious East, or the teeming West.   The world was all
before her; and possessed of a pension of fifteen hundred
pounds per annum, regularly paid in good honest sovereigns out of the British exchequer, her future looked
bright enough.

The Lady Hester was unfortunate at the outset of
the voyage.   The vessel in which she sailed was shipwrecked off the Island of Rhodes, and her ladyship nar-
rowly escaped with life.   She proceeded to Constantinople—sojourned there for some months, whiling away
the time by inditing a voluminous correspondence, the
subject-matter of which was mainly the glorification of
Napoleon Bonaparte and herself!

Finally, this eccentric lady settled at Dar Joon, in
Syria, not very distant from St. Jean d'Acre.   Whilst
there her spiritual visions assumed a distinct shape.   The
Millennium was close at hand, and she was the chosen
bride of the Messiah of Nations—chosen from before the
foundations of the earth were laid;—whose advent she
hourly expected, and not less confidently after, by the
lapse of time and the indulgence of vicious habits, she
had withered into a smoking, chewing old crone, whose
chief occupation was swearing at the "black beasts" her
servants.

Many persons from Europe visited her at Dar Joon.
The most distinguished of them was M. Lamartine, who,
in his *Eastern Travels,* plentifully bedaubs her with plaster-of-paris artistically coloured.   Lady Hester had condescended to prophesy high things of the French poet;
her chief avowed reason for assuring him that he would
rise to eminence in his own country being, that although
he could not pretend to an exalted instep like her own,
which a kitten might creep under, water would flow be-

neath his pedal-arch without wetting it. Lamartine positively repeats this craziness, as if he were transcrib-·ing the sayings of a Plato. Lady Hester also vouchsafed to show M. Lamartine two foals, curiously marked on their backs, upon which the Messiah and herself would make their entry into Jerusalem!

The chosen bride of the Messiah had strangely enough grown oblivious of the maxims of common honesty. A pension of fifteen hundred pounds per annum must have been an enormous income at Dar Joon; but her ladyship could not, somehow or other, make both ends meet. Creditors became clamorous, and some of the wiliest of them instructed agents in London to apply to a Court of Equity for relief. The pension—at least a considerable portion of it—might, they thought, be set aside for the liquidation of her ladyship's debts. That, however, could not be done; but Lord Palmerston, then Secretary for Foreign Affairs (1838), apprised of the circumstances by Colonel Campbell, the English Consul at Beyrout, wrote to her ladyship, politely intimating that payment of the pension would·be suspended, unless she would make a *bonâ fide* effort to settle with her creditors.

This "impertinence to a Pitt" was warmly resented by Lady Hester, and not condescending to reply direct to the Foreign Secretary, she addressed a letter to the Queen of England herself, threatening to give up her pension, and with it the name of an English subject and the slavery which it entailed. As to Colonel Campbell, her ladyship had half a mind to shoot him, either herself or by proxy; he having richly deserved that fate, "for having alienated from the queen and the country a person whom great and small must acknowledge had raised the English name in the East higher than any one had before done, besides having made philosophical researches of every description for the benefit of mankind in general."

The final renunciation of the pension was, however,

postponed; and soon a more potent creditor than those who had invoked the intercession of Colonel Campbell put in his claim. Lady Hester Stanhope died suddenly in June 1839. The favourite and beautiful niece of the great William Pitt fills an obscure grave in the Syrian wilderness, her only bequest to the world being the sad moral of her life.

BEAU NASH.

There are many kinds as well as degrees of celebrity. Lord Chancellor Brougham once, under the influence of an access of acrid humour, observed, in illustration of his argument, and pointing towards the Dukes of Wellington and Cumberland, who were conversing quietly together on the cross-benches of the House of Lords, that the one was illustrious by his deeds, the other illustrious by courtesy.

Quite true. The remark is of every-day application, and takes in a wide range of character. Richard Nash, esquire, master of the ceremonies and king of Bath, was, equally with George IV., king of England, illustrious by courtesy. His Majesty of Bath, with all his weaknesses and follies, was, however, a far more respectable man than his Majesty of Britain. This must be conceded even by those who recognise the truth as well as admire the caustic force of the verses attributed to Lord Chesterfield. In what was then known as " Wiltshire's Ball-room, Bath," a statue, life-size, of Beau Nash was placed between the busts of Newton and Pope. Chesterfield wrote :

> " The statue placed these busts between
> Gives to my satire strength;
> Wisdom and wit are little seen;
> And folly at full length."

The right of fribble Chesterfield to sit in judgment upon fribble Nash may be disputed, but there can be no doubt as to the strict applicability of his lordship's lines. For all that, the Beau of Bath was a superior man to Lord Chesterfield. A trifler, sycophant if you will; but Beau

Nash, as I shall presently prove, had a heart in his bosom ever responsive to the sad music of humanity. The noble lord who, if we accept the dictum of Doctor Johnson, published a book which taught the morals of a prostitute and the manners of a dancing-master, was, morally estimated, far below the standard of Richard Nash,—and that was not a high one.

Richard Nash was born at Swansea, Glamorganshire, on the 18th of October 1674. His mother was niece to Colonel Poyer, who made a gallant stand for Charles I., when that monarch's fortunes were utterly desperate, and whom Cromwell crushed with an effort as slight as it was merciless.

The king of Bath was educated at Jesus College, Oxford; but his genius, or inclination more properly, lying in the direction of fine clothes and elegant deportment, it is not surprising that he did not take a degree. He left the University considerably in debt; a petty liability for which he considered the property he left behind him —one pair of boots, two volumes of plays, a fiddle, and tobacco-box—sufficient security.

Arrived in London, he contrived to raise a sufficient sum of money to purchase an ensigncy. The temptation must have been the uniform, for assuredly no man was ever less fitted for the vocation of a soldier than Beau Nash. The commission, however, served his purpose, by introducing him to the society of persons in high life, with whom his obsequious deference for every one who had any claim to social distinction soon made him a favourite—Nash repaying himself for lip-homage by his success as a gamester, a profession in which he was an early adept.

It was at this time that the first striking instance occurred illustrative of the double nature of this vain popinjay of a man. He was introduced to and fell in love with a Miss Verdun. She was beautiful, and possessed of a moderate dowry. The father, who had risen from obscurity, and looked with reverence upon the elegant fop who was hand-and-glove with nobility, insisted upon his daughter's acceptance of Nash's offer. The lady had, however, formed a prior attachment, and candidly confessed it to her exquisite suitor, who behaved admirably. Nash sought an interview with the father, and finally prevailed upon him to allow his daughter to marry the man of her choice. Nash himself gave the bride away; a sorry gift, for the woman eloped with her footman after a few months only of married life. Nash, upon being informed of what had occurred, entertained a gay party at the Smyrna Coffee-house, and having related the disinterested part he played in promoting his rival's suit, remarked that the result was a striking illustration of the moral aphorism which declares that virtue is its own reward. The husband, looking at the matter from a different point of view, committed suicide.

Scared by war's alarms, brought home to him by the ominous fact that his regiment was about to be sent on active service, Beau Nash, who had had an instinctive horror of vile guns, sold his commission, and entered himself in the Middle Temple. He would become a famous barrister, and glimpses of the great seal flashed across his ambitious vision. That dream did not last long; Richard Nash was not slow to discover that he had no more genius for law than for war. His refined manners, elaborate yet elegant courtesy stood him, however, in good stead. Upon King William III.'s accession to the throne, that monarch, in compliance with time-honoured custom, accepted an entertainment at the Middle Temple. The Benchers requested Nash to do the honours, the ceremonial speechifying; and so well did he acquit himself that the king offered to confer upon him the honour of knighthood. The reply of Nash was apt and prompt: "If your Majesty should condescend to create me a knight, I would humbly beg that it should be one of the poor Knights of Windsor, as I should then have a modest income wherewithal to support the dignity." The king did not take the hint. Honour he was quite willing to bestow, but money and profitable places were required for very different claimants.

Nash was also treasurer to the Benchers of the Middle Temple, and when, for the last time, he made up his accounts, one item therein greatly surprised the auditors: " For making one man happy, ten pounds." Mr. Nash explained that he had made a present of the ten pounds to a man who declared that such a sum would be his salvation—" would make him the happiest man in the world." The Benchers, not for a moment doubting his word, passed the item. This anecdote is a proof not only of Nash's good nature, but of the confidence which the Benchers must have had in his integrity.

The barrister's gown, like the ensign's uniform, was cast off, and Beau Nash, with no resource but his skill at play, ostentatiously devoted himself to the pursuit of pleasure—of sensuous but refined enjoyment. It is curious, too, that this man, whose hand was open as day to relieve indigence and misfortune, had an inveterate dislike to paying his debts. A gentleman to whom he owed twenty pounds, having often and often applied to him in vain for payment, hit upon the expedient of asking a mutual friend to affect distress and borrow thirty pounds of Nash. The mutual friend did so, and Nash lent the money. On the next day the creditor called upon the gentleman, who was always generous, if not just. After the common interchange of courtesies, Mr. Nash said, " Ah, I suppose you are come about that twenty pounds? Well, I daresay that in the course of a few weeks I shall be able to pay you."

" You have told me that story, my dear friend, a hundred times," was the reply, " but there is no necessity to tell it again. Mr. ——, to whom you lent the thirty pounds yesterday, gave me twenty, and I have now to return you the difference." Nash, upon hearing that, flew into a violent rage, swore he had been swindled out of his money, and had he not been a rigorous disciple of the peace-at-any-price doctrine, would probably have kicked his clever friend down stairs.

Richard Nash, esquire, now determined upon a provincial tour; but his first essay was unfortunate. He must needs try his comparatively 'prentice hand at York, where he was completely cleaned out—lost every shilling he possessed. The sharpers by whom he had been fleeced were not altogether bad fellows of their sort, and agreed to return him fifty guineas if he would consent to stand in a white sheet for half-an-hour at the door of the Cathedral. Nash consented, and being recognised by one of the clerical dignitaries, to whom he had been introduced in London, said, in answer to the dignitary's astonished inquiry as to what such an exhibition meant, that " it was a Yorkshire penance for keeping bad company!" Another proof of the low state of his exchequer at that period is that a man of his fastidious habits won a large wager by riding naked through a village upon a cow!

For some time Richard Nash, esquire, remained under a cloud; but at last he turned up resplendently at Bath, the medicinal waters of which city had attained fashionable celebrity by a visit of Queen Anne, and the benefit it was alleged her Majesty had derived from their use. Nash was not only a man of fashion, an universal gallant, but a professed, and, upon the whole, highly successful gamester—so successful, that he was before long enabled to set up a coach drawn by six gray horses, and although often put to degrading shifts, managed to maintain a fictitious splendour, till he died in extreme old age—an apparent pauper.

His ascendency in Bath society was quickly achieved, and so firmly established that his claim to be King of Bath was never disputed. Nash was a veritable despot of ball-rooms, and, it must be admitted, a judicious one. Dancing began at six precisely, and terminated at eleven. This rule was peremptory, and never broken during his reign. The Princess Amelia, it is stated, was refused another dance after the fixed hour had chimed.

Some of the regulations framed by Beau Nash display sense and some slight humour. Duels, fought in hot blood, were frequent in those days; and to diminish the evil, and give time for reflection, the King of Bath refused to allow swords to be worn at either the Pump or Ball-rooms. Amongst the rules which he had printed and framed were these:

"No gentleman shall give his ticket for the balls to any but gentlewomen.—N.B. Unless he has none of his acquaintance.

"No gentleman or lady must take it ill that another dances before them, except such as have no pretence to dance at all."

The anecdotes related of him are amusing enough.

He one night played a game of piquet for two hundred pounds, and won the stake. One of the on-lookers, a poor gentleman with whom he had a slight acquaintance, exclaimed in a subdued, soliloquising tone, but quite audible to the sensitive ear of Nash, "My God, how happy that money would make me!" "Take it, then," said Nash, without an instant's hesitation; "take it, and be happy."

The distressing case of a clergyman was brought under his notice. The income of the reverend gentleman was thirty pounds per annum, upon which he, his wife, and six children starved. Nash at once zealously exerted himself to relieve the unfortunate divine's necessities, raised a handsome subscription, and did not cease importuning his influential friends till he had obtained him a living worth two hundred and sixty pounds per annum. Whilst the subscription was going on, Sarah Duchess of Marlborough entered the Assembly-room, and, addressing Nash, said, "I have come here without money. You must put something in the plate for me." "With pleasure, your grace. One, two, three, four, five ——" "Stop, Nash; five guineas are surely enough." "Consider the eminent position filled by your grace, and the clergyman's cruel necessities. Six, seven, eight, nine, ten, eleven——" "Nash," remonstrated the Duchess, "you will drive me mad." "Twelve, thirteen, fourteen," —Nash did not stop till he had counted as far as thirty, when, finding the Duchess was becoming furious, he held his hand.

Another creditable anecdote is thus told: One Colonel Montague, a ruined gamester, endeavoured to inveigle a young lady of great beauty into contracting a marriage ruinous to both. Beau Nash baffled his scheme, and the enraged colonel forthwith challenged his Majesty of Bath. The "King," like a sensible man, refused to fight. The Colonel left Bath, and joined the Dutch army in Flanders, where he served for some years in the ranks, and returned to England in such deplorable destitution that he was fain to join a company of strolling-players exhibiting at Peterborough. Meanwhile the young lady, who had never concealed her partiality for the Colonel, had come into possession of fifteen hundred pounds per annum. Beau Nash, who knew of the condition and whereabouts of Colonel Montague, invited the damsel and her mother to accompany him to Peterborough, giving no hint of his real purpose in going there. Arrived at Peterborough, the party went to the theatre. The piece played was *The Conscious Lovers*, in which Colonel Montague, in the assumed name of Egerton, was to play Tom. The lovers instantly recognised each other, and there was a new scene of Conscious Lovers enacted. The young lady fainted; "Tom" bolted, and another actor had to walk on for the part. Finally, au interview was arranged, and Beau Nash, joining the hands of the loving couple, exclaimed, "Take her, Colonel; and d——, say I, whoever attempts to part you."

The consideration shown by Beau Nash for the Earl Townsend was marked by a real magnanimity. The young nobleman had a perfect mania for gaming, but was utterly deficient in skill. He played with Nash, and lost every thing — estate, carriages, horses, furniture. Nash gave back all, upon condition that he would not play again, and give a written promise to pay him, Nash, five thousand pounds, should he ever stand in need of the money. The time did come when the King of Bath was in pressing need of the money, but before that Earl Townsend was in his grave. Nash applied to the heirs, who honourably discharged the obligation.

This curiously-constituted man, cringingly servile to the possessors of wealth and rank, so lavishly bountiful to the needy, who had worked for many months and with great ultimate success, in conjunction with Dr. Oliver, to found a General Hospital in Bath, and who, as his feeble foot-fall approached nearer and nearer to the setting sun, manifested a terror of death as abject as did George IV. or Doctor Johnson, lived on—if his last years can be called life—till his eighty-eighth year. The day after his death the Corporation met, and voted fifty pounds to defray the cost of the " King of Bath's" funeral. The worshipful Corporation did more even than that for the man whom they had left to die in indigence, as the following epitaph, engraved upon his tomb, in commemoration of his merit and the magnanimous liberality, which induced them to perpetuate his memory, will testify:

" Richard Nash, Esquire,
Died February 13th, 1761, aged 88.
He was by birth a gentleman,
and educated at Jesus College, Oxford.
He erected the City of Bath into a Province of Pleasure,
and held sacred Decency and Decorum.
Of his Noble Public Spirit
and
warm grateful heart,
the Obelisk in the Grove
and
the Beautiful Needle in the Square
are Magnificent Testimonies."

SIR GERALD MASSEY, KNIGHT.

I DO not know if Sir Gerald Massey, knight, who died at Halifax, Yorkshire, in 1792, at the ripe age of ninety-six, was a progenitor either of Gerald Massey, the poet, or Mr. Massey, M.P. and Chairman of Committees in the House of Commons. That, in a small way, he was both poet and politician, is not of course decisive evidence of such relationship. Sir Gerald was, at all events, a very odd fellow, not to be matched, I should suppose, by many of the tens of thousands of self-proclaimed odd fellows—the mass of whom I rather think are pretty even with the world.

Sir Gerald Massey was "picked up" in a field about two miles out of Halifax, by a shoemaker of the name of Cross. Not at all an appropriate cognomen, Charles Cross being a man of remarkable benignity, who, with not very large means—though he was one of the principal tradesmen in Halifax—"went about doing good." The child was about seven years old when found by Mr. Cross. He was clothed—if clothing it could be called—in dirty rags, and had fallen asleep in a gravel-pit from fatigue and exhaustion. The only account the boy could give of himself was that his mother and father were travelling tinkers, and that when he awoke in the morning they were gone. He had tried to find them, but could not; and hungry, weary, laid himself down, he believed to die. His mother, the boy said, could read and write, but was the slave of her husband—not the boy's father—who cruelly ill-used her. He was always called Jim; but his mother, who might have known that her husband was determined to rid himself of the encumbrance, had written something on a piece of linen only a day or two before he was abandoned, and stitched it on the inside of his trousers. Mr. Cross examined the piece of linen, but could only make out clearly two words, "Gerald Massey." More had been written, but the ink had run, and the sentence, whatever it was, could not be read.

Mr. Cross took the boy home, and, having no children, was gradually so won upon by the boy's endearing ways, that he adopted Gerald Massey as his own son. Gerald was placed at school, received a good plain education, and when of the proper age was put to learn the craft of a cordwainer.

Gerald was a good boy enough, but he was refractory as to shoemaking. He could not abide it. A taste for tinkering—out-of-door tinkering—possessed the lad. With the pocket-money allowed him by Mr. Cross he procured the few tools and the materials necessary for the tinker-trade, and one day, before his benefactor had risen, set off " to seek his fortune" by mending pots and kettles. He earned sufficient to keep body and soul together, and inspired probably by the example of John Bunyan, with whom he had at least this resemblance, that both were tinkers, and conscious of possessing considerable talking ability, he commenced the practice in his twentieth year, perhaps earlier, of preaching on Sundays in the open air. At that period of life his creed was Calvinism—Calvinism in its most outrageous form— its blasphemous denial that the fountain of God's infinite mercy is ever, and will for ever remain, open to all. This fit of fanatical enthusiasm brought Gerald Massey to grief more than once. He was finally cured of his preaching propensity by a long spell in the stocks, supplemented by a terrible whipping, at the cart's-tail, through the Yorkshire village of Upham, or Updown. It seems hardly credible that even in those cruel days such punishment could be awarded to a man guilty only of preaching without a license what he believed to be the Gospel. I cannot, however, find that any other charge was preferred against him.

Gerald Massey was not the stuff of which martyrs are made. He discontinued preaching, and made his way back to Halifax.

Mr. Cross, whose health was fast failing, received the ungrateful truant kindly, and was willing to let bygones be bygones, if he would thenceforth lead a steady, quiet life. Gerald Massey promised to do so, and kept his promise, till one day a woman, stylishly dressed, and attended by a servant, entered the place, inquired for Mr. Cross, and asked that person if it were true that he had found a boy, as she had been informed he had, in a gravel-pit, about two miles from Halifax, in 1696? Mr. Cross admitted that he had. The woman or lady said she was the boy's mother, and mentioned the circumstance of her having stitched a piece of linen with his true name written upon it inside the child's trousers. She also described some natural marks upon young Massey's body, and no reasonable doubt could be entertained that he was, as she alleged, her son. Times had changed with her. The tinker husband had died—she had married Mr. Gerald Massey, a gentleman of fortune, the father of her illegitimate son. He too had been several years dead. She was in tolerably affluent circumstances; resided at a place near Appleby, Westmoreland, and had, after much difficulty, found by God's mercy her son and only offspring. Gerald Massey was out when the widow Massey called, and when he returned did not recognise his mother. The image of the mother, which dwelt in his memory, was that of a tall woman with dark hair. This woman was not more than a medium height, and her hair was brown, whereas the almost invariable tendency of age is to darken and whiten hair, as the case may be. Still Gerald—but seven years of age when he lost, or was separated from his mother, and over twenty years having passed since then—could not confide in the faithfulness of his memory, even with regard to that mother's personal appearance. Besides the temptation to believe, or affect to believe, Mistress Massey was his mother, would half unconsciously perhaps tinge his recol-.

lection—not sickly it over with the pale cast of thought, but shedding the glow of a luxurious future over the life of an aspiring young man who had suffered the ignominy of the stocks, and been publicly whipped at a cart's-tail. Gerald Massey left Halifax with his real or pretended mother for Stone Hall, Appleby.

This narrative will be an imperfect one. I cannot discover any thing of importance in the life of Gerald Massey till the close of the year 1727, when he went up to London to present an address of congratulation to George II. upon his accession to the throne; of condolence also, I suppose, for the loss of his father, George I. The new king knighted him—in very bad English—but it sufficed, and Sir Gerald Massey returned to his seat near Appleby in high feather. It is pleasant to know that his benefactor, Mr. Cross, having fallen into difficulties, Sir Gerald paid all his old and first friend's debts, aud made his age comfortable and happy. Mr. Cross died in 1738.

When Mrs. Massey died I have not been able to discover. I should judge about 1740. At all events, Sir Gerald Massey, soon after her death, entered the army; was present in 1743 at the battle of Dettingen; behaved very well, was badly wounded, and—though the French were defeated ahd compelled to repass the Rhine with precipitation—had the mischance to be taken prisoner. After confinement in a fortress for two years, he managed to escape, with the aid of a Frenchwoman who had nursed him whilst he was suffering from the wounds received in the battle. He safely reached England—the woman with him—where Sir Gerald married her; in London probably. Her maiden name was Marie Lefranc. Sir Gerald appears to have been ardently attached to her, and she bore him several children.

Soon after his marriage, Sir Gerald, who had given up his commission in the army, became infected with a mania for cock-fighting, dog-fighting, bull-baiting—entered with all his heart and soul into those refining amnsements—converted one of his best rooms into a cock-pit—baited bulls in his own park, freely admitting, spite of the remonstrance of his French wife, all the lowest rabble to witness the sports, at which he assisted, dressed in the highest style of fashion. These cock-fights and bull-baitings were immensely attractive; and hugely rejoiced was the small farmer or humbler rustic if he was permitted to make a wager with the eccentric knight, as Sir Gerald always paid if he lost, and refused the wagerer's money if he won. He never betted with gentlemen or with men of wealth. This game went on for several years, and Sir Gerald had gained a character for one of the best and oddest gentlemen in the whole country side. A man of rare pluck, too, was the knight. Ralph Button, a brawny pugilist of local celebrity, was given to cruel practical jokes. One hot day Sir Gerald, a great walker, finding himself some thirty miles distant from Stone Hall, and at a place where he was personally unknown, entered a humble hostelry, called for refreshment of some kind, and sat down amidst a number of rude peasants. It was Sunday—the time, afternoon. Ralph Button was there, swaggering and bullying after his usual fashion; but one especial object of his enmity and spite was a gray-haired man named Travis. The old man was guardian to a niece who would in a few weeks be entitled to the splendid fortune of one hundred pounds. That one hundred pounds was much coveted by the brutal pugilist, and the rejection by John Travis of his request to go a-courting the niece was savagely resented. After a good deal of bitter chaff on Button's part, he affected a wish to make it up, be good friends, and offered his hand to the old man in token of his sincerity. The pledge of amity was accepted, and then Button, grasping the hand of Travis in his own, "and keeping the fingers straight," pressed them together with a vice-like force. Many people know by experience that this inflicts excruciating torture; and the old man yelled with pain. Sir Gerald, who was eating powdered beef, sprang up and struck Button in the face with such right good will, that blood spurted from his nose and mouth, and he let go the old man's hand. The brutal pugilist turned fiercely upon Sir Gerald. Had he mentioned who he was, Bully Button would not have dared to assault a titled, wealthy county magistrate, or the rustics present, who must all have heard of "good" Sir Gerald Massey, would have immediately interfered, and settled Button's business in a twinkling. Sir Gerald disdained to do so. A regular turn-up fight ensued, and after a contest which lasted nearly an hour the thews and sinews of the pugilist prevailed. Sir Gerald was beaten into a state of insensibility, but not till he had inflicted severe punishment upon his adversary.

A doctor was sent for, and the injuries which Sir Gerald had received being very serious, and in the medical gentleman's opinion might possibly have a fatal result, the patient's pockets were searched to ascertain whom he might be. To the astonishment and consternation of the landlady, and great delight of the doctor, it was found by papers or letters he had about him that the man who had fought a vulgar public-house fight with a low professional bully was Sir Gerald Massey, of Stone Hall, near Appleby! Button fled the county, and enlisted in the army.

Sir Gerald quickly recovered, and so little malice did he feel towards the brute by whom he had been so severely beaten, that he made the fellow's mother, a paralytic woman, who had been dependent upon her son for support, a present of ten guineas, and allowed her five shillings per week during life.

Not long afterwards, Sir Gerald Massey was engaged in a more serious contest than that with the pugilist. Captain Goldsworthy, a handsome *roué*, had dared in some way to insult Lady Massey at a ball given by Sir Lewis Leavenworth. It was afterwards alleged that the lady, in consequence of her imperfect knowledge of English, had misunderstood or misconstrued the words addressed to her by Captain Goldsworthy. That, however, upon the face of it, is unlikely. Women know perfectly well when they are insulted, though they may not have a nice appreciation of the oral language in which the insult is conveyed.

Be that as it may—a duel with swords was fought between Sir Gerald and Captain Goldsworthy the same evening. Goldsworthy was run through the body, and died of the wound four days afterwards, protesting to the last that the offensive compliments he had addressed to Lady Massey were merely playful badinage.

The death of Goldsworthy had a painful effect upon the mind of Sir Gerald Massey. He had gone to ask the dying man's forgiveness, which was not given, and the white, ghastly face of the moribund, with its expression of hate and despair, haunted him for ever afterwards. It helped to cloud Sir Gerald's never very clear intellect.

Not long after Goldsworthy's death, an aged man, dressed in tattered apparel, and whom Thomas Barnes, an ancient servitor, recognised as a travelling tinker whom he had seen many years before, arrived at Stone Hall, and requested to see Sir Gerald. The request was refused; but the man would not be denied, scribbled something upon a piece of paper, which procured an immediate interview with Sir Gerald. The interview was a long one, and at its termination the travelling " tinker" left the Hall, seemingly in the highest spirits, and " chinking gold money in his pockets."

Sir Gerald was not seen by any of the servants for several days after the tinker's visit. Lady Massey was taken ill, and had not recovered when the tinker returned —this time in high feather—and accompanied by Mrs. Justin, a youngish widow, and it was soon given out the relict of the nephew of the late Mr. Gerald Massey, who, but that the son had been discovered, would have inherited the Massey property. High words—fierce wrangling between the new-comers and Sir Gerald and his lady, were overheard by the servants, though they did not catch the cause of the dispute. At last a compromise, it seemed, was effected—the old tinker and the young wife went their ways, and were not again seen together at Stone Hall.

Lady Massey's illness, owing, it was said, to nervous agitation, terminated fatally. Sir Gerald, in pursuance of a promise—it was exacted from him on her death-bed by his wife—became a member of the Romish Church, and a devout one. He left Stone Hall for London, returned in about a year, bringing with him a bride, no other than the widow Justin, niece-in-law to Sir Gerald's reputed father. She had a grown-up daughter. Both were ugly, bitter-tempered viragos, and soon made the house too hot to hold Sir Gerald's own children. They left Stone Hall one after the other, fairly provided for, it is estimated, probably by an ante-nuptial settlement previous to the last marriage. Sir Gerald, after they were gone, seemed to weary of his life—took again to cock-fighting, bull-baiting, found the old pastimes flat, stale, unprofitable—essayed jockeyship, won a cup at some race, and horsewhipped Sir Claude Gregson, who refused, upon some futile pretence, to pay him a heavy bet.

All would not do. There was secret grief—some sting of remorse rankling in his bosom; at least, it was so believed by those who had opportunities of observing him closely. Domestic strife helped to embitter his life—to weaken his intellect. Quite certainly a very hideous skeleton was hidden, but ever present to himself at Stone Hall.

At last, a few days after a visit from his confessor, Sir Gerald Massey disappeared. He had left no trail behind. There was search, languid search made by order of the widow, but nothing could be heard of him—nothing authentic, that is to say. One report, to which more than one witness testified, was that Sir Gerald Massey had been seen pursuing the trade of a travelling tinker. This may be, and I think was true, notwithstanding that in 1762 he suddenly returned to Stone Hall, infinitely to the disgust and dismay of Lady Massey and her daughter, Charlotte Justin, who was on the point of marriage. The contract was broken off—postponed at all events. Sir Gerald appeared to be vehemently desirous of attending at the court of the young

King George the Third, and ordered a very expensive dress in which to appear before the sovereign. Again a fit of caprice or insanity seizes him: he once more vanishes, and is afterwards seen by many persons in the streets of London, and its most frequented coffee-houses, always glitteringly attired, and known as the "Mad Baronet," though baronet he was not. He was very charitable, especially to the class of "unfortunates," and this without giving cause for any serious stain upon his moral character—in that regard at all events. Sir Gerald had taken care at his last visit to Stone Hall to secure to himself a regularly paid and sufficient income. The end came, as it will come to all, whether they be eccentric or wisely self-governed. On the 18th August 1792, a man—the mere skeleton of a man rather—was found in a kneeling posture by the grave of the first Lady Massey. There was no difficulty in determining that it was the corpse of Sir Gerald Massey, of Stone Hall.

MARGARET FULLER.

This *very* eccentric American lady, daughter of Timothy
and Margaret Fuller, was born in the State of Massa-
chusetts on the 9th of May 1810. She is known in
Europe by her *Woman in the Nineteenth Century*, a clever
book, but far from justifying the prophetic laudation
which she bestowed upon herself in comparatively early
days. It is a striking illustration of the propensity of
all strong-minded ladies to monster nothings. "Mine,"
she wrote, " is a large, rich, but unclarified nature. My
history presents much superficial temporal tragedy. The
woman in me kneels and weeps in tender rapture; the
man in me rushes forth, but only to be baffled. Yet the
time will come when from the union of this tragic king
and queen shall be born a radiant sovereign-self." Strange
hallucination! Amusingly wonderful the microscopic in-
trospection which could magnify, transform mere fluent,
erratic cleverness into even the semblance of creative
genius! It is only the air of America which can fill
such self-glorifying trumpets as that blown by Margaret
Fuller.

This intellectual prodigy—this spiritual king and
queen, of which, in the fulness of time, was to be born
a radiant sovereign-self—could not boast of the beauty
of the tenement which enclosed so divine a soul: a defect,
it has often been observed, common to intellectual female
prodigies, and especially true, it seems, of this "mountainous me," another amusing trick of self-description
quoted by Margaret Fuller's biographer, Mr. Emerson.
Pity that a "mountainous me" announced, with flourishing of trumpets to deafen one, to be in travail with a

new and more perfect Evangel, should invariably present the hopefully-expectant world with a tiny *ridiculus mus!* Mr. Emerson says, "the unpleasing cast of her features was increased by a disagreeable habit of opening and shutting her eyelids, and the nasal tone of her voice." This last peculiarly-national characteristic ought not, in fairness, to have been flung in Margaret Fuller's face, plain as it may have been.

The home-nurture of "Mountainous Me" was not a judicious nurture. Mr. Fuller, who, though a thorough business man, prided himself upon his knowledge of Greek and Latin, no sooner ascertained that his daughter had a capacity for retaining words in her memory, than he determined to rigorously educate her according to the classic and now well-nigh exploded formula. The child was relentlessly drilled into a knowlodge superficial as, except in rare instances, such knowledge, if it deserve the name, must necessarily be. When only six years old, she could read Latin—at seven, Greek. The intellectual and moral education of Margaret Fuller had been accomplished. She knew the names of many things in three languages at least, and her mind had been elevated, purified by the study of Ovid's Metamorphoses, Martial's Epigrams, and other classicality. Mr. Fuller, a rigid Puritan, had no objection to his daughter amusing herself during the intervals of Sabbath worship with that refining literature; but when he caught Margaret on a Sunday afternoon with a volume of Shakespeare in her hand, he was exceedingly wroth. To read *Hamlet* on a Sunday was profanity—a desecration of the holy day. Could she not be content with Catullus or Petronius Arbiter? The pride of being able to read, however haltingly, imperfectly, Greek and Roman authors in the original, strangely blinds men to the filthiness of many classic writings.

The stern discipline which compelled incessant study of Greek and Roman literature was equally enforced with respect to other branches of learning, and the consequence was broken health, hectic nervousness, and spectral illusions. She would frequently start up in the night and flee shrieking from the horrible shapes with which her overwrought brain peopled her bed-chamber. *Positive* insanity might probably have been the result but for the soothing influence, the compassionate tenderness of her mother, to whose worth Margaret Fuller testifies in a passage which does honour both to Mrs. Fuller and her daughter:

"My father's love for my mother was the one green spot on which he stood apart from the commonplaces of a mere bread-winning existence. She was one of those fair and flower-like natures which spring up even beside the dusty highways of life—a creature not to be shaped into a merely useful instrument, but bound by one law with the blue sky, the dew, and the floric buds. Of all persons I have known, she had in her most of the angelic—that spontaneous love for every living thing—man and beast and tree—which restores the golden age."

Windy exaggeration this, no doubt, but redeemed by filial love. And what were the first-fruits which this sternly-enforced semi-pagan education produced in Margaret Fuller? Chiefly a belief in the influence of the planet Jupiter, in omens, in *sortes*, in talismans, and in the occult power and signification of precious stones. "When I first met with the name of Leila," wrote this transatlantic prodigy of intellect — this Mountainous Me—"when I first met with the name of Leila, I knew it in a moment, and said 'it is mine.' I knew that it meant night—night which brings out truths."

Margaret Fuller herself was a precious stone of the masculine gender—a living carbuncle! Carbuncles, she said, were of two kinds, male and female. "The female casts out light, the male has light within itself. Mine is the male." When writing to friends for whom she had a strong regard, Margaret Fuller always put on her finger a male carbuncle. If she were writing to less-valued acquaintance, she would use an onyx or amethyst. She was, moreover, a firm believer in the mummeries of Mesmerism. A pet project of Mountainous Me was to get up a female congress in Washington as a rival to the male bipeds who congregate in the Capitol,—herself to be president, because, I suppose, of her quality as male carbuncle. The assembly would be female carbuncles casting out light; but a president, whose chief duty it would be to keep order, maintain the decorum of debate, could require only the inner light. This serious silliness appeared at one time to have a chance of being adopted, and lively controversies, *pour et contre*, were printed in the American papers. The notion was perhaps not more ridiculous, more absurdly American, than the institution of baby-shows. It, however, like the babies, fell through.

All this while her contributions to the not very luxuriant literature of "the greatest nation on the face of the universal airth" were criticisms written for the *New York Tribune* and the *Dial*, poor pretentious stuff about upon a par with Horace Greeley's political articles. John Sterling, son of the real old original Thunderer, whose life Carlyle has written, was, according to Miss Fuller, a poet of the highest order, Longfellow a mere rhymester; Beethoven's music she declared to be the sublimest expression of which the soul of man is capable, and distinct, positive, literal in its meanings as human speech; an old, long-since exploded German extravagance, the assumption being pretty nearly as tenable with respect to music, as of colour, perfume.

And yet the woman who could write such outrageous folly was, for a long period, the observed of all observers in the literary circles of Northern America—the lion, or should it be lioness?—of *bas-bleu* coteries. The literati of the New World acquiesced with deferential recognition in the truth of her self-estimate, when before a numerous company she said, "I am acquainted with all the people worth knowing in America, and I have found no intellect comparable to my own." Mr. Emerson says he was both delighted and astonished at her talking gifts. Surely there *must* have been something in this much-bepraised woman, although written records of her "philosophic eloquence," if they ever existed, have been lost or mislaid.

Miss Fuller was a teacher in several establishments of high standing, and she was accustomed to say, with the quiet assumption of superiority which habit had made natural and easy to her, looking down upon her audience as she spoke from the lofty stilts of a self-conceit unmatchable in this used-up Europe, "that she had formed the minds of hundreds of young girls and men upon the model of her own unmatched intellect, as closely as natural inferiority would permit."

There was no intellectual achievement to which Miss Fuller, if we are to take her at her own valuation, was not equal. Like Horace Greeley, of the *New York Tribune*, she was a zealous protectionist, and more than once expressed a wish that she might be a member of the British House of Commons, in order to have an opportunity of extinguishing once and for ever the free-trade orators of that assembly—Sir Robert Peel, Richard Cobden, John Bright, and others.

One Sunday morning it was announced at the chapel frequented by Margaret Fuller that the minister—one of the great pulpit-guns of a distant State (Illinois, if I remember rightly)—had been seized with sudden illness, and as there was no substitute immediately available, the service would only consist of prayers and psalms. This was a great disappointment to the crowded congregation. Margaret Fuller beckoned to the chief officebearer after the minister of the chapel, and offered to preach a sermon. Taken by surprise, the bewildered gentleman wonderingly acquiesced. Margaret Fuller mounted the pulpit and delivered a very eloquent oration,—quite as well, however, suitable to a temple of Jupiter Olympus as to a Christian church. This bold *démarche* of strong-minded Margaret Fuller was not flatteringly commented upon at the time; but social religious life is very crowded in America—extravagance succeeds extravagance—one pushing out the other in endless succession, and impulsive Miss Fuller's escapade was soon forgotten. One of her friends has affected to doubt the truth of the story. I must not omit to mention that a few weeks after the death of her father, of cholera, in 1835, a calamity under the influence of which her proudly-worn mantle of self-glorifying arrogance fell partially off, Miss Fuller, divesting herself for the nonce of her paganish fantastic eccentricities, warmly interested herself in behalf of the miserable female outcasts shut up in the prison of Sing-Sing, and ou Christmas preached from the text, "The bruised reed he will not break; the smoking flax he will not quench." About this time she enunciated in the columns of the *Tribune* her belief that had Shelley lived twenty years longer, he would have become a Christian, and so have attained the mental harmony necessary to him. The filthy rags of philosophic paganism woven by her early studies were falling off, giving to view the white vesture beneath them of a Christian maiden.

Margaret Fuller, finding teaching — but especially writing—"was mighty dead work," that "much study was a weariness to the flesh," determined upon visiting England in company with a Mr. and Mrs. Spring. This was in 1847. Before leaving America it was arranged that Margaret Fuller, in a series of letters to be published in the *Tribune*, should repay with compound interest the libels on the social life of the wondrous republic perpetrated by such malignant scribblers as Frances Trollope, Charles Dickens, and others. "I will lay bare, anatomise that monstrous sham, English society," wrote this formidable damsel; "and I regret that the keenness of the sacrificial knife may be perhaps dulled by the memory of an English lady, the first angel of my life, whom I met with in youth. But private feeling must yield to public duty." Alas for England!

Before following this very singular lady to the old worn-out country, I may relate a few anecdotes of her early youth at the time when she made the acquaintance of "the first angel of her life."

Her first vivid experience was, she says, one of

death—the death of a sister, "a sweet playful child, in whom death and life were alike beautiful;" a bitter, enduring sorrow. There can be no doubt that there was in Margaret Fuller a fount of womanly tenderness—sympathy which, allowed free play, would soon have swept away the incrustations created by a radically-vicious education overlaying a true and generous spirit.

Her meeting and brief acquaintance with the English lady, "first angel of my life," the recollection of whom would, she feared, blunt the point of the sword intended to smite England under the fifth rib, I shall describe in her own words:

"I was reading *Guy Mannering*, and my eyes were wet and dim with tears drawn forth by the loss of little Henry Bertram, when an English lady of surpassing beauty, on a brief visit to that part of America, observing me, approached and accosted me. She did not question, but fixed on me looks of beautiful love. She did not speak many words; her mere presence was to me a gate of Paradise. I laid my head against her shoulder and wept, dimly feeling that I must lose her and all who spake to me of the same things—that the cold waves would rush over me. She waited till my tears were spent, then rising, took from a box a bunch of golden amaranths. They were very fragrant. 'They came to me,' she said, 'from Madeira.' The departure of the lady threw me into a deep melancholy, from which I was with difficulty roused. I kept the amaranths during seventeen years. Madeira for long, long afterwards, was pictured in my imagination as an Island of the Blest. And when ships sailed past the coast, their white wings glancing in the sunlight, I fancied they must be bound to happy, fortunate Madeira!"

This erratic young lady did some audacious things, but they were always dictated by a generous spirit. She, when about sixteen, was on a visit to an aunt and cousin, Mrs. Paulding and her daughter, who resided about ten miles from Boston. Mrs. Paulding's only son, Arthur Paulding, had not long before married against his mother's consent. It appears that his mother's decided aversion to the match was not so much caused by the wife's inferiority of social position, as that her family had grossly insulted and defrauded Mrs. Paulding's deceased husband. The widow was inexorable, and mentally registered a vow never to forgive, never to willingly set eyes upon her son—never, if he were starving, to afford him the slightest assistance. The rash young man very soon had pressing need of pecuniary help. He was desirous of going west with his young wife, but had no means adequate to the purchase of a wagon, horse, implements, and many things essential to such an enterprise. He wrote many letters to his mother, asking forgiveness and money. His sister Caroline sympathised with him, but could do nothing. A letter from him arrived when Margaret Fuller was on a visit to her aunt and cousin. It was a request for a loan—merely a loan —of five hundred dollars. The letter was read by Mrs. Paulding, and cast contemptuously aside.

" ' Caroline,' " said Margaret Fuller, having previously taken care to place the appropriate carbuncle upon her finger ; " ' Caroline,' " said Margaret to her weeping cousin, " ' you must act in this momentous affair for aunt, for your mother's better self. She will live to bless you for so acting. From Arthur's despairing, bitter letter, I fear poor Arthur—and we know his impulsive, yet positive disposition—will commit suicide. That would kill your mother by slow, lingering torture. You write aunt's letters, draw and sign her cheques. Well, draw one for the five hundred dollars in favour of Arthur. I will deliver it to him with my own hand, and make some excuse to prevent his writing to acknowledge its receipt. Aunt is rich ; she never examines her banker's or any other account, leaving all to you : you are, we may assume, your mother's only child. Her money, regarded from a moral point of view, is as much yours as hers. It is your duty, your positive duty, to do for aunt that which, temporarily dominated by unreasoning passion, she refuses to do for herself.'—Much more I urged to

the same tune, and finally prevailed with Caroline, by
the power which strong natures exercise over weak ones!
The cheque was drawn, and I myself placed it in Arthur's hands. About two months afterwards my aunt
was attacked with serious and, it was feared, mortal illness. The approach of Death, whose dread steps she
fancied sounded nearer and nearer every hour, awakened,
not alarm only, but remorse in her bosom. She bethought herself of the outcast Arthur; and calling Caroline to her side, bade her at once send Arthur one thousand dollars, and assure him of her forgiveness. A
cheque for five hundred dollars was sent immediately,
and the matter was happily terminated. I believe that
I rightly advised Caroline."

The voyage to England was a pleasant one: Margaret
Fuller brought with her numerous letters of introduction
to Carlyle and other literary celebrities of the land which
she had promised to smite with the flashing sword of her
incomparable wit and sarcasm. She carried out that
promise to the best of her ability. Her letters on England are certainly not more stupid nor half so malignant
as the rantipole rubbish lately written and printed by
Hawthorne.

Margaret Fuller rather patronised Thomas Carlyle.
She seemed to admit that the author of "Sartor Resar-
tus" might almost take rank with the writer of "Woman
in the Nineteenth Century." No other English man or
woman could she for a moment think worthy of being
placed on so lofty a pedestal. Of English society, English
manners, English people generally, Margaret Fuller, who
had thoroughly gauged, analysed that "compound of
sham," during her ten days' sojourn in England, spoke
with serenity—superior, good-natured disdain—in that
nasal tone of hers, and with full play of the unpleasant
habit of opening and shutting her eyelids. France was
much more fortunate than England, but for no Frenchman or Frenchwoman did she feel such esteem, such admiration as for Madame Dudevant (George Sand). She,

if you like, was a model woman, cruelly maligned, espe-cially by her numerous lovers, who must have known better than the outside world how good, amiable, charm-ing she was, not perhaps according to the orthodox stand-ard of an obsolete world, but judged by her own tran-scendental sense of right and wrong and the eternal fit-ness of things. Margaret Fuller had at last found an intellect equal to her own, or pretty nearly so.

Miss Fuller having exhausted, finished with France in something less than a fortnight, determined to visit and dissect Italy. There an event befel which saved the land of Dante and Tasso from being withered up, as England had been, by Margaret Fuller's scathing pen.

A Marquis,—a real live Marquis,—the Marquis Gio-vanni Angelo Ossoli, made Margaret Fuller's acquaint-ance at Rome. He was a disciple of Mazzini, a Republi-can *pur sang*, and an idolater of the famous republic destined in the near fulness of time to absorb the uni-verse. No wonder that, although the illustrious Marquis was miserably poor, was never quite sure that he would be given this day his daily bread, "was unacquainted with books, destitute of enthusiasm, and remarkable only for good sense and good temper," he should have found favour in those everlastingly opening and shutting eyes of Margaret Fuller. Would not she by acceptance of that hand of his—empty as it might be—become the Marchioness d'Ossoli? Ah! if it were ever worth while, which I doubt, to catch in a matrimonial sense a strong-minded woman imbued with stern republican principles, you can find no surer bait than a title. Ladyship is a great thing—but Marchioness! good heavens! The Mar-quis d'Ossoli knew very well what he was about; a well-principled, gifted woman, if a little given to strange fan-cies, whose facile pen commanded a considerable revenue —in Italian estimation, was not so bad a prize to draw in the lottery of marriage. The "daily-bread" difficulty would be got rid of; and the end was that Margaret Fuller became (1848) Marchioness d'Ossoli. The happy pair intended to leave almost immediately for the then

United States; and the following paragraph went the round of the American papers: "Our highly-gifted country-woman Margaret Fuller, now Marchioness d'Ossoli, is expected to arrive with her husband, the Marquis d'Ossoli, at New York, in the course of the next month."

Circumstances detained them in Italy—the Marchioness d'Ossoli became the mother of a fine boy, who was baptised Angelo, after his father. Marriage and maternity wrought a marvellous change in the lady. The supercilious pedant disappeared, and in her place was seen a true, trustful woman. An American lady acquainted with her since she was a child, and who had often been repelled, disgusted by her haughty self-sufficiency and petulant temper, was astonished at the transformation: "How unlike is she to the Margaret Fuller of former days! The masculine intellectual gladiator ready to challenge all comers, is now so delicate, so simple, so confiding, so affectionate, with a true womanly heart and soul, and, what was to me a still greater surprise, possessed of so broad a charity that she could cover with its mantle the faults and defects of all about her." There could scarcely be a more striking illustration of the great truth, that a woman's natural, healthful life is the Christian life.

The revolution broke out in Italy. The Marquis d'Ossoli, an enthusiastic Mazzinian, was drawn into the vortex, and the Marchesa, fully sharing her husband's political principles, cheerfully accepted the office of directress of one of the hospitals for wounded soldiers during the siege of Rome by the French—one of the blackest spots in the pages of the history of France, in which there are very many black spots.

Rome capitulated—yielded after a valiant, stubborn resistance to overwhelming force. Garibaldi, his true wife Anita, with a remnant of his gallant followers, had previously left the Eternal City; and the Marquis d'Ossoli, who was deeply compromised, reached Florence in safety; the Marchesa, with her darling Angelo, soon joined him.

They remained in Florence till May 1850, supported in modest respectability by the proceeds derived from contributing to the American press by the untiring pen of the Marchesa d'Ossoli. The lady pined for home, to again embrace her mother; and on the 15th of May 1850 the husband and wife, with their infant son and a servant of the name of Celeste, embarked from Leghorn in the Elizabeth, an American barque, James Harley master. Forebodings of shipwreck, common to continental landsmen, haunted the mind of d'Ossoli, and, from sympathy, I suppose, were shared by his wife. D'Ossoli recalled to mind that he had been warned long since to beware of the sea, an injunction which almost all inland Italian mothers address to their sons. The Marchesa appears to have feared chiefly for her son, lest "he should be devoured by the howling waves or die in unsolaced illness." For herself she took very high ground indeed. "I am quite content," she wrote,—"I am quite content, if it *should be thought I need so much tuition in this planet,* to stay my threescore years and ten; but it is borne in upon me that my earthly career will soon close. It may be terribly trying, but will not be a very prolonged agony; God will transplant the root, if He wills, to rear it into fruit-bearing." She prayed that if one was doomed to perish, all three—herself, husband, and son—might die together.

Her prayer was granted. On the morning of the 16th of July the Elizabeth, an ill-built, unskilfully-handled ship, after labouring through the night in a fierce hurricane, went ashore on Fire Beach, off the Jersey coast, America. Mr. Channing, in his graphic, solemn narrative of the afflicting catastrophe, says:—"After twelve hours' communing face to face with Death, a sea struck the forecastle, carrying with it the deck and all upon it —the steward and Angelo were washed upon the beach, both dead, though warm some twenty minutes afterwards —Celeste the servant and d'Ossoli were caught up for a moment by the rigging, but the next wave swallowed them up—Margaret sank at once—when last seen she was seated at the foot of the foremast, clad in a white night-dress, with her hair fallen loose upon her shoulders."

Thus untimely passed away a gifted, high-principled, eccentric woman, who, for the healthy development of her very considerable powers, seems to have required but a prolongation of the better, the natural life which she had but recently embraced. Let us hope that the belief embodied in a sentence of hers, penned during the vigour of life, sustained her in the trying death-hour: "I have faith in a glorious explanation which will make manifest perfect justice, perfect mercy, perfect wisdom."

THE EARL OF PETERBOROUGH.

THE names of Cromwell, Marlborough, Wellington, are household words in the country which gave them birth; but how many Englishmen, speaking in a comparative sense, are familiar with the marvellous, if eccentric, career of Charles Mordaunt, Earl of Peterborough and Monmouth, as daring a soldier as either of them?—the man to whom it is mainly owing that the magniloquent boast of Louis XIV., when he supposed his grandson the Duke of Anjou would ascend the throne of Spain, and by the French monarch's aid maintain himself thereon, "There are no longer Pyrenees," became an empty vaunt.

The date of the birth of this remarkable man was 1658, or thereabouts. His father was a zealous royalist, but Charles, Lord Mordaunt, the son, long before he had lived to manhood, hated and despised the restored Stuart, King Charles II., and his brother James, Duke of York. In his eyes they were both contemptible, worthless men. The military and naval glory of England achieved under Cromwell excited and inflamed his imagination. "The Protector's burial," he once observed to Algernon Sidney, "was, it is said, a grand affair; but what funeral honours ever paid to a hero could be compared with the thunder of De Ruyter's Dutch cannon in the Thames—echoing the shouts of a vile populace shouting in triumph over the exhumed bones of Cromwell and others, gibbeted by order of the second and worst Charles Stuart!"

A spare small man was the great earl—spare and small as Nelson, but, like the great admiral, of an unconquerable, fiery spirit. He was the firm friend of Algernon Sidney and Lord William Russell, and passionately resented the murder of those true heroes. Nevertheless, he managed to keep clear of the clutches of the law. Judge Jeffreys himself could find no pretence to hang him, ardently as he desired to do so. There is a laughable anecdote which may account for Jeffrey's baffled anxiety to weave a hempen necklace for Lord Mordaunt. This happened before the judge was raised to the judicial seat; at least I conclude so, though the data upon which I ground this supposition are confused and contradictory.

Jeffreys, I have to say, whether barrister or judge, courted, not honourably, a peasant lass living as servant to a Mrs. Curtis, at Parson's Green. The girl's name was Sophia Crowe. Jeffreys had made an assignation with the silly wench, who was to meet him at some place near Fulham, in a hack-coach which he would send for her. By some means the young Lord Mordaunt became acquainted with what was going on. The *Gentleman's Magazine* opines that he was smitten with the damsel himself. At all events he took care that the assignation should not be kept. Possibly he made a confidant of Mrs. Curtis. Be that as it may, Sophia Crowe did not keep the appointment, and Lord Mordaunt did. The coach was to arrive at an appointed spot at a particular hour—evening. It did so, and a nicely-attired young lady, but wearing a thick muffler, was in waiting. She gave the signal agreed upon, entered the coach, and was driven off to London. Jeffreys welcomed the lady with rapture, and presently found that the charming damsel upon whom he was lavishing his endearments was—Lord Mordaunt! Very provoking, one must admit.

A very wild slip was Charles, Lord Mordaunt. Admitted behind the scenes of courtly and clerical life—such as that courtly and clerical life was in the days of Charles II., he was early an entire sceptic, not only as to the Divine Right of Kings—but Revelation. It may be doubted that he believed in a future existence. He had a sovereign contempt for "popular preachers." One would fancy he was writing about Mr. Spurgeon when

he says—after the great and learned Selden, by the way
—"To preach long, loud, and damnation is the way to
be cried up. They love a man who d——s them, and
then run after him to save them." This fatal scepticism
—open, avowed scepticism—made him innumerable enemies, and was one main cause of his disparagement by
the chroniclers of his time. He had, it seems to me,
something of Percy Bysshe Shelley's spirit, though not
gifted with poetic genius. He would in a spirit of antagonism have torn up and cast into the furnace all the
creeds in the world, though sadly conscious that there
was nothing which could fill their place. The whole
family would appear to have been afflicted with the like
bigotry of unbelief; the despair of a future. Philip Mordaunt blew his brains out after inditing the following
doggrel:

> "L'opium peut aider le sage;
>   Mais, selon mon opinion,
> Il lui faut au lieu d'opium
> Un pistolet et du courage."

Both Charles and Philip Mordaunt were members of the
"Hell-Fire" club—an association of "noblemen and
gentlemen" who not only discountenanced Christianity,
but engrafting stupidity upon scepticism, denied the existence of a Creator. Blasphemy has never been so rampant in England—has never raised its brazen front in
high places with such audacity as during the reigns of
the sons of the Stuart of pious memory—whose execution for high treason in making war upon his people, if
we are to accept the dictum of cleric flunkeyism, can only
be expiated by the consumption of salt fish and egg-
sauce on each successive twenty-ninth of January.

Charles, Lord Mordaunt, led for some years a wild,
eccentric life. At eighteen years of age he fell into a
love-craze for a pretty actress of the name of Barton, and
had she not been a wife, though living apart from her
husband, might possibly have married her. As it was,
the young lord joined the company of strollers to which
she belonged, passing under the name of Nepas, and

played Benedict to her Beatrice at Worcester with tolerable success. The love-fit passed away; and the young nobleman, aware that the chief cause of the temporary dissolution of partnership between Mr. and Mrs. Barton was the "woful want o' siller," visited the husband at his lodgings in Great Titchfield Street, London, and bluntly proposed to make him a present of five hundred pounds, upon condition that he returned to cohabitation with his wife. Mr. Barton gladly consented, and, for aught that appears to the contrary, they lived afterwards happily together. Lord Mordaunt had borrowed the money upon his personal bond.

At last an opportunity was afforded of entering upon the state of life for which nature had fitted him. The depredations of the Barbary pirates upon British commerce had reached such a height that even the pusillanimous Government of Charles II. found itself compelled to send a fleet to the Mediterranean under the command of Sir John Narborough. The mode in which Blake had dealt with those gentlemen was to be feebly imitated. Lord Mordaunt volunteered his services: they were accepted, and he joined the English squadron. Sir John Narborough was not Blake, and little was done except by an attack with boats under the command of Lieutenant, afterwards Sir Cloudesley Shovel, in the harbour of Tripoli. The Algerine corsairs, moored under the shelter of batteries and armed with, for that age, powerful artillery, deemed themselves perfectly secure, there not being sufficient depth of water for the much heavier English ships to close with them within cannonshot. The corsairs were mistaken. The English boats dashed on to the attack, the pirate ships were carried, captured, burned, and one of the foremost in the fray was Charles Mordaunt. "He is true metal, and if he has a chance will go far," remarked Cloudesley Shovel in one of his letters.

Mordaunt had no opportunity of "going far" at that time. The heart of England, tested by the Government of England, had collapsed—at least was only capable of

slight, spasmodic action. Peace at any price was advocated in the Sybarite court of Charles II., as it is in the
counsels of a noisy, if in an essential sense utterly uninfluential, party of the present day. Lord Mordaunt had
no option for a man of his temperament but to plunge
again into the licentiousness and laxity of London life.

But a better time was coming. The Stuart incubus
would be speedily thrown off. Charles II. outwardly professed Protestantism during his scandalous life, though
he died with the Host sticking in his throat; but James
II. honestly avowed himself to be a Roman Catholic.
The dynasty was doomed; and no one saw that with
clearer insight than gay, giddy, reckless Charles Mordaunt. The marriage of the English Princess Mary with
William of Orange naturally attracted the eyes of the
English people towards that prince, and Lord Mordaunt
was one of the first of eminent Englishmen who went
over to Holland to endeavour to prevail upon William to
make a descent upon England, and free her from the
yoke of a Papist king. The prince listened, but could
not commit himself by a positive declaration. The English army, numbering forty thousand men, he remarked,
and commanded by Lord Churchill too (afterwards Duke
of Marlborough) would be far too many for such Dutch
troops as he could transport to England. The English
army, Mordaunt assured him, would not fight for James.
Churchill himself was disaffected. The prince gave heed-
ful audience to all that Mordaunt had to say; but the
young gallant returned to London, unassured that the
Prince of Orange would really embark in the enterprise
of delivering England, and placing the greatest crown of
all the earth upon his brow. The enterprise, not at all
an audacious one, was, we all know, finally resolved upon
by William of Orange. James was the mere simulacrum
of a king. His troops, who, had they been willing to
fight for the Papist king, would have made short work
of the Dutch deliverers, deserted James; the nation had
withdrawn from him; and that which is known as the
glorious revolution of 1688 was accomplished with the

utmost facility. Lord Mordaunt played his part—not a very conspicuous one—in the drama, but does not appear to have gained much favour at court. No command of importance was offered him, and he again subsided into the restless unrest of London life.

An amusing anecdote is related as having occurred just about the time of the flight of James. Mordaunt was in love—it may, indeed, be doubted that he was ever out of love. Mordaunt was in love with a lady who had a fancy to a beautiful canary belonging to the proprietress of a coffee-house near Charing-cross, and insisted that her noble lover should at any price procure it for her. Lord Mordaunt endeavoured to do so, but the landlady refused to part with her pet for any sum of money. The lady insisted. He must bring the canary, or not presume to see her face again. Thus goaded, Mordaunt hit upon a clever expedient. Searching the depôts of bird-fanciers, he found a canary closely resembling the superb songster which had so charmed his lady-love; but it was a *hen* canary, and could not chirrup a note. Hastening to the coffee-house, Lord Mordaunt contrived to get rid of the landlady—a Catholic, and devoted loyalist—for a few minutes, and adroitly substituted his female for the male canary. After a considerable time, he called at the coffee-house and asked the proprietress if she did not regret having refused the handsome offer he had made for her bird. "Oh dear, no," said the woman; "he is more precious to me than ever; for do you know that since our good king was compelled to leave his kingdom he has not sung a single note!"

Here is another freak of his. Driving along King Street, Covent Garden, in his coach, on a muddy day, he noticed a comedian dressed out in extravagant fashion. The man was probably going to dine with some grand friends. The sight stirred the bile of Mordaunt, who at once stopped the coach, sprang out, and drawing his dress-sword, pricked the astounded player, principally in his calves, "which were out of proportion," till the man, despairing of rescue—there were no day-police in those good old times—and running for his life, slipped down, and was bemired in the slush of the street. Lord Mordaunt sheathed his sword, helped the bedevilled player up, and on the morrow made such ample money amends that the player said "the mad freak of the eccentric lord was about the best benefit he was ever likely to get."

On the 19th June 1697, Charles Mordaunt succeeded to the earldom of Peterborough. Stirring events cast their shadows before. The death of William III., the accession of a woman, Queen Anne, to the English throne, was deemed a fit opportunity for realising the dream of Louis XIV.—that he was destined to restore the empire of Charlemagne—not immediately, perhaps, in its entirety —but to a great extent.

The "Grand Monarque" was much mistaken. The Queen of England happened to have in her service two great men, the Duke of Marlborough and the Earl of Peterborough. Her valiant soldiers and seamen would be well commanded, and to discerning eyes the horizon was bright with the coming glory of England.

England, victorious England, met Louis XIV. in the Low Countries, under the guidance of Marlborough. In Spain, the Earl of Peterborough trampled into dust the pretensions of the French king to annex practically Spain to France.

An expedition was prepared in 1705 at Spithead, and placed under the joint command of Sir Cloudesley Shovel, Lord Charlemont, and the Earl of Peterborough. The military force consisted of between three and four thousand men. They were an undisciplined set of men, but being made of the true soldier-stuff, something might be made of them under energetic leadership.

The destination of the force was Barcelona, Spain; and its purpose was to assist Charles III. in resisting the pretensions to the throne of St. Ferdinand of Louis XIV.'s grandson.

The expedition was only saved from ignominious failure by the eccentric earl. The fortress of Monjuich commands Barcelona, and Lord Charlemont, Sir Cloudesley Shovel approving, decided that the English force was utterly inadequate to storm it.

The Earl of Peterborough demurred to that counsel, and resolved to ascertain personally if the defences of Montjuich were so utterly unassailable as was asserted. To do so, he disguised himself as a peasant—a French peasant—charged with conveying to the commandant of the fortress a written message in cipher. The letter written in cipher was not fictitious. Lord Peterborough had intercepted, but not opened it. A courtesan of Barcelona, with whom he had formed acquaintance, informed him that the Count Beauvilliers, disguised as a peasant, was the bearer of an important missive to the commandant at Monjuich, and would sleep at her house. The Earl's measures were swiftly and silently taken. Monsieur le Comte Beauvilliers was rudely awakened at the dead of the night, and hurried away to strict confinement; the missive, or letter, having of course been taken possession of. It was from the Spanish General Las Torres.

Armed with that document, Lord Peterborough boldly presented himself at the citadel, was admitted, and the genuineness of the document he carried being known to the governor of the fortress, not the slightest suspicion was felt. The supposed Count Beauvilliers was treated with the highest distinction, and allowed to roam at his pleasure over the castle. He soon came to the conclusion that Monjuich could not be carried by open assault, and returning to the English camp, agreed with Charlemont that the enterprise was a hopeless one, and that the troops ought to be at once re-embarked. Preparations to do so were immediately commenced. The garrison of Monjuich were thus thrown completely off their guard, and whilst lulled in that fool's paradise, and keeping slack watch and ward, were surprised in the night by the Earl of Peterborough, who, stealthily creeping up to the walls under cover of night, succeeded in surprising and mastering the garrison. The capital of Catalonia was lost to the French Pretender to the Spanish crown. Charles

III. wrote the Earl a very complimentary letter upon his bold and fortunate achievement. Lord Charlemont did not second Peterborough's daring. He was left alone in his glory. He practised, and, as far as I know, was the inventor or originator of a new system of war-tactics. The problem to be solved was, how he, with one hundred and fifty dragoons, could drive the army of Las Torres, numbering some ten thousand men, out of Valencia? Rather a hard nut that to crack. Peterborough did it. His entirely unscientific strategy was to despatch a few of his troopers, previously well instructed, and whom he could trust, to the enemy's lines. They were deserters, and informed Las Torres that an army, thrice as strong as his own in numbers, was advancing rapidly, in the hope of taking him at a disadvantage. A few dragoons, the advanced guard of an overpowering force, would herald the approach of that overpowering force. The device succeeded. The army of Las Torres, panic-stricken at the sight of the "advanced guard" of dragoons, fled precipitately, and Peterborough, by like artifices and dash, daring, consummate skill, his renown rapidly attracting thousands to his standard, released the northern proviuces of Spain from the Anjou yoke, and rendered, as I have before remarked, the grandiloquent phrase of Le Grand Monarque—"*Il n'y a plus de Pyrénées*—an empty vaunt. But it is not my purpose in this paper to dilate upon the military skill of the Earl of Peterborough— to sketch, however briefly, his wonderful Spanish campaign. It was successful; Charles III. owed his crown to the English earl. That is eulogy enough. It is the end which crowns the work. Earl Peterborough, though a disbeliever in the inspiration of Scripture, could not deny the truth of one of the sacred texts—"Put not your trust in princes." The recompense for his great services was a royal request that he would quit Spain. The Spanish officers were jealous of the great Englishman. It was ever thus. The Conde de Toreno, for a short time Prime Minister of Spaiu, wrote a book a few years ago to prove that the great battles in the Peninsula, where England met Napoleon, were mainly won by Spanish soldiers! But the other day an official paper, published at Vienna, enraged with Lord Palmerston for his denunciation of the atrocious aggression upon valiant little Denmark by the two preponderant German powers—great in no sense of the word can they be called—said that after all there might be some truth in Baron Muffling's assertion that it was the Prussians who really won the battle of Waterloo—Prussia, that had not one soldier killed in the conflict, which finally checked, for nearly fifty years, the tide of French impetuosity and success. This, however, by the way.

Lord Peterborough was, fortunately for himself, not dependent upon the favour of kings. He returned to England, took his seat in the House of Peers, and made a short, sensible speech there, when an attempt was made by the right reverend bench of bishops to pass an Act of Parliament making it penal to speak against the Thirty-nine Articles. "I am content," said Lord Peterborough, "with a parliamentary king, but I refuse to acknowledge a parliamentary religion—a parliamentary God."

Like many other men of original genius, he appears, notwithstanding his military proclivities, to have held the gewgaw glories of the world very cheap. High, fashionable society wearied and disgusted him. He was in the habit of taking long walks into the country, and upon one occasion met with a remarkably pretty girl, with whom he was much struck. She was the daughter of a miller, one James Smithers, and a modest, worthy girl. On the following day Lord Peterborough, giving the name of Copp, and attired in homely fashion, presented himself at the mill, obtained an interview with James Smithers, and offered a large sum—the amount is not specified—to be taught the art and mystery of the miller's craft, making, no doubt, some plausible excuse for the request, which was complied with; and Charles Mordaunt, Earl of Peterborough, under the name of Richard Copp, positively worked in a mill near the village of Wheatstone, for several weeks, in the hope of ingratiating himself with Jane Smithers. He did not succeed; "pretty Jane" was engaged privately to the son of a neighbouring farmer, and one fine morning it was discovered that she had secretly married a week previously. The Earl was fiercely wroth, and in his rage revealed his rank. One can hardly suppose that John Bunt, the successful rival, and husband of "pretty Jane," would have appropriated the miller's daughter had the Earl tempted her with a coronet. As it was, he had not only lost his love and the money-premium paid to the miller, but got himself laughed at, sung in ballads, and altogether made to cut a very ridiculous figure. The authenticity of this anecdote has been questioned; but there can be little, if any, doubt of its essential truth.

The celebrated soldier was soon again over head and ears in love. This time the lady was Miss Anastasia Robinson, a singer on the public stage. The Earl was so struck with her charms that he immediately sought an introduction. This was refused; the noble lord's character being but too well known, and the beautiful Anastasia a young woman of virtue and high principle. She lived at Chelsea with her father, who always escorted her home. He was but a feeble man, who could only afford her moral protection. One night, at one of the most solitary spots on the road to Chelsea, at that time really a suburban village, their hack-coach was stopped by two craped horsemen, and their purses demanded under pain of immediate death. The lady was fainting with fear, when the gallop of horses rapidly approaching was heard, and the visored ruffians fled in apparent terror and dismay. The horsemen rescuers were the Earl of Peterborough and two of his servants; the pretended highwaymen also were his servants. His lordship's introduction to Anastasia Robinson was thus effected under very favourable circumstances; though one can hardly believe that so shallow a device—the precedent circumstances considered—could have imposed upon a lady, of whose clear insight of men and things the Earl thought so highly: "She reads a love-swain," he wrote, in his usual affected style—"she reads a love-swain as easily as she does a love-song."

Deceived in the highwayman affair or not, the Earl could only obtain Anastasia Robinson by making her his countess. They were married; but, to the Earl's dishonour, he insisted that the marriage should be kept secret, and the Countess of Peterborough, whilst openly living with her husband, continued to sing on the stage as Anastasia Robinson. This gave occasion for a striking dramatic incident. The lady happening to tread upon the professional toes of one Signor Senesimo, that individual taunted her with being the *mistress* of Lord Peterborough. The insult was bitterly resented. The Earl happened to be in the theatre—probably behind the scenes—when informed by his wife of what had taken place. Signor Senesimo had gone on again, and was flourishing away in a favourite bravura, when he was suddenly assailed by Lord Peterborough, and most unmercifully caned; the audience, though ignorant of "the reason why," greatly applauding such an unexpected episode in the opera. They knew that the assailant was Lord Peterborough, and that he was caning an Italian foreigner. *Sufficit.* After this incident, the marriage of the Earl to Anastasia Robinson was acknowledged, and the Countess retired from the stage.

The marriage was kept secret so long for no better reason, it appears to me, than that Peterborough was laying pretended siege to the heart of Mrs. Howard—the mistress of George the Second, and by him created Duchess of Suffolk. The Earl's fulsome love-letters, written, no doubt, for the purpose of obtaining, through the favourite's influence, some employment in which he could win additional honour or fame, have been published, as have also the lady's answers. The Duchess fooled him to the top of his bent. Her vanity may have been gratified; but the great soldier's honeyed phrases did not beguile her into a belief of his sincerity. She accepted his homage, but did not, for a moment, think of rewarding it—and the ridiculous correspondence

ceased without the Earl profiting in the slightest degree
thereby.

The dreams of ambition faded away—the eccentric,
wayward, defeated life of the Earl of Peterborough was
drawing to its close, and he withdrew with his good and
faithful wife to a residence on Bevis Mount, about a mile
distant from Southampton, and commanding a view of
some of the most charmiug scenery in the world.   There
he for a time rallied iu both mental and bodily health.
It was but the last flicker of a lamp of which the oil is
spent.   Advised that a warmer climate might benefit
him, he embarked for the Azores, and died during the
voyage out. The last object upon which his glazing eyes
were bent was his wife; the last name which trembled
on his lip was hers—Anastasia!

SIR SAMUEL SMITH,

ATTORNEY-AT-LAW.

THE first start in life, upon his own account, of this English worthy and true gentleman—a life which exceeded by five years, within a few days, the orthodox span of man's existence—was an unpromising one. It lived but faintly in his own memory. He recollected, dimly recollected, that he once lived in a pretty house, was nicely dressed, and that having been put to bed as usual, he upon awakening found himself in a donkey-cart, wrapped in rags. He must have been about five years old, not perhaps quite so much, and being terribly frightened, began to cry bitterly. This, a man and a woman in the cart, whom he had never seen before, put an immediate stop to by cruel chastisement. They gave him nothing to eat but bread, which his stomach rejected, for which daintiness of appetite he was again severely beaten. Sleep, as darkness drew on and the earlier stars glinted forth, relieved his misery, and when he awoke, the donkey-cart was motionless and empty, standing before a house in which loud revelry was going on—a public-house, no doubt. The street was crowded with people, and the poor little boy contrived to creep out at the back of the cart, drop without much hurting himself on the pavement, and ran off with the intention of getting back home. He had been running some time, becoming every moment more terrified, when, whilst passing a street, a brewer's dray ran against him. He was knocked down, and remembered nothing more till he found himself in bed in a strange place, sedulously attended to, and, though in great pain, comforted by the

I

kind looks of the people abont him. His right leg had been broken by contact with the dray, and he had been carried to St. Bartholomew's Hospital, Smithfield. The child's leg was set; his blood was in a healthy state, and he got rapidly well. When asked his name and where he came from, he could give no further information than that the gentleman's name was Smith, himself Sammy Smith. This gentleman came to see him sometimes, and was always cross. Once a lady came, who kissed him and cried very much. This was not long before he was kidnapped. There was but one servant kept in the pretty house, an elderly woman, who was very kind, but forbade him to ask any questions about any thing. He could not tell the name of the county where the house was situate, though he should be sure to know the place again. Barbara would, he was sure, cry bitterly when she found he had been stolen away. This was all. The rags he had on when brought to the hospital afforded no indication. The only course would be to send him t the poorhouse as soon as he was fit to be removed.

This would have been done had not a casual nurse in the hospital, the wife of Edward Lovegrove, a journeyman watchmaker, who lived in Hosier Lane, Snow Hill, taken a fancy to the friendless boy, and having but one child of her own, a girl named Fanny, about his own age, decided, with her husband's consent, to adopt the little fellow. Fanny and Sammy grew up together as brother and sister, and received the same homely education. Inquiries were set on foot by the hospital and parish authorities, but without substantial result. One man called in the dusk of evening and left fifty guineas for Samuel Smith the foundling, together with a note expressing a wish that the said foundling should be bound either to Lovegrove himself or some other tradesman, to induce him honestly to earn his own bread by the sweat of his brow. The donor left no name. Once, in the dusk of evening, a lady clad in deep mourning, the lady who kissed him and cried, met him on Snow Hill. She seemed to have been waiting for him. She caught the boy up in her arms and almost smothered him with kisses, sobbing passionately the while. The gentleman "who was always cross" came up, and with angry words, "the meaning of which, except that they were angry words, I did not understand, took the lady away. A coach was waiting for them, into which they got and drove off. The lady had left a big purse in my hand. It contained fifty guineas. This was a god-send to my benefactor Lovegrove. He was, I afterwards knew from his own lips, much in debt (for him) at the time, owing to a fall in Church Lane, by which his right wrist was strained, and he rendered incapable of work for many months. This was a grand chance for me— though I could then have had no notion of its import-ance—to return the mighty obligation I was under to my honoured benefactor and benefactress."

Mr. Lovegrove thought to teach his adopted son the trade of watchmaking, but the lad felt no vocation for the business. For some years he had a mania for tend-ing the sick in Bartholomew Hospital, whither he often accompanied his foster-mother, as we may call Mrs. Lovegrove. He had great tenderness for suffering, a heart readily responsive to the sad music of humanity, and became an immense favourite with both the pro-fessors and patients in the hospital.

This whim of the boy mainly determined the course of his life. Antony Firmin, an attorney in large prac-tice, residing in Cursitor Street, Chancery Lane, whilst passing beneath or near to a scaffolding in East Smith-field, was knocked down and grievously injured by the falling upon his shoulders of a hodful of bricks. A labourer going up a ladder had missed his foothold, fell himself, was killed on the spot (the man was drunk), and the bricks falling in a compact shower upon Mr. Antony Firmin's head and shoulders, prostrated that gentleman with terrible violence—made him bite the dust, in classic phraseology. An action for assault and battery would clearly have lain against the hodman had not the grim serjeant Death superseded it by his final *ca-sa*. Mr. Firmin was forthwith conveyed to St. Bartholomew's Hospital. The case was a serious one; removal to the sufferer's own house impossible. "For seven weeks it was not certain that he would outlive the day or night; Mr. Firmin was a bachelor; had no relatives; none, at least, who cared for him, or for whom he cared. Mrs. Lovegrove was his nurse; but his constant, assiduous attendant was young Samuel Smith. The lawyer, discerning the intelligence of the boy, and appreciating his kindly nature, took a great fancy to him. The end so far was that Samuel Smith entered the office of Mr. Firmin as copying clerk; when older, and having proved his integrity, the young man was articled, the expenses being defrayed by his master, Mr. Firmin.

The vulpine, if eccentric intellect of Samuel Smith had found its true vocation. Mr. Firmin had a good criminal as well as civil practice. The former was chiefly attended to by Smith, and his success in getting up cases in defence of accused persons became notorious. He was not a valuable ally in prosecutions—very far from it; and more than once was known to have privately given hints to counsel for prisoners, to help to convict whom Mr. Firmin was fee'd, which led to their acquittal. When he had convinced himself, rightly or wrongly, that a client was innocent of the imputed crime, there was no device to which he would not have recourse to free him or her from the meshes of the blind, iron law.

The case of Phœbe Somers will be remembered by those who are fond of groping amidst the dusty records of the criminal courts. Phœbe Somers was accused of attempting to poison her master, Edwin Cartwright, a bookseller, established at 157 Holborn, and his family. Phœbe was a very pretty girl about seventeen years of age. Samuel Smith, then over twenty, fell in love with her at the first interview in Newgate. She, standing within the shadow of the scaffold, heard the young lawyer's avowal of enthusiastic passion with astonishment. She, too, an illiterate country maiden, "who could scarcely read, and could not write,—she readily promised to become his wife, his "true, faithful wife," if he should succeed in saving her from the dreadful doom which apparently awaited her.

The circumstances were peculiar. I do not remember to have read of a more complex, involved business. Phœbe Somers being, as I have before said, a girl of singular beauty, found herself within a short time after her arrival in London from High Barnet, her native place, an object of attraction to her master, Edwin Cartwright, and to Joel Dunstane. Both were married men. Dunstane, a master-baker in Gray's Inn Lane, served the Cartwright family with bread. Cartwright and Dunstane had both married shrews—vixens. The criminal overtures of both the rascals were rejected with disdain by Phœbe Somers, who gave notice to leave, but without informing her mistress of the reason why she did so. Thereupon a plot was concocted by Cartwright and Dunstane to entrap the beautiful orphan into their power. The *Gentleman's Magazine* says there were two single plots and one double plot. I do not understand this. All which appears certain is, that Phœbe Somers was accused of attempting to poison the Cartwright family. The case in some particulars resembles that of Eliza Fenning, whose judicial murder not so very many years since so strongly moved the national conscience. The Dean of Faculty, pleading at Glasgow for Madeleine Smith, charged with having poisoned her lover, Langelier, made, it will be remembered, effective use of that terrible catastrophe.

Phœbe Somers was, I repeat, accused of having attempted to poison the Cartwright family.

These were the circumstances:—Phœbe Somers made a cake, a rich cake, the occasion being the birthday of Caroline Cartwright, a girl ten years of age, her father's eldest child. All who partook of the cake were taken ill, but not, as it proved, dangerously. Phœbe Somers did not eat any portion of the cake. There was nothing in that, as she was not allowed to eat pastry of any kind by Mrs. Cartwright. Neither did Mr. Cartwright eat of the cake, "though he was known to be fond of sweet stuff." The cake was eaten, every crumb consumed, and, as before stated, the consumers were seized with violent sickness, though of brief duration. A medical inquiry was ordered, and the conclusion arrived at was that poison—mineral poison—had been administered, and in the cake. There does not appear to have been any scientific chemical analysis of the contents of the stomach of either sufferer; but a conclusive proof that mineral poison had been mixed up in the cake was held to be that the blades of the knives with which the cake had been cut had turned blue. This absurd conclusion was pronounced to be decisive by no less than three learned physicians—Doctors Forsyth, Leadbetter, and Jennings.

The dough of which the cake was made had been delivered at the house by one Frederick Jenkins, a young man in the employ of Dunstane. He had the same morning delivered other parcels of dough. They were all specially directed. A split flat piece of stick with the name of the customer written upon it was stuck into each lump of dough. This was all he (Jenkins) knew about the matter, so he said; but 'cute Samuel Smith, who was in the police-court unnoticed, Mr. Firmin not having been then retained, afterwards recalled to mind the deponent's white face and his shaking speech whilst giving evidence.

Phœbe Somers was committed for trial on the capital charge of attempting to poison the Cartwright family. There was no great hubbub about the business. Newspapers were few and guarded. It was very different from now, when rumours, unsifted rumours, which practically prejudge the accused, take the wings of morning and fly to the uttermost corners of the earth. That gross injustice is a modern institution.

I now give an almost literal transcript from Samuel Smith's diary. The spelling is changed, and a considerable amount of surplusage made up of lover-rhapsodies omitted. There is, however, quite enough retained.

"CHRISTMAS DAY: I have now seen Phœbe Somers

for the fourth time since we have been engaged by Mr. Barstone of High Barnet for the defence. Pity is, they say, akin to love. I think and am sure it is. I first pitied the sweet girl, and now I adore her with an extravagant fondness. We understand each other. The deep, the unsuspected deep of a fount of tenderness in my heart is broken up. The ecstasy of a new joy overwhelms me. I know she was guiltless of offence—of the shadow of crime. I did not require her to assure me of that. I felt even annoyed that she should assure me of her innocence. But I am not the world. I must act, not dream. I shall struggle with fate till I come off victor. To dally with danger is to be lost."

"JANUARY 2ND: Dunstane has a servant lass of the name of Nugent, Susan Nugent. I have met her several times at private theatricals in Greek-street, Soho. She goes out by the sly, and is a clever, unscrupulous devil, if I am any judge of character. A comely lass too. Would like to be married to a theatrical husband, and go on the stage. I once played Romeo to her Juliet. She is of a warm temperament, and, for such a girl, represented the Veronese bride with fire and spirit. The best of it is, that she only knows me as Greville Arlingford, my theatrical name, and believes me to be a young man of quality who has run away from his fine home in the country. I daresay that I, by hints and innuendoes, suggested that belief. She must have thought me a little crazed, too—not far wrong in that, perhaps. I always, when attending these private theatricals, dressed in fine fantastic attire, and sported a spruce young-beau costume hired for the occasion. I was a favourite with her. I have not the slightest doubt she would condescend to marry me, did I solicit so great a favour. Something, I thought, might come of this intimacy. My suspicions point to Dunstane, the more steadily that he has through this very Susan Nugent conveyed hints to Phœbe that he and he only can save her from the scaffold, clear her good name, and make manifest her innocence. This was

very cautiously glanced forth—as one may say, conveyed
—previous to the final commitment, to the prisoner by
looks, nods, gestures, rather than by absolute words.
Yes, yes; Susan Nugent is in the black secret."

"This terrible business quite unhinges one. I feel
as if oppressed by nightmare. The world seems dark at
noon-day. The weather, to be sure, is gloomy, even for
this gloomy time of the year. I have seen Cartwright in
my proper capacity as Mr. Firmin's confidential clerk.
He is a thorough wretch, a villain of the deepest dye.
With a diabolic leer, for which I could have stabbed
him, he said it was possible he might be induced not to
press the prosecution. That would depend upon the
young girl herself. I endeavoured to make him speak
more explicitly. He is too wily a fox for that. What
is to be—what can be done?

"I have met Susan Nugent by appointment in Hat-
ton Garden. She is certainly a very clever girl. Somehow she seems to divine my thoughts. Her hawk-eye
pierces through one like a sword. She has inquired con-
cerning me of Mrs. Lovegrove, having by some means
discovered who and what I am—that I am Samuel Smith,
parentage unknown, possibly base, instead of Greville
Arlingford. She is not, however, the less friendly. She
seems to be governed by romantic crotchets. Fancies
that I shall turn out to be a lord or lordling, and is
ardently desirous of sharing my fortunes, shadowy as
they may be."

"Nugent can save Phœbe Somers if she choose to do
so; I feel almost sure of that. It is a moral conviction
only; but not the less firmly held. Frederick Jenkins,
the lout who delivered the dough, is as madly attached
to her as I am to Phœbe Somers. It is by him I think
she would work out Phœbe's deliverance, if I would but
pay the price."

"A very fanciful price. Susan, I have said, has a
notion that I am a stray slip (at the worst) of some
grand family; and that some day I shall be converted
into a rich, prosperous gentleman; emerge suddenly

from my grub-chrysalis state, and soar, like a richly-gilded butterfly—she, Madam Butterfly, accompanying—into the empyrean of fortune and fashion. Till that blessed time shall arrive, which can hardly be anticipated till the third volume of this improvised Minerva-press romance of life approaches completion, we can pass life charmingly away, having first been united in the holy bonds of matrimony, as Mr. and Mrs. Greville Arlingford, as first actor, first actress in a provincial strolling company of players. It is very comical. I laugh obstreperously—miserable as I am in mind. Susan is, however, perfectly serious; and knowing the strength of the ligature by which I am bound, has no doubt of being able to noose me. Truly I should be a precious prize."

Samuel Smith was, laugh as he might, securely noosed. The day of trial for Phœbe Somers wore on. A true bill for the capital crime of attempting to murder the Cartwright family was found, and the opinion of the counsel consulted by the prisoner's solicitor unmistakably foreshadowed a verdict of "Guilty," with the regulation "sus. per col." to follow within forty-eight hours. In the good old hanging times, execution was done within that number of hours from the delivery of the judgment to die. The maker of a bill of exchange or promissory note had then as now *three* days' grace allowed, which clearly shows that the wisdom of our ancestors accurately appreciated the immense difference between the value of men and money.

The Old Bailey sessions sometimes lasted three or four weeks. The trial of Phœbe Somers would not come on in less than nine or ten days from the finding of the true bill. But what would avail that brief respite? Smith was in despair. Mr. Firmin did not believe there was the slightest chance of the deliverance of Phœbe Somers from the frightful doom of an intentional murderess. Very likely there were links in the chain of circumstantial evidence which, from the imperfect reporting of those days, have dropped out of the narrative. This I

cannot but think must have been the case, as upon the
face of the matter the evidence appears utterly insuffi-
cient, not only to warrant a conviction, but to justify the
commitment for trial.

There was but one way. Samuel Smith finally determined to pursue that one way. He sent a scrawl by
a sure hand, requesting to see Susan Nugent at the Sa-
lutation Tavern, Newgate Street, without delay. The
girl came at once. The interview is given at great
length by Smith, but the substance can be compressed
into a small compass. It is a very queer story. Its truth
alone makes it interesting.

Susan Nugent declared with a positiveness which imposed upon Smith, that she could save Phœbe Somers,
but her price was marriage with *him!* Overwhelmed
with despair, and after an afflictive farewell with Phœbe
Somers, he again met Nugent, and agreed to be her husband. The nuptial knot was to be tied on the morning
of the day fixed for the trial. The marriage was celebrated at St. Sepulchre's, the Reverend Mr. Onwhyn offi-
ciating, at half-past eight in the morning. At about
eleven the trial came on before Mr. Justice Goold, the
Recorder assisting.

The proceedings will be best understood, and the
story told, by a summary of the examination of the witnesses.

Cartwright called. Said he had partaken of a cake
made by the prisoner. He was very ill afterwards. His
wife and children, who had eaten of the cake, were also
seized with violent pain in the stomach—retching. Had
been informed that the cake contained arsenic.

Cross-examined by Mr. Serjeant Bowles: He was not
aware that the prisoner could have any motive for poison-
ing himself and family. Had he (the witness) ever solicited the prisoner in an improper way? Witness did not
understand what was meant by the question. Serjeant
Bowles: "Oh, no one can understand the question more
clearly than you do, Mr. Cartwright." Here Mr. Justice
Goold remarked that counsel must not make speeches

under cover of cross-examination. "My lord, I made a remark, not a speech, or the fragment of a speech," returned Serjeant Bowles. "Well, well," said the Justice, "go on." Serjeant Bowles to witnesss: "Did you ever solicit the prisoner in an improper manner?" "No." "Have a care, sir. Have you not done so indirectly?" "No." "You have spoken with Samuel Smith, Mr. Firmin's clerk?" "Yes." "Did you say it depended upon the prisoner herself whether or not you would prosecute?" "I do not remember." "You do not remember? That will do." Mr. Justice Goold thereupon remarked that he did not see what essential bearing the questions of Mr. Serjeant had upon the case. Mr. Serjeant retorted warmly. There was a sort of scene, which, however, does not appear to have lasted long. The trial proceeded. Dunstane was called. He looked pale and trembled very much. He said that the dough he had sent to Cartwright's was the same he sent to all other customers. He would swear to that. Being asked and much pressed by Mr. Serjeant Bowles as to whether he had not given a powder to his man, Frederick Jenkins, to be mixed with the lump of dough to be delivered at Mr. Cartwright's, Dunstane fainted, and was carried out of court. The medical testimony was given, and though it was much shaken by the learned serjeant's cross-questioning, it evidently made a strong impression upon the jury. The case for the Crown was closed, and no one in the court doubted that the prisoner would be convicted. Mr. Justice Goold asked Serjeant Bowles what possible answer he could make to such a case. "My lord," said the serjeant, "were I allowed to speak I could make a sufficient answer, humble as may be my abilities, to the case for the prosecution, without calling one witness for the defence, and——" Mr. Justice Goold (interrupting) said, "I will have no speeches, Mr. Serjeant, in defence of felons." Serjeant Bowles: "That is a remark which your lordship ought not to have made." Mr. Justice Goold: "How? What is that? Do you presume to correct me?" "I presume," said the serjeant, "to do

my duty to the unhappy girl whose case is intrusted to me.
My client is *not* a felon; and no man, though he be seated
on the bench, has a right before conviction to call her so."
Here there was applause in court, several of the jury joining therein. Mr. Justice Goold rebuked them, and said he
made use of the term "felon" not as specially applicable
to the prisoner, but in the sense that counsel were not
allowed to address the court and jury on behalf of persons accused of felony. After some further talk the
learned serjeant called Susan Nugent. She was sworn
by that name, though she had been married to Smith
three hours previously. The young woman deposed that
she knew her master, Mr. Joel Dunstane, had a liking
for the prisoner, Phœbe Somers; knew it from various
circumstances; also knew that he had sent to her to say
that "if she would promise to be kind" no evidence
worth a straw would be brought against her; she herself
had taken the message. Frederick Jenkins could, however, tell all about it. He was Mr. Dunstane's man.
Cross-examined by Counsellor Sherlock: "Frederick
Jenkins was a sweetheart of hers?" "Yes." "Would
do or say or swear any thing if he thought it would
please her?" "Did not know about that. Thought not."
"You are going to be married to him?" "I don't see,
Mr. Counsellor, why you should catechise me about that;
suppose I am, and suppose I ain't, what then?" "You
are a smart damsel." "Many better-looking men than
you have told me that." (A laugh.) Counsellor Sherlock had no more to say to the bright-eyed, sharp-tongued
damsel.

Frederick Jenkins, called by Mr. Serjeant Bowles.
Said he was in the employ of Joel Dunstane. Remembered taking a "lump of dough" to Mr. Cartwright's.
His master and Cartwright were very intimate—very—
often talked together. One morning Mr. Dunstane
called him into his private room. He said, "Fred, you
want to marry Susan, and she won't have you?" "Well,
perhaps not." "I know," says he, "she won't unless
you can get a little money to set her up in some little

way of business." "I said that was true." "Now," says he, "can you be trusted?" "Yes," says I, "when it's worth my while." "Ah," says he; "yes, and I'll make it worth your while. Now," says he, "look here ——" Mr. Justice Goold, again interrupting, said, "Be careful, young man; be careful. I don't like your manner, I promise you. It is too glib. Be careful; speak the truth, the whole truth, and nothing but the truth,—this you have been sworn to do; and *remember* that you have sworn to tell all the truth, and the truth only." The young man said he knew that very well. He declared that he saw his master mix something with the lump of dough which was sent to Mr. Cartwright. It was a white powder shaken out of a blue paper—a little bag. "He did not know that I saw what he was doing. He afterwards told me to be sure that I delivered the *right* lump of dough to Phœbe Somers, Mr. Cartwright's servant, as it was made of very fine flour and mixed with milk instead of water." Witness promised to do so—to be *very* particular. Did not think much of the matter at the time. Knew master had said to the prisoner's friend from Barnet—did not remember his name—that all would be right if she would promise not to be a fool.

Upon cross-examination, the witness said he had not mentioned the circumstance of having seen his master mix powder in the dough till he heard of the illness which had overtaken the Cartwright family; and then, perhaps two or three days afterwards, to Susan Nugent. Susan Nugent did not advise him to go before the magistrate and state what he knew. She said he had better keep quiet. She *had* persuaded him to come and "speak up" at the trial. That was the reason he had come. "Were he and Susan Nugent sweethearts?" "Well, yes." "Any thing more than sweethearts?" Witness boggled and blinked, and said he didn't quite know. (A great laugh.) "Were he and Susan going to be married?" "That's just as it may be." "No doubt as it may be, but when will it be?" Witness could not say, and wouldn't if he could. "It is no business of Mr. Counsellor."

"Will it be next week?" "Mayhap yes, mayhap no." "Susan Nugent is a particular friend of one Smith, Mr. Firmin's clerk, he that is employed to defend the prisoner?" "Smith is a sweetheart of the prisoner. He had told him so, and said Susan is a cousin of his, and had known each other from childhood. She (Susan) wished her well, and said that she could get her out of her trouble. Knew nothing about the white powder; it might be sugar of lead, anything in creation, as far as he knew. Did not want to know either. It was no concern of his. What should the counsellor badger him so for?"

It is needless to dwell further upon the report—the halting, imperfect report of the trial. The result was the acquittal of Phœbe Somers, the jury, however, having taken more than six hours to consider their verdict. Had the Scotch-jury system prevailed, "Not proven" would no doubt have been the verdict. The jurors would seem to have been neither satisfied that the prisoner was guilty or innocent; and it is possible that the charge of Mr. Justice Goold, which was dead against the prisoner, by exciting a feeling of antagonism in the minds of the jury, may have helped to the liberating verdict. At all events, the testimony of Nugent and Jenkins had cast so much doubt upon the prisoner's criminality, that the jurors gave her the benefit of that doubt.

So far Samuel Smith's conduct, judged by ordinary rules, is intelligible enough. It is true that few young men would have married one girl whom he did *not* love for the chance of saving the life of another girl to whom, though he madly loved her, he must thenceforth be as a stranger—brother we will say. Still, in the exaltation of a fervid, romantic passion, such a piece of folly, shall we call it? may be understood. But how are we to comprehend Samuel Smith's motives for bolting away from London on the morrow of his beloved's acquittal, merely leaving a brief note for Mr. Firmin, which duly stated that the writer was disgusted with the law and London, and should not again appear at the office. Dr. Southey has hazarded an opinion—which, however, the sequel of the story does not, as I think, bear out—that the evidence given on the trial—imperfectly, tamely, as I have said, reported—convinced Smith that Phœbe Somers was really guilty. In the distraction of mind induced by that belief he resolved to leave his familiar haunts for ever, to seek in new scenes oblivion of the past and peace for the future. Whether he took formal leave of Mrs. Lovegrove and her husband is not stated; I should suppose he did, for he was warmly attached to them. He may not have said upon what mad errand he was bound or with whom he was about to journey.

It is pretty clear that he left London about a week after the acquittal of Phœbe Somers, without seeing the damsel of his affections, and in company with his bride. They departed upon a strolling expedition, and obtained an engagement at Rochester, Kent. The acting was done in a barn, or large outhouse. The salaries were not very magnificent, we may be sure, and not so regularly paid as dividends on Consols. The pair managed to live, exist, vegetate, during three years and upwards, at about the end of which period Samuel Smith appeared as clown in Richardson's booth in Bartholomew Fair.

He was then the father of two children, who were taken care of by Mrs. Lovegrove, whose lovingkindness for her *enfant trouvé* was constant and unabated. The wife, towards whom Samuel Smith appears to have comported himself with unvarying kindness, finding from doleful experience that she had no real *paying* talent for the boards, had taken service with a family of the name of Sawkins in Cheapside.

Mrs. Lovegrove—her husband was dead—grieved, to the heart to see her adopted son figuring as clown at Bartholomew shows—his clown name, by the way, was Rayner—took upon herself to see Mr. Firmin, the attorney. She found wifeless, childless Mr. Firmin in a state of rapidly-declining health. He had made inquiries after Smith without success, and was much grieved and disquieted about him. He at once penned a letter.

which he gave Mrs. Lovegrove to be delivered to Smith without delay. Every thing was to be forgiven and forgotten. Samuel Smith was requested and implored to return to the office; a liberal salary would be secured to him, and a home provided for his wife and children. Smith, thoroughly tired of his Bohemian existence, accepted the offer, resumed his former employment, cohabited again with his wife, had his children home, and lived happily with them. Mr. Firmin died and left the business and a large sum of money to Samuel Smith—all he possessed, with the exception of some trifling legacies. Samuel Smith, attorney-at-law, was a moderately rich man, with the prospect of becoming much richer.

Sad misfortunes, which we are truly told come not single spies, but in battalions, befel him. His wife—a good, loving wife—sickened of fever and died. Mrs Lovegrove caught the infection, and soon followed Mrs. Smith to her long home. Then the children in quick succession were carried to their graves. Samuel Smith was a lonely, melancholy man.

He had not heard of Phœbe Somers since he left London, a few days after her acquittal; had made, as I take it, no inquiry after her—at any rate, only occult inquiries, which led to nothing. But it may be presumed she had never been absent from his thoughts.

Mr. Firmin had left many bundles of papers, which Smith examined at his leisure. They chiefly related to bygone, concluded transactions, which possessed no interest, and were burnt as soon as read. One evening, while so engaged, he lit upon a note, much less discoloured by age than the others, which gave him a real heartquake. It was in the handwriting of Phœbe Somers —a sorry scrawl which he knew well. It was a request for money assistance. Mr. Firmin had relieved her before, but she had been unable to obtain a situation, the verdict of acquittal not having effaced the stain of guilt which public opinion had branded her with; and this was a humble, very humble, request for further aid. It was also asked if any tidings had been heard of Samuel

Smith. There was no address; if there had been one, it
must have been torn off. A *mem.* in Mr. Firmin's hand
was subjoined to the letter: " I shall send the poor creature two guineas. She will soon, I fear, be on the town.
Poor thing!—poor thing! But I am afraid she was
guilty, and so must S. have thought, or why did he run
away?"

This fragment of a paper was too much for Mr. Samuel
Smith. He had recourse to all sorts of agencies—had
bills posted, one of which is to be found in the British
Museum, describing her, with, I should suppose, much
flattery. It was all in vain; he did not hear of her, nor
the faintest inkling of her whereabout. She was dead,
probably; had passed from crowded life, unmarked, un-
cared for.

I shall not add another line of my own. Sir Samuel
Smith must himself conclude this, I fear, tedious and
assuredly not very lucid narrative.

"The business grew apace: I made money rapidly.
But glitter of gold is not sunshine of the soul. Odd,
too; but I was a very odd fellow, every body said. Odd,
too, that I gained much of my money by that very oddness. That peculiarity took this shape, at least this was
one of its shapes. I used to hunt about the purlieus of
the two big theatres, about Ranelagh, peep under gay
ladies' bonnets in the hope of discovering her beneath,
at whose glance the latent fire in my heart had leapt to
flame. This behaviour of mine excited curiosity—caused
amusement. ' He, that youngish-looking man in green
spectacles (coloured spectacles were a new, a comparatively new invention)—that youngish-looking man, but he
is no chicken,' I have heard people say, ' is Mr. Samuel
Smith, Attorney-at-Law. He, don't you remember? who
conducted the great suit of Tredgold *versus* Cummins,
and was complimented in open court by the Chief Justice.' ' Ah, I know: a queer card, ain't he? Something
wrong in the upper works? Something about a woman?'
' Very likely, but I don't know.' That is about a fair

sample of the remarks upon my singular self I used to hear.

"But I could not find Phœbe Somers. Though I was most anxious about that girl—I could not help thinking of her as a girl, though at the time I am now writing she could not have been much less than forty. I come to the crisis of my life. Any one, any unfortunate who had a grievance or a supposed grievance that might be redressed, came to me. I obtained great praise, as all the world knows, for undertaking the suit of Charlton *versus* Charlton, the defendant one of the richest men in Suffolk. He married privately, but by regularly published bans, Mary Shepherd, a pretty, nice girl, under the name of Rogers. He thought to evade the obligation of marriage by that shallow device. I showed him the contrary—no great merit on my part. No man can avail himself of his own wrong. But I am babbling —a bad habit, though it is only upon paper. The only thing was that I had conducted the suit at my own cost, and risk—very unprofessional, no doubt of that.

"I was sitting in my private-room one afternoon, chewing the cud of sweet and bitter fancies—the former very faint, scarcely discernible—when a clerk announced Miss Danby. I bade him show the lady in.

"Miss Danby was young, very young—not more than eighteen. I judged that at the time, and knew so afterwards. She was dressed in half-mourning, and wore a thick black veil. I invited her to be seated, and presently she lifted her veil. Heavens! how startled I was! The lady was Phœbe Somers, young, fresh, radiant as when I first saw her. To be sure the radiance was somewhat eclipsed by the atmosphere of Newgate, but its starlit purity pierced through.

"'Miss Somers!' I exclaimed impulsively. 'No, sir; my mother's maiden name was Somers. I come from her to you.' I sank—fell back into a chair, overwhelmed with a rush of emotion. Her mother! The train of ideas set in motion by that word swept through my brain like lurid lightning; and, ridiculous fool that I was, I burst into a passion of tears. That ever a middle-aged man and lawyer could be such a spoony, beggars belief—fact, nevertheless.

"I at first listened to Ellen Danby's story like one in a dream. I heard what she said, but did not catch, realise the sense, the meaning. My thoughts were far away. I was living again in the old time. Rousing myself, I apologised for my inattention, and asked her to begin again.

"'My mother, Mrs. Danby, I was saying, sir, is very ill, cannot leave her bed. My father is also indisposed. You appear to be suffering, sir. Shall I go away, and return after a while?'

"'No, no,' I said, 'go on; a sudden spasm, nothing more.'

"'My mother only knew where to find you a few weeks ago, and then by the merest accident. (The business had continued to be carried on as Firmin and Co.) You once rendered her the greatest service, she says, that one person can render to another, and in addition she owes entirely to you the splendid position she has occupied for twenty years, and from which, if you cannot help us, she will be cast down. My mother thought to have written and sent you a full statement of the trouble she is in, but afterthought suggested. to her that I had better call and have a personal interview with you.' (I understood that quite well. Phœbe Somers knew the effect which the apparition of her second-self would have upon me.)

"'Go on, Miss Danby, go on. But first tell me what you meant by saying that Mrs. Danby owes to me the splendid position she has occupied during the last twenty years.'

-"'The explanation is very simple, sir. A lady who, as I understand, took great interest in you when you were a child, having seen reports in newspapers—newspapers which mentioned your name in connection with the infamous accusation brought against my mother—endeavoured to find you out. She was then a widow—'

" ' Her name ?'

" ' Mordaunt; Mrs. Mordaunt of Beach Hall, Essex.
Not being able to obtain news of you here, sir—you had
gone away, as I understand, no one knew whither—Mrs.
Mordaunt sought and found my mother.   The result was
that Mrs. Mordaunt engaged her as companion.   The
time passed; no one heard of you.   Archibald Danby,
Mrs. Mordaunt's nephew, fell in love with my mother.
They were married with Mrs. Mordaunt's full consent.
They have lived happily together.   We are nine children,
sir.   Nine: mother has not lost one.   Do I pain you,
sir ?'

" ' No, no; go on.   Why do you come to me ?'

" ' Mrs. Mordaunt, sir, died about a twelvemonth
since, leaving all the property to my mother.   An elder
nephew of hers—elder to my father—has now stepped in,
and claims every thing as heir-at-law.   It appears that
by ante-nuptial settlement,' continued Ellen Danby, reading from a memorandum in her hand,—' it appears that
by ante-nuptial settlement between Julia Royston and
Philip Mordaunt, it was agreed that only in case of their
dying without issue could the survivor dispose by will of
the property.'

" ' Well, yes; I understand.   Go on again, I say.'

" ' My mother, sir, believes that you are the true,
direct heir—that the property is yours.'

" ' What do you say ?   Your mother believes that I
am the direct heir of a Mr. Mordaunt?   What mockery
is this ?'

" ' It will, I hope, be found to be no mockery, sir.
But you had better, sir, read this paper—drawn out by
my mother—yourself.'

" I read it, and, ridiculous donkey that I was, should
have passionately kissed the writing—well known to me
—but for the young girl's presence.   The substance may
be briefly stated: Mrs. Mordaunt's marriage had been a
clandestine one, contracted in defiance of the well-known
will of Philip Mordaunt's father.   The consequence was
that I, the offspring of the union, was brought up in

concealment, and called by the name of Smith. There were documents, it was said, which would prove that I was the legitimate heir. Mrs. Danby, having by accident heard that I was alive, and where I was, had determined upon appealing to me. She preferred being in my hands rather than in those of Sir Gervoise Mordaunt, the grasping nephew who was the eager claimant for the estates.

"After the affair was, legally speaking, finally disposed of—my legitimacy and heirship proved—I, for the first time, ventured upon a visit to Beach Hall. Phœbe Somers (Mrs. Danby) was but slightly changed. What the Americans describe as an Indian summer—a summer of the soul—shed its light, its mellow light, over her well-remembered countenance. The children were charming children, the husband a mild-mannered man. All were depending upon my fiat. Never shall I forget the thrill of ecstasy which flashed through me as, rising to depart, I presented Mrs. Danby with a Deed of Gift, conferring upon her the whole of the property, real and personal, to which I had been proved to be the heir! Never!

"After all, though people have called me madman, eccentric dotard, and all sorts of pleasant names for so acting, I made no very wonderful sacrifice. What did I want with the three or four thousand a-year derived from the Mordaunt estate? My business is a lucrative one—very lucrative. I am rich. Ellen Danby's marriage-portion was a handsome one. I danced at her wedding. Shall I hope to do so at the wedding of her brothers and sisters? Danby and I are cronies, and it is agreed that when I leave off business I shall take up my abode at Beach Hall."

Mr. Samuel Smith was knighted in reward of his successful exertions in the case of Throgmorton *versus* the Earl of Bute.

AMAZON SNELL.

THERE is no denying that the glare and glitter, the pomp, pride, circumstance of war, have a strong fascination for the great mass of mankind; ay, and not only of men, but of women. There are thousands of undeveloped Jeannes d'Arc, Maids of Saragossa, in the world. It is useless to indite homilies in rebuke of this propensity. No sylvan pipe can stir the blood, or quicken the pulse, as does a trumpet. If the teachings of the New Testament have failed to bring about effective abhorrence of war, the Society of Friends, now the fast-diminishing disciples of a fallen faith, may well despair of the task. Amazon Snell was one of such bellicose girls, but has not, like the French and Spanish heroines, been so fortunate as to have her exploits celebrated by a Lamartine and Byron in magniloquent prose and verse. Amazon Snell's eccentric heroism will have a far humbler chronicler, though her courage was as great, her patriotism as ardent, as those of the maids of Orleans and Saragossa.

Amazon Snell by popular, Hannah by church baptism, was born in Fryer Street, Worcester, in 1723. Her father was a hosier and dyer, and she was one of a family of nine children, three sons and six daughters, all of whom, with one exception, became soldiers or sailors, or the better-halves of soldiers and sailors. The sensible exception, Mary Snell, married one James Gray, a house-carpenter, who finally settled in Ship Street, Wapping, London.

They were a very martial family; enthusiastic partisans of the Protestant succession, and inveterate haters of the expelled Stuart dynasty. Samuel Snell was the

first to enlist, and got his *quietus* at the battle of Cullo-
den. It was a stirring time. The "Pretender" was as
great a bugbear to the simple English folk of that day
as Bonaparte was some sixty years agone. Mrs. Snell
was a good ballad-singer; had a fine, if not highly culti-
vated voice, and mainly educated her children by warlike
songs. Hannah had also a fine organ, but cared little
for music except that of the fife and drum. The young
girl actually organised a company of boy-soldiers, nominated herself captain, and used to parade the city of
Worcester at their head. It was thus she earned the
sobriquet of Amazon Snell. She was a good-looking
damsel, and captivated the affection of one of her youth-
soldiers—the son of a principal goldsmith established in
Worcester—to such a degree that his father's suspicion
of the danger to which his only son was exposed being
aroused, he insisted upon the discontinuance of the amateur soldiering and the acquaintance of the too attractive
Amazon. The poor youth fell ill, and so seriously that
the alarmed father sent for Mrs. Snell, waived his opposition to the match, and took his son into partnership as
soon as he attained his twenty-first year. It wanted but
about seven months till then. The doctor had said it
would have a beneficial effect upon his patient if Hannah
would see him. Mrs. Snell was in ecstasies. Such a
match could not have been hoped for. Her husband was
equally delighted. The fortune of the family was made,
Mr. Sawyer being reputedly worth twenty thousand
pounds at the very least, and ailing—ageing too, very
fast. He was a widower, and had no other child. It was
thought he would, being senior alderman, be elected to
the dignity of mayor in the following year. An immense
lift in life this for the Snell family. Well, yes, it looked
so; but the same agency which "gave the infant world a
shog," and furnished a theme for the *Paradise Lost*, up-
set also this woman's promising project. Amazon Snell
—Snell is a disagreeable name for a heroine; but it cannot be helped—Amazon Snell consented to visit her rich
lover—she did so. The cordial proved effective, real

elixir-vitæ, and Sawyer junior was soon convalescent. Not for long. The enamoured swain had not comprehended—certainly had not fully appreciated—the force of eccentricity which prompted a young woman to form a company of juvenile soldiers, and march at their head —drums beating, flags flying—through the streets of Worcester. He no doubt looked upon it as a passing, romantic whim—something to make merry about during their blissful honeymoon. He was dreaming in a fool's paradise, as so many of us have done in the morning of life, "when the blandishments of passion," to quote Johnsonian pomposity, "take the reason prisoner." Amazon Snell, as soon as he was quite recovered, suddenly checked his rapturous aspirations by the announcement that she would never be married except to a soldier. The insipidity of trade-life disgusted her. Could he prevail upon his father to obtain him a commission in a horse or foot regiment? If he could, she would be his wife, follow him faithfully to the wars; if not she would remain single. Sawyer junior, who had not the slightest vocation for soldier-life, decidedly demurred to such a proposition. The world, with all its substantial comforts and elegancies, would be theirs. Why on earth, therefore, should he dress himself up in a red coat for the express purpose of being shot at? The Amazon expressed her profound disdain of such unheroic reasoning. He, Charles Sawyer, was, it was quite evident, "of the earth—earthy," and no fit mate for her. The amazed lover appealed to the damsel's parents. They were quite as indignant as he, and angrily remonstrated with their daughter upon her folly. But the warrior-soul of the Amazon was no more to be subdued by parental threats than mollified by a lover's tears. Feeling that coercive measures might be had recourse to, the damsel set off, *without* beat of drum, for London, and took refuge with her sister, Mrs. James Gray. This was in 1741, when she had consequently reached her eighteenth year. The wilful girl was not reclaimed by father or mother, and the forsaken lover consoled himself, before many months had passed, with a wife of less combative proclivity. A good exchange, in a marital sense I mean, with all respect for the Amazon's heroic qualities.

While staying with her sister, Hannah made the acquaintance of one Jan Summs, a Dutch mariner, belonging, as she believed, to the Dutch Military Marine. This was an infamous deception. Jan Summs, so-called, was really Jan Spyk, who had run away from his home and entered as a common sailor on board the Jung Frau, a ship hailing from Rotterdam. Happening to make Hannah's acquaintance at Wapping, and struck with her comeliness, he and she, mutually deceptive, it is asserted (though how the bride, residing at a ship-carpenter's in Wapping, could have assumed to be any thing better, in a worldly sense, than she was, is difficult to understand), were married on the 16th of January 1742. After a few weeks' cohabitation, Jan Spyk disappeared, and was never seen by his wife again.

The Amazon in due time gave birth to a child, which opened its eyes upon another world, after having unclosed them upon this a few hours only. Deserted by her husband, for whom she appears to have felt a real affection, and impatient of her actual position, Amazon Spyk borrowed a suit of James Gray's clothes, had them altered to fit her own person, walked off without acquainting any one with her purpose or destination, and found her way, after enduring much hardship, to Coventry. General Guise's regiment was statioued there. The Amazon enlisted in Captain Miller's company, in the name of her brother-in-law, James Gray. The new recruit was oft at drill, and got through her duties creditably, but came to great grief through an act which reflected honour upon her. One of the serjeants of her company, named Davis, had a design upon some poor and pretty girl in Coventry, whom he purposed to seduce under promise of marriage. The Amazon knew he was married already, and privately informed the girl that he was, requesting, however, that the name of the informant should not be disclosed. This condition was not adhered to. Serjeant Davis discovered

who it was that had "betrayed his confidence," and resolved upon taking a signal revenge. It was easy in
those days of martinet militaryism to inflict almost any
amount of punishment upon a "common soldier," at the
suggestion of an officer, whether commissioned or non-
commissioned. It was thought essential to the discipline
of the service that a charge preferred by an officer against
one or more of the men should, without more than a
formal inquiry, be visited with condign punishment.
Serjeant Davis accused James Gray of insubordination,
neglect of duty, &c., and the unfortunate aspirant for
the honours of war was sentenced to receive one hundred
lashes. This sentence was rigorously recorded upon the
Amazon's back. This first instalment of "glory" was
very distasteful to the valorous woman. But for shame,
she would have returned to Worcester, or, at all events,
to her sister, Mrs. Gray. Reflecting, however, that the
glorious profession of arms could not possibly number in
its ranks many Serjeants Davis or Captains Miller, she
would seek service in some other corps. The Amazon
accordingly stole off and trudged on to Portsmouth on
foot.

There was a great danger to be encountered. The
deserter would be actively pursued, and if retaken, death,
or worse punishment, would certainly be her fate. "If,
peradventure, my sex did not save me; I had dependence
upon that, remembering the case of Charlotte Watkins.
That gave me courage."

The day was already high when the Amazon, about
five miles out of Coventry, saw a number of pea-pickers
at work. She had gone across fields, and the locality
was a solitary one. The pea-pickers, that morning, it
being the month of June and very hot, had divested
themselves of their outer clothing, which they had de-
posited under a hedge. Mrs. Jan Styk took the liberty
of exchanging her soldier-coat for one of the rustics', and
so disguised went on her way rejoicing. She arrived
safely at Portsmouth, enlisted as a marine, and was in
a few days drafted on board the Swallow, sloop-of-war.

There she might have been comfortable enough, had not the sister of a marine, Reuben Cheeres, who came frequently on board to see the brother, taken a violent fancy to her. So violent a fancy, that when George Henshaw —the Amazon's new alias—she had an uncle of that name—repulsed her advances with perhaps inconsiderate rudeness, the love-sick damsel jumped overboard. The young woman was saved with difficulty, but refusing to be comforted, Mrs. Jan Styk was compelled to reveal the secret of her sex to the half-demented maiden. The cure was, of course, instantaneous—complete; and the confidence reposed in the girl was not abused.

It was not long before the Swallow was ordered to join Admiral Boscawen's fleet, then stationed in the West Indies. The Swallow was an unlucky vessel. Twice she had to put back to Portsmouth from stress of weather, and when at last she proceeded on her voyage, sprang so large a leak, that it was with difficulty she made Lisbon. There the Swallow, after having undergone a thorough repair, continued her voyage, and ultimately joined Boscawen's squadron, which had received orders to proceed to the East Indies. It arrived at Madras, and there disembarked the troops and marines on board. Mrs. Spyk was soon in the thick of the fight with the French. Her first serious experience of war was not, to ordinary apprehensions, a very exhilarating experience. She was put to work in the trenches, and had hardly been so placed five minutes, when a cannon-ball smashed the head of a marine who was working by her side. This man, Richard Perkins, had been her especial friend as well as constant comrade. She was besprinkled with his blood. "This baptism of death made me furious. I caught up the slain man's loaded musket—mine was uncharged as it chanced, took steady aim at the cannonier who fired the gun, and shot him dead. At least I supposed so, as he fell backward with a yelling scream."

Amazon Gray received five wounds in about as many hours. Only one, in the groin, was serious. It was, of course, impossible to consult the regimental surgeon, if she would conceal the secret of her sex. The brave woman had recourse to the aid of a native woman who had a reputation for skill in surgery. The ball was extracted, the Amazon recovered her health; but the unfaithful black doctress disclosed the secret of her sex to Captain Mellor. That gentleman became in consequence importunate with the charming marine, and before long so much inflamed that he offered her marriage. The Amazon frankly told him she was already married, and that her husband, she had no reason to doubt, was alive. Thereupon the gallant captain appears to have waxed wroth; and to avoid his persecution the Amazon Gray absconded, and after suffering much danger, and passing through many vicissitudes, reached Bombay. The details of her journey are wanting. At Bombay she entered as a common sailor in the Elthorn man-of-war, commanded by Captain Lloyd. Misfortune still pursued the misguided woman. She was accused of stealing one of the seamen's shirts, and flogged; the shirt was subsequently found. Captain Lloyd expressed his regret for what had occurred. The ship put in at Lisbon, and there the Amazon, having revealed her sex, was at her own request discharged.

Amazon Spyk must have saved some money, as she remained in Lisbon over three months without employment. She then entered as a common sailor on board a vessel bound for Genoa. There she fell into the company of Dutch seamen, one of whom being questioned by her as to whether he had ever heard of Jan Spyk, replied that he did know Jan Spyk, who about a twelvemonth previously had been hanged at the yard-arm of his ship, the Jung Frau, for inciting the crew to mutiny. The relater was one of the crew, and always having been friendly with Jan Spyk, the latter "conversed with him earnestly before his execution." Amongst other confidences, he said that that which troubled his conscience, and lay heaviest at his heart, was a circumstance in his life which occurred in England. He had there married a beautiful girl of the name of Hannah Snell, and after a short time cruelly abandoned her. The little property that he possessed—watch and chain, twenty-five Dutch ducats—he had left with the captain of his ship in trust for his English wife.

This queer story rests upon the authority of the Amazon herself, who says, after " a great pother" she obtained the watch and money.

The Amazon returned to England, got a regular discharge from the service, and, thanks to the good offices exerted in her favour by the Duke of Cumberland, obtained a pension of two shillings per diem during life.

A curious phase in the vagrant life of this strange woman now occurred. She was sitting in a coffee-house in Cheapside, dressed, as was her wont, in male attire, when her attention was attracted by a youngish gentleman of the name of Rawle, whom she had known at Worcester. He seemed much disturbed in mind, and at last confessed the cause of it. He had written and published a scurrilous libel upon a Major Pierrepoint. The major, to whom he was personally unknown, had sent him a challenge by letter, which he would be obliged to accept or be for ever disgraced. Now he (Rawle) was not of a valorous temperament, would rather fight with tongue or pen than with sword or pistol. Besides the constitutional objection to risking his life in a duel, was superadded the consideration that he was about to wed in a few days a young, blooming, rich widow. And he had no skill with either sword or pistol. He had, however, sent off an acceptance of the challenge, and the meeting was to come off early the next morning at Chalk Farm. Being in want of a second, and being a comparative stranger in London, he had written a note to a military gentleman with whom he had a slight acquaintance, proposing to meet him at the Falcon Coffeehouse, where they then were. He had not arrived, and had not, perhaps, received the note. (I do not quite understand whether Rawle knew the Amazon as well as she did him. Possibly he mistook her for one of her brothers.)

Amazon Spyk reflected for a few moments. She knew Major Pierrepoint, and the stuff he was made up of, quite well. The printed libel which Rawle handed to her was, she also knew, true in every particular.

"Mr. Rawle," said she, "this Major Pierrepoint has not seen you, and does not know you personally? You have no doubt upon that point?" "Not the slightest doubt." "Very well. You are well off, unskilled with sword or pistol, and about to marry a rich young widow. On the other hand, I am very poorly off, can handle sword or pistol indifferently well, and am not going to marry a rich widow. Now, what will you give that I appear as principal in the duel, you the second?" "The poltroon Rawle," says the Amazon, "was delighted with the proposal, and after some higgling paid me down one hnndred guineas to be his substitute. I was equally pleased. The next morning we went in a coach to Chalk Farm. Major Pierrepoint—a major of militia—had, I afterwards knew, heard that Rawle was a wretched craven —a very handsome one, by the bye—and had no doubt that an abject apology would be tendered on the ground. The major himself, I knew, was no fire-eater—very far from it. Arrived on the ground, where we found the major and his second, a Mr. Snodgrass, a suggestion was made by the latter that an apology for the libel should be made, in which case the affair would be at an end. 'Yes,' said I, 'an apology for the libel, the libel, the affronting libel contained in the letter of challenge. Here it is. Major Pierrepoint calls me a slandering scoundrel. I must have a very ample written apology for that.' My bold countenance quite put out the feather-bed major. He turned all sorts of colours, which finally resolved themselves into a deadly white. I saw my advantage. 'But it's of no use talking; Mr. Snodgrass,' said I, 'measure the ground, and let us settle this little affair out of hand. It won't last long. My hand will have lost its cunning if it doesn't settle the major by one click of the trigger.'

"The horribly terrified major beckoned to Snodgrass

and whispered him earnestly. 'What apology do you require, Mr. Rawle?' 'A written one, and an order upon the major's banker to pay me a hundred guineas as compensation for having been detained in London to attend this meeting, to the neglect of urgent affairs which required my immediate presence in Worcester.' 'That cannot be listened to,' said Mr. Snodgrass; 'it is preposterous.' 'Very well; then let us take our places at once. I am the challenged party, and object to a greater distance than ten paces.' The major again eagerly whispered with Snodgrass. The result was an agreement with my terms. We adjourned to the nearest tavern, where the gallant major, as soon as good liquor had sufficiently steadied his hand, wrote a very humble apology, for which I did not care a tittle, and an order on Roberts, the city goldsmith, for one hundred guineas, payable to James Rawle or bearer. I had made two hundred guineas very easily."

The next we read of Amazon Snell is, that she was engaged to sing at Goodman's Fields. She had considerable success in that vocation, and was still engaged therein when she died, in 1779, in her fifty-seventh year.

This brief memoir of her erratic career differs essentially from any previously written one; but is, I believe, strictly accurate as far as it goes, though unavoidably incomplete. It is thought, for example, that Amazon Snell was present in a great naval battle fought in the West-India waters; but I can find no record of the fight in any authority which I have been able to consult.

CAPTAIN MOWBRAY.

PHILIP MOWBRAY, a brave soldier, inveterate duellist, notorious gambler, and an earnest eloquent preacher, strange as such a conjunction appears, was born at Shrewsbury in the year ——. He was a posthumous child. His father, the Rev. Tobias Mowbray, had been many years in the enjoyment of a good living, and had left his son between five and six thousand pounds. Having been long a widower, he left his friend Thomas Charlwood trustee and guardian. At his father's death Philip Mowbray was sixteen years old. Mr. Charlwood took the youth to his own home, Dovecote House, engaged a private tutor, and caused him to be carefully educated. The young man had a strong devotional bias, with a very decided inclination towards religious extravagances; with that was combined a spirit of fun, of practical joking, exuberant, inexhaustible. He was an adept, too, at all athletic sports; could kill a partridge before it was a foot above the herbage from which it had been started. Colonel Hawker makes a passing allusion to "Mowbray's remarkable skill as reported." He was also singularly skilful with the pistol and small-sword—a skill acquired by constant practice. It is said that the anecdote related in one of his novels by Sir Bulwer Lytton (I forget which novel), where he makes the hero of his book shoot a bird on the wing with a pistol-bullet, was suggested by that seeming impossibility having been achieved, and more than once, by Philip Mowbray. This may or may not be correct.

His love of the small-sword exercise brought sore discomfiture and no slight danger to Enoch Burfield, an invalided serjeant of dragoons, in the service of Mr. Charlwood as a sort of valet, groom of the chamber, and groom of the stable. The worthy veteran having some skill in fence, or having once had before his sinews became stiff and feeble with age, was coaxed, pestered, hectored by Mowbray into perpetually practising with him. Of course foils were used, but not always, it would appear, wire masks for the face. "Where is Burfield?" one day inquired Mr. Charlwood. "In bed, sir," was the reply; "the doctor is with him, and so is Master Mowbray." "What is the matter?" "Master Mowbray, sir, has poked Burfield's right eye out, sir, with one of those swords with buttons at the end of them, which they are always playing with." Whilst they were thus talking, Mowbray came into the room. "What is this I hear about Burfield?" demanded the master of the house. "Well, sir," replied the hopeful youth, who was greatly moved and excited, "poor Burfield ran one of his eyes upon the point of my foil, and the unfortunate truth is, that he has lost it; the eye, I mean, not the foil." "It is a very shocking affair," said Mr. Charlwood. "Yes, very shocking, sir; I am much grieved," replied Mowbray. "There is one consolation—it is his bad eye, the one that squinted, you know." This was not unfeeling badinage. Mowbray arranged with his guardian that the poor fellow should be allowed thirty pounds per annum as compensation for the "bad eye which squinted."

Master Mowbray must next take it into his featherhead to fall in love with a "plain Quakeress," which means a damsel or matron who has not swerved from the strict rules of the founder of the sect: abjures bright colours, music, &c., and feels somewhat surprised that in the-councils of God at the creation it was decreed that the world should not be drab-coloured, or that even a bird were allowed to sing. This votary of an obsolete faith was Anne Gurney, and a very pretty girl. This she perhaps considered to be a kind of sin. The combination of rose and lily in her face could not be quite right, though laid on by Nature's own sweet and cunning hand.

Master Mowbray did not think so; and, finding "sweet Anne" to be inexorable in her determination to decline the acquaintance of any one who was not, like herself, a conscientious, pure, and simple disciple of "the plain and pure apostle of Quakerism," he at once put off his fine clothes, in the cut, colours, and fashion of which he had taken pride, and assumed the garb of plainest Quakerism.

He did more than that. Anne Gurney—not, we must conclude, convinced by clothes—continuing to look coldly upon the aspirant for her favour, he regularly joined the Society of Friends; and upon more than one occasion, being moved by the spirit—which we can easily believe—he held forth, "to the great admiration of the assembled friends."

But it nothing availed with the obdurate maiden. She preferred a "born plain Quaker"—John Rice—and frankly told the enamoured Mowbray that she did so, when he pressed her for a final decision. Thereupon Master Mowbray, flinging off his drab-coloured suit, arraying himself in his gayest attire, and taking two stout cudgels in his hand, waylaid the successful rival, offered him the choice of cudgels, which being mildly declined, Master Mowbray so belaboured John Rice with one (or both) of them that the bridegroom expectant "did not rise from his bed for more than a month."

Master Mowbray's guardian and trustee was fain to compromise so gross an outrage, and paid a large sum of money, though doubting if he had a legal right to do so, out of the funds left by the reverend rector. "I had, however, confidence in the youth's honour, the fullest confidence. I knew that when he attained his majority he would make it all right. A strange young man, but the very soul of honour."

A very strange young man. Dissatisfied, as it seems, with the failure of his love-chase, refusing to be comforted by Miss Charlwood, who, there appears reason to believe, would have been quite willing to heal up his spirit-wounds, Master Mowbray, having made acquaintance with a son of Captain Clements, commander of the frigate Pallas, thirty-two guns, ran off, or went off—there had been an unpleasantness, or quarrel, between the guardian and guardee (it may be respecting Miss Charlwood; this, however, does not clearly appear)—and entered on board the Pallas, then at Sheerness.

The Pallas not long afterwards sailed for the Irish coast, and was one of the three ships—Æolus, Brilliant, and Pallas—despatched by the Duke of Bedford, Lord-Lieutenant of Ireland, to put an extinguisher on Captain Thurot, who, in command of a considerable French squadron, had been playing the mischief in the Bay of Carrickfergus. Thurot's career, as most of us are aware, was closed in a battle fought near the Isle of Man, upon which occasion Master Mowbray so behaved himself as to obtain from Captain Clements a certificate that there was no more promising youngster in the service.

As far as the naval service was concerned it was promise unfulfilled. The attainment of his majority, the possession of his "fortune," and some obscure quarrel with one of the gun-room officers of the Pallas, induced him to abandon the naval profession; though there was no doubt he would have creditably passed in due time for the grade of a lieutenant.

We next glimpse Philip Mowbray at the court of George the Third in 1763. How introduced is not very clear; but he was page of honour or page in waiting, whichever may be the more appropriate phrase. At all events he managed to fall in love with a maid or lady of honour, the Honourable Cecilia Barrington. This calamity was a heavy one, far more pardonable than his passion for the plain Quakeress. The Earl of C——, the name is not given at length—an Irish peer, also admired the Honourable Cecilia Barrington. The lady, as was natural, inclined to the peer. This offended, as was but natural too, Philip Mowbray, Esquire, and he determined upon settling with the Irish lord after a summary fashion. They used to meet at a fashionable gaming-house, and Mowbray with malice aforethought cheated so audaciously—pretended to cheat, I should say, for there can be no question that he intended to return the money he won—that the Earl of C—— loudly called him a rogue and swindler. An immediate duel was the consequence. It took place in a garden at the back of the gaming-house. This was precisely what Mowbray wanted. He gave his oppenent the choice of weapons. The Earl of C—— chose the small sword, and received a wound severer than the Honourable Cecilia's eyes could have inflicted, though not through the heart, as it happily chanced. The Earl recovered; the nobleman had influence at court; the occasion of the duel was related after the manner most favourable to the Earl—most discreditable to Mowbray. To be sure the latter had taken pains to furnish his detractors with ample materials. Philip Mowbray, Esquire, was dismissed from his office of honour or page in waiting; the Honourable Cecilia Barrington declined the honour of his acquaintance, and my gentleman was literally thrown upon the world and his own resources; Mr. Charlwood, his guardian, having died in the interim.

Mr. Philip Mowbray did not shine forth very brilliantly for some years after this misadventure. He took to gaming and dicing. I must not, however, forget to mention a characteristic and honourable anecdote of this "strange person." On the day of the marriage of the Earl of C—— to the Honourable Cecilia Barrington—if Barrington were her true sirname—the noble lord received a sealed packet from Mowbray containing six hundred odd guineas, the amount unfairly won at the game which led to the duel. A note was enclosed—this disjointed, incoherent one:

"MY LORD,—You are one of the luckiest scamps in the world. I did not succeed in killing you; shall not probably have another chance. You are married—the devil confound you—to the most beautiful girl in England; ay, or in twenty Englands! and now I return you the money which I unfairly won—unfairly won in fact, but not in intention. I never intended to keep your dirty dross. It may, perhaps, amuse your bride to know that I have myself this morning espoused Charlotte Beath, the daughter of a chimney-sweep—a master chimney-sweep—do not forget that; he does not now climb chimneys himself, has not done so since he was twelve years old. This he assures me of, upon 'his honour.' And I tell you what, you cowardly Hibernian—how *could* you have been born in Ireland? I tell you this, you cowardly Hibernian, you could hardly hold the sword in your shaking hand: it was no credit to me to run such a fellow through his preposterous belly. Yes, I tell you, you rascally Hibernian, I shall be happier to-night than you. I should think so! It will be just as well not to pretend to be a real husband. Leave your bride at the church-door, you emasculated, incapable thing.

"PHILIP MOWBRAY."

"N.B. If you do not think this letter sufficiently insulting, I will improve upon it at the slightest hint."

There cannot, I think, be two opinions as to Philip Mowbray's state of mind when he penned the foregoing epistle. It was quite true that Philip Mowbray, "the gifted, gentle, handsome Philip Mowbray," had married Charlotte Beath, the daughter of a chimney-sweep—a master chimney-sweep. If we are to take the evidence of her portrait—said to be her portrait, painted by a great master, in the Vernon collection—she was a very charming creature. Education, high thoughts,—her husband's teachings, not by words and discourses only, but bold, valiant, glorious deeds—though not trumpeted forth to the world by the post-horns of the time, must, no doubt, have greatly improved and refined her, when the portrait was painted. She wears a red cardinal, and the face is one of the *sweetest* ever limned.

Philip Mowbray married in a passion. His fancy had been caught by the plebeian beauty, though the Honourable Cecilia still dominated over his imagination. Ah, well! he soon learned to forget the Honourable Cecilia. Meeting the Earl of C—— one day in Pall Mall, a few months after an extraordinary run of luck at cards, he said, " My dear fellow, I heard last night at the Club that you were infernally hard-up. Now that is an unpleasant position. I have a right to say so, as I speak from experience; *will* a cool five hundred be of any use to you?"

The astonished Earl said it would be of the greatest use to him—would in a sublunary sense, be his salvation. "Here then are the notes," said Philip Mowbray. The Earl was profuse in his acknowledgment, and offered to sign any paper necessary to secure repayment of the loan at a given day. "No loan at all, my lord," retorted Mowbray. "It is but an instalment of a great debt I owe your lordship." "Debt—debt—what debt—debt? (His lordship seems to have had a habit common at that time of repeating himself. The King set the example.) Debt, debt! I don't understand you, Mr. Mowbray." "The explanation is very easy, my lord," said Mowbray; "your lordship kindly relieved me of a brimstone lady, now the Countess of C——, thereby enabling me to marry the daughter of a chimney-sweep, for which benefit five hundred pounds is a poor repayment."

Philip Mowbray had no children. This was a cankering grief, though it did not disturb the marital harmony. Ennui, however, grew upon Philip Mowbray. He longed to have something to do in the world besides eating, drinking, and gambling. The war with America had broken out. He was acquainted with Colonel Tarleton, one of the most dashing cavalry officers that have ever charged, from Tamerlane to Murat. He obtained a commission in that officer's regiment,—a cornetcy, and embarked with it in the Glasgow frigate for America. He would not, however, enter into the service, great as were the temptations to a mind constituted like his, till the "master chimney-sweep's daughter" consented to go with him. There does not appear to be any reluctance on her part, and the pair safely reached Boston.

Cornet Mowbray attained a captaincy; was present and distinguished himself in all Colonel Tarleton's raids

At the "Cowpens," the only positive defeat sustained by Tarleton, Captain Mowbray, one of the very last to leave the field, shot one of two American officers who were riding against him, and then threw the discharged pistol in the face of the other with such force and direct aim that the Yankee, stunned and blinded, fell from his horse. Captain Mowbray escaped without a scratch.

The most singular of his military adventures occurred a few weeks before the war with America substantially terminated. Lafayette at the head of the French force, and Washington in command of the Americans, were besieging Yorktown, in which Cornwallis had permitted himself, with about four thousand men, to be cooped up. Tarleton had long since discovered the military imbecility of Cornwallis, seen through the hollowness of his Indian reputation, and chafed like a madman at the unhappy thought of surrender which was entertained by the titled general. He offered, it is well known, to break through the hostile beleaguerment, and join Clinton, if Cornwallis would give him but two thousand men. Cornwallis hesitated. How could he attempt such a thing, not knowing the enemy's strength? What part of his line could be attacked with a chance of success? Tarleton said he knew a man—Captain Mowbray—who would soon ascertain that. Leave was given to make the experiment. Mowbray's consent was promptly obtained, and he agreed to set out upon the enterprise before the lapse of an hour.

"Reflecting upon the matter after Tarleton left, I could not do away with the impression that Cornwallis would never, whatever my report might be, attempt so bold a venture. I talked with my wife. She agreed with me. Cornwallis would surrender. The troops might be kept prisoners till the war terminated, which would be only heaven knew when. I must, she argued, do my duty, of course. At the same time, whilst doing that, we had a right to provide for our own safety and freedom. I agreed; and the result of our deliberations was, that we should disguise ourselves as negro minstrels, creep, under cover of night, out of the camp, and present ourselves boldly before the French or American general, when opportunity offered. We should be patriotic negroes who had been captured by the English, and who knew all the secrets of their camp; that is, of their position and means of defence. The reason of our pretended minstrelsy was that we were hasting away to our home in Louisiana, and did not wish to be detained on the road, even by the patriotic forces. Our rude music was to pay our way. We both were pretty well up in the negro dialect, knew several negro songs, and two rude guitars made up a sufficient orchestra.

"We got away very well; were, as it was certain we should be, captured, taken first before Colonel Symes, and after some preliminary talk, shut up in a rude sort of hut-dungeon. The next day we were led before the two generals. There was mighty questioning. I told my story pretty well, but was not trusted. My wife was even less successful; but by God's especial grace, and the favour of a sentry—handsomely paid for it, as we had not been searched—we stole away in the night. After much peril and suffering we gained General Clinton's lines. Next we started for England."

A deep sense of the depravity of war had seized the mind of Captain Mowbray, and he thenceforth determined "to fight only with Satan, the enemy of souls." He hired a chapel in Southwark, in or close by Bermondsey, "and did much godly work." His wife officiated as clerk. A volume of his sermons has been printed. They breathe a spirit of earnest faith and piety. But the old Adam within him was unsubdued. The breaking out of the French Revolution kindled the smouldering ashes of his old war-spirit to flame. He solicited military employment. The request was granted; he was appointed to a company in one of the regiments—number not mentioned—which formed part of the force placed under the command of the Duke of York. He was killed at the siege of Valenciennes. The daughter of the master sweep was with him during the campaign, and closed his eyes when he died from a severe wound received in the trenches.

Captain Mowbray died poor. The petition of his widow to the king is a curiosity in its way. Charlotte Mowbray sets forth "that her husband fought for his king and country in many battles in both worlds, had wrestled with Satan to the advancement of Christ's kingdom, and when dying told her to rely upon the justice of God and the king." She (Charlotte Mowbray), therefore, "humbly solicited such a provision for her age as would suffice to keep soul and body together till such time as God would require the first—earth and worms the latter. And the petitioner would every pray, *et cetera.*" The petition was so far successful that Charlotte Mowbray was allowed twenty pounds a-year. She did not live to enjoy the king's magnificent bounty more than about two years.

DANIEL DE FOE.

THE world does not recognise—not, at least, ostensibly—its chief benefactors. Splendid monuments are erected over the dust of statesmen and warriors, and glorifying titles are inscribed upon them; but men who have shed light and mirth—who will continue to shed light and mirth as long as the language in which they wrote shall endure—find scant stone or marble recognition. It is, perhaps, well that it should be so. Their works, instinct with the life of life, are their true monument. "Si requiris monumentum, circumspice" is the grand epitaph of Sir Christopher Wren inscribed over the front of the chancel of St. Paul's. That epitaph has a wide application; and to few men it more directly applies than to the author of the *History of the Plague* and of *Robinson Crusoe*. It is not embodied in brass or bronze, but is written indelibly upon the hearts of millions.

He was an odd wrong-headed man this Daniel De Foe, the author of *Robinson Crusoe*. He did not even know or suspect, till he was sixty years of age, that he could write fiction; did not, before then, imagine that he had a *Robinson Crusoe*, a *Citizen's Account of the Plague of London*, &c. &c., in him. An altogether wayward man, and suffered the penalty which all incur who persist in knocking their heads against the orthodox granite walls by which " Society" is bounded and enclosed.

Daniel Foe was his real name; the " De" was added in afterlife, when, with venial weakness, he was desirous it should not be known that his father, James Foe, was a butcher long established in London. He was born in

1661 in the parish of St. Giles's, Cripplegate. James Foe was desirous that his son should have nothing to do with trade, and he himself being a dissenter, he resolved that Daniel should be a dissenting minister. But Daniel was not made of the right stuff for that vocation. He was a very refractory, unpromising pupil of a Mr. Moreton, who kept a dissenting academy on Newington-green; but at which academy he, nevertheless, acquired a smattering—scarcely more—of five languages, mathematics, logic, geography, and history.

. The "principle" of dissent—that of refusing submission to, or acquiescence in, authoritative teaching—took firm hold of Daniel Foe's mind, which was essentially combative and antagonistic. At the age of twenty-one, and just towards the close of Charles the Second's infamous reign, when unblushing licentiousness had full sway in high places, he must needs write a biting satire upon the clergy, entitled *Speculum Crapegownorum*. There was nothing very terrible in that paper thunderbolt—a weak flutter only of the young eagle's literary plumes. Disappointed that his pen failed to overthrow the half-Romanised Church, Daniel Foe had recourse to the sword, and joined, when but twenty years old, the Duke of Monmouth's rebellion against James the Second, much against the sage counsel of a friend, who advised him that, since he felt no aptitude for preaching, it would be wise to follow his father's trade—slaughter beasts, not men—which vocation he would find to be as much more profitable as it was decidedly more moral. Daniel Foe, who had not then cut his wisdom-teeth, demurred to his good friend's advice; ran off from the "academy" set up for teaching the young idea how to shoot in an evangelical direction, and was quite in time to take part in the battle of Sedgmoor. We have the testimony of Lord Macaulay, that never was the stubborn bravery of peasant Britain more conspicuously displayed than by Monmouth's mob—a mob ill-furnished with efficient arms—than in that fatal fight. It is doubtful that the victory would have been with James's disciplined troops, had it not been for cannon which the Protestant Bishop of Winchester enabled the Royalist commander to bring up against the " Rebels." This prelate lent his carriage-horses to drag the guns into action against men who were fighting to prevent the subversion of the Church of which his lordship was one of the mitred chiefs. Foe often alluded to this circumstance with great bitterness.

How the rash young soldier escaped the vengeance of the triumphant party is not shown with distinctness. There are several versions of his hair-breadth escapes from the hunters. According to one account, he was at a farm-yard in the capacity of swine-, sheep-, and cow-herd, when it was visited by a party of " Kirke's Lambs," as the murderous ruffians were popularly named. They were, as usual, in search of victims. Instead of concealing himself, Daniel Foe, whose secret was known to the farmer and his wife, waited, in a ploughman's guise, upon the soldiers, and " made merry with them."

Be that true or not, he escaped the myrmidons of James; and instead of figuring in a dock at the Bloody Assize, we find him working for bread as a commercial traveller for several London houses who dealt mainly in hosiery. Skill in stockings was hardly to be expected in Daniel Foe, and yet so speedily was it acquired, that in 1687 he was chief buyer, for eminent houses in the trade, of the provincial producers. It was then he assumed the aristocratic prefix " De" to his name. " It gave him consideration with the manufacturers. He also, being free by birth, became an enrolled citizen of London."

A great event was now on the eve of accomplishment. The nation was in travail with the Revolution of 1688. The army, it was well known, from the exultant shouts, when news reached them of the acquittal of the bishops, had become thoroughly disaffected to King James, and could no longer be made the instruments of his cruel rage. William of Orange was known to be actively preparing for a descent on England; the tongues and pens of numerous speakers and writers were loosened, and the agitation, the enthusiasm of the people, especially of the Londoners, hourly increased. Daniel De Foe rushed at once into the *mêlée*. He had made a great advance in dialectic power, and was by no means one of the least formidable of the king's assailants.

The Revolution itself was hailed by De Foe with transports of joy; and he ever after kept the 4th of November, the anniversary of William's landing, as a festival. After that monarch's decease, no Orangeman in Ireland ever drank the glorious, pious, and immortal memory with more hilarious gusto than De Foe. He, moreover, buckled on his sword again, and joined a royal regiment of volunteer-horse, who made a gallant show upon the occasion of William and Mary's first ceremonial visit to Guildhall..

The Revolution established, the Constitution settled, the enthusiasm of the nation for the "Delivered" visibly cooled; the main cause of which appears to have been that he was not an Englishman. This waywardness on the part of the nation greatly incensed De Foe, who again rushed into print in defence of his hero. This time it was a satirical poem, entitled *The True-born Englishman*. It is written with rough vigour, and proves, what no one ever doubted, that the inhabitants of this island are a race compounded of many races of men,— Welsh, Saxons, Danes, Normans, Germans, French, Scotch, Irish, &c.,—for which reason he argued, with curiously-twisted logic, that the true-born Englishman, according to the popular idea, was a myth, and that in a real sense King William was as much an Englishman as any one born within the sound of Bow bells. The king was so much pleased with the poem that he sent for De Foe, and highly complimented him upon his genius and good sense; the sincerity of which praise was proved by the monarch's frequent consultations with De Foe on important matters of state during the latter part of his reign.

The king's favour, if it conferred a sort of factitious fame on De Foe's literary efforts, did not fill his purse. It was very pleasant to be a man whom a king delighted to honour—in words—but a man with a wife, and a fast-coming family, could not be content even with regal breath, and Daniel De Foe turned again to the vulgar stocking-business.

He enlarged the sphere of his commercial operations; set-up as a shipowner and merchant, trading with Spain and Portugal, and failed;—not, however, discreditably. No doubt, as struggling men generally do, he committed some faults in the hopeless endeavour to recover his position. They could not, however, have been very serious faults, as his creditors accepted the composition offered, and consented to accept his own personal security for its due payment.

Dr. Johnson, in his *Dictionary*, gives as one definition of patriotism, that it is the last refuge of a scoundrel. It may also, 1 may observe inter alia, be the resource of a highly moral person, as witness the learned Doctor's pamphlets, in which the right of England to tax the unrepresented American Colonies was urged with all the Doctor's ornate pomposity of style and forcible feeble argumentation. Those pamphlets, nevertheless, gained him his pension of three hundred per annum.

De Foe was not so learned in dead languages as the famous lexicographer, but he was a man of original inventive genius, which Doctor Johnson certainly was not in any just sense. The peculiar eccentricity of the broken-down merchant or trader was never more strikingly illustrated than by the mode hit upon by Daniel De Foe to regain a good position in the world.

He had sadly failed to provide ways and means for the support of himself and family; but, nothing deterred by that trifling failure, he at once addressed himself to the task of instructing the Government as to how they should provide for the "ways and means" of the nation. His counsels were appreciated, some of his suggestions were adopted, and his expedient for "raising the wind" had a double effect. The financial measures of the ministry derived a certain success from his suggestions, and he in requital obtained a situation with other favours, which placed him in a position of modest competence.

Daniel De Foe had nothing more to fear in a worldly sense. He had gained at last one of the minor heights of society, and might, perched thereon, have passed his days in contentment.

But De Foe was not a man to pursue the safe beaten paths of life, though he had given hostages to Fortune in a beloved wife and children. He was off at a tangent again. The accession of Queen Anne to the throne was the signal for an outburst of bigotry such as has been rarely witnessed in this country. The High-Church party had solved Pontius Pilate's question, "What is truth?" to their own entire satisfaction, just as the Spanish inquisitors did. Very earnest persons, thoroughly self-convinced men are indeed always persecutors, and this from motives of benevolence. " Why should I permit my brother to perish? Let us put down false teachers by the strong hand of authority." Mr. Samuel Pope and Mr. Lawson are modern teachers of the world-old dogma of bigots, succinctly expressed by the French princess in the often-quoted sentence, "*Il me semble qu'il n'y a que moi qui a toujours raison*" ("It seems to me that I only am always in the right").

Against this theory of slavery,—spiritual slavery,—a thousand times more galling than chains, which only bind the body—the combatant spirit of Daniel De Foe fiercely revolted; yet, spite of all that has been urged in his defence, it must be admitted that his pamphlet, entitled *The Shortest Way with Dissenters*, was not happily compiled. The High-Church party were rampant, and, inflamed by the teachings of Dr. Sacheverell, a university preacher, a furious mob swept throught the streets of London, demolished Dissenting places of worship, burned the dwellings, and obtained such a brutal ascendency that it was not safe for any known Dissenter to be seen in the streets.

Such a triumphant combination of fierce intolerance with brutal stupidity had naturally excited the wrath of

De Foe; but he mistook his audience in thinking that by exaggerating the High - Church " principles," arguing those principles to a natural conclusion in a logical sense, he would make them revolting to the common herd. It was a clever caricature of the High-Church party, but so subtilely coloured that the more blatant of that party deemed they had never been limned by a more skilful appreciative artist. De Foe had out - Heroded Herod; enunciated in glowing language the really true and only effectual mode of dealing with Dissent. The Dissenters were astounded—written as the pamphlet was by one of their professed zealous champions. These two facts amply prove that De Foe's arrows had gone awry; that he had failed to hit the mark aimed at.

"High Church" appears to have first become aware of the true esoteric meaning of the pamphlet. A prosecution was instituted against him for seditious blasphemy. The ostensible purpose of the book was hypocritically assumed to be the real one. To burke his defence and insure the punishment of "one of the most profligate of men," he was persuaded to plead "Guilty," under the most solemn assurances by high-placed people that the queen's pardon would be immediately extended to him. De Foe's keen sagacity must have failed him at this trying crisis. He was rudely awakened from his dream. Directly his plea of "Guilty" was recorded, he was sentenced to be pilloried three times, have his ears snipped off, to pay a fine of one hundred marks, be imprisoned during the queen's pleasure, and upon liberation find sureties for good behaviour during seven years. He was about to pay dearly for having broken with the solemn dignified hypocrisy of the world. With all his keen insight of mankind, he had not measured the influence, the power of that solemn dignified hypocrisy.

Pope's infamous line in allusion to De Foe in the pillory,

"See where on high stands unabashed De Foe,"

is interpreted by the courageous thinker and writer of his life his highest eulogy. The selfish cringing meanness of Pope brings out by comparison the defiant firmness of De Foe in brilliant relief. Admitted that Daniel De Foe could not have written the *Rape of the Lock;* neither could he have grovelled in the dust before stars and garters, titled gentlemen and ladies, drunken and noble lords and demireps, as Pope did.

To be sure, Pope made "a better end," in common estimation, than "the unabashed De Foe"—but the true end is not here. And even *here* now at the present day, the moral estimate of Daniel De Foe is infinitely higher than that entertained for Alexander Pope.

It would have been a great loss to England, and to the world, had Daniel De Foe not been an eccentric man; if he had been content to dwell in conventional decencies after attaining his place. No nation has ever been deficient in "respectabilities." They are the dust of grave-yards; the spots where they lie, in crowded heaps, signalised by lying tombstones. Daniel De Foe lives with hearty vigorous life in tens of hundreds of thousands of homes in both worlds.

De Foe was equal, superior to his fate. He recovered, when cast down into apparently remediless ruin, his pristine mental vigour. He penned a *Hymn to the Pillory* during his bravely-borne imprisonment, and commenced his *Review*, and re-engaged in political-pamphlet warfare with as much energy and fierceness as ever. He abated not one jot of heart or hope. The Whigs, for whom he had so strenuously laboured, abandoned him to his fate. The Tories, to whom he had always been strennously opposed, were more generous, more just towards the wayward, wilful, high-principled writer. Upon the accession of Harley, through the influence of Mrs. Masham, to power, that minister induced her majesty to order De Foe's liberation from prison, and even prevailed upon the queen to liquidate from the privy purse his fine and expense. This was not, perhaps, a piece of purely Quixotic generosity; Harley and Bolingbroke having been, no doubt, anxious to secure for their party the pen of so vigorous and versatile a writer. The horizon brightened rapidly. Harley commissioned De Foe to act as confidential agent at Edinburgh in endeavouring to bring about the union of Scotland and England; a duty of which he creditably acquitted himself.

Still this utterly unpractical man would not lend his talents to the advocacy of the Tory measures of the cabinet. He, however, refrained from writing against them. His obligations to Harley commanded such a negative service as that.

He determined to withdraw from the active conflict of parties. He had suffered much more from his reputed political friends than enemies. Unwarned, however, by the persecution brought upon him by *The Shortest Way of Dealing with Dissenters*, he must needs launch forth a similar *brochure*, by which, to ordinary minds, he appeared seriously to propose the bringing in of the Stuart Pretender, to the exclusion of the Hanoverian dynasty. This was done, as in the former instance, by caricaturing and exaggerating the arguments of the Jacobites. The irony was not understood by the commonalty. One Benson, an ardent partisan of the Whigs, honestly thinking that De Foe was in covert league—(his official, or officious connection with the Harley-Bolingbroke ministry giving force and colour to this suspicion)—with the exiled Stuart, petitioned that Daniel De Foe might be tried for high treason. A judge was found to commit the unlucky pamphleteer to Newgate for presuming to write in defence, or rather explanation of the inculpated pamphlet, after Benson's accusation had been preferred before the grand jury—a true bill found—and he had been compelled to find heavy bail to surrender for trial. But for his ministerial friends it might have gone hard with him, so inveterate were his enemies, so obtuse the public as to the true meaning of the pamphlet. Harley, to avoid all danger to a man whose talents he respected —much as he laughed at his erratic follies—covered him with a royal pardon; an incident to which he afterwards alluded with much humour.

The accession of George the First put the finishing

stroke to De Foe's political career. He had no longer one single influential friend—was sixty years of age—had once been struck with apoplexy—was lonely, and afflicted with gout and stone. Under these exhilarating circumstances this peculiar, indomitable man betook himself to romance writing! His first essay was the immortal *Robinson Crusoe.* The idea was suggested by the story of Alexander Selkirk, a Scottish seaman who had sailed in the ship commanded by Captain Rogers, in his voyage round the world. Selkirk was *marooned* for some offence, and left upon the Island of Juan Fernandez in the Pacific, where he contrived to exist for four years. Cowper has some verses upon the subject, beginning with "I am monarch of all I survey." The idea was derived from Selkirk's story, but the treatment of the narrative is incomparably striking and original. "The great beauty of this fiction," remarks an Edinburgh Reviewer, "consists not in the hero, but in his situation, and the admirable manner in which he is made to adapt himself to it. Human sympathy attends his every action, and the simple, natural pathos of a plain, unsophisticated man, and the sublimity and awfulness of perfect solitude, moves more than would all the feeling and eloquence of Rousseau, had he attempted a similar story. No wonder this tale has been translated into every European language, and even into Arabic, according to the testimony of Burkhardt."

This criticism is just, as far as it goes, but to render it *perfectly* just, it should have been added, that only the first part of the book, before the Spaniards arrive on the island, is invested with the indescribable charm which has made the work popular throughout the world. But the same may be said of Milton's *Paradise Lost.* The first six books are magnificent—the others pale their intellectual fires in the blaze of glory which illuminates those first chapters. The mightiest wing would flag and droop before the termination of so exhaustive a flight.

The other romances of Daniel De Foe have fallen out of the current literature, are practically dead and buried.

Moll Flanders, Colonel Jack, Captain Singleton, have disappeared, though they were not without much merit. The pre-eminent quality of De Foe as a writer of fiction was his power of *realisation*. Any one would go before a magistrate and make an oath that, to the best of his belief, *A Citizen's Account of the Great Plague of London* was a simply-told narrative of what had really, and to the writer's knowledge, taken place. This is a very rare quality in an author.

Ah! yes; but genius when not combined with discretion, when its possessor refuses to be bound by the shackles and *safeguards* of conventionalism, will rarely have a good balance at his banker's. De Foe, though his writings had a large sale, was beset with pecuniary difficulties, embittered by domestic affliction. Himself on the verge of both gaol and grave, he was doomed also to experience—how sharper than a serpent's tooth it is to have a thankless child. His son, to whom he had made over in trust some property for the benefit of his wife and daughters, appropriated the whole to himself. The sad story will be best told in the following touching letter—the last of the writings of the author of *Robinson Crusoe*, addressed to Mr. Baker, an eminent naturalist, who had married De Foe's favourite daughter, Sophia:

"DEAR MR. BAKER,—I have your very kind and affectionate letter of the 1st instant. It did not reach me till the 10th: how it has been delayed I know not. As your kind manner and kinder thought, from which it flows—for I know all you say to be sincere, Nathaniel-like, without guile—is a particular satisfaction to me; so the delay of a letter, however it happened, deprived me of that cordial too many days. I stood so much in need of it, to support a mind sinking under a weight of affliction too heavy for my strength, and looking on myself as abandoned by every comfort, every friend, every relative, except such only as are unable to give me any assistance.

"I was sorry you should say in your letter you were debarred from seeing me. On the contrary, it would be a greater comfort to me than any I now enjoy, if I could receive your agreeable visits with safety, and could see both you and my dearest Sophia, could it be without giving her the grief of seeing her father in his present situation, bowed down under the load of insupportable sorrows. I am sorry I must open my griefs so far as to tell her it is not the blow I received from a wicked, perjured, contemptible enemy that has broken my spirit. She well knows I have borne up against greater disasters. But it has been the inhuman dealing of my own son which has ruined my family and broken my heart. As I am at this time under a weight of very heavy illness, which I think will be a fever—and a fatal one—I take this occasion to vent my grief in the breasts of those who I know will make a prudent use of it; nothing but this has conquered or could conquer me.

"I depended upon my son; I trusted him; I gave up my two dear unprovided children into his hands; but he has no compassion, and suffers them and their poor dying mother to beg their bread at his door, and to crave as it were as alms what he is bound under hand and seal, beside the most solemn promises, to supply them with, himself at the same time living in a profusion of plenty. It is too much for me. Excuse my infirmity; my heart is too full. I can say no more; my heart is too full. I only ask one thing of you as a dying request. Stand by them when I am gone, and let them not be wronged whilst my son is able to do them right. Stand by them as a brother; and if you have any thing within you owing to my memory—I, who have bestowed upon you the best gift I had to give—let them not be injured and trampled upon by false pretences. I hope they will want no help but that of comfort and counsel; and that they will indeed want, being too easily led by words and promises.

"It adds to my grief that I must never see my little grandson. Give him my blessing, and may he be to you both your joy in youth, your comfort in age, and never add a sigh to your sor.ows.   But that, alas! is not to be expected.   Kiss my dear Sophy once more for me; and if I must see her no more, tell her this, that her father loved her above all to his last breath.

" Your unhappy D. F.

" About two miles from Greenwich, Kent,
    ". Tuesday, August 12th, 1730."

This great and good, but uneonfined and unconfinable man did not cast off the burden of mortality so soon as, when he penned the foregoing letter, he expected.   He lingered on till the 24th of April 1731, when he sank to his final rest.   He died where he was born, in the parish of St. Giles, Cripplegate, and was buried in Bunhill Fields.   He would have been more fortunate had he been less highly principled.   But 'twas ever thus.   Whoever attempts to stem the torrent of the time is sure to be whelmed in it.   To sail with the tide is the only chance of reaching pleasant pastures.   To be sure, those who go with the multitude will, like that multitude, fill forgotten graves: but it is a cruel irony upon human life to say of a rarely-gifted man like De Foe, that he died in misery and lives in fame.

THE HONOURABLE JOHN LOFTUS.

THIS highly variegated and vivacious gentleman is assumed to have been a stray scion of a distinguished family who had large estates both in England and Ireland. The fact mainly rests upon his own assertion; but how, in such case, he could legally or by courtesy be entitled to the prefix of Honourable, puzzles one.

There is, however, proof, though shadowy and indistinct, of the truth of the statement in the remarkable, strongly contrastive life he led up to Christmas-Day, 1782, when he perished, in his thirty-fourth year, in a manner as heroical and self-sacrificing as ever shed an aureole round the brow of warrior, priest, or king.

John Loftus was born, or, to speak by the card, is believed to have been born at or near Carrickfergus, Ireland, in the year 1748. As to what surroundings accompanied his birth and boyhood, nothing trustworthy is known. He certainly received a fair education—was a gay, frolicsome boy, fearless as frolicsome, and very good-looking. He had very considerable talent for mimicry and personation, and gained much applause at amateur private theatricals in Dublin, where business or pleasure had taken him when he was in his twentieth year. He must have moved in or been admitted into what is named good society, as he was known by sight and name to the Duke of Bedford, then Lord-Lieutenant of Ireland, a nobleman of somewhat debauched habits, but not destitute of administrative talent.

His excellency, not long after young Loftus arrived in Dublin, indulged in the undignified whim of making one at Donnybrook Fair, disguised, of course, as com-

pletely as might be.   He was accompanied by two of his
suite only, both metamorphosed, like his grace, into Irish
peasants.   That Loftus knew of the Duke's intention is
not positively stated.   The rollicking young man had
merely, perhaps, determined, independently for himself,
to assist at a scene where an Irishman was proverbially
to be seen in the full blaze of his glory.   However that
may have been, the Duke and his companions entered
with such gusto into the spirit of the fair—its boisterous,
riotous fun—that he got singled out at last by a powerful
countryman, and challenged to fight by the usual prelude
to such encounters—a crack upon his excellency's skull,
inflicted by a stout shillelagh.   This was carrying the
fun much too far.   To discover himself was impossible,
except in the last extremity to save his life.   John Loftus,
who must have been eagerly watchful of what was going
on, and either knew beforehand or had penetrated the
Duke's guise—he himself being habited as a rough country lad—rushed forward and felled the assailant upon his
grace with one tremendous blow.   The din and riot going
on prevented immediate attention being paid to so unusual an incident as the interposition of a third party
between two combatants; but it being well known to
Loftus that the Duke's adversary belonged to a "faction,"
which, as soon as they heard what had happened, would
rush furiously to the rescue, the young fellow whispered
hastily to his grace : "Leave this place, my Lord Duke,
without delay; you are in great danger; your horses are
without; I and some rough acquaintances shall manage
well enough to insure you a sufficient start."
    The Duke and his elderly friends did not wait to be
told twice; they bolted forthwith, and reached Dublin
Castle scatheless, except for the crack upon his grace's
crown, given without the slightest malice or suspicion,
by the man, whom it was he had assailed, in pure *gaîté
de cœur*.   Loftus and his friends made a fierce fight of it
with the help of some of the "boys" who belonged to a
faction opposed to that to which the man who assaulted
the representative of royalty belonged, and got clear off

with no more than the ordinary average Donnybrook damage to themselves.

Young Loftus was not one to neglect improving such a singular chance. The very next day he presented himself at the Castle, handsomely attired, and sent in a note addressed to the Duke of Bedford, marked " private and very important." He had not long to wait for an audience, a lengthened one. The Viceroy was naturally anxious to " hush up" so scandalous a story; Loftus solemnly assured him that he had been recognised by himself only. It need hardly be said that Loftus promised to keep the adventure inviolably secret—of course, in consideration, the perfectly well-understood consideration, that he should receive a handsome *quid pro quo.* The Duke believed himself to be quite safe with respect to his courtly companions. He was not wrong in counting upon their fidelity as long as his viceroyalty lasted. That terminated, their tongues were loosened—in accordance with the theory of moral ethics which teaches that political gratitude can only in the eternal fitness of things, and its highest sense, be held to mean no more than a keen sense of favours *to come.* The story was circulated amongst the fashionable circles of Dublin, with many varieties and additions. One was that his grace *knighted* his young champion on the spot. Who the young man was that so promptly interposed in favour of the Lord-Lieutenant was not known, except to the Duke and John Loftus, till some years afterwards. The story was flatly contradicted by " authority;" but the denial did not weaken the credence attached to it by the gossips of Dublin.

The substantial result to Mr. John Loftus was, that he obtained the commission of cornet of cavalry, and the post of attaché, or something analogous, at the Viceroy's court. No post of the kind could, I suppose, have made Loftus an Honourable, even in Ireland.

About this time (1759) the French monarch made a great combined effort by the fleets assembled at Dunkirk and Brest to redress the catastrophe of Minden by descents on the British and Irish coasts. The main design was defeated by Hawke's splendid victory in Quiberon Bay. A gallant French captain, of the name of Thurot, achieved, spite of the vigilance of the British fleet, some small successes amongst the western islands of Scotland. Thurot's squadron consisted originally of five frigates. One of the largest of these became unserviceable through stress of weather, and was sent back to France. Another of the remaining frigates foundered at sea. Not abating one jot of heart or hope, Thurot sailed with his shattered force to the Bay of Carrickfergus, where on the 21st of February he effected a landing with about 700 men. Colonel Jennings, with four companies only of raw recruits, was in the open town of Carrickfergus. He made a resolute, but of course an unsuccessful resistance, then retired to the dilapidated castle, in which there was neither store of provisions nor ammunition, except the small quantity he could carry in with him. *En revanche* there was a breach about fifty feet wide in the crumbling wall. The colonel, in the hope of being quickly succoured by regular troops, filled up the breach with rubbish, and gathered up heaps of stones to use instead of bullets and balls. Let us leave the gallant colonel with his bulldog resolution, and return to John Loftus, cornet unattached, in Dublin.

The successes, such as they were, of Thurot greatly irritated the English people, and threw a shade even upon Hawke's victory. What!—was the nation who had so signally discomfited the French upon their own coasts and harbours to be harassed by a beaten enemy on its own seaboard, he finding no check? The Duke of Bedford was subject to much abuse by the Press, and to implied censure by the Cabinet, and was very desirous of signally restoring his tarnished reputation for watchfulness and vigour. News came of Thurot's doings at Carrickfergus, where his ships were in the bay. Messengers from Jennings succeeded in reaching Dublin, from whom his excellency learnt that Jennings could not hold out many hours, although he had repulsed the French at the first attack. Thurot had, it was also reported, received intelligence that the regular troops were within a few marches of Carrickfergus, and the French commander was preparing to embark his troops and leave the bay with all possible expedition, and in order to do so had offered to accept the surrender of the castle upon the easiest possible terms. The English soldiers were to be at once exchanged for the same number of French sailors or soldiers who had chanced to be made prisoners. The castle was not to be blown up, nor the town of Carrickfergus to be burned or pillaged.

The Duke of Bedford had despatched three frigates —the Æolus, the Pallas, and the Brilliant—to Carrickfergus Bay, their mission being to extinguish Thurot once and for all. But should the French frigates have left before their arrival, the Lord-Lieutenant would have no chance of setting himself right with the British people and British ministry. How could he make sure that the English frigates, when they opeued up the bay, would there find Thurot's ships? That was the question which he determined to discuss without a moment's delay with Cornet Loftus, whom he knew to be a Carrickfergus man, and in whose dash, bravery, and fertility of resource he had much confidence, notwithstanding certain bizarre peculiarities which he frequently indulged in. In fact, the cornet's life was one long practical joke, broken fitfully by serious, earnest deeds.

One of his jests has, apparently, been reproduced by Christopher North, in the " Noctes Ambrosiauæ," originally published in *Blackwood's Magazine*. It is necessary to relate it in this place, or the adventure at Carrickfergus would scarcely be credited. The story told in the " Noctes," and admirably told, is—I quote from memory—that Professor Wilson (Christopher North) caused an advertisement to be inserted in oue of the Edinburgh papers to the effect that an elderly gentleman, of large means, was desirous of entering into the bonds of matrimony with a suitable partner—he, a bachelor, never having experieuced the bliss of that state of life. In order that any lady who might be disposed to entertain the proposition should have an opportunity of personally viewing the candidate for connubial honours, the advertiser would seat himself, towards the "gloaming," on the morrow of the day when the advertisement appeared, at a particular spot on the Calton Hill. Christopher goes on, in richly humorous description, to describe the throng by whom he was beset, their jibes, sarcastic derision, &c.

The real adventure of the Honourable John Loftus differs in its minor accessories from the imaginary one of Professor Wilson. Loftus, I have previously remarked, was a handsome young man. That beauty was of a feminine type, stout-hearted, courageous as he in scores of instances proved himself to be. He had fine flowing dark-brown hair, which he was clever at arranging in female fashion. He would in other respects cleverly "make up" as an interesting young lady—or elderly lady for that matter—so cleverly that he more than once danced at the Viceregal court balls as a Miss M'Clarty, or M'Carthy of Roscommon—a distant relative of his, I apprehend—a left-handed one probably—if, indeed, there was any such person in existence, for whom he had himself procured the necessary order of admittance. Upon neither occasion was the cheat discovered by those most intimate with Cornet Loftus.

Now, Cornet Loftus had a grudge or pique against Captain Robert Brady, also an attaché of the Viceregal court. Brady was an especial favourite of the Lord-Lieutenant, who would have secretly, though not perhaps openly, resented any quarrel fastened upon him provocative of a duel, or no doubt Loftus would, in the spirit of the time, have chosen that mode of avenging himself upon Brady. He hit upon a plan of much more refined, artistic vengeance.

One of those advertisements so common now, but novelties at that time, alleged by Loftus to have appeared in a Dublin paper, set forth that a young lady of high family, considerable personal attractions, and a fortune of thirty thousand pounds at her own disposal, was desirous of becomiug the wife of a military officer *not* under the rank of captain. He must be a handsome man, not more than thirty years of age, and of ancestral descent equal to her own. Money she cared not for, having plenty for both. At such a time, on such an evening, the lady would be found at the entrance of a wood in Roxby Park, near Swords, attired in a riding dress, and with a riding whip in her hand. This was signed C. M'C.

A post-scriptum added, that the candidate for her favour must wear a white rose in his button-hole. The lady would, on recognising the sign, raise the whip in military-salute fashion; and both would then exchange more intimate courtesies, as if old acquaintances. If the officer —not below the rank of captain—this was indispensable —answered the description given, and could give unexceptional testimonials to character—this was also indispensable—the ceremony might take place as soon as the bridegroom wished.

Into this clumsily-contrived trap poor Brady rushed at a run. He was a handsome man, no one would deny; and as to descent, he claimed for one of his ancestors no less a personoge than Brian Boirhomme himself; and he was, without doubt or question, very poor—poor to extreme indebtedness.

Cornet Loftus, who for some time had been very assiduously "making it up" with Captain Brady, and had succeeded in doing so, suddenly rushed into the gallant captain's quarters one fine morning with a slip of printed paper in his hand, which he declared he had just cut out of a Dublin paper. The "slip" contained the two paragraphs I have quoted. As to its having been cut from a Dublin newspaper, that was an invention, like the rest. He had caused the "slip" to be printed "in confidence."

"Captain Brady," exclaimed Loftus,—it is the cornet himself who tells the story,—"Captain Brady, my fine fellow, fortune, an immense fortune, is in your grasp.

You have but to close your hand.   Read—read, captain,
read.   You are the angled-for—the very man.   Ah, it is
true, as the fellow says in the play, *some* people have
greatness thrust upon them.   That, I fear, will never be
my case; whilst you——"

"I do not understand," interrupted the puzzled captain.   "In what way can this absurd advertisement concern me?"

"My dear fellow, it concerns no one but you.   Hear
me out.   Have I not heard you say that you once had
the honour, not long ago, to dance at a Castle ball with
Miss Charlotte M'Carthy of Roscommon; a lady——"

"Honour be——" angrily exclaimed Captain Brady.
"Three times, and in quick succession, the jade trod on
that corn of mine—three times, as if she knew exactly
the place to pitch upon.   I thought I should have fainted.
The devil take Miss M'Carthy!"

"Thou pray'st not well, my noble captain.   It will
not be the devil, but a devilish good fellow, for all that's
come and gone, that will take Miss M'Carthy; namely,
your fascinating self, you lucky son of a gun."

"By the powers, Loftus, you have been drinking; and
it is not quite ten yet.   But perhaps it is last night's
drink, not slept off."

"You have, I suppose, slept it off."   It does not seem
so, though; for a foggier-brained fellow I have seldom
met with.   Can't you understand 'M'C——' means Charlotte M'Carthy? and what captain besides you within a
circuit of fifty miles is handsome, highly born, not more
than thirty years of age, and decidedly poor, eh?   Answer me that!"

The gallant captain began to listen with both his
ears.   He began to dimly comprehend what his enthusiastic friend was driving at.   Miss M'Carthy was a hand-
somish hoyden; but thirty thousand pounds!

"I had no occasion," continues Cornet Loftus, "to
extra butter the bait; he swallowed it like sack and sugar,
and I left him quite sure that he would be punctual to
the appointment.   Of course I had told him that Miss

M'Carthy was for a time residing, to my knowledge, with an aunt at Swords. That was 'confirmation strong as proof from Holy Writ.' I often quote plays, and without exactly knowing it at the moment. I once thought in my *very* green salad days I should like to turn player. I mean in the ordinary sense. Is not 'all the world a stage, and all the men and women merely players?' The only doubt I experienced when I left that prince of conceited fops, Brady, was whether, when the curtain fell upon the decisive scene of the little comedy I had invented, it would be found I had been playing the knave or fool! I went on for knave, but in the transformation scene I might be wearing motley and the cap and bells!—an unendurable thing! If it should so fall out, I would kick the puppy, defiant of Bedford's choler!"

There were quartered at Swords at that time six companies of Irish dragoons, the officers of which were amongst the gayest, most rollicking of those proverbially gay and rollicking spirits. With these Cornet Loftus was an especial favourite, and they were, of course, secretly apprised of the matrimonial adventure about to be engaged in by Captain Brady. Cornet Loftus did not give them his entire confidence, nor nearly. To have done so would have spoiled the fun, and marred his main purpose.

At the appointed time and place the blushing M'Carthy found herself the object of the admiration of all the dragoon officers, and all wearing white roses, in full dress. But to none did she condescend to show the sign of favouring recognition by giving the military salute with the riding-whip. All the sugared, high-flown compliments paid could not elicit a word or a smile. She was stern, silent, inexorable.

The thing was getting tiresome, no captain having appeared, and they were about returning to Swords, when the lady's eyes, which had been steadily fixed in one direction, suddenly lightened, and a bright smile parted her lips. Captain Brady had at last put in an appearance. He was walking very slowly, as if doubtful of the propriety of his conduct in answering personally such an advertisement, and its likelihood of success. It happened, from the peculiar curve of the road, that the gallant captain was seen before he had glimpsed either the lady or her numerous military wooers. There being now a certainty of sport, the dragoon officers at a signal from one of them, Charles O'Reilly, the plotter's especial crony, the whole party disappeared within the wood, where, unseen themselves, they could witness the sport.

Captain Brady was most graciously received by the lady. Words breathing ardent devotion were stammeringly poured or rather gurgled forth from the gallant officer's bewitching lips. The modest acquiescence of the gratified fair one was accompanied by a soft, smiling allusion to their former meeting at the Castle ball, which must, one would suppose, have elicited a painful reminiscent twinge from Captain Brady's corn-toe. But thirty thousand pounds! That was a salve for all sores; and the golden goal being won, or as good as won, who can be surprised that the enraptured officer—his itching palm already closing in imagination upon the splendid fortune of his betrothed, as the M'Carthy might now be called—should plump down on his knees, after a nervous glance around to ascertain there was no witness of the scene except the blushing bride expectant, and vowing, swearing —A guffaw of many voices interrupts him; the gallant captain leaps to his feet, and, flaming to the colour of a peony, is obliged to hear the compliments, the congratulations of the dragoon officers. They were too late, one of them said, by a few minutes, or, by the powers, the captain would not have carried off the precious prize so easily. During this rude badinage, Brady looked daggers at the intrusive roysterers, who at last, tiring of chaff, went off in the direction of Swords. It was some time before their boisterous laughter died away in the distance.

Of course Captain Brady was very irate, much disturbed—who so circumstanced would not be? Never mind. *"Il rit bien qui rit dernier."* He should have the last laugh. And so, composing his ruffled plumes as best

he could, the captain renewed his billing and cooing in
the most dulcet tones. He declared that her image had
been ever present to him since the night of that fairy
ball; and had it not been that a friend of his, Cornet
Loftus, had privately informed him who C. M'C. was, he
should never have thought of coming to the enchanted
spot where he now breathed the air of Paradise, &c. &c.

As to the lady's fortune, that to him was of total insignificance. Indeed, he almost wished she was entirely
portionless, that he might be able to prove beyond all
doubt his disinterested devotion. It is hardly credible
that a man of mature years and of the world could have
made such a gaby of himself, and possibly the mocking
narrative of the Honourable John Loftus may be somewhat highly coloured.

"It was now my cue to speak," continues the Honourable John Loftus, in very fair English, by the way,
improved by his national brogue—"It was now my cue
to speak. 'That generous declaration,' said I, 'has
mightily relieved me, since, to confess the truth, the
thirty thousand pounds is—is a——'

"'Is a what, Miss M'Carthy?' gasped Brady, turning all the colours of a dying dolphin. 'Is a what, Miss
M'Carthy?'

"'Is a dream, dear captain—an illusion. In short,
I do not possess thirty thousand farthings. It is true
that my aunt may, at her death, leave me a few hundreds——'

"'D—— your aunt! Let me go, will you?'

"'Why, you false, perfidious man—did you not say,
only a minute ago——'

"'Never mind what I said; let me go, I say.'

"'But I won't let you go, you false, deceitful villain.
I'll let you know what it is to insult a M'Carthy—you
beggarly spalpeen!'"

The gallant and utterly bewildered captain found
himself seized by the throat-collar with a grasp of iron,
and the accursed riding-whip, to be lifted by agreement
in the fashion of a military salute, was laid most un-

mercifully across his shoulders with heartiest good-will, Brady struggled fiercely, but could not for a time release himself from the grasp of "the female fiend," who nearly throttled him. At last he broke away, in a frantic state, running at top speed, pursued by that dreadful Miss M'Carthy. He, at last, seemed to have dropped her, and having wiped his streaming forehead, and readjusted himself generally, the crest-fallen captain walked with as much nonchalance as he could, at such short notice, assume, into the mess-room of the dragoons. He did that, probably, under a confused impression that the virago, from whom he had with such difficulty got free, would never dare to follow him there.

Error! delusion! unfortunate captain. He had no sooner begun to apologise for his disordered appearance, caused by a smart run—he was fond of running—than in bounced Miss M'Carthy—flew at the wretched man, who vainly attempted effectual resistance to the athletic young rascal in whose power he had placed himself, and got unmercifully beaten; the accompaniment to which unmerciful beating was the lady's furious abuse of the poor fellow for having dared insult a M'Carthy—amid the screaming laughter of the dragoon officers. At last, the terrible fair one stayed her wearied arm, and sailed out of the mess-room, remarking that Captain Brady would not be insolent to an Irish lady of family—one of the ould stock—again in a hurry. The captain disappeared next day from Swords, and in a few days afterwards from Dublin. It was clearly impossible he could remain there. The story of his having been whipped by a lady had taken the wings of the morning, and was known all over Dublin before the flagellated captain had left Swords—that, to him, for-ever-memorable village. What became of him is not recorded. He vanished into space. The Honourable John Loftus was of opinion that he believed himself to have been whipped and pummelled by a young woman to the day of his death. This anecdote does not show the Honourable John Loftus in a very favourable light. The vengeance taken, all

things considered, was monstrously disproportionate to
the offence.

This lively young gentleman was the chosen of the
Duke of Bedford to out-general or out-manœuvre Thurot,
the skilful and daring French sea-captain. Loftus accepted the mission, for the accomplishment of which he
possessed peculiar facilities, with alacrity, and took leave
of his excellency with an assurance that he would so
manage matters that the English squadron should find
that of France in the Bay of Carrickfergus.

The Honourable John Loftus had an intrigue with a
pretty girl in the service of one John Donovan, a silver-
smith and jeweller of Dublin. The girl's name was Mary
Rearden. John Donovan was the brother of a well-to-do
farmer residing in the immediate neighbourhood of Carrickfergus. Both were arrant Jacobites, and well known
to be such, although no overt act of treason could be
proved against either of them. The brothers had not
seen each other for years; nor had either seen a maiden
sister since they were children. This lady's domicile
was somewhere in Ulster. She, like her brothers, was
a Jacobite *enragé*, and it was known to Loftus through
Mary Rearden—the intrigue I have spoken of, as we shall
presently see, was not a criminal one—it was known to
Loftus through Mary Rearden that the sister had at last
made up her mind to visit her brothers, him at Dublin
first, next him living near Carrickfergus.

Other particulars, more detailed information from the
same source, enabled the Honourable John Loftus to
plan, mature, and carry out a very notable scheme.

Mrs. Donovan, a very nice elderly lady, with a bright
complexion that did not at all harmonise with her gray
locks, reached Dublin and her brother's house several
days before she was expected. An excellent excuse was
made. The Carrickfergus brother had been taken suddenly ill, and she, Mrs. Donovan, being desirous of seeing
him, had taken Dublin *en route*, where she could only
stay a few hours. John Donovan was pleased to see his
sister, very pleased, and feeling anxious for his brother

and his niece Anne, that brother's daughter, who might
be left destitute by her father's death, he gave his sister
a letter to James, assuring him of his sympathy, and also
that he had whispered in her ear certain matters which
it was of importance should be communicated to the
Liberators." Loftus had succeeded beyond his hopes.
A scrap of introduction was all he had hoped for; but
the letter would at once give him the political confidence of James Donovan. That was very important.

Loftus started at once for Carrickfergus in his cornet's uniform, with the make-up of an elderly dame
packed away in a valise or knapsack. Arrived within a
not very great distance from Carrickfergus, he exchanged
his man's for woman's apparel, hired a vehicle of some
kind, and was driven to the abode of James Donovan.
He was most cordially received; the daughter was delighted to see her aunt, embracing her over and over
again; a demonstration "which I quietly checked, as it
might lead to dangerous consequences." Miss Donovan
was a remarkably pretty girl.

Cornet Loftus could not, besides, trifle with time.
He found that Thurot, alarmed by rumours of the rapid
advance of a large English force, and that a British
squadron would soon make its appearance in the bay,
was, after granting highly favourable terms to Colonel
Jennings, working with hot haste to get his troops, &c.
on board, and be off with the least possible delay. This
precipitation would greatly impair the efficiency of his
ships, two of the frigates being under repair, and the
squadron not half victualled.

If Loftus was to prove worth his salt, he must check
that precipitate flight. Twelve hours' delay, less than
that, would insure the destruction of the French arma-
ment, signally avenge the outrage to British pride of a
successful invasion of Ireland, in a small way no doubt,
by a contemptible French force relatively considered,
after the defeat of Conflans had seemed to render such
an event of impossible occurrence.

James Donovan was in immediate communication

with Captain Thurot, who thoroughly trusted him. The
French commander knew him to be in communication
with the principal Jacobites of Ireland, and on more
than one occasion had proved the trustworthiness of
intelligence obtained by his agency. Loftus assured
Donovan, as from his Dublin brother, that the troops
assembling for the relief of Carrickfergus could not reach
that place in less than four days at earliest, and that the
ships about to be despatched by the Duke of Bedford—
only one of which had arrived in Dublin Bay—could
not, be wind and weather ever so favourable, make their
appearance off Carrickfergus in less than that time.
Donovan hastened off with the news to Thurot. The
French commander did not, perhaps, attach implicit
confidence to the report; but it so far influenced him
that he did not hurry his preparations for departure
with such impatience as before. More than twelve hours
would be gained. Loftus felt satisfied of that, and that
he himself should be handsomely rewarded for so signal
a service by his Excellency the Lord-Lieutenant.

There was an under-play going on in the Donovan
household, the full details of which Loftus, in his character of aunt, was speedily made acquainted with by her
woe-stricken, sobbing nieee, the charming Mary. Her
father, feeling that he was too deeply compromised to
remain in Ireland—that if he did so, an often-recur-
ring imaginative halter tightening unpleasantly round his
throat might become a terrible reality—had determined
to depart with Thurot. To that end he had converted
into cash every thing he possessed of marketable value.
His daughter was to go with him, and worse than even
that, in the damsel's estimation, was to become the wife,
before embarkation, of a Lieutenant de Poncy—a man
whom she greatly disliked, and who was old enough to
be her father. That dislike had been within a few days
intensified to abhorrence—one Charles Sullivan, an old
sweetheart, who had been for many months absent from
that part of the country, having returned, and at their
first stolen interview renewed his vows of attachment

and constancy—vows supplemented by the agreeable fact that he had succeeded to a considerable property in the West of Ireland, of which it was his soul's desire to make her mistress. But Sullivan was not only a Protestant, but notoriously loyal to the House of Hanover; and Donovan père consequently hated him with an absolute hatred. Donovan was not in other respects a harsh father. The niece poured her sorrows into the sympathising bosom of her aunt, who bade her be of good cheer, as she would not fail to work out her deliverance, jealously as she was watched and guarded. She was enjoined to believe in her aunt's sincerity, notwithstanding she might appear to coincide with the father's views and favour the pretensions of Lieutenant De Poncy.

Commodore Thurot will delay no longer. The air is thick with rumours of the swift approach of British land and sea forces. Thurot has dallied with the time, and must not lose another moment. He resolves to sail soon after dawn on the morrow. Donovan's effects—portable effects—are on board the flag-frigate. Donovan himself goes on board just as the first rays of light pencil themselves upon the eastern horizon.

His daughter will quickly follow. Lieutenant De Poncy is in waiting at the house to escort her to the boat; he has a French seaman with him. They will stand no nonsense; the damsel's tears, prayers, expostulations, will not avail her. Her lot is cast irrevocably; her doom sealed. The aunt is with her, but even if she could be melted by the tenderness of tears, *her* sympathy would practically avail nothing.

A mistake! as M. le Lieutenant De Poncy found to his cost.

"'*Allons!*' exclaimed the lieutenant, addressing the mourning bride (I am quoting just literally from Loftus); '*allons!* we must be gone. The squadron will lift anchor in less than a quarter of an hour. We shall be the last to leave this *maudit* shore.'

"'It was of your own choice you came to this

"cursed" shore,' said the aunt; 'though not, perhaps, quite of your own will that you go away.'

"The Frenchman stared at me. Then he said, '*Bonne femme*, be pleased to speak in a more polite, respectful tone when addressing *me*. Now then, mademoiselle, come with me at once. I do not wish to use force without necessity, having your father's sanction and authority.'

. "*Boom!* The report of a heavy gun shook the air.

"'It is the signal for departure,' exclaimed the French lieutenant, excitedly. '*Nom de Dieu!* we shall be left behind. Here, Jacques,' he added, calling to the French sailor,—'Here, Jacques, help me to master and bind this young lady, who refuses to obey her father's commands!'

"Poor Mary Donovan was in despair, and looked at me with an expression so piteous, so reproachful, that knowing as I did there could be but little doubt of her successful rescue, the French having all embarked except the enamoured lieutenant and his man, I burst into a fit—an immoderate fit of laughter. I cannot account for it, but I am generally affected with spasmodic bursts of merriment when excited and about to engage in some exploit out of the common mode. It was so then. Mary Donovan stared at me through her fast-falling tears. The lieutenant stared also, and there was a certain expression of doubt and surprise. He detected, I fancy—for I had dropped the female falsetto—the ring of a man's voice in the few words I uttered.

"'Let that young lady alone!' I exclaimed in my own natural voice, pitched in its fiercest key—'let that young lady alone! Do you hear me?' (I spoke in French.) 'Diable!' said the Frenchman, 'what does the old lady mean?' 'I mean this,' said I, suddenly drawing forth a pistol. The lieutenant started. 'Diable!' was repeated in a less jeering tone—'diable!' 'Go away, lieutenant,' I said; 'get on board your ship before she weighs anchor. This jeune demoiselle remains with her aunt.' '*Sacré tonnerre!*' exclaimed the lieutenant, 'do

you think I am to be baulked by a cursed old woman?"
His sabre was out in a twinkling, and he rushed at me.
He meant, I daresay, only to disarm me, unless he suspected, guessed, or imagined I was a man disguised in
female attire. My pistol-bullet was swifter than his
sabre-stroke. He fell with a scream prone upon the
floor—dead! The sailor went off with all sails set."

The Honourable John Loftus gave Mary Donovan
into the safe keeping of Sullivan, and had the honour of
being best-man to the bridegroom. He had also been
entirely successful in his political mission. Thurot's delay, though but for a few hours only, in the Bay of Carrickfergus, was fatal to him. The English squadron
overtook and captured the French ships, after a severe
fight, in which the gallant Thurot was killed.

Cornet Loftus was a "bright particular star" at the
Viceregal Court for some months after his Carrickfergus
exploit, and won so much upon the favour of a ducal
family that he would have been accepted as a suitor to
his grace's niece. She was neither young nor handsome
—far from being so; but the Duke promised a dowry of
ten thousand pounds. "It was a tempting bait," remarks
Loftus; "but I had courage and virtue to say, 'Get thee
behind me, Satan.' I had conceived a fervid attachment
to Mary Rearden. Not mere boyish passion—straw on
fire. So I turned my back on the Duke's niece, and
married Mary. The union was kept secret for a while,
as his excellency had more than half promised to obtain
me a good appointment. I took lodgings for my wife at
the village of Howth. It was not very long before it
was whispered about that Cornet Loftus had married a
serving-girl. The Duke sent for and questioned me. I
did not deny the fact. Being brought to bay, I faced the
matter boldly out, and gloried in what I had done. His
grace was indignant; I insolent—my blood being up. We
parted in extreme wrath.
    "I had but a few shillings over twenty guineas,—that

was all my worldly wealth. I tried friends, but might as well have attempted to reap the wind. So, after much dubitation, I and Mary hit upon the scheme which has given us so much notoriety. She sang well, especially in part-music, having a fine natural ear. So we started off upon an itinerant tour—dressed in the extreme of fashion, both of us. I gave out, at every town we came to, that we were playing at wandering minstrels for a large wager. That is to say, I hinted it mysteriously to the landlords or landladies of hotels and taverns. We had to make up a great sum in a given time. The success was great. People believed me to be a lord, my wife a lady. I played, she played; and both sang very well. No one presumed to offer us less than a silver piece; and sometimes gold was tossed to us. My wife's beauty had much to do with it. We made money fast—passed over to England, where we made it much faster. I had two children—flowers of Paradise; and had saved a large sum, when an advertise-ment appeared in the Irish and English journals, stating if John Loftus, who formerly resided at Carrickfergus (I had sold my cornetcy), would call or communicate with Messrs. B——, Merrion-square, Dublin, he would hear of something to his advantage."

The Honourable John Loftus did communicate without delay; and the result was that his wayward, wander-ing life ended in his settling down at a place called Chevers, in the County Galway, Ireland—an estated gentleman. His descendants still, I understand, inhabit the fine old mansion bequeathed by the will of the Earl of ——; and one gentleman, a member of the present Parliament, and a relative of his, I suppose, in a left-handed way, only the names are totally dissimilar, ex-hibits eccentricities which go far to prove that oddness or eccentricity of character, though differing in type and fashion, runs in the blood of the family.

JONATHAN SWIFT, D.D. AND DEAN OF SAINT PATRICK.

THERE can be no doubt of the audacious eccentricity of this reverend and dignified gentleman,—dignified by position, not by character, nor by seemly observance of even the common decencies of life. It is difficult to understand how Swift acquired his great reputation. Sir Walter Scott, in the feeblest paper he ever wrote (1824), pronounced him to be one of the greatest men this country had produced. One feels astounded that such a sentence should have flowed from such a pen. No question that Dean Swift possessed a vigorous, sledge-hammer kind of intellect. He was a sort of clerical William Cobbett, wearing a gown instead of a smock-frock, but utterly deficient in the tenderness for women which was the most amiable characteristic of the Hampshire ploughman. With the exception of *Gulliver's Travels*, nothing of Swift's really lives in the popular mind. The taste of readers has so far improved since his time that indecent coarseness no longer passes for wit, nor irreverent mockery of all that constitutes the grace and glory of life for profound, searching wisdom. The true solution of the enigma presented by the career of Dean Swift is, in my my judgment, this—that he was in a certain morbid sense insane from an early age. The mental malady grew upon him with advancing years, and at last became apparent to the dullest observer, fully justifying the second line of an often-quoted couplet :

> " Down Marlboro's cheeks the tears of dotage flow,
> And Swift expires a driveller and a show."

This much-talked-of Dean is commonly claimed by Irishmen as a countryman of theirs. No one would grudge the Isle of Saints such honour as that circumstance might be supposed to confer : but the fact is not so ; except, to use a trite vulgarism, a man is a horse if he happens to be born in a stable. Jonathan Swift's father was a Yorkshireman, and married Mrs. Abigail Erick, of Leicestershire. Famous people were the Swifts of Yorkshire, if we are to believe the Dean's historiographers; though not by any means equal in historic lustre to the Ericks,—Mrs. Abigail Erick having been a direct descendant of Erick the Forester, who flourished in the days of William the Norman!

Mr. and Mrs. Swift, though rich in ancestral honours, were poor in an actual money sense. The father of the celebrated Dean was the youngest son of his father, and inherited a youngest son's portion. He accepted the situation or office of steward to the Society of King's Inn, Dublin; went to reside in that city; and there was born, before the expiration of the honey-year, if such a phrase be permissible, the subject of the present sketch, on the 30th of November 1667. His father died when he was about a year old, leaving his widow almost penniless. She had recourse to her deceased husband's brother, reputedly a rich man, but not really so. Godwin Swift befriended her to an extent much beyond his real ability. Jonathan's education was secured, and ultimately he entered Trinity College, Dublin. He was not very successful in his studies there, and prone to all sorts of vagaries. He incurred seventy penalties for gross offences against the discipline of the college, and was compelled to make a most humiliating apology to Mr. Owen Loyd, the Junior Dean. He, however, obtained a degree, which seems to have been conferred upon him more from compassion than as a guerdon of merit. Swift was already at war with the world; but with the astuteness which is often found in men of unsound but powerful intellect, he early determined to be on the *right* side of the world, which he secretly scorned and despised. He sketched the first rough outline of his *Tale of a Tub*, and showed it to his college friend Mr. Warying, who did not greatly approve of the High-Church dogmas which it set forth. He did not, however, suspect that the production was a sample of Jonathan Swift's rabid insincerity.

Pecuniary troubles again clouded the never-very-bright morning of young Swift's life. Godwin Swift was unable any longer to afford "supplies." Dryden William Swift filled up the gap for a while, not very efficiently; but his cousin Swift, settled abroad as a merchant, came to the rescue in the very nick of time. Jonathan Swift was at his wits' end—and that, whatever we may think of his moral character, was a long way to go—when the captain of a merchant-vessel came to Trinity College, and having found out the person he was in quest of, presented him with a considerable sum of money, a gift from the cousin. Young Swift was overjoyed, as well he might be. He offered the captain a large fee for his fidelity in the transaction, which the honest sailor refused to receive.

Swift meanwhile had made great progress in what was, and still is, esteemed learning. He was a fair Greek and Latin scholar, and he had given evidence of the possession of a fluent biting tongue and coarsely-sarcastic pen.

His worldly prospects still, however, looked gloomy enough, when a ray of light, though but a faint one, pierced through the clouds. He attracted the notice of Mr. Temple, who procured him a situation as secretary or amanuensis to his uncle, Sir William Temple, of Moor Park, Hampshire, brother of the then Lord Palmerston.

The connection was not an agreeable one to either Swift or Sir William Temple. The former thought himself undervalued, which was true enough; and the baronet, whose lofty opinion of himself is well known, was annoyed by the supercilious assumption of the secretary. A truce was, however, for a time patched up. Sir William Temple had drawn up a series of papers upon state affairs, for the edification of King William the Third, and sent them by his secretary, who was charged to make clear to his Majesty any point or passage which the monarch might not distinctly comprehend.

Swift acquitted himself so well of this duty, "that his Majesty offered me," says the facetious Dean, "the command of a troop of horse, and to show me how to cut asparagus the Dutch way." Whatever may have been the Dutch mode of *cutting* asparagus, the manner of eating it seems to have been extraordinary. Some time after his interview with the King, Swift was dining with an acquaintance, who heartily partook of the asparagus on the table, and pronounced it excellent. "How is it, then, you do not eat it?" exclaimed Swift. "You have left the stalks." "Of course I have; who the devil could eat the stalks?" "Sir, his gracious Majesty eats the stalks. The King, sir, when, as I was just now remarking, he offered me a troop of horse, showed me not only how to cut asparagus, but how to eat it. He and his nation always eat the stalks." If the King had offered Swift a lucrative post in the civil service instead of a troop of horse, we may be sure that the asparagus joke, if joke it can be called, would never have been uttered.

In 1692 we find Mr. Jonathan Swift at Oxford University, where he obtained the degree of M.A., and wrote Pindaric odes, not much worse than those of Cowley or Donne. His cousin, John Dryden, to whom he sent a copy, wrote slightingly of them, an offence which the High-Church author of *A Tale of a Tub* never forgave.

Jonathan Swift, M.A., returned to Moor Park, but not to abide long there. He and Sir William Temple had an angry quarrel, the secretary not being as decorous in his life and conversation as the baronet was desirous he should be. That being so, Mr. Swift announced his intention to go to Ireland, and there take holy orders. He went and took holy orders; but as that initiatory ceremony is barren of desirable fruit unless supplemented by a living, the Rev. Mr. Swift wrote a penitential letter to Sir William Temple, soliciting his pardon and good offices with the Lord Deputy of Ireland, who had livings in his gift. The good-natured baronet was at once mollified, freely forgave his reverend correspondent, and so warmly commended him to the favour of the Lord Deputy, that that high officer presented the young clergyman with the living or prebend of Kilroot, in the diocese of Connor, worth about one hundred pounds a-year.

Previous to this, the Rev. Mr. Swift had wooed Jane Warying, sister of his college-friend, and promised to marry her as soon as circumstances should enable him to do so with prudence. The courtship lasted four years, and was chiefly carried on by letter. At last the lady, wearying of the long delay, asked that some day should be fixed for the celebration of the marriage. To this the reverend suitor replied that he had changed his mind; he had discovered she was too ugly for his wife. This lady he was accustomed to address by the name of "Varina." Swift had a fancy for such *noms d'amant*—though genuine lover he never was throughout his chameleon life.

A curious anecdote, variously reported, is related of the Reverend Jonathan Swift. Whilst vegetating at Kilroot, and preaching to a congregation which sometimes reached the unusual number of seven persons, the clerk inclusive, he, being out for a walk, met a poor clergyman — one much poorer than himself, as he had to maintain a wife and eight children upon forty pounds a-year. It is only in the pages of the poet—a true poet notwithstanding—who lamented the good old times of England when every rood of ground maintained its man, that a parson can be passing rich upon that stipend. And yet, as the story goes, this starving clergyman bestrode a fine black mare, his own property. The Reverend Mr. Swift was desirous of doing the poor curate a good turn, but naturally expecting some recompense for a charitable deed, asked for the loan of the horse. As the Reverend Swift was, we may presume, personally known to the poor parson, the request was complied with. Shortly afterwards, according to Sir Walter Scott, the prebend of Kilroot was vacated by Swift, and presented to the indigent clergyman, the Reverend Jonathan retaining the black mare as a fee for the conversion of forty into one hundred pounds per annum, through his, the Reverend Swift's, influence and exertions. It is a strange story, and scarcely credible, though believed in by Sir Walter Scott. Lord Orrery—no friend of Swift's —gives a very different version of the affair; but as his imputations are not sustained by proof, it would be unfair to quote them. The truth of the matter I suppose to be this: Swift had obtained of Lord Berkeley, one of the Lord Justices of Ireland, a promise of the rich deanery of Derry, and being about to leave Kilroot, recommended the clergyman with a wife and eight children to the vacated prebend, and accepted the " fine black mare" as a present of gratitude.

The Reverend Jonathan Swift was grievously disappointed in his expectation of the rich deanery of Derry. The Lord Justice's private secretary had an insuperable objection to the arrangement. Another candidate, anxious to be the instrument of saving souls in that particular deanery, was willing to hand over one thousand pounds for the possession of the blessed privilege. The Reverend Jonathan Swift had not, perhaps, a thousand pence. A sufficiently rich client was found, the secretary of the Lord Justice pocketed the thousand pounds, and Swift's anger found impotent expression in a letter, wherein he exclaimed, with reference to the Lord Justice and his secretary, " God confound you both for a couple of scoundrels!"

The Lady Berkeley was friendly to Swift, and through her influence the youthful divine obtained the vicarages of Laracor and Rathbeggan, with the prebend of Dunlain—the gross income derived from which amounted to four hundred pounds a-year.

About this time the Reverend Jonathan carried out a practical joke which caused much amusement. One John Partridge published a Prophetic Almanack, which had a large sale. It was not, perhaps, more absurdly

audacious than our modern Francis Moore and Zadkeil's
publications. It, however, so stirred Swift's bile that he
sent a letter to the papers, subscribed " Isaac Bickerstaff,
the Modern Merlin," in which he foretold the death of
Partridge, naming the day and hour when that sad and
solemn event would take place.

Poor Partridge was terribly annoyed: the prediction
seemed likely, as sometimes happens, to fulfil itself. He,
however, survived the day upon which Isaac Bickerstaff,
as interpreter of the stars, had foretold that he would
die. He announced that important fact in the belief
that it would put his persecutor to shame. Not at all;
very far from that. The only notice taken by Swift of
the Almanack-maker's assertion that he was alive and
well was the publication of a monody on his death. The
assertion of his being alive was coolly ignored. Vainly
did the persecuted Partridge write again to the newspapers, " Blessed be God, John Partridge *is* still living
and in health, and they are all knaves who report otherwise." Strange to say, the Stationers' Company believed
Isaac Bickerstaff, and prohibited the publication of Partridge's Almanack—forasmuch as that person was de-
funct. In his extremity, Partridge engaged the facile
pen of Dr. Yalden, who wrote a pamphlet which set
forth the pros and cons of the argument, very elaborately
summing up the case by a hesitating opinion that John
Partridge *was* still in the flesh. The Doctor was a wag
and a friend of Swift's. John Partridge was never able
to successfully prove his own identity, and at last he
appears to have been himself somewhat doubtful of it.

I shall pass rapidly over those sad episodes, so to
speak, in the life of this misplaced man, which repute
has connected with Miss Esther Johnson and Miss Vanhomrig—the Stella and Vanessa of his repulsively selfish
egotistical verses. Esther Johnson he met with at Moor
Park. She was his pupil, and a beautiful girl. He
gained her affections, and with her sister, Mrs. Dingle,
she followed him to Ireland. Miss Vanhomrig was a

later acquaintance, and she also pursued the fascinating parson to the Emerald Isle. Ultimately Swift married Esther Johnson (Stella), privately, in Dublin—the condition being that the union should not be acknowledged till such time as he himself chose to announce it. That time never came. Miss Vanhomrig (Vanessa) died of a broken heart, to use a conventional phrase, which sometimes expresses a substantial truth. A great reverse in life, whether it arise from disappointed affection or baffled ambition, will often so weaken and depress the vital force of life, that the slightest physical disorder will extinguish the flickering flame.

The Reverend Jonathan Swift had not, and did not care to have, an extensive cure of souls. His congregation usually consisted of about half-a-dozen hearers, and upon one occasion he had only one auditor, the parish-clerk, one Roger Coxe, whom, on commencing his sermon, this facetious champion of High-Church orthodoxy addressed as " Dearly beloved Roger !"

The Reverend Jonathan Swift, in sooth, cared but for the emoluments of the Church, though he did write a pamphlet upon the best mode of promoting the advancement of religion. A Whig in politics, he, finding Harley and Bolingbroke in favour with Queen Anne, abandoned his former friends, and employed his bitter pen to vilify them. He was constantly in London soliciting and importuning for preferment—money! " If the Queen," wrote the high-flying Churchman to Stella, " does not give me a thousand pounds, I am ruined."

When in London, Swift used to frequent Button's Coffee-house, where he was known as " the Mad Parson." He rarely spoke to any one, and was in the habit of pacing the room to and fro in moody silence. He broke that silence one day by an odd sally. A country gentleman in mud-bespattered boots came in. Swift instantly accosted him with " Pray, sir, do you remember any fine weather in the world ?" The country gentleman thanked God that he had in his lifetime known much fine weather.

"Well, sir, then your experience and mine differ. The weather is always too hot or too cold, too wet or too dry." Recollecting his Church livery, Swift sanctimoniously added, "However, God contrives it is all well at the end of the year."

Dr. Arbuthnot, who now and then dropped in at Button's, tried a fall with the mad parson, and got the worst of it. He had written a note in the coffee-room, and stepping up to the "mad parson," asked if he could favour him with a little sand to dry the ink. "No, sir," said Swift; "I have no sand; but I could accommodate you with a little gravel."

Lord Wharton, of not very odorous reputation, was appointed Lord-Lieutenant of Ireland, and was, of course, pursued by the importunities of Swift. He was unsuccessful. Dr. Loyd, who was on sufficiently intimate terms with Lord Wharton, had observed that an attendant upon her ladyship, upon whom she had bestowed the sobriquet of Foysdy, was an especial favourite with his lordship. Dr. Loyd made vehement court to the young lady—actually proposed marriage to her; upon hearing which Lord Wharton exclaimed, with the fervour inspired by a great .deliverance, "Why, then, he shall have the first bishopric that falls vacant." Dr. Loyd was in no hurry to make dear Foysdy Mrs. Loyd. He waited till a bishopric did fall vacant—that of Cork, and immediately married Foysdy. Lord Wharton endeavoured faithfully to fulfil his part of the bargain, but Queen Anne could not be persuaded to nominate Loyd Bishop of Cork, and that eminent divine was compelled to accept a not very lucrative deanery in the North, as the best *solatium* obtainable for his disappointment. Swift indulged in much coarse merriment at Dr. Loyd's expense.

Mrs. Masham, the influential favourite of Queen Anne, was a steady friend to Swift, and but for his irritable temper, might have succeeded in procuring him the bishopric of Hereford. There were, however, *two* favourites—the Duchess of Somerset, and Mrs., subsequently

Lady Masham. Her majesty alternately listened to the advice of one and of the other. Swift knew that her Grace of Somerset disliked him, and in a fit of petulance wrote and caused to be printed a scurrilous libel, in which he charged her with the murder of her first husband. At the earnest request of Lady Masham, to whom he had sent a copy, and who knew how much it would offend the queen, he gave orders to the printer to destroy all the copies. He was too late. The duchess had obtained one of them, which she showed to the queen, who was exceedingly indignant that such a charge should be made against a person whom she held in favour and esteem. The Archbishop of York also opposed himself to Swift's pretensions, and spite of Lady Masham's powerful support, the bishopric, which he believed himself to be in almost actual possession of, became a rapidly-dissolving view. He afterwards avenged himself, after his fashion, by the following couplet:

> " By an old murderess pursued,
> A crazy prelate, and a royal prude."

At last he so far succeeded in the struggle for the loaves and fishes of the Church as to obtain the deanery of St. Patrick, Dublin. There being nothing more to hope for from the English Ministry, Swift determined to set up for a flaming Irish patriot,—he, who had always proclaimed his disgust with Ireland and all things Irish. Once at the town of Kells, he asked the landlord of the tavern in which he was staying his name and country. The reply was, " My name is Jonathan Belcher, and I am an Englishman by birth." " Good heavens !" exclaimed Swift, " an Englishman baptised Jonathan *here!*"

The Dean preached political pamphlets, not sermons; and soon came to be very popular in Dublin. He had not to wait very long for an opportunity of displaying his newly-kindled Irish zeal.

William Wood was authorised by royal patent to coin copper-money for Ireland to the amount of one hundred and eight thousand pounds. This would have been a perfectly legitimate, unobjectionable transaction, had it not oozed out that the patent had been obtained through the influence of the Duchess of Kendal, the king's mistress, who was to share half the profits with Wood.

Swift at once took up the cudgels nominally against Wood—really against the Ministry. He wrote under the name of " A Drapier," and his vigorous Billingsgate produced immense effect. Harding, the printer of the letters, was thrown into gaol, and a reward of three hundred pounds was offered for the discovery of the writer. Every body knew the Dean was the author—the moral proof was conclusive, but legal evidence of the fact was not obtainable. Harding steadily refused to give up the name of the author. Swift himself was a witness of the man's constancy. He visited Harding disguised as an Irish peasant. Whilst there, Government emissaries arrived; they came with liberal offers from the viceregal government if Harding would enable them to convict the seditious pamphleteer. Harding refused—preferring to remain in prison rather than betray the confidence which Swift had reposed in him. The Dean found himself nevertheless in great jeopardy. A servant who had taken the manuscript to Harding and brought back proofs, presuming upon the possession of so perilous a secret, replied to the Dean in an insolent manner, hinting that he might be induced to claim the reward offered by the Government. " Strip off your livery!" exclaimed the enraged Dean. " Begone, and do your worst!" The man begged pardon and was forgiven.

One curious incident in this absurd imbroglio deserves notice. Swift attended a levée held by Lord Calcot, the lord-lieutenant, and bursting through the brilliant *entourage*, fiercely demanded how his lordship dared to keep such an honest man as Harding in gaol. Lord Calcot, who knew perfectly well, as every one else did, that Swift was the Drapier, replied with a good-humoured classical quotation, and the matter ended. The obnoxious patent was ultimately cancelled.

There are innumerable anecdotes related of the Dean, all, or nearly all, exhibitive of a coarse, offensive nature. Nasty is the true word. His deanship did not engage a servant without first questioning him or her as to their willingness to perform the most servile, unpleasant offices. If the answers given were satisfactory, showing the requisite slavish spirit, the man or woman was engaged, not otherwise.

One *not* unsavoury anecdote told of this man is that when " Mary Cook" sent him to table a leg of mutton overdone, he rang for and desired her to take it away, " and do it less."

The fierce, erratic intellect rapidly gave way at last. He was himself conscious—had for years felt conscious that his brain was flawed. It was a morbid sympathy with unfortunates afflicted with mental derangement which prompted him to found the Hospital for Idiots. One day, reading his *Tale of a Tub*, he suddenly exclaimed, " Good Heavens! what a genius I had when I wrote that book! It is gone now—gone—gone for ever!" This reminds us of the anecdote of Marlborough, who, when in his dotage, gazing upon a portrait of himself when he was in the flush and heyday of life, exclaimed, in a childish, treble voice, " That *was* a man!"

When strolling with a friend in the country, Swift gave utterance to the dismal forebodings which had long possessed him. They came upon a noble elm, the topmost branches of which were withered. " Ah, my friend!" exclaimed Swift, " like that tree, I shall *die at the top!*"

Prophetic words—soon to be realised. Dean Swift died raving mad, leaving little behind him, spite of great talents, which the world has not willingly allowed to die.

LADY MARY WORTLEY MONTAGUE.

THE Lady Mary Pierrepoint was the eldest of the three daughters of the Earl of Dorchester, afterwards Duke of Kingstown. She was his favourite, very beautiful as a child, and of that type of beauty which maturity perfects and enhances. A singularly precocious girl was the Lady Mary Pierrepoint; her talent, genius—such talent and genius as she possessed—not only budded, but flowered early. The splendour and the perfume were, in a comparative degree, but the suppliance of a minute—sweet, not lasting—forward, not permanent.

The first distinct view we have of her ladyship is at the once famous Kit-cat Club in 1698. It was the custom at that very aristocratic *réunion* to assemble at the commencement of the London season, to nominate the lady who should be their standing toast for the year, have her name inscribed upon their drinking-glasses, and her portrait painted in Kit-cat fashion—head and bust merely. In the year named, 1698, the members of the Club were somewhat puzzled as to the choice of a lady who would accept the honour. To end the difficulty the Earl of Dorchester proposed his daughter, the Lady Mary Pierrepoint. There was some demur to the proposal, no member of the Club having seen the young lady. To obviate that objection the earl said he would go at once and fetch her if the members were willing that he should do so. There could be no possible objection, and it was not long before the earl returned with a beautiful girl not quite nine years old. She was received and nominated with exuberant acclamation. The members were delighted, and the Lady Mary received their compliments with a grace and sweetness almost womanly, which won upon the hearts of all. She herself was in an ecstasy of delight. The incense of admiration intoxicated her at that child-age. "Pleasure," she afterwards wrote, "pleasure were too poor a word to express my sensations; never again throughout my life have I spent so happy a day." There is in these few words a self-revelation which gives the key to her wayward ladyship's whole life—a life of which the master-passion was vanity, insatiable vanity, a craving after notoriety, from the attainment of which she would certainly not be hindered by old humdrum prejudices.

The charming nominee of the Kit-cat Club was born in 1690, at Thoresby, Nottinghamshire. She was in her fifth year when the Countess of Dorchester died, since when her studies had been directed by the earl, her father. The curriculum adopted was identical with that pursued by her brother, the Earl of Newark. The girl soon distanced the boy. He was nowhere in Classics. When she was still in her early teens the Lady Mary had mastered the Greek and Latin languages, and acquired so true an insight into the social and political condition of England, that she translated *Epictetus*, after a fashion, and sent the manuscript to the Lord Bishop of Salisbury, accompanying it with a long, laboured epistle, in which she proved to her own perfect satisfaction that the "sinking liberties of England" could only be saved from speedy and total wreck by the patriotic fortitude of soul which his lordship was known to possess. The *elixir vitæ* recommended by her young ladyship for the effectual renovation of England, whose fine ladies, this pretty minx of fifteen assured the bishop, were more atheistic than the loosest rakes, was the enforced education of English girls and women in the dead languages; which means that they should be consecrated to Christianity by the baptism of Pagan moralists. What answer was returned by my lord the bishop to this silly stuff does not appear. Mr. Stuart Wortley, the present Recorder of London, if I mistake not, is of opinion that that early flight of genius showed that the charming girl's talents would bear her very high in the literary empyrean.   His Recordership's law, we may be permitted to hope, is sounder than his critical acumen.

It is difficult, if not impossible, accurately to estimate Greek and Latin scholarship.   In ninety-nine cases out of a hundred it is a pretentious sham.   Porson, the most famous of Greek scholars, used to admit in his cups that he really knew less of the Greek language than an ancient Greek cow-boy.   Mr. Gladstone would probably make the same admission.   Professor Porson, moreover, denied that the scholastic Germans knew any thing of Greek:

> "The Germans in Greek
> Are sadly to seek,
> Not one in ten score,
> Nor yet in ten more,
> Except my friend Hermann,
> And Hermann's a German—"

There are other tests more decisive than mere critical dicta.   The highly-cultivated classic taste of Lady Mary Pierrepoint was of so refining a quality as to cause her to revel with delight over the highly-intellectual pages printed at the Minerva Press, to admire and effusively sympathise with Corydons, Celias, Grandisons, Aramintas, who sigh, simper, maunder, and preach through dreary records of impossible life.   The English dramatic writing which this young lady (whom her biographers would have the world believe could not only read in the original but fully appreciate Sophocles and Euripides) most highly esteemed, was not Shakespeare's.   She seems to have condescendingly patronised the author of *Hamlet* something after the supercilious fashion of Mrs. Montagu and the author of *Irene*.   Her admiration of the British stage culminated in Lilly's magnificent *George Barnwell*. The force of genius could not soar a loftier flight than was evinced in that immortal drama.   After this, the anecdote of the enthusiastic Scotchman who, standing up in the pit, after the successful representation of Home's tragedy of *Douglas*, exultingly exclaimed, looking down upon the English audience from the immeasurable height of Caledonian conceit—"What do you think of your Wooly Shaksperè noo?"—reads like the utterance of a sensible man.

Beautiful Lady Mary was, it would seem, by her own confession, by no means fastidious as to personal cleanliness. One of her French intimates remarked that her hands were not so clean as they might be. "*Mes mains! C'est vrai; mais si vous voyiez mes pieds!*" ("My hands! It is true; but if you could see my feet!")

A frolicsome girl was this daughter of the Duke of Kingston, destined, in that age of literary gourd-tribe luxuriance, to attain rapidly as lofty as spurious a reputation for genius. She ordered a boy's fantastic dress of many colours, very picturesque, becoming in a certain sense no doubt, and used to delight in riding a favourite pony boy-fashion, at a pace which made the attendant groom, though well mounted, toil after her in vain. She was, perhaps, as good a horse-woman as Queen Victoria.

Her eccentricities, whilst she was still young—not unsexed, un-Englished, by a cosmopolitan cynical scepticism—often inclined to virtue's side, to use a much-quoted namby-pambyism. An elderly person in the establishment had been guilty of some impertinence towards her, which coming to the Earl of Dorchester, or the Duke of Kingston's knowledge (the date of the anecdote is not so clear as the fact itself), the woman was discharged without notice. She was poor. The Lady Mary—her anger, excited by the servant's want of manners, having subsided—managing, under pretence that she required a considerable sum of money for the replenishment of her wardrobe, to obtain fifty guineas of the earl or duke, went herself to the woman's dwelling, and handing her the fifty-guinea purse, said, "Now mind, you very impudent creature, that if you ever dare mention that I have given you money, not only will I never give you another farthing, but I will have you hunted out of the country. Remember that!" The woman, or some other person cognisant of the circumstance, must have mentioned it, as it soon became known in the Lady Mary's father's establishment, and the servant was before

long readmitted to the situation from which she had
been abruptly dismissed.

The home-education of the Lady Mary Pierrepoint
was well adapted to early-fashion a girl of her peculiar
idiosyncrasy and temperament into a self-willed, vain,
self-confident girl-woman of the world. She was mistress of her father's household, presided at her father's
table when she was in her sixteenth year. The conversational contact incident to such a position, in a house
where the guests were chiefly men, could not be otherwise
than destructive of the maidenly modesty of manner
which constitutes the charm of girlhood.

Still she was a much-admired, much-toasted young
lady, not only at the Kit-cat Club, but other resorts of
fashionable gentlemen. No wonder that her not very
powerful, though to a certain extent creative brain was
turned by the adulation of society, that the incense lavishly burnt before the shrine of the noble young beauty
by a multitude of titled fools and tuft-hunters should
have developed her organ of vanity — originally large
enough, in all conscience—to a prodigious extent. Beautiful — fascinating, when she chose to be so—and declared to be the wittiest woman of that or any other
age, it is not surprising that she esteemed herself to be
superior to all the men and women in the world—in
that hallucination presenting a marked resemblance to
Margaret Fuller, the American phenomenon, who made
her brilliant *début*, passed across, and made her sudden
exit from the stage of the world a century and a half
after her English prototype. Well, the Lady Mary was
certainly witty—not with the wit of Rosalind or Beatrice,
or its faintest reflex, but she could string together shining
sentences. Not much in them, but the gold varnished
glittered. There have been, are, and I suppose always
will be, adepts in that art. They resemble the artist-
workers of Birmingham, who, it is said, can manufacture
a thousand pounds' worth, sale-worth, of jewelry out of
a sovereign and a copper coalshute.

Lady Mary was especially proud of her epistolary

powers. " Do not destroy or mislay my letters," she wrote, with laughable *égoïsme.* " Forty years hence they will be as highly esteemed as those of Madame de Sevigné."

I give a specimen of one of the compositions which were to rival, possibly surpass, those of the *spirituelle* Frenchwoman. Lady Mary was on a visit in Yorkshire, whence she addressed the following barren, blotting-paper imitation of the De Sévigné style to her friend Anne Wortley, the granddaughter of Admiral Montague, Earl of Sandwich. She is writing of the Yorkshire beaux:

" In the first form of these creatures is a Mr. Vanberg. Heaven, no doubt compassionating his dulness, has inspired him with a passion which makes us all ready to die with laughing. 'Tis credibly reported that he is endeavouring at the honourable estate of matrimony, and is resolved to lead a sinful life no more. It is hard to say whether pure holiness inspires, or dotage turns his brain. 'Tis certain he attends the Monday and Thursday market assemblies constantly, and for those who don't regard worldly advantage much, there's extra good and plentiful choice. I believe there were two hundred pieces of woman's flesh—fat and lean—last Monday. But you know Van's taste was always odd. His inclination for ruins has given him a taste for Mrs. Yarborough. He sighs and ogles so, that it would do your heart good to see him, and she is not a little pleased, in so small a proportion of men amongst such a number of women, that a whole should fall to her share."

The Lady Mary had a multitude of lovers, admirers, and danglers; not one of whom did she regard with the slightest real favour. But she amused herself mightily with them. One desperately enamoured and very rich young gentleman, a Mr. John Beauchamp, who made impassioned love to her, and who, when she had just passed her eighteenth birthday, sent a formal offer in writing to her noble father. The young gentleman was a wretched horseman. He had been brought up effeminately by " a timid, fearful aunt." A John-Gilpin equestrian, he preferred a walking pace while on the back of a horse, or at the worst a very mid amble. Mischievous Lady Mary resolved to give him a practical lesson upon the folly of seeking to unite himself in the blessed bonds of wedlock to a lady whose tastes, habits, proclivities were so directly opposed to his own.

John Beauchamp, esquire, attended in the forenoon at the duke's mansion to receive, as he phrased it, his life or death-warrant. He barely escaped, in grim reality, the latter alternative. Lady Mary Pierrepoint was waiting for the sighing swain in the fore court-yard; her high-blooded pony was ready, as was another equally high-blooded animal, though in appearance meek, mild to a fault. "You will take a ride with me?" said her young ladyship, flashing upon her dazzled suitor one of her most brilliant smiles: " I have had the quietest mare in the stable saddled on purpose for you. We shall have a delightful ride on this beautiful day." What could the ardent lover do but accept so flattering an invitation, whatever his misgivings as to the quietest mare in the stable? I am almost sure, by the way, he was the Honourable John Beauchamp, so called, at all events, if I remember rightly, in an old number of the *Gentleman's Magazine*, from which I derive the anecdote. Whether honourable or not, the highly-flattered, dreadfully-frightened lover mounted the meek mare with a groom's assistance, and away went the fast pony with her faster ladyship, the quiet mare following suit with a will. It was cruel, terrible—sit upright, holding on solely by the bridle, the Honourable John Beauchamp could not, at that terrible pace; and stooping down, like Cowper's hero, he grasped the mane with both his hands and eke with all his might. Ah, my Lady Mary, it is useless to wave your handkerchief, as, half-turning round in the saddle, you do, by way of courteous encouragement, to that frightfully scared swain. The quietest of mares has become unusually excited—wondering and perplexed, no doubt, as to the kind of animal which bestrides her. She passes the pony like a cannon-shot, and makes straight for a five-barred gate, which she has leapt a hundred times. The Honourable John Beauchamp screams with terror, but holds on, nevertheless, like grim Death, to the mare's mane and neck, till the terrible leap takes place, when he is shot out of the saddle like a stone from a sling. The Lady Mary and groom ride up, and the frolicsome maiden was a good deal alarmed by the result of her practical joke, as she looked upon the white face of her lover, and the blood oozing from the back of his head. The Honourable John Beauchamp was, fortunately, not killed, though the escape from death was a narrow one. It does not seem that he ever again renewed his offer of marriage, or requested a more decisive reply to that which he had sent. He was quite satisfied, and in after years, when the Lady Mary had developed into the bluest of *bas-bleus*, the strongest of strong-minded women, was wont in his convivial hours to rejoice in the memory of that tremendous ride. Bitter in the mouth, but sweet in the stomach.

Meanwhile, a marriage between her eccentric ladyship and the Honourable Edward Wortley Montague was initiated. Mr. Wortley Montague, a solemn, methodic gentleman, an incarnation of red-tape routine, became enthralled by her lovely ladyship—by her face and figure—a merely sensuous passion. Lady Mary Pierrepoint met the gentleman one day at his sister's. He, like most dull pedants, affected contempt for feminine acquirements, feminine genius. Lady Mary put forth all her powers to compel the practical retraction of that cynical creed; the artillery of her eyes, and general personal beauty, being infinitely more effective, we may be sure, than smart flippancy of tongue, which never since the world began enchained the affections of a man. It was especially hopeless to attempt doing so in this particular instance. Had the Lady Mary been gifted with genuine wit or humour, it would have been as useless attempting to cut blocks with a razor, as to have sought the subjugation of Mr. Wortley Montague by such a weapon. At their first interview, it came out that her ladyship's

classic curriculum did not comprise Quintus Curtius.
This afforded Mr. Wortley Montague an opportunity of
sending his charmer a copy, on the flyleaf of which he
wrote the following dreary doggrel :

> " Beauty like hers had vanquished Persia shown,
> The Macedon had laid his empire down,
> And polished Greece obeyed a barbarous throne,
> Had wit so bright adorned a Grecian dame,
> The amorous youth had lost his thirst for fame,
> Nor distant India sought through Syria's plain,
> But to the Muses' stream hither had run,
> And thought her lover more than Ammon's son."

This supremely dull and pompous personage was, however, unmistakably in love with the Lady Mary's beauty.
He could not escape its influence, though nervously desirous of doing so. The Reverend Sydney Smith used to
say that he must have recourse to an umbrella to shield
himself from the "Norton" rays. Mr. Wortley Montague
contemplated the adoption of a far more effective defence
against such sun-strokes—that of flight. But he could
not convert purpose into action ; he could not break his
chains. His correspondence with the eccentric enchantress was commenced through the medium of his sister,
Anne Wortley. Wortley Montague wrote the letters, the
fervour of which, supposedly uttered by female lips, would
have been insipidly absurd. One of the Lady Mary's re-
plies is explicative enough—is only another illustration
of the instinct by which *l'esprit vient aux filles:*

"I am infinitely obliged to you, my dear Miss Wortley, for the wit, beauty, and other fine qualities you bestow upon me. Next to receiving them from heaven,
you are the person from whom I would receive gifts and
graces. I am very well satisfied to owe them to your
own delicacy of imagination, which represents to you the
idea of a fine lady, and you have good nature enough to
fancy I am she. All this is mighty well, but you do not
stop there. Imagination is boundless. After giving me
imaginary wit and beauty, you give me imaginary passion, and you tell me I'm in love. If I am, it is a love

of ignorance, for I don't even know the man's name. I passed the days of Nottingham Races at Thoresby, without seeing or wishing to see one of the sex. Now, if I *am* in love, I am very unfortunate to conceal it so industriously from my own knowledge, and yet reveal it so plainly to other people. 'Tis against all form to have such a passion as that without giving one sigh for the matter. Pray tell me the name of him I love, that I may, according to the custom of lovers, sigh to the woods and groves hereabout, and teach it to their echo."

Miss Wortley died, and the thin, transparent device of wooing by proxy—lisping love for a woman by the voice of a girl—was necessarily given up. Mr. Wortley Montague courted in person instead of by attorney; but the trumpet gave an uncertain sound, and the replying echoes were still more uncertain.

"You think," said the lady, "that if you married me I should be distractedly fond of you for one month, and of somebody else the next. Disabuse yourself of that notion. Neither would happen. I can esteem, I can be a friend, but I don't know whether I can love. Expect all that is complaisant and easy, but never what is fond in me." Mr. Wortley proposed that immediately the nuptial knot was tied, the "happy pair" should retire to the glades, permanently it would seem—the world forgetting, by the world forgot. A paradisal hermitage was dimly pictured in his foggy imagination. The Lady Mary had no such stuff in her thoughts. "Retirement," said the strong-minded young lady, "would soon be disagreeable to you. A face is too slight a foundation for happiness. You would soon be tired of seeing every day the same thing." Again: "Love is a mere madness— the passion of a child for a well-dressed doll. It delights him till in a short time the tinsel covering wears through, and he discovers that it is mainly made of sawdust." Truly a plain-spoken damsel, perfectly secure of her victim, if she elected to lead him to the altar of sacrifice. In another of these amiable rejoinders she says: "Make no answer to this. If you can like me on my own terms, 'tis not to me you must make the proposals. If not, to what purpose is our correspondence?"

Lord Wharncliffe remarks in his poorly and partially-written biography of his ancestors that Mr. Wortley Montague was horribly afraid of uniting himself for better for worse with such a very original damsel, and struggled fiercely to break through the meshes in which she had bound him; "but every struggle to get free left him still a captive, galled by his chain, yet unable to break one link of it effectnally."

Who can control his fate? Mr. Wortley surrendered at discretion, and made a formal proposal for the hand of the fascinating daughter to the Earl of Dorchester. The proposal was accepted with reservations as to how the property should be settled. Mr. Wortley, inspired by his lady-love, who differed with society—"high" society, it is well understood—*crême de la crême*—with respect to the justice of the laws of entail and primogeniture, refused to entail the whole of his landed estate upon the oldest male issue of the proposed marriage, who might, he remarked with prophetic truth, prove a spendthrift, an idiot, or a villain. Lady Mary was decidedly of opinion that the fathers and mothers of children should reserve joint power to make such disposition of their property as they saw fit. The Earl of Dorchester would not listen to such revolutionary doctrines, and the marriage negotiation was abruptly broken off.

Principle and passion are very unequally matched antagonists. A new and, in the opinion of the Earl of Dorchester, more eligible suitor for the hand of Lady Mary Pierrepoint appeared suddenly in the field. This gentleman, who was very rich, would sign and seal to any documentary settlement the earl chose to dictate, and readily agreed to maintain a town establishment. This cardinal point had never been distinctly conceded by Mr. Wortley. The Lady Mary hesitated. She preferred Mr. Wortley. But the earl, her father, threatened that if she did not marry the man of *his* choice, he would forthwith pack her off to some out-of-the-way country

place and keep her locked up till she came to her senses.
I cannot but think it would have been happy for the
wilful young lady had the earl been able to carry out
his purpose. But the Lady Mary's organ of combative-
ness had been called into play; and it was an organ of
much more than ordinary size and development. The
wedding-dresses were ordered, sent home. It was im-
perative to decide at once. The Lady Mary cast off her
indecision, though tremblingly. An elopement was arranged. The following extract of a letter, written on its
eve, lets in betraying light on the lady's character:

"I tremble for what we are doing. Are you sure you
will love me for ever? Shall we never regret the step
we are about to take? I fear, and I hope. I foresee much
that will presently happen. My family will be furiously
incensed. The world generally will blame my conduct;
the friends of —— will invent a thousand stories to my
discredit; yet 'tis possible you may compensate me for
all. In your last letter, which I much like, you promise
me all that I wish. [The town establishment?] Since
I wrote so far, I received your Friday letter. I will be
only yours, and I will do as you please."

The elopement was successfully carried out, though
as the bride was in her twenty-fourth year, and as a consequence at her own disposal, the necessity of such a proceeding does not clearly appear. Lady Mary Pierrepoint
was married to Mr. Wortley Montague in May 1713.

A miserable marriage! The lady's mind daily becoming "stronger" in the social-science sense of the
phrase, enabled her to mentally tear asunder—I think
only mentally—the flimsy conventionalisms, the coloured
cobwebs, which have nevertheless sufficient power to
hedge-in the sanctity of domestic life, with the mass
of ladies—not, indeed, transcendental femalities—but
wives not too bright or good, as Wordsworth expresses
it, for human nature's daily food. The hectic fever of
passion was soon chilled by satiety: Mr. Wortley Montague cared nothing for his wife; the wife despised her
husband. *Vanitas vanitatum!*

P

Mr. Montague, through the Duke of Kingston's interest, was appointed to the post of British Ambassador at Constantinople. The "Ambassadress" accompanied him. The female domestic life of the Orient amused her wayward fancy. She sympathised with its indolence, with its practical creed of "eat, drink, and be merry, for to-morrow we die." She audaciously asserted, in letters that "in forty years after they were written would be esteemed as highly as Madame De Sévigné's," that married women in Turkey, where a wife can to this day be sewed up in a sack and flung into the sea at the pleasure of a husband, enjoy more real liberty than English wives. One remark of this beautiful oddity is a curious one. She, from frequently seeing the Turkish ladies at the baths, was impressed with a notion that were the superfluities of dress dispensed with, which, but for a false delicacy would be quite practicable in sunny eastern climes, the faces of women in comparison with their figures would attract no attention. Lady Mary Wortley Montague, also, in these laboured letters of hers, constantly bemoans her piercing insight into the realities of things, and sighs to think that a simple milkmaid, by whom "the burden of the mystery"—not the Lady Mary's phrase, but her meaning—had not been felt, was necessarily much happier than such lofty intelligences as herself!

Returned to England, she fluttered about the English Court, flirted with Pope the great poet—so nominated in the history of English poets, though it would puzzle his admirers to quote one inspired line in all his melodious verses—laughed at him, and never more mockingly than when she expressed her joy that, having done with the humdrum day-world,

"They would meet with champagne and a chicken at last,"

—next definitely separated from her husband (1739), and again left England for Turkey, where she resided for upwards of twenty years, though often implored to return by her daughter, Lady Bute.

Oriental sensualism is not so keenly enjoyed at seventy

as at seventeen, and her husband being dead, Lady Mary Wortley Montague returned to England in 1761, and occupied the brief remnant of a weary life in gaming, scandal, speculation in South-Sea bubbles; and dying, left no other memorial of her life than a collection of cosmopolitan letters, industriously puffed into circulation and celebrity, but utterly destitute of genius, and, worse than all, containing no spark of womanly feeling, tenderness, or truth.

CHRISTINA OF SWEDEN.

THE readers of the *Legends of Montrose*—and who has not read them?—will remember the enthusiastic eulogies of Gustavus Adolphus, King of Sweden, Lion of the North, Bulwark of the Protestant Faith, &c., unctuously enunciated, in season and out of season, by Dugal Dalgetty. It would seem that he never heard of Christina, the only offspring of the Northern Lion, but for whom the victories of Gustavus Adolphus would have been fruitless, the cause of scriptural truth itself lost, and been mortally stricken down with its metaphorical immortal champion at the battle of Lutzen in Upper Saxony. The sun of England has, we know, set for ever, very many times,—a phenomenon which the British people rather enjoy than otherwise; perhaps because custom or habit becomes a second nature. Be that as it may, Sweden felt itself doomed, given over to perdition, when, in the year of grace 1632, news reached Stockholm that the great King and Lion of the North had fallen in victorious battle.

Amidst the general dismay, Chancellor Oxenstiern, the reputed original author of the saying—though a truth so trite must have been uttered a thousand and a thousand times before Sweden was a nation—"Behold, my son, with what little wisdom the world is governed!" —gave a striking illustration of his theory or platitude by reminding the hastily-assembled States that the glorious king had left a daughter, who, though about seven years of age, might, if immediately recognised as Queen of Sweden, save the vessel of the State from foundering. He concluded by introducing the child, who was immediatcly acknowledged to be the picture in little of the Gustavus Adolphus. "Behold," exclaimed a leading peasant deputy, "Behold the very features of the grand Gustavus. We will have her for our sovereign. Seat her on the throne, and at once proclaim her *King*." This was done, and Sweden *ipso facto* saved.

Christina herself was no less enchanted than the nation to whom she was the herald and sign of salvation. The enthroned girl, many years afterwards, when she had developed into a Brummell-Brummagem royal celebrity, thus wrote of herself and the occasion: "I was so young that I knew not either my own worth or my great fortune; but I remember how delighted I was to see all those men kneeling at my feet and kissing my hand." She adds, with touching modesty: "It was Thou, O God, that didst render the child admirable to her people, who were amazed at the grand manner in which I enacted the part of queen upon that first occasion. I was little, but upon the throne displayed an air and countenance that inspired the beholders with respect and fear. It was Thou, O Lord, that caused a girl to appear thus who had not yet arrived at the full use of her reason. Thou hadst impressed upon my brow a mark of grandeur not always bestowed by Thee upon those Thou hast destined, like me, to glory, and to be Thy lieutenant over men."

This innate greatness of Christina had been foreseen, predicted by the astrologers, whom Gustavus Adolphus, Bulwark of the Protestant Faith, had consulted with respect to the child with which Maria Eleanora, his queen, was in travail. Both their majesties imparted their dreams to the wise men, who, having interpreted them by the light of the signs in heaven,—the Sun, Mars, Mercury, Venus, being in conjunction,—declared the coming child would be a boy, and that if he outlived the first twenty-four hours, which that mischievous Mercury rendered doubtful, he would attain as great celebrity as his father. The sex of the child was a sad stumbling-block to the soothsayers at first, but soon removed, as easily as John Cumming, D.D., will explain in 1867, that his prediction of the end of all sublunary things in 1866 was a figure of speech, having reference to the extinguishment of the Maori tribes, and the passing away, as a heathen country, of New Zealand from the map of the world. The mistake of the Swedish soothsayers was, after all, a merely verbal one; the girl, Christina, "having been born with the head of a Machiavelli, the heart of a Titus, the courage of an Alexander, and the eloquence of a Tully." Who would not be entitled, speaking of an incarnation of such heroic qualities, to exclaim, "This is a man!"

Gustavus Adolphus, though ardently desirous of a son, bore the disappointment with greater equanimity than at first did the astrologers. His sister, the Princess Catherine, was the first to announce that the expected boy was, in sad truth, a girl. "Sister," said the king, "let us return thanks to God. I trust this daughter will prove as valuable to us as a son; and may the Almighty, who has vouchsafed her to us, graciously preserve her. She will be an arch girl," the king added, "who begins to play tricks upon us soon." This was an allusion to the announcement of the attendants at the birth, who, momentarily misled by the thick hair which encased the child's head, the thick down upon her face, and the harsh, loud cry with which she greeted the world, proclaimed that a man-child was born.

The Lion of the North was resolved that though this child would be queen by sex, she should be a king—a warrior king, like himself, thereto fashioned by education and custom. He, the Bulwark of the pure Christian Faith, diligently instilled into his offspring a taste for the pomp, pride, and circumstance of glorious war. "When but three years of age," delightedly exclaimed the Champion of Christendom, "she, as a soldier's daughter should, crowed and clapped her tiny hands at the blare of trumpets and roar of canon."

The Lion of the North promised his very promising child, when she could have but dimly, if she did dimly, comprehend his meaning, that she should one day be a partner of his in real glories;—the slaughter—scientific slaughter of impious people who declined acquiescence, or were coerced by their rulers into resisting, *vi et armis,* the Gospel of Peace, as interpreted by the great Gustavus. "To my irreparable misfortune," sighingly simpers this once much-belauded lady,—"to my irreparable misfortune, Death (a terrible promise-breaker in a vicarious sense is Death) prevented him from keeping his word, and me from serving an apprenticeship in the art of war to so complete a master."

Concurrently with a taste for the glories of war, the great Gustavus was very desirous that his daughter should be thoroughly grounded in the Lutheran Faith, and, especially, should be versed in Holy Scripture, the ground of all true knowledge. An odd *mélange.*

In subsidiary matters the masculine, military propensities of Christina were developed by the system of instruction devised by Gustavus Adolphus, who sought from her cradle to mould the infant Queen of Sweden into a reflex of himself. He was so far successful that in a very few years she had acquired, and loudly expressed, illimitable contempt for women—her own mother compassionately excepted—and was constantly regretting she was not a man; not that she cared much for men—but they had this advantage, they were not women. Her own portrait has been given by a graphic hand. A more accurate pen-and-ink sketch has seldom been drawn:

> "By her petticoat so slight,
> And her legs too much in sight,—
> By her doublet, cap, and dress,
> To a masculine excess,—
> Hat and plume, and ribands tied
> Fore and aft in careless pride,—
> By her gallant, martial mien,
> Like an Amazonian queen,—
> Nose from Roman consul sprung,
> And a fierce virago's tongue,—
> Large eyes, now sweet, anon severe,
> Tell us 'tis Christina clear."

This mentally unsexed girl was not unattractive as to

personal charms.   Her figure was *petite*, but well-enough
formed.   She had fine hazel eyes, and a profusion of
bright-brown hair; her teeth were fine and regular,
which a more constant use of a tooth-brush would have
improved.   Her mouth was large, her lips coarse as the
boisterous laughter and frequent oaths in which the girl-
queen lavishly indulged.   Christina was devoured by a
restless energy, which made her the torment of all about
her.   "The men and women," she wrote, "who waited
upon me were in despair, for I gave them no rest night
or day.   They had the audacity to propose retiring from
their posts.   They should have known that I would not
permit them to escape the bondage in which I held them.
Incensed by the application, I made their yoke more
galling.   I did so upon principle, and no one ever afterwards dared propose to quit the Sovereign's service."
Queen Christina was indefatigably studious, at least she
herself says so, and it is certain she rapidly acquired a
showy, superficial knowledge of the Greek, Latin, two or
three modern languages, geography, astronomy, mathematics, philosophy, and divinity.   Her theological studies did
not, however, include the only commandment with direct
promise—Honour thy father and thy mother—for so intolerable a life did she lead the Dowager Queen, that
that lady fled secretly to Denmark, leaving a note upon
her toilet-table declarative of her intention rather to beg
her bread elsewhere than live with all the appliances, the
outward show of royalty, at her daughter's court!   The
two Queens were, however, ultimately reconciled, and
Maria Eleonora returned to Stockholm.

It has been truly said that the possession of absolute,
irresponsible power would corrupt and debase an angel.
Christina, though no angel, affords a striking illustration of that truth.   The prime article of her political
creed was the divinity of monarchs.   They were the
gods of the earth, to whom all sublunary power had
been delegated by the Eternal.   She remorselessly exercised that absolute power when but a mere child.
"Those," she writes, "who believe that childhood is the

scason when a princess that will one day wield the sceptre hears wholesome truths, are mistaken, for in the cradle they are feared and flattered. Men fear the memories of royal children as much as their power, and handle them as they do young lions, who can only draw blood now, but hereafter will have strength to tear and devour."

Christina as child-queen proved herself quite equal to the representation of the royal *rôle*. She had scarcely passed her seventh birthday when, seated upon a lofty silver throne, she received ambassadors from Muscovy in great state. Chancellor Oxenstiern and others sought to fortify the mind of Christina, in order that she might acquit herself creditably at the audience. "Why," said the self-confident child, "why should I be afraid or timid before men with long beards? You also have long beards, and am I afraid or timid before you?" There could be but one answer to that question.

At fifteen Christina openly presided in the senate, "and became at once," wrote home the French ambassador, "incredibly powerful therein. She adds to her quality as sovereign, the graces of honour, courtesy, and the art of persuasion, so that the senators are astonished at the influence she gains over their sentiments." A very shallow gentleman this French ambassador: Christina herself could have whispered in his ear the true secret of her influence over the sentiments of the senators. The daughter of Gustavus had reached an age when, if so willed, she "could tear and devour." A fact, we may be sure, never for one moment absent from the minds of the grave and reverend Swedish senators.

The nominal regency of Chancellor Oxenstiern expired on the 18th of December 1644, Christina's eighteenth birthday, and the Queen no longer affected to be swayed by any other influence than her own imperious will. She was remorselessly indefatigable in the exercise of absolute power, regulating every detail of government by the simple magic of "such is my will." Taxation, the freedom or limitation of commerce, questions of war and peace, were decided by her peremptory "shall" or "shall not." Having no taste for the elegance of dress, she issued sumptuary decrees forbidding Swedish ladies to wear lace or coloured ribbons; prohibited any festal rejoicings at betrothals, bridals, baptisms. People sometimes drank to excess at such meetings, and that, Christina, who was a total abstainer just then, could not tolerate. Funerals, it was also decreed, should never exceed in cost about five pounds of English money; and gaming was forbidden under severest penalties. How a nation could quietly submit to such extravagance of despotism is a marvel.

In other than government matters the wayward, eccentric girl exhibited the same love of capricious domination. In a fit of educational enthusiasm, Christina endowed universities, academies, appointed largely-salaried professors, and suddenly changing her mind, dismissed them all with abuse and contempt. Two solemn philosophers, whom she had taken into favour, she one day, brusquely interrupting a grave colloquy, compelled to play at shuttlecock with each other as long as they could move their arms. Three of the most eminent scholars in Sweden she made pirouette before her in a Greek dance, she screaming with laughter the while, and urging the musicians to play faster, faster, until one of the venerable men fainted and fell on the floor. Descartes, whom she had induced by the most flattering promises to take up his residence at her court, she literally worried into a consumption, by insisting, in that terrible climate and the season winter—a more than usually rigorous winter—upon his presenting himself in her library punctually at five o'clock every morning. The young queen's manner was always very suave, almost caressing, like Ferdinand VII.'s of Spain, when she had once decided upon the death or ruin of any one who had offended her. The velvet covering concealed a terrible claw. Christina was but nineteen when Captain Bulstrode, a Danish officer, and said to be one of the handsomest, most accomplished men of his time, being present upon some mission from his sovereign at her court—he was, I suppose, a subordinate member of the Danish embassy—attracted her notice. She honoured him with her hand in a dance, and on several occasions comported herself very graciously towards him. The handsome officer misconceived the motive of the young Queen's graciousness, and was indiscreet enough to boast that he should one day be King Consort of Sweden. This silly, impudent vaunting was reported to Christina, whom it deeply offended. She had always boasted of being an adept in the art of vengeance, and now gave a signal proof of her skill in the demoniac science. Captain Bulstrode found himself treated with more pointed favour than ever, and at last it was confidentially intimated to him that if he obtained the royal license of his sovereign the King of Denmark to throw up his allegiance to that monarch, and become naturalised as the subject of Queen Christina, there was nothing he might not hope for. Bulstrode swallowed the bait with avidity, knowing as he did that the Queen could not marry the subject of any other potentate than herself. The King of Denmark consented, Bulstrode's connections being very influential, and all rejoiced at the great fortune in store for their handsome relative. Other necessary preliminaries were completed, and the gallant captain was to all legal intents and purposes the subject of the absolute Queen of Sweden. He, in a state of overflowing jubilant vanity, solicited the honour of offering his devoted homage to the new sovereign to whom he had sworn fealty—a request promptly granted. The triumphant captain was ushered with much ceremony into "the presence." Christina was alone, and emboldened by the flattering reception given him, this military Malvolio threw himself at the sovereign's feet, and poured forth a high-flown declaration of passionate love. Christina's answer was characteristic. She listened with a smile of withering scorn, and in reply said, " Poor witless fool! I will teach you what it is to falsely boast at your filthy orgies of the favour of a queen." Summoning her attendants as she spoke, "Take this man, who has dared to insult me, to prison. Let him be guarded securely, and fed during my pleasure upon the coarsest prison fare. Not many days will have passed before it will be necessary to confine him in a prison for lunatics during life. That shall be his fate. Away with him!" The astounded dupe was never again heard of. He died in either an ordinary prison or one specially reserved for the reception of lunatics. The saying of Solomon was terribly true, till the English people struck down kingly despotism in the person of Charles the First, giving fluukeyism, to quote Carlyle, a crick in the neck, from which it has never since fully recovered, and is not likely to recover. "Curse not the king," wrote the royal sage, who had found that all was vanity under the sun—"Curse not the king, even iu thy bedchamber; for a bird of the air will carry the news, and that which hath wings shall tell the matter."

Queen Christina's determiuation, in opposition to her Chancellor's counsel, to finish with the thirty years' war, is creditable to her judgment. She boasted to have been born "in the palms and laurels thereof," but the cypresses so thickly intertwined with those bloody palms and laurels seem to have at last made an impression even on her by no means sensitive conscience. The year following the Peace of Westphalia, Christina indulged herself in the caprice of being solemnly crowned King with great splendour. On the afternoon of that day of high festival the Queen or King issued an order commanding that the illuminations in Stockholm should be continued in unabated splendour till the dawn of day.

By this time the Swedish people, with whom the Queen was universally popular, spite or possibly because of her eccentric vagaries, were exceedingly anxious that Christina should marry, lest peradventure they should, some disastrous day, find themselves queenless—a doomed nation, with not even a child six years of age to save them from perdition. The crown being, as her Majesty smilingly observed, "a very pretty girl," there were abundance of suitors for the sacrificial honour of dividing the glittering burden with her. The Kings of Spain, of

Poland, of Naples, with no end of electors, dukes, margraves, were willing to undertake the onerous duty; but Christina begged to decline the assistance so generously proffered. Neither heaven nor earth, she vowed, should compel her to marry, "an act which required far more courage than to fight a battle." Taking pity, however, upon her loyal people, who were daily becoming more and more demented by the dreadful risks they were daily running of sinking into insignificance by being reduced to the condition of lost fatherless and motherless sheep, — an unhappy flock, destitute of shepherd or shepherdess,—Christina suddenly nominated her cousin, Charles Augustus, Crown Prince of Sweden, whereupon the alarm of the people subsided.

Wearied at last by the very indulgence of her petulant, capricious humours, disgusted with the sameness of the dissipation in which she had so long lived, and was living, Christina, by way of change, fixed her thoughts upon heavenly joys. She admitted to her confidence several clever Jesuits, who, having succeeded in converting her, or, more correctly, cajoling her into the belief that she was converted to the faith of Roman Catholicism, advised her to "put money in her purse"—abundance of money—and then exhibit to the world the edifying spectacle of the daughter of the crowned archheretic, Gustavus Adolphus, renouncing an earthly for a heavenly crown. Sacrifice so heroic and sublime would insure her a glorious immortality in this world and the next; canonisation would follow in due course, and no name in the holy hierarchy of heaven would be more frequently invoked than that of Saint Christina!

The children of Loyola were too strong for her. As no Roman Catholic could, by the fundamental law, wield the Swedish sceptre, she determined upon resigning the crown in favour of the but recently-nominated Crown Prince. The solemn act of abdication took place on the 6th of June 1654, in presence of the Assembly of States. Whitelock, Cromwell's envoy, was there. This the wilful woman did in defiance of the remonstrances of her wisest and most attached counsellers. The English envoy reported the speech delivered by the Marshal of the Boors upon the occasion, which is conclusive as to her general popularity amongst the masses of the population. "O Heavens! madam," exclaimed the rude, coarsely attired, but common-sense country-fellow,—"O Heavens! madam, what are you about to do? It humbles us to hear you speak of forsaking those who love you as well as we do. Can you be better than you are? You are queen of all these countries, and if you leave this large kingdom, where will you get such another? If you should do it—as I hope you won't for all this—both you and we shall have cause, when it is too late, to be sorry for it. Therefore, my fellows and I pray you to think better of it, and keep your crown upon your head; then you will keep your own honour and our peace; but if you lay it down, in my conscience you will endanger all. Continue in your gears, good madam, and be the forehorse as long as you live, and we will do the best we can to bear your burthen. Your father was an honest man, a good king, and very shining in the world. We obeyed and honoured him whilst he lived. You are his child, and have governed us very well. We love you with all our hearts; and the Prince is an honest gentleman. When his time comes we shall be ready to do our duties to him as we do to you. But as long as you live we are unwilling to part with you, and therefore I pray, madam, do not part with us."

The entreaties of the blunt-spoken Marshal of the Boors did not prevail; the formal act of abdication was accomplished, and Christina hastened out of the kingdom, taking with her an enormous amount of treasure in gold, silver, and jewels. A few weeks afterwards she openly renounced the reformed religion, and was solemnly received into the fold of Rome. "The greatest scandal she could afflict us with," remarked the Pope, when the intelligence reached him, "unless the idea of writing a book in defence of the faith should unhappily seize her."

Cardinal Mazarin, the prime minister of France, differed from the Pope, and despatched a French troop of comedians for the express purpose of giving *éclat* to so illustrious a conversion. Balls, plays, concerts, masquerades, succeeded each other for many weeks in celebration of the great event. The conversion, we need hardly say, was false, factitious, the vagary of a hot brain ambitious of notoriety. When leaving the play one evening, Christina remarked to a lady, *sotto voce*, "They could do no less than treat me to a play after I had indulged them with a farce." That particular mind-fever soon passed off. The woman would seem to have doubted the existence of God. "If there is a God," she whispered to a confidant, after finishing her first confession,—"If there is a God, I shall be prettily caught." In a letter addressed at the same period to the Countess Sparre, she wrote, "My chief employments are to eat well and sleep well, to study a little, chat, laugh, see French and Italian plays, and pass my time in an agreeable dissipation. In conclusion, I hear no more sermons, and utterly despise all orators. As Solomon said, 'All wisdom is vanity.' Every one ought to live contentedly, eat, drink, and be merry."

Christina could not herself follow Solomon's advice. The remainder of her ruthless life was chiefly consumed in vain efforts to regain a crown, that of Sweden or of Poland, and in quarrelling fiercely with successive popes. One dogma she strenuously insisted on, her divine right of taking the life, with or without cause, of any of her former subjects. She carried this article of her political creed into execution. Suspecting her chamberlain Monaldeschi of having betrayed or threatened to betray her interests, she ordered the captain of her guard to stab, murder him almost in her very presence. His piteous screams for mercy availed nothing. The crime was consummated, and afterwards defended by her as a legitimate exercise of authority committed to her by God, which she had not and could not give up! The plea was allowed by "the gods of the earth." The murder was

committed at the Palace of Fontainebleau, and even the
philosopher Leibnitz was of opinion that Christina was
justified by her inherent royal power! Christina died,
having shortly before obtained plenary absolution of the
Pope, in April 1689, in the sixty-third year of her erratic, bizarre, blood-stained existence.

JOHN ABERNETHY, SURGEON.

This eccentric humorist, skilful surgeon, and excellent man, was the son of John and Elizabeth Abernethy. He has been claimed as an Irish and a Scotchman, but it has been clearly established that he was born in London, and was christened at St. Stephen's Church in 1764. He received his preliminary education at a day-school in Lothbury, and at a comparatively early age was sent to a high-class seminary at Wolverhampton. He does not appear to have taken kindly to the classics. Dr. Robertson, the master of the school, did not regard him with favour. His task one day being to translate into Latin a chapter in the Greek Testament, the erudite doctor was amazed at the fluency and correctness of the Vulgate version. A rigid investigation took place, and it was discovered that John Abernethy had a Greek Testament with a Latin translation in contiguous columns; which Latin translation he had faithfully copied. His reward was that the book was shied at his head by the irate doctor. He not long afterwards left Wolverhampton, and at the early age of sixteen was apprenticed to Mr. Blick, afterwards Sir Charles Blick, surgeon of Saint Bartholomew's Hospital.

John Abernethy had now found his true field of action—one in which he was destined to reap abundant, blessing harvests. Such a labour of love to him was the healing art, so rapidly did he master the science of surgery, that at the age of twenty-two he was appointed assistant-surgeon to the hospital, and a few months afterwards promoted to the chair of anatomy and surgery. For so young a man this was an unparalleled honour.

I do not propose to go into the history of this great man's life. The anecdotes which I quote will best illustrate his character: show how kind, how good a heart beat beneath an undemonstrative exterior; how sympathising, compassionate the nature which the rough tongue at times perplexingly interpreted.

Mr. Abernethy had a crotchet: all clever men have. They discover a truth, and in some measure unconsciously exaggerate its importance. Mr. Abernethy was disposed to attribute all, or nearly all, the diseases to which flesh is heir to a disordered stomach. Opinions differ upon that point; but no one, we suppose, will dispute the soundness of his dictum, exemplified through life, that "operations are a reflection on the healing art; that the habitual operator is a savage in arms, who performs by violence what a civilised person would accomplish by stratagem."

A curious anecdote is vividly illustrative of Abernethy's persistent practice in this respect: A poor Irishman, not long after Mr. Abernethy had succeeded to the post of chief-surgeon at St. Bartholomew's, was brought into the hospital. He was suffering from a diseased leg. Amputation was advised, but Abernethy refused his consent, and finally succeeded in curing the diseased limb. Going one day through the hospital with his pupils, the Irishman, thrusting the leg out of bed, shouted out, "That's the leg, your honour; that's it. Glory be to God. Your honour's the boy to do it, and to the devil with the spalpeens who said your honour would cut it off." Abernethey, improving the occasion, lectured the pupils upon the folly of hastily crippling a person for life, whilst there was a chance of curing a diseased member of the body. Paddy endorsed all the doctor said, repeatedly tossing his recovered leg into the air, and exclaiming, "Divil the lie in it. It's all true. That's the leg, gintlemen."

There are many anecdotes of the native goodness of this, in many respects, eccentric gentleman. I relate a few of them without reference to date.

Mr. Abernethy was going to attend a very poor man,

from whom he never had received, and never would receive a fee. The Duke of York called and said the Prince of Wales wished to see him immediately. Mr. Abernethy could not for some hours attend his Royal Highness: he was going to visit a suffering patient. "But surely you will first wait upon the Prince?" said his Grace of York. "If not, I must call upon ——." "Do so. He will suit the Prince better than I should."

A pupil of Abernethy was sent for to attend a case in an obscure quarter of London. The house was one of the meanest and dingiest of the mean and dingy locality. The patient, an elderly, much-afflicted man, received the surgeon with a grace and amenity which convinced that gentleman that the sufferer had fallen from a considerable social height upon evil days. The proper remedies were prescribed, and the surgeon was about to leave, when the invalid tendered the customary fee. It was politely declined. The refusal excited the old gentleman's ire to such a pitch of rage that the doctor was fain to accept the proffered honorarium. "Had you persisted in your refusal," said the patient, "I would never have seen you again. I wished for your advice," he continued, "because I knew you had studied under Abernethy. *He* visited me once, and declined to receive his fee. 'By God! sir,' exclaimed I, 'you shall take it.' 'By God! sir, I won't,' was his answer, as he bolted out of the room. I shall never send for him again." The patient succumbed to the disease which had fastened upon him, and it was found that he had a considerable hoard of money by him. *He*, also, appears to have been a very eccentric person.

A foxhunter, somewhat stricken in years, consulted Abernethy. The man's digestion was not so good as it had been. He had lost his appetite; man delighted him not, nor woman either. "Sir," said Abernethy, "you drink a great deal." "Now," said the foxhunter, when relating the interview, "now, supposing I do drink a great deal, what the devil was that to him?"

A literary gentleman called upon him. He, too, had

a disordered stomach. "Of course you have," said Abernethy; " a half-blind man could tell that by your nose."

He used to have his wine of a merchant whose name
was Loyd. He one day called to pay for a pipe, and
thrust a handful of papers containing fees into the wine-
merchant's hand. "Stop—stop, doctor," said Loyd.
"There may be much more here than you have to pay!"
"Never mind, Loyd. I can't stop. You have them as
I had them."

He was very careless of money. He would receive a
heavy fee, place the money on the table, and forget all
about it. "Lead me not into temptation" is the holiest,
because the humblest prayer. Some few of his pupils
were led into temptation. The loss of money was so
considerable that the surgeon determined to ascertain
who was the delinquent. He marked his money, and
appearing suddenly before his pupils, said, "Now, young
gentlemen, be pleased to show me your purses." The
thieves were discovered and dismissed.

He was one day about to perform an operation—a
painful one. As was his custom, he took care to see
himself that all the required instruments were at hand,
and in first-rate order. "I think every thing is all right,"
said one of the assistants. "No, sir, every thing is not
all right," replied Mr. Abernethy. "Get a napkin to
conceal those terrifying instruments. The man need not
be horrified by the sight."

Abernethy was offered a baronetcy by the Earl of
Liverpool. He announced the proposal to his family by
saying, as they were about to sit down to dinner, "Lady
Abernethy, permit me to hand you to your seat." He
afterwards explained that he had been offered the title,
but, for cogent reasons, declined the honour.

The memory of Mr. Abernethy was singularly active
and tenacious. A friend, of a poetical turn of mind,
composed some verses complimentary of Mrs. Abernethy,
which he recited after dinner on her natal day. Abernethy listened attentively, and immediately the reading
terminated, exclaimed, "Come, that is a good juke to

attempt passing those verses off as your own original composition. I know them by heart;" and Abernethy at once repeated them without the mistake of a·word. The "poet" was astounded, mystified, angry! The amused host explained, and offered to repeat *verbatim* any piece of about the same length which any one in the company would recite.

There is a droll anecdote told of a certain major, which Mr. Abernethy used to relate with great·humour and contagious laughter. The major dislocated his jaw. The accident was a trifling one, and easily remedied. It was, however, likely to occur again. The surgeon of the regiment was as expert at the simple process as Abernethy himself. One day, however, the gallant officer, dining at a considerable distance from the regimental quarters, thoughtlessly indulging in a fit of laughter, dislocated his jaw. The nearest Medicus was sent for. That gentleman did not understand how the accident should be remedied; pulled the unfortunate major's jaw about for a considerable time, inflicting great agony, during which manipulation the major, who could not speak, manifested by furious pantomime his indignation at, and contempt of, the clumsy practitioner. His rageful action thereupon decided the doctor that the major was distraught, and he forthwith sent for a strait-jacket, which he fastened upon the furious major, had his head shaved, applied thereto a blister and placed the victim in bed. The ill-used gentleman foamed with rage, but finding that his wild gesticulations availed nothing, subdued himself into seeming acquiescence, and made intelligible signs that he desired to be furnished with writing materials. This was done; and the major wrote, " For God's sake send for Mr. Abernethy or the surgeon of the regiment." Mr. Abernethy was as quickly as possible in attendance, and the major was relieved and released. He fiercely threatened, upon recovering his voice, to bring an action against the medical man by whom he had been so maltreated, but was persuaded by Abernethy to forego his purpose. " You cannot doubt," said Mr. Abernethy,

" that the clumsy dunce was actuated by what a certain unmentionable place is paved with—good intentions."

Benevolence in Mr. Abernethy was largely developed. He was much more gentle with poor or pauper patients than rich ones. He was just stepping into his carriage to attend a duke, when a message was delivered to him soliciting his immediate attendance upon a' sufferer who acknowledged he was without means of tendering a fee. " I cannot go to him at present," said Abernethy, getting into his carriage. " If you do not go at once," said the messenger, "it will be useless to go at all." The carriage was moving on as these words caught Abernethy's ear. He pulled the check-string. "Where," said he, "did you say this poor gentleman lives?" The address was given, and Abernethy ordered the coachman to drive there. "The Duke must wait," he muttered. " Besides, *he* can command the services of twenty surgeons."

A widow brought a child to him from the country. She had heard of the skill in the treatment of such complaints of the great London doctor, and had managed to raise sufficient money to pay the proper fees. ,Abernethy cured the child, receiving his fees the while, but returned them to her when she was about to return to her home, with the addition of a cheque for fifty pounds !

Another widow came to the hospital to have an operation performed. She was carefully prepared to undergo it; but on the eve of the day when it was to come off, the woman announced her intention to leave the hospital. Abernethy was greatly annoyed, enraged, and expressed himself in very angry terms. " Her father is dying in the country," interposed an assistant, "and wishes to see her." The wrath of Abernethy was instantly diverted from the woman to the assistant. " You confounded fool !" he exclaimed, " why did you not tell me that before ?" He apologised to the woman, said of course she must go, gave her money that she might travel easily, and bade her return to have the operation performed as soon as she possibly could.

Such traits of character are an ample set-off to the

rudeness of manner which Abernethy occasionally exhibited. A lady in consultation with him remarked that when she lifted her arm-pit higher than usual, the pain was intense. "Then why the devil do you, madam, lift your arm higher than usual?" was the gruff response. Another lady who consulted him was so annoyed that she threw his fee upon the table and said sharply, "I had heard of, but never witnessed your vulgar rudeness before." He had written a prescription. "What am I to do with this?" the lady asked. "Any thing you like: throw it on the fire, if you will." She did so, and left the apartment. Mr. Aberriethy hastily followed to return the fee. The lady did not condescend to notice him, and he flung the money after her.

Abernethy, at all events, was no flatterer. He went to sit for his portrait to Sir Thomas Lawrence. Whilst he was waiting to see the fashionable painter, he fell into a conversation with a stranger-gentleman who was contemplating a newly-finished portrait of the Duke of York. "Beautifully painted and an excellent likeness," remarked the gentleman." "Yes, a good painting." "And a capital likeness; the express image of his Royal Highness," persisted the stranger. "No," retorted Mr. Abernethy; "it is *not* the express image of the Duke. He is not half so handsome." It was the gentleman's first turn for a sitting. Mr. Abernetny followed after. "So," said Sir Thomas Lawrence, "you have, I find, been telling Lord Castlereagh that you do not think my portrait of the Duke of York is a faithful likeness." "Lord Castlereagh! Why, I had never seen him before. But, my dear sir, it is *not* a likeness. You painters—and especially *you*—flatter so constantly and cleverly. Now mind, you must not flatter *me*."

Mr. Abernethy had a country-seat at Enfield, Middlesex. Whilst journeying there one day, he was run over and severely bruised. The people who picked him up proposed to send for a doctor. "D—— doctors!" was the reply. "Get me a hackney-coach."

These anecdotes might be indefinitely multiplied;

but enough has been told of the oddly-compounded nature of the man—an essentially noble nature, the specks and flaws of temper showing only like spots on a white robe, by contrast with the purity of the general texture.

John Abernethy died at Enfield on the 20th of April 1831.

CAPTAIN MORRIS.

This flighty and amiable gentleman first opened his eyes upon the world in the dingy locality of Love Lane, leading from Leadenhall Street to Billingsgate Market. His father, Joel Morris, was a fishmonger in a large way of business. Arthur, his sole surviving child, was petted and spoiled. Joel Morris was a widower before the boy was five years old. He doated upon his son and determined he should be a gentleman. That which Morris senior meant by gentleman was the common signification attached thereto : the possessor of fine clothes, a fine house, a carriage, and abundance of money. To so provide his son, the well-meaning, fond fishmonger toiled incessantly, rose early, sat up late, and ate the bread of carefulness. He did not neglect young Arthur's education ; his natural shrewduess suggesting that to be really a gentleman, it was necessary to have a decently-cultivated mind. That part of the gentlemanising process he got through at little cost. He had sufficient interest to place the lad in Christ's Hospital, or Blue-coat School. Being a boy of large capacity, he, spite of a constitutional indolence—his own excusative phrase—proved an apt scholar, and knew as much when he left as the teachers.

Morris senior had managed to scrape together between thirty and forty thousand pounds ; and finding himself growing prematurely old and infirm, he made up his mind, though with much reluctance, to dispose of his business, the goodwill of which would net a handsome sum. The result was, that at his father's death, Arthur Morris found himself in possession of over 40,000*l.*

cash, besides some house property; and was contracted
by his father's will and a signed agreement with the
lady and her father, a wealthy goldsmith, to Arabella
Smithson, a person of mature years, rigid principles, and
a devotedly pious, plain Quaker.

Now this sort of lady was not at all suited to the
taste of Arthur Morris. He was fond, extravagantly
fond, of fine clothes ; "the happiest day of his life was
that upon which he finally cast the slough—the blue
coat and yellow stockings of Christ College." He piously
respected the last wishes of his father ; and would perhaps have unhesitatingly complied with them—especially
as, if he refused to consummate the marital bargain upon
which his father had set his heart, half his fortune would
go to the disappointed damsel—but that, having been
in the habit of secretly frequenting the theatres (utter
abominations in the eyes of Joel Morris), he had contracted an intimacy with Emily Melville, a stage song-
stress and dancer. Melville was probably an assumed
theatrical name. Be that as it may, the fascinations
of the actress ultimately prevailed over those of the
plain Quaker, gilded though these were with 20,000*l.*
His mode of announcing the decision he had come to
was characteristic. Mr. Smithson, I should have stated,
was a relative, and Joel Morris was himself inclined to
Quakerism :—

"Friend Smithson,—After careful consideration I
have concluded that it will be more conducive to the
happiness of Arabella that she take the 20,000*l.* instead
of me. I am not worthy of her, my aspirations being
much less spiritual. Your sincere well-wisher,

Arthur Morris."

This note could hardly have been delivered, when
Arthur Morris and Emily Melville were united in the
bonds of holy matrimony at St. Paul's Church, Covent
Garden. He appears to have been devotedly attached
to her, and the brief summer of their bliss was unclouded

by a passing shadow. She died of fever within six months of the marriage. Her mother had lived with them. She must have been an amiable woman, something under forty years of age. The dying daughter's anxiety was concentrated upon that good mother, whom she commended to her husband's tenderest care. Kneeling by her death-bed, he made a vow, scarcely audible for his sobs and groans, that he would honour and cherish her as long as he lived. The expiring wife accepted that vow "with a heavenly smile, in the sunshine of which she passed from earth to heaven."

Arthur Morris determined to enter the army, and lodged the price of a commission in the Line with the proper agents, but whilst waiting till a vacancy should occur,—some two or three years,—fell into wild courses, and at last found himself enmeshed by the wiles of another actress, whose name is not given. He knew her to be unworthy; that if he married her, Mrs. Melville would be compelled to leave his home; and, conscious of his own weak, impressionable nature, he adopted the singular expedient of securing himself against a violation of the vow he had made to his wife, by proposing to marry her mother. There was no absolutely legal impediment to the union, and he espoused Emily Melville the elder, in the same church where he had joined hands, till death should them part, with her daughter.

There is a droll anecdote connected with this union. Arthur Morris was fond of convivial society; he sang a capital song; and stayed out late at night in taverns, the Wrekin, Covent Garden, being his especial place of delectation. On the evening of his wedding-day, he betook himself to the Wrekin; sang, diced, drank, till the small hours of the next morning, utterly oblivious of his bride, till reminded about three A.M. that he had been married the morning before. "Good heaven!" he exclaimed, starting up, "that is true; and I had totally forgotten it."

The commission was obtained, and Lieutenant Morris joined the 27th of the Line, then stationed in the island of Jersey.　Major-General Don was the Lieutenant-Governor of that "Peculiar of the Crown of England," to use the phrase of Falle, the quaint historian of the island.　Lieutenant Morris, who had left his wife in England, comfortably provided for of course, soon became very intimate with General Don, and it was he, there can be no doubt, who suggested the brilliant idea to the Lieutenant-Governor which, in a local sense, has immortalised his name.　The island of Jersey, when General Don arrived there, was in a miserable plight as to roads; the towns and villages were unpaved, unlighted, and the people rebelliously averse to being taxed to remedy those evils.

The problem to be solved was, "how to do it?" whether by loan from the Imperial treasury,—which could scarcely be hoped for,—or inducing the "States" of the island to impose a tax upon the inhabitants, whose peculiar privilege and boast had been from time immemorial that they were an untaxed race.　The "States," it was soon ascertained, would consent to no such proposition.　Better muddy, dark streets, almost impassable roads, than to be mulcted by the tax-gatherer!

Lieutenant Morris worked out the problem in very simple and effective fashion.　When matured in his own mind, he sought a special interview with General Don, and laid it before him.　Very likely the Lieutenant-Governor gave it additional touches, altered or amended some of its details, but substantially Lieutenant Morris was the author.　He proposed to repair, widen, and keep in repair the island roads, light and pave the towns, without the disbursement of a shilling, and yet the work should be honestly paid for.　The scheme was simple as effective.　Every person who possessed a house, every one by whose grounds or fields ran a road, was obliged to sign bank-notes to the amount of the cost incurred in paving and lighting before their house or houses — of widening and levelling the portion of the road contiguous to their fields and grounds.　These notes they would be obliged to give silver for on demand; but inasmuch as they were guaranteed by the Vingtaine or parish authorities, they could be immediately sent into circulation again by the changers. The writer of this paper was once in a barber's shop in St. Helier's, when a man brought in a note to be changed, to which the barber's signature was attached. The barber's bank happened to be at that moment in a very sorry state. Silver and gold the hapless shaver had none; a few coppers being the whole of his " reserve." Of little consequence that. Taking the presented note in his hand, he left the shop with it, stating that he would return with the silver in a minute or two. He merely stepped into a neighbouring baker's, bought a loaf, received change for the note, came back with the loaf under his arm, the silver in his hand, and honestly acquitted himself of his obligation as an issuer of bank-notes payable on demand.

Curiosities of currency, as developed in the Channel Islands, would gladden the hearts of English paper-money maniacs. There are thousands of notes issued of which it is set forth upon the face of them, that the sole security for their redemption are the Methodist chapels in the island which those notes built. A certain tradesman in the town had, however, undertaken, for a consideration of course, to cash Methodist chapels' " promises to pay,"—though under no legal obligation to do so. It puzzles one to understand how the holder of a handful of such promises could manage, should the gentleman who had undertaken to give silver for the notes abdicate his function. This system, substantially invented by Captain Morris, though popularly ascribed to General Don, is in full vigour to this day. It must have collapsed long ago—the importation of soft and hard goods from England being taken into consideration—were it not for the great number of English officers on half-pay who have taken up their quarters in the Channel Islands. The drafts forwarded to them always command a considerable premium, and are returned to England, in payment of manufactures, as fast as they are received. Sovereigns, Bank-of-England notes, in like manner, make

unto themselves wings, and fly away to the country
where they were coined and issued. The metallic currency of the island is almost exclusively composed of
French five-franc and one-franc pieces. There is, however, a good deal of copper money afloat, coined in Birmingham.

The eccentric genius of Captain Morris soon led to
the adoption of a vocation which would seem to be very
opposite to that of inventor of paper-money. It is, however, one in which large sums of solid cash are often
netted without the trouble and expense of its manufacture. Arthur Morris—who, in writing to Friend Smithson, declined to marry the pious Arabella, had given as
one ground of his refusal that his aspirations were less
spiritual than hers — became suddenly affected by the
wildest religious enthusiasm. He had been paying a
visit to the North of England, where a great "revival,"
as it is now the fashion to call such spiritual masquerades, was brought about by the fervid teachers of Wesleyan Methodism. Captain Morris' caught the infection.
Benevolent as he was imaginative, the gallant officer was
horrified at the tremendous truth that "every day, every
hour, every minute that passed, hundreds of human souls
were falling through the Mirza bridge of Life into the
gulf of eternal perdition, where the worm dieth not, and
the fire is not quenched, whilst the means of saving themselves from so inexpressibly terrible a doom were always
within reach, if they could only be persuaded to ask for
it in sincerity and truth." Deeply impressed with this
conviction, conscious of possessing considerable powers of
illustration and a fluent tongue, Captain Morris was soon
himself amongst the Prophets. He did not, however,
join the Wesleyan sect—preferring to pursue an entirely
independent course. He became a favourite with the
people, and might possibly have founded a Morrisonian
Church, but for an untoward accident.

The old Adam within him had been rebuked, but not
vanquished. Very far indeed from that. He had always
been very pugnacious; could relish and put away com-

fortably a couple of bottles of wine at one sitting—not at all an extraordinary performance in those days. The chains of evil habit are with much difficulty broken. He could sing a capital song; had made acquaintance in Jersey amongst the garrison-officers, several of whom were Irishmen, and by their own admission could sing "The Night before Larry was stretched" (hanged) as well as, if not better than, any native of the Emerald Isle.

As the Father of Mischief would have it, the head-quarters of the regiment with whose officers he had hob-nobbed in Jersey were quartered in Ipswich, Suffolk, where it had been announced he was to preach on a given Saturday. The people were invited to assemble in a field near the town, the use of which had been kindly granted by a Mr. Selward. Thursday was chosen, from its being market-day, and a large attendance might be hoped for after the traffic of the day should be comcluded. Several of his old comrades or companions were still with the regiment, and all the officers unanimously resolved to witness the performance of Captain Morris in his new character of preacher. The time fixed was six in the afternoon of a summer's day. The concourse was large; but the captain, in the opinion of his admirers, was not so ferveut and unctuous as usual. He had caught sight of the merry faces of his former acquaintances, and the amused expression which gleamed from their eyes and wreathed their lips. 'The officers had dined, and were elevated, to use a mild phrase, with wine,—one, the most rollicksome of them, Patrick Blake, a lieutenant and excellent mimic, more so than the rest. However, decorum was fairly maintained till the conclusion of the discourse,—a very short one; after which Captain Morris gave out the number and first verse of a psalm or hymn. Before the hymn or psàlm could be commenced by the improvised field choir, Patrick Blake burst out with "The Night before Larry was stretched," in closest imitation of the captain's peculiar voice and manner; his comrades joined in obstreperous chorus. Those of the

auditory who were disciples or admirers of the captain
were immediately scandalised, but the majority cheered
and shouted in sympathy with the irreverent officers.
Finally, Captain Morris, unable to control his risible
muscles, joined in the almost general guffaw, jumped off
the cart which had served for pulpit, and attempted to
hurry off. He was intercepted by some of the officers,
and carried away captive to the principal hotel tavern
in Ipswich. It was a genuine self-consciousness which
dictated the avowal to Friend Smithson, that his was
not a highly spiritualised nature in the conventional
sense of the phrase. His imagination had been inflamed
by the passionate oratory of religious fanatics; but his
understanding had not been convinced, his heart had not
been touched. He remained with his old acquaintance
till early morning, and most likely was encored more
than once in " The Night before Larry was stretched."

He left the next day without beat of drum, and a few
days afterwards got a friend to write a letter for him to
the editor of the Ipswich newspaper. This letter, dictated by himself, announced his own death, "partly in
consequence of the debauch in which the Enemy of Mankind induced him to take part, and partly from remorse
of conscience. He died truly contrite," it was added,
"and begged forgiveness of. all his former friends for
the great scandal he had brought upon a sacred profession for which the infirmities of his fallen nature—
not suspected by himself, till he was tried in the balance, to be so gross as they proved to be—totally un-
fitted him."

This effusion was duly printed in the Ipswich newspaper, in the following number of which weekly sheet an
announcement appeared signed by a regular Wesleyan
preacher, the Rev. Mr. A——, who "declared his intention to address his hearers on the evening of the next
Sabbath, upon the awful lesson read to mankind in
general, and the inhabitants of Ipswich in particular, by
the sudden cutting off of Captain Morris, a man of gifts
and considerable worldly knowledge, who had prema-

turely perished for having put his hand to the plough
and looked back."

This sermon *in petto* reached Captain Morris, who resolved without a moment's hesitation to be present in the
body at his own funeral sermon.   He felt a strong suspicion that he should be roughly handled by the Rev. Mr.
A——, and felt desirous of viewing himself in the mirror
to be held up before him by that saintly, snuffling gentleman.

The convetincle, or chapel, was crowded.   Captain
Morris, coarsely attired, his face enveloped in bandages,
as if he were suffering from combined toothache, earache,
and tic-douloureux, and unrecognised by the crowd, el-
bowed his way to the foot of the pulpit-stairs.

Preliminary prayer and praise concluded, the Rev. Mr.
A—— commenced his sermon in a moderate key, but
gradually kindling into holy fervour, went on crescendo,
till having fully worked himself to the requisite pitch, he
avowed his opinion that the reprobate backslider, unless
he had been saved by a miracle of God's mercy at the
last moment, which could scarcely be hoped for by the
most charitable, was at that moment gnashing his teeth
in hell.   This was too much.   Captain Morris, stripping
off his facial disguise, sprang up the pulpit-stairs, and
seized the astounded preacher by the throat, pommelling
him soundly, shouting the while, "You are a lying rascal!
I, Captain Morris, am here, and you are much nearer hell
than he; and I have a good mind to pitch you headlong
out of the pulpit which you disgrace."   There was a great
uproar; but in the end the captain contrived to escape,
though not without considerable damage to his person.

The next four or five years are a blank in the published history of the wayward impulsive captain.   Those
years were years of calamity: his wife had died, the immediate cause of her death being a shock to her nervous
system.   One Jane Evers, who had been her schoolfellow
and attached friend since they had known each other, had
for some cause or other—a love-disappointment is glanced
at—gone mad.   She was confined in Bedlam or Bethlehem

Hospital, where she was visited by Mrs. Captain Morris.
The treatment in those days of lunatics, real or presumed,
was very different from that which obtains in the present
time; "a dark house and a whip" were held to be the
only curatives, and these were applied to both sexes.   It
must be presumed that Mrs. Captain Morris saw Jane
Evers in Bedlam when the unfortunate young woman
was in a very pitiable condition; not only when she was
mad, but had been scourged for madness!   Mrs. Morris
was *enceinte* at the time; and the distracted husband lost
at one terrible blow wife and expected child.   The captain was prostrated for a time by so cruel a stroke of
fate; but ultimately recovered his physical, if not his
mental health in its entirety.

His restless energy now took one direction, in compliance with the dying request of his wife.   He *would*
rescue Jane Evers from the tomb in which she, living,
was immured.   He first thought to release her by force,
and he initiated several combinations with that object.
The notion was ridiculous; a conclusion to which he himself reluctantly came.   His next move was to petition
the ministers, especially Earl Bathurst, with whom he
appears to have been on friendly terms of acquaintance-
ship.   It was useless; he could get no one to believe in
the alleged mismanagement of Bedlam—the cruelties to
which real or supposed lunatics were exposed.   A sort of
inquiry was instituted, but the managers of the establishment, sustained by the statements of eminent medical
men, refuted, to the satisfaction of an indifferent Home
Secretary, all the charges made against the mode of treatment practised in the asylum.   Very likely those charges
contained many exaggerations.   It is a common error
with enthusiastic men possessed of one idea to overstate
their case; a great error when you have to deal with
astute and unscrupulous opponents.

Captain Morris was not convinced by the meagre
official report—very far indeed from being so; and casting about in his inventive brain for some practical means
of proving that his assertions were well-founded and called

for peremptory interference, he hit upon an expedient which, read by the light of common sense, would be conclusive that he himself was a fit candidate for Bedlam. There is no doubt, let me not forget to state, that Mrs. Captain Morris firmly believed, and impressed that belief upon her husband, that Jane Evers, if ever afflicted in the brain, was perfectly sane when she visited her, and was dying of the cruelly coercive treatment to which she was subjected.

"Friend Smithson" and fortunate but still unappropriated Arabella had taken up their abode at Stamford Hill. Captain Morris, who was a frequent visitor at their house, had vainly endeavoured to interest them in his efforts to liberate Jane Evers. They believed he was labouring under an illusion, or that some motive more powerful than a promise made to his dying wife induced him to make such strenuous exertions in her behalf. Morris perfectly divined their but half-expressed thoughts, and formed his plans accordingly. In less than a fortnight after his final resolve was taken, Friend Smithson and his daughter were quite convinced that Captain Morris was mad as a March hare. He would start up of a sudden, seize a decanter of wine, fling it under the grate, or smash a pier-glass, and immediately break into a fit of wild, maniacal laughter. Friend Smithson was much alarmed. Medical opinions were obtained. Captain Morris was placed under immediate restraint, and to confirm beyond doubt the opinion of the doctors that he was insane, a paper was found upon him which could only have been dictated by a man conscious of mental infirmity. It was to the effect that if the malady which he felt was obtaining mastery over him should not be subdued, he wished to be confined in the Bethlehem Hospital, in the same building with his beloved Jane Evers, till it should please Almighty God to restore him. This wish was complied with, and Captain Morris was soon in a condition to prove on oath from actual experience the course of discipline which governed Bedlam. He wished for no further enlightenment; and when the doctor next visited him he demanded his release, alleging that he had perfectly recovered his senses, and was no longer labouring under any illusion whatever. The hospital Medicus smiled incredulously, said his liberation for some time, perhaps for years to come, could not for his own sake be consented to. The real madness of his conduct flashed upon the captain. He remonstrated, threatened the doctor and all concerned with direst vengeance, and finding all he could say unavailing, threw himself upon the doctor, and might have throttled him, but that instant effective help was at hand. The now really mad captain was seized, a strait-waistcoat strapped upon him, and he was taken to the ward appropriated to violent lunatics. "There," he writes, "I languished, eating my heart away with impotent rage, for more than two years. I was sometimes indulged with the sight of a newspaper, and one day I read that General Don was in London, and had attended the royal levée. Hope revived in my heart. One of the keepers was a very decent man, who in his heart believed I was as sane as himself. I offered him a heavy bribe, to be paid thereafter, if he would secretly procure me pen, ink, and paper, and post a note which I would write to General Don. He agreed to do so, and fulfilled his promise. The very next day General Don, accompanied by a still more influential personage whose name I am not at liberty to mention, visited the hospital. The General demanded to see me. I told my story, was believed, and the next day I was liberated by order of the Home Secretary. Poor Jane Evers had died several months previously. My mad freak produced beneficial results. Bethlehem Hospital was placed under strict supervision, from which resulted much benefit to the afflicted inmates."

The busy world into which Captain Morris had again emerged was to him a desert, and by General Don's advice he applied for and obtained active service in the army. Shortly afterwards he exchanged into a regiment under orders for India, served there with credit, if not distinction, and closed his erratic career at the storming of Rangoon in the Burmese war. "He fell," wrote Major Thompson, in a note subjoined to his friend's diary—"he fell at the moment of victory, which he as much as any soldier there had helped to win. A braver, a better man never lived, and but for his impulsive, wayward nature, he might have attained high rank in the service."

J. M. W. TURNER, R.A.

It is in no spirit of detraction that I string together a number of descriptive anecdotes of this great painter's eccentricities of character and manner. They afford another illustration of the world-old truth, that the life of the highest and the best of us is woven of a mingled yarn of good and evil. Social shortcomings or extravagances, deviations from the beaten path of decorum, are little noticed in ordinary men. There is no violent contrast to strike the eye—no fine gold seen in incongruous mixture with common clay. The dazzling mantle of genius reveals and magnifies such spots. This is one of the penalties of intellectual greatness.

Joseph Mallord William Turner was born in 1773, in Maiden Lane, Covent Garden, nearly opposite the Cider Cellars. His father, William Turner, was a barber. Some of the admirers of the greatest of English landscape-painters have endeavoured to attenuate the disagreeable fact that he was born in such a vulgar locality, by pointing out that Andrew Marvel occupied a second floor there in the days of Charles the Second, and that even M. de Voltaire, the prince of persiflage and a bright particular star in the galaxy of French celebrities, lodged there for several years at the sign of the White Peruke. J. M. W. Turner, R.A., may be excused having been born in a street or lane so patronised.

William Turner, the barber, and his father were natives of South Molton, Devonshire. The barber was an illiterate, close-fisted, but not ill-natured man. When, in after-life, Turner was reproached with his penurious way of life—how nobly redeemed, all England knows—

he would reply, "You would not be surprised if you knew the lessons instilled into me during boyhood. My father never praised me except for having saved a halfpenny."

William Turner did not neglect his son's education. Comparatively with his scanty means he was liberal in that respect. J. M. W. Turner was sent for the benefit of his health to an uncle and aunt who kept a butcher's shop in Brentford. Whilst there he was sent to an academy, opposite the Three Pigeons—the master of which "academy" was a pedagogue of the sternest kind. His name was White. The future Royal Academician was next sent, at the age of thirteen, to a school at Margate, then a little fishing-village. It was there he formed an acquaintance which coloured, and in a moral sense ruined, his future life. He fell in love with the sister of one of his schoolfellows; tremblingly declared his passion when on the point of leaving, and was accepted. Young Turner, then a sprightly youth, trod the empyrean. It had long since been determined he should be a painter. Feeling with the instinctive consciousness of genius that he was certain to attain eminence in his art, he looked with confidence to the future. At nineteen he left for a lengthened tour in the North, to sketch scenery from the great book of Nature, after first exchanging vows of mutual fidelity with Miss ——. He wrote constantly, but the young lady was not permitted to see one of his letters. Her stepmother, who did not approve of the contemplated match, intercepted them. Miss —— believed herself to be forgotten, forsaken, and finally consented to receive the addresses of a new lover. The day was fixed for the marriage, when Turner, who, spite of not having received an answer to one of his letters—the cause of which he must have divined—had never for one moment doubted his beloved's constancy, came back to London, and forthwith betook himself to the young lady's abode. When informed how matters stood, he was wild, mad—passionately implored Miss —— to break off an engagement into which she had been inveigled. The lady, believing she had gone too far to recede, refused. The marriage was soon afterwards celebrated. A most unhappy one it proved to the bride. To young Turner the marriage-bells sounded the death-knell of his hopes. The blow was mortal: he never recovered from it; and to it must be attributed, in an almost entire degree, his misanthropic manner, his neglect of appearances, and his contempt of the world, except as a place in which money might be scraped together. One unbroken idol at whose shrine he might worship remained to him—Art, and to that worship he for the future devoted himself with all his heart and strength.

The goddess rewarded her votary with her especial favours—inspired, inflamed his genius, but for many years was niggardly of temporal gifts.

Turner took up his abode in his old dingy bedroom over the barber's shop in Maiden Lane, drew sketches, which when he had gained recognition would have brought hundreds of pounds, for three or four shillings each. He acquired the art of engraving, greatly excelled in it, and was much patronised by the print-publishers, with whom, till he became celebrated, he was perpetually at war—at such low prices did they require him to work. Throughout his life he cherished a bitter hatred of publishers.

The sole relaxation which this remarkable man permitted himself, besides certain potations—but it was not till late in life that he at times over-indulged—was fishing. He might be seen wending his way to the riverside, dressed in the oddest fashion,—a flabby hat, ill-fitting green Monmouth-Street coat, nankeen trousers much too short, and highlow boots, with a dilapidated cotton umbrella, and a fishing-rod. From early morning till nightfall would he sit upon the river's bank, under pelting rain, patiently, shielded by his capacious umbrella, even though he did not obtain a single nibble. He was not, however, an unskilful angler, and was very proud of a good day's sport. He often fished in the Thames at Brentford.

Turner engraved for a livelihood; he painted for

fame, and fame came at last. The world of London awoke to the knowledge that a great painter had arisen amongst them. Yet was the recognition for some time doubtful, hesitating. The critics of the press abused unmercifully his painting of "Carthage," exhibited at the Royal Academy. The gentleman who had ordered and was to pay one hundred pounds for it refused on account of those strictures to complete the bargain. Not very long afterwards Turner was offered thousands for the same work. "This is indeed a triumph," he exclaimed, with natural exultation. He was at last at the top of Fortune's wheel. His paintings commanded any price he chose to ask for them, and he accumulated money at an astounding rate. He had removed to 48 Queen-Anne Street West, a street north of Cavendish Square—a house subsequently known as "Turner's Den." Truly a den. The windows were never cleaned, had breaches in them patched with paper; the door was black and blistered, the iron palisades rusty for lack of paint. If a would-be visitor knocked or rang, it was long before the summons was replied to—up to 1812 by a wizened, meagre old man, who unfastened the chain sufficiently to see who rang or knocked, and the almost invariable answer was, "You can't come in." After the old man's death, Mrs. Danby, an elderly woman with a diseased face, supplied his place.

A profound melancholy shadowed not only the social, but artistic life of Turner, relieved by occasional, far-between flashes of merriment. Mr. Ruskin has remarked upon this in his usual forcible language—"Sunset and twilight on ruins were his favourite effects." Speaking of the Liber, the great art-critic goes on to remark—"A feeling of decay, of humiliation, gives solemnity to all his simplest subjects, even to his views of daily labour. In the pastoral by the brookside, the child is in rags and lame. In the hedging and ditching, the labourer is mean and sickly, the woman slatternly. The mill is a ruin; the peat-bog dreary."

Nothing could be more true. Even his glorious picture of the last of the Old Téméraire, is the Téméraire going to be broken up. "Ah! the fallacies of hope!" was his frequent exclamation when he was in the full blaze of his fame and rolling in riches. "Ah! the fallacies of hope,"—a thought which, if seldom uttered in words, is ever burning in the brain of finely-organised poetic natures, and Turner's was a finely-organised poetic nature, if there ever was one. The burden. of the mystery is too heavy for them. The highest poetry of the nineteenth century is but the melodious echo of this deep-seated feeling, this religion of despair.

Turner loved to mystify people. His great picture of Polyphemus, the one-eyed Cyclops whose eye Ulysses put out, with a tree pointed like a stake, when the monster was asleep, the subject of which was taken from the. *Odyssey*, had an immense success. One day Turner dined with a large party, amongst the guests at which were the Reverend Mr. Judkins, and a lady, who greatly admired Turner's pictures. They were sitting opposite Turner and talking in whispers. "I know what you are talking about," exclaimed Turner, his keen eyes glittering with fun; "you are talking of my picture." This was true, the lady having expressed great admiration of the Polyphemus; "a sweet picture," she called it. The Rev. Mr. Judkins intimated assent; they *were* talking about his picture. "And where do you think I got the subject from, sir?" asked Turner. "Why, from the *Odyssey*, of course." "Not a bit of it, my dear sir; I took it from Tom Dibdin. Don't you remember the words?—

> 'He ate his mutton, drank his wine,
> And then he poked his eye out.'"

One Mr. Gillat, a wealthy manufacturer of Birmingham—it was the wealthy merchants and manufacturers, not the aristocracy, by whom Turner was chiefly patronised—Mr. Gillat was determined, if possible, to possess himself of some of Turner's pictures. With that fixed purpose he came to London, called at the Den, 48 Queen-

Anne Street, rang the bell again and again, till at last it
was answered by the old woman with a diseased face.
He told his business, and the usual reply was given—
"You can't come in." The Birmingham gentleman was
not so easily beaten. He had got his foot in the doorway—the housekeeper had incautiously unhooked the
chain—and Mr. Gillat made a forcible entry. He had
hardly gained the first landing when Turner, hearing
strange footsteps, rushed out of his particular compart-
ment in the Den and angrily confronted the intruder.
"What do you want here?" "I am come to purchase
some of your pictures." "I have none to sell." "But
you won't mind exchanging them for some of mine? You
have seen our Birmingham pictures?" "Never 'eard of
'em." "I will show you some," rejoined the gentleman
from Birmingham, pulling out a roll of Bank-of-England notes to the amount of five thousand pounds. "You
are a rum one," said Turner. "Those are pictures, too,
that must not be copied." The Birmingham gentleman
was successful, and carried off five thousand pounds'
worth—now perhaps worth five times that sum—of the
great artist's creations.

Turner could not bear to sell a favourite painting.
It was a portion of his being; to part with it was a ren-
dering up, the blotting out of that space of his life spent
in its creation. He was always dejected, melancholy,
after such a transaction. "I lost one of my children
this week," he would sadly exclaim, with tears in his
eyes.

At a meeting at Somerset House, presided over by
the late Sir Robert Peel, it was decided to purchase
Turner's two great pictures, the Rise and Fall of Carthage, for the National Gallery. A Mr. Griffiths was
commissioned to offer five thousand pounds for them.
"A noble offer," said Turner, "a noble offer; but no,
I cannot part with them. Impossible." Mr. Griffiths,
greatly disappointed, took leave. Turner ran after him.
"Tell those gentlemen," he said, "that the nation will,
most likely, have the pictures after all."

Long before this Turner had matured a purpose which continued to be his dominant idea till the curtain fell upon the incongruous drama of his life. This was to bequeath to his country a Turner's Gallery of noble pictures, and amass one hundred thousand pounds at least, to build and endow an asylum for decayed artists. It was for this great end that he scorned delights, except such cheap luxuries as fishing, and the indulgence, at times, of somewhat ignoble tastes; consented to be esteemed a miserly curmudgeon, lived in a state of almost absolute squalor, dressed in such a Paul-Pry fashion—Paul-Pry run to seed—that country friends, as well as his aristocratic acquaintances, gave him the sobriquet of Old Podgy.

His resolve once made could not be shaken. A wealthy merchant of Liverpool offered him one hundred thousand pounds down for the art-treasures rolled up in dark closets—hanging from dripping walls in the Den, Queen-Anne Street. "Give me the key of the house, Mr. Turner," said the would-be purchaser, "and here is the money." "No, thank you," replied Turner; "I have refused a better offer," which was true.

Upon another occasion an eager speculator called upon him to effect purchases. Turner happened to be in one of his jocose moods, and he displayed his wonderful sketches bound up in volumes. The purchaser expectant was in ecstasies as the gem-like pages flashed one after the other upon him. His bid for them rapidly increased till it reached the sum of one thousand pounds per volume. "You would very much like to have them, I daresay?" "Yes, very much." "Well, then, you won't."

Yet this large-souled man—a mighty spirit prisoned in the shabbiest of shells—could be guilty of the most niggardly meanness. He caused a tablet to be placed in St. Paul's. Some masonry work was required to fix it; the charge for which was seven-and-sixpence, which one of the churchwardens, paid, believing of course, that Mr. Turner would immediately reimburse him such a trifle. Mr. Turner was much pleased with the tablet, but his mood changed when the little bill was presented. "Send me a receipt from the mason," said Turner; "I won't pay it till you do." It was not worth the trouble' to do so, and the churchwarden lost his money. "He a great man!" growled a Southend boatman, one of two whom Turner used to hire to pull him about the Thames shore whilst he was sketching. "He a great man! over the left! Why, he takes out a big bottle of gin regular, and never axes us to have a nip."

Yet even with respect to that least-significant sign or evidence of true benevolence, indiscriminate alms-giving, the great artist was often, very often, impulsively, lavishly generous. An old Irish beggar-woman impor-tuned him in the streets, to his great annoyance. He rebuked her angrily, but presently repenting of his harsh-ness, ran back and slipped a five-pound note into her hand.

He was sometimes munificent, even during life, in affording help to those who he knew really needed it. A gentleman who used to buy his sketches when he was working in the dingy bedroom over his father's shop in Maiden Lane, and always prophesied high things of him, fell into difficulties, and was about to sell the timber on his estate. Turner heard of this, and sent many thou-sands—twenty it is said—anonymously to the gentleman's steward. The embarrassment was temporary only, the gentleman recovered himself, and Turner received back his twenty thousand pounds.

Especially for struggling artists he felt an ardent sympathy, and was ever ready to assist them with advice and money. One young man who had painted "Galileo in the prison of the Inquisition," showed the work to him. "It is a good picture," said Turner; "full of pro-mise." Then seizing a brush, he dashed in some geome-trical figures upon the prison walls. This was worth fifty guineas to the young painter.

One incident gives high proof of the native genero-sity of his nature. He was one of the hanging com-

mittee, as the phrase goes, of the Royal Academy. The
walls were full when Turner's attention was attracted by
a picture sent in by an unknown provincial artist of the
name of Bird. Turner examined it carefully. "A good
picture," he exclaimed; "it must be hung up and exhibited." "Impossible," responded the committee of
Academicians. "The arrangement can't be disturbed.
Quite impossible!" "A good picture," iterated Turner;
"it must be hung up;" and finding his colleagues to be
as obstinate as himself, he hitched down one of his own
pictures and hung up Bird's in its place.

Another time Sir Thomas Lawrence exhibited a painting which was hung close by one of Turner's. The ex-
ceeding brightness of the latter rendered the dulness of
Sir Thomas Lawrence's repulsively apparent. The courtly
portrait-painter was much annoyed, but there was no
help for it. The next day, a friend called upon Turner,
and asked what, in the name of heaven, he had been
doing with his picture. The colour was all smudged out.
"Yes, yes—Lawrence looked so miserable. But it's only
lamp-black; it will easily wash off."

Turner never entertained any one, never gave a dinner during his life. Upon one occasion he had no option
but to do so. He had paid a visit to Edinburgh, and
whilst there had been hospitably entertained by a Mr.
Thompson. He had, in fact, made that gentleman's
house his home. Mr. Thompson came to London, and
Turner could not do less than invite him to dinner.
The invitation was accepted, greatly to the consternation
both of Turner and his father. There seemed, however,
to be no help for it, when fortune came to their relief.
Mr. Thompson called upon a nobleman, who pressingly
invited him to dine at his mansion the next day, the last
he should remain in town. Mr. Thompson pleaded his
previous engagement with Turner. "Bring Turner with
you," said the nobleman. Mr. Thompson delivered the
message. Turner, secretly delighted, affected to hesitate. "Well, I suppose I must, but—" "Go, Billy,"
exclaimed the father, furtively opening the door, on the

outside of which he had been listening. "Go, Billy; the mutton need not be boiled."

The suffering of his friends grievously affected Turner. Their death encompassed him for a time with the gloom of an inconsolable despair. He had, unhappily, no religious convictions, and the thought of annihilation was to him a source of constant terror and dread. The death of his jovial-hearted friend Chantrey, the sculptor, deeply affected him. He could never be induced to enter a sick-room, and would not visit at the house where a friend or acquaintance had died.

At last the sere of life had fallen upon this great genius. He felt, though he refused to acknowledge it to himself, that he was fast approaching the setting sun, that the universe was fading from his sight, crumbling at his feet. He strove to escape from himself, as it were: "He would give all his wealth to be twenty years old again." He was recognised at the Yorkshire Stingo by a very slight acquaintance. He may have indulged in potations at times. "I shall often come," said the man, "now I know you frequent the house." Turner never went there again; but the world was a blank for him: he had no cheerful fireside—no home in its true saving sense.

Becoming more and more conscious of the swift approach of death, and fancying, perhaps, that a change of scene—seclusion from society—might retrim the expiring lamp, he suddenly left Queen-Anne Street with merely a change of linen, as if he were going out for a walk, and took lodgings in a cottage at Chelsea, next door to which ginger-beer was sold, and not far from the present Cremorne Pier. It was a long time before his whereabout was discovered by his old faithful housekeeper, Mrs. Danby, by accident.

He had not then many days to live. A medical gentleman whom he had known at Margate—Margate, which he was never weary of visiting, and the memories of which were present to him in his last hours—had been sent for, and he had no sooner looked upon the moribund than he gently but firmly announced that the last hour was at hand. Turner was greatly shocked, and refused to believe that his end, that "annihilation" was so near. "Go down-stairs," trembled from his ashen lips, "go down stairs, and take a glass of wine. Then come and look at me again." The medical gentleman did so, returned, and again interpreted in the same words the doom of inevitable death written unmistakably upon the great painter's brow. A few hours afterwards, on the 19th of December 1851, J. M. W. Turner, R.A., expired, aged 79 years. He was buried in St. Paul's.

By his will he bequeathed one hundred and forty thousand pounds to found an asylum for poor artists born in England, and a magnificent art-treasure to his country. This latter bequest was, however, coupled with the condition that his Rise and Fall of Carthage should be hung up in the National Gallery between Claude's Sea-port and Mill.

LORD NORBURY.

THE Mr. John Toler who, by force of unblushing sycophancy, unparalleled impudence, and a pair of hairtrigger pistols, became Lord Norbury, and Chief Justice of the Court of Common Pleas, Ireland, was of respectable parentage, notwithstanding that his only fortune when launched upon the world was fifty pounds and the hair-trigger pistols. These qualifications sufficed in those days—although he knew little of law, in a comparative sense of course, and was utterly destitute of eloquence—to clear his way to the high offices of Solicitor-, Attorney-General, Chief Judgeship, and to place a coronet on his truculent brow.

This man, called to the Irish bar in 1771, was in person fat, podgy, with small gray cunning eyes, which ever sparkled with good humour, irrepressible fun, especially when he was passing sentence of death. He was never so jocund as then, especially if there was a large batch of criminals. Lord Norbury was at once Sancho Panza and Judge Jeffreys. He had not, and did not care to have, a particle of moral courage; but was animally brave, or pretty nearly so, as a bull-dog is. He was always ready with his pistol. He fought some half-dozen duels, one with fire-eating Fitzgerald; frighteued James Napper Tandy, who died a French general, nearly out of his small wits by the threat of one; and Sir Jonah Barrington's very respectable brains he would probably have blown out, but for a ludicrous mishap. Of these incidents more presently. Lord Norbury, it must be admitted, only followed the fashion of the times. Lord Chancellor Clare "went out" with the Master of the Rolls, John Philpot Curran. There was a mania for

duelling. To have stood fire, at least once, was held to
be the only stamp of a *raal* gentleman. It was a customary query for a father or mother to put to any one
who advocated the pretensions of a suitor to his or her
daughter's hand: "What family is he of? Did he ever
stand a blaze?" Judge Fletcher, a learned, humane,
bibulous man, and a terrible glutton, when summing up
the evidence in the case of the King *v.* Fenton, who was
indicted for the murder of Major Hillens, said, "It is my
duty to tell you, gentlemen of the jury, that to kill a
man in a duel is by law murder. It is my duty to say
that; but upon my honour, gentlemen, a *fairer duel* I
never heard or read of." Fenton was of course acquitted.
What a distance, looked at from our present point of
view, seems to have elapsed since such sayings and
doings were possible in high judicial regions! The
march of civilisation and refinement may be slow, but
it is palpable and decisive.

Notwithstanding that Lord Norbury was seen by
dullest eyes to be a coarse vulgar embodiment of a mean
rascality, unredeemed by the faintest gleam of honour or
patriotism, the man was tolerated by society for his convivial talents. He could sing a capital song, often did
so in miscellaneous company, long after he was Chief
Justice of the Common Pleas, and sometimes delivered
smart, if not exactly witty, sayings. His best songs
were "Black-eyed Susan" and "Admiral Benbow." His
character will be best portrayed by anecdotical pen-
strokes. In so doing it will be necessary to mix up the
tragic and the trivial, the savagery and jocoseness, which
made up Lord Norbury. It would, indeed, be impossible
to separate in his moral portrait those characteristics
from each other. His judicial ferocity was invariably
tinged with a sort of ghastly fun, just as his jocosity was
ever spiteful, venomous, brutal.

Mr. John Toler, become Attorney-General, prosecuted,
on the part of the Crown, John and Henry Sheares, young
barristers of good family, who had rashly mixed themselves up with one of the abortive rebellions rife in that

troubled exciting time. They were the dupes and tools of more astute and cunning conspirators. This was especially true of Henry Sheares, a young man of weak, not to say cowardly, spirit. The trial, which took place before Lord Carleton, was a lengthened one. Mr. Curran, when the case for the prosecution closed, asked for an adjournment, he being physically incapable of addressing the jury with effect. "What do you say, Mr. Attorney?" said Lord Carleton. Mr. Attorney Toler objected. He was as much exhausted as the counsel for the rebels. Such adjournments, he added, were prejudicial to the public interests, and a waste of time. The trial went on, the accused were convicted—sentenced to death. Mr. Attorney immediately rose and prayed that execution might take place on the following day. The prayer was granted.

Mr. Attorney-General Toler had a purpose in view. He was aware that Sir Jonah Barrington, one of the most loyal of men, and held in high esteem by the Lord Lieutenant, had been acquainted with the prisoners— that he felt great commiseration for them, and would do his utmost to avert or mitigate their doom; and Mr. Attorney-General could not endure that the quarry which he had hunted down should be rescued by any impertinent interference. Mr. Attorney's was a well-calculated haste. Henry Sheares wrote a letter, immediately after sentence was pronounced, to Sir Jonah Barrington, imploring him, in the most pathetic phrases, to see the Lord Lieutenant, and intercede for his, the prisoner's, life. The letter itself was abundant proof that the craven who wrote it could never have seriously contemplated rebellion. Lord Clare yielded, and sent a respite staying execution, in the hope that the doomed man might be able to make revelations which would justify him, the Lord Lieutenant, in granting a full pardon. Sir Jonah Barrington hurried off, and arrived before the gaol in just sufficient time to see and hear the executioner hold up Henry Sheares' head, and exclaim: "This is the head of a traitor!"

There is only one step, we are told, from the sublime to the ridiculous: in the instance of this man there is but one, and a short one, so closely do they approximate, from the horrible to the funny—the ludicrous. Take, for example, the following anecdote:

Lord Redesdale, appointed Lord Chancellor for Ireland, a dull, prosaic man, who believed himself to be a wit of the first water, was anxious to exhibit himself to advantage in his first social intercourse with the Irish bar, the rollicking humour of whom was well known. He fared but badly, Mr. John Toler contriving to turn the laugh against him at every tilt of repartee. Lord Redesdale mentioned that when he was a lad cock-fighting was in vogue, and that ladies went to see the exhibition full-dressed, and wearing hoops. "Ah," exclaimed Toler, "now we get at the etymology of cock-a-hoop." This was thought very clever, and a general laugh followed. His lordship subsequently remarked—the conversation having turned upon skating—that in his youth skating was not a dangerous pastime, inasmuch as that the skaters fastened bladders under their arms, so that if the ice broke beneath them, they would be suspended above water by the bladders. "Ha, ha!" shouted Toler, "now I understand what blatherum-skate means." Poor stuff, no doubt, but there was not much superior to it in Lord Norbury's motley coat of many colours.

The Right Honourable John Toler crept, crawled, bullied his way into the Irish House of Commons, when it was really worth while to be a member of that assembly. The English government were bent upon abolishing the Irish parliament, and votes for the Union were to be purchased at any price. The Right Honourable John Toler was very useful in flattering all voters with his praise, and in bullying the opponents of the scheme, it being well known to all that a skilfully-pointed hair-trigger would echo his insults at a moment's notice. His first onslaught was upon Mr. George Ponsonby. He told the honourable gentleman that if he had heard any one utter such words out of the House as he, Mr. Ponsonby, had within it, he would have seized the ruffian by the throat, and trampled him into the dust. Mr. Ponsonby took no notice of the right honourable gentleman's Billingsgate. Mr. Toler next fell foul of the Honourable Jonah Barrington, and having dined and drunk very freely, was more than usually abusive. Sir Jonah Barrington curtly replied: "I shall only give him the character which he deserves; this, that he has a hand for everybody and a heart for nobody." The instant Sir Jonah sat down, Toler gave him an unmistakable hair-trigger wink with one of his small gray eyes, and out of the House hurried both the honourable gentlemen. They were not, however, quick enough. The Serjeant-at-Arms' assistants were ordered to follow, and bring the honourable members back into the awful presence of the Mace. Toler was captured. His coat-tails were caught in a doorway he was passing through; and though, tugging with might and main, he at last freed himself at the cost of his tails, the delay was fatal. He was seized and brought back to the House. Sir Jonah got as far as Nassau Street, where he was overtaken, rudely seized, carried back by four stout fellows, and flung like a sack of sawdust upon the floor of the House. Both members were ordered to declare "upon their honour" that the affair should proceed no further. The Right Honourable John Toler rose to explain—to defend himself; but his appearance, denuded as he was of the skirts of his coat, was so ludicrous, that the House burst into roars of laughter. As soon as he could make himself heard, Curran, with great apparent indignation, rose and exclaimed: "A more intolerable insult has never been offered to this House. One honourable member has positively dared TO TRIM THE JACKET of another honourable member within these walls, and nearly within view of the Speaker!" This sally intensified the merriment, amidst which the comical fracas evaporated, so to speak.

The Right Honourable John Toler voted for the destruction of the Irish Parliament; a wise measure, it may be, but carried by infamously corrupt means. The right honourable gentleman drove a famous bargain with the government—a peerage for his wife, already an old woman, and the chief-justiceship of the Common Pleas for himself, with the title of Lord Norbury. Upon this being communicated by Lord Castlereagh to the Lord Chancellor Clare, that learned dignitary replied, "No, no, that will never do; make Toler a bishop, an arch-bishop even, but not a chief justice." The Lord Chancellor was obliged to yield, the Union was carried, and Lord Norbury was placed in possession of the seat and salary of the chief justice. "You have sold your country," said an Irish lady, not having the fear of hair-triggers before her eyes; "you have basely sold your country." "Very lucky for me that I had a country to sell," was the rejoinder. "I wish I had another."

Lord Norbury, as Chief Justice, reflected no honour upon his office or upon those who had appointed him to it. Anecdotes of his conduct on the bench of justice are numerous. I select a few. He never would nonsuit a plaintiff; he had a *constitutional* objection, forsooth, to withdraw the decision of any case from a jury. Upon one occasion he was urged in bolder terms than were ordinarily employed by the counsel for the defendant to grant a nonsuit. "For once, my lord, have the courage to grant a nonsuit." "I tell you what, Mr. Wallace," rejoined the Chief Justice,—"I tell you what, Mr. Wallace; there are two kinds of courage—courage to shoot and courage to nonshoot. I hope I have both. But nonshoot now I won't."

Lord Norbury, it has been already said, had a strong liking for capital punishments. He was never so hilarious as when putting on the black cap. It happened, however, that upon one occasion, during a trial of some interest, he manifested considerable emotion. Mr. Harvey Grady, a barrister of ability, who had been chafed by some of the judge's remarks, thereupon said, "The incident reminds me, my lord, of a judge who was never known to weep but once, and that was in a theatre." "Tragedy—deep tragedy, Mr. Grady," said Lord Nor-

bury. "No, indeed, my lord. It was in the *Beggars'
Opera*, when Macheath was reprieved." Lord Norbury
tried the unfortunate Robert Emmett for high treason,
conducting himself throughout the proceedings as a Jeffreys or Scroggs might have done. "My lord," said the
high-minded, if mistaken, young man, irritated by a
brutal taunt,—"my lord, there are men concerned in
this conspiracy who would disgrace themselves by shaking
your blood-stained hand." The judge revenged himself
by passing sentence of death in a sneering, mocking
tone, omitting to add the usual formula, "And may the
Lord have mercy upon your soul."

"Some of Lord Norbury's impromptus are apt and
humorous. He was told by a gentleman that he heard
an old enemy of his was dead. "Do you believe it?"
asked his friend. "I don't know," said Lord Norbury.
"He is villain enough to live or die, just as it suits his
own convenience."

Again. During a session of the Irish Parliament,
when a strong effort' was made to induce the House of
Commons to pass a Catholic Emancipation Bill, the
friends of the measure hit upon the notable expedient of
inviting over from England Edmund Burke's son, for
the purpose of drawing up the petition to be presented
to the House. The father was an eloquent writer, and
it was concluded that his son must be the same. The
young gentleman failed to please his patrons. The petition was nevertheless presented, and an acrimonious
debate ensued. Young Mr. Burke was in the gallery,
but, becoming much excited, walked down and entered
the House itself, and walked up towards the chair. As
soon as the audacious act was noticed, loud cries of
"Privilege," "There is a stranger in the House," arose
on all sides. "Serjeant-at-Arms, do your duty," roared
Mr. Speaker. The intruder was dumb-foundered, paralysed with terror. Thunder had fallen upon him. The
imminence of the peril partially restored his faculties; he
turned; the Serjeant-at-Arms, with a drawn sword in
his hand, blocked his way: instantly doubling, he was

stopped by the Clerk of the House: turning again, he fairly took to his heels, followed at full speed by the door-keepers. He, however, escaped. The incident produced some excitement amongst the members, one of whom observed that he did not believe such a thing had ever happened before. "I beg your pardon," exclaimed the Right Honourable John Toler; "I found the same incident, a few days hence, in the cross-readings of a newspaper. Yesterday a petition was presented to the House of Commons—it fortunately missed fire, and the villain ran off."

This, again, is tolerably smart. A gentleman had been tried for arson and acquitted legally, though not by the verdict of general opinion. This gentleman attended a Castle levée. "I am glad to see you *here*," said the Right Honourable John Toler. "It will be my last visit for a long time," said the gentleman, "as I am about to become a Benedict." "Ah, well," said the Right Honourable John, "St. Paul says it is better to marry than *burn*."

The Chief Justice of the Common Pleas was as averse to signing bills of exception as to directing a nonsuit. One was tendered against his lordship's ruling by the late Daniel O'Connell, between whom and Lord Norbury there was perpetual feud. They hated each other bitterly. If a judge refuse to sign a bill of exceptions, he is liable to a penalty of five hundred pounds. Lord Norbury was yet more loath to pay five hundred pounds than to sign a bill of exceptions. "Surely, Mr. O'Connell," he exclaimed, "you cannot be serious." The great Daniel replied that he was never more serious in his life. The duty he owed his client required him to insist either that his lordship should sign or refuse to sign the bill of exceptions. Lord Norbury was sure Mr. O'Connell would always do his duty towards his clients. He was a bright example to the bar in this respect. But he was disinclined either to sign the bill or refuse to sign it. "I wish your lordship had spared me the infliction of your praise. I must insist either that your lordship signs or refuses to sign." "Certainly I shall not refuse to sign, nor sign now. Come to me by and bye at chambers, and we will see about it." Mr. O'Connell attended at chambers, and the bill of exceptions was signed.

In another tilt with Lord Norbury, Daniel O'Connell did not come off so well. The late Sir Robert Peel, when Secretary for Ireland, had challenged Mr. O'Connell to mortal combat, in consequence of some offensive expressions made use of towards him by the celebrated agitator at a public meeting. Mrs. O'Connell, discovering what was going on, caused her husband to be arrested and bound over to keep the peace with all the king's subjects in Ireland. Mr. Peel immediately started for Ostend, first sending a written message to O'Connell that he intended to do so. Mr. O'Connell followed shortly, was again arrested in London, and bound over by Lord Ellenborough, in heavy penalties, to keep the peace with all his Majesty's subjects. Mr. O'Connell returned to Ireland, and a short time afterwards was arguing a knotty point of law before the Chief Justice. Lord Norbury paid little attention to the argument, preferring to fondle a Newfoundland dog he had with him on the bench. "My lord," exclaimed Mr. O'Connell, "I am afraid your lordship does not apprehend me." "I beg your pardon, Mr. O'Connell," replied the Chief Justice with a sneering chuckle, "no one is more easily apprehended than Mr. O'Connell *when he wishes to be.*"

Irish gentlemen are proverbially the most hospitable race in the world. Lord Norbury was an exception. He was, however, liberal enough in his invitations, but there was very lenten entertainment grudgingly placed before such persons as, not knowing his lordship, ventured to accept them. He once pressingly invited an elderly lady and gentleman, with whom he had been long acquainted, to come and spend a week at Cabra, his lordship's seat, at a considerable distance from Dublin, little imagining his invitation would be accepted. He was mistaken. The lady and gentleman packed up such necessaries as would be required during a week's sojourn at Cabra, where they safely arrived, and were most politely received by Lord Norbury. "Well, now, this is kind," said his lordship; "I am so happy to see you both, and must insist—now, no excuse—that *you stop and take dinner.* You must, indeed: I will take no refusal,—certainly not."

The Chief Justice once, when passing sentence of death, at Carlow, upon a lot of rebels, was attired in a masquerade dress! He had, some weeks previous, been present at a grand masquerade given by Lady Castlereagh, where he appeared in the character of Hawthorne in Love in a Village. His dress was green tabinet, with mother-of-pearl buttons, striped yellow-and-black waistcoat, and buff breeches. When about to dress on the morning of the day when so many sentences would have to be passed, and the weather being extremely hot, he examined his wardrobe to select the lightest, coolest dress he could find. This happened to be his masquerade costume, which he at once decided upon. When he took his seat on the bench, his robe concealed the underdress; but soon overpowered by the heat, Lord Norbury threw back his robe, disclosing his masquerade attire to the amazement of a crowded court, and went on with his pleasant labour in a comfortable state of both body and mind.

Lord Norbury clung to the great office which he disgraced to the last. At length the Government determined to abate so pernicious a scandal, and a private intimation reached him that he would be required to resign the Chief Justiceship. The intelligence made him wild—furious; life would be valueless if not enlivened by the power of passing death-sentences, a delectation which the absurd chicken-heartedness of modern legislators had already shamefully curtailed. The Chief Justice quickly resolved upon his plan of campaign. Mr. Gregory, the Lord Lieutenant's private secretary, would be the person selected to present him with his Excellency's compliments, and politely intimate the request of Government that he would tender his resignation. Lord Norbury sent for Mr. Gregory at once, conducted him to a private room, carefully closed the door, turned the key, and then with the fierce glimmer in his eyes which his auditor well knew indicated mischief, thus addressed him : "My dear Gregory, you are my oldest friend. There is no one I respect so much. It seems that our mock king in the Phœnix Park is about to publicly insult me, and I never yet brooked a saucy look. I am to be asked to resign my seat on the Bench! Of course the sham monarch himself cannot be punished, but the minion, whoever he is, whom he intrusts with such a message, shall be; I will have his life. Gregory, my old, my valued friend—you will stand by me, I am sure. *The hair-triggers* are ready as in the days of Tandy and Fitzgerald." Mr. Gregory, who had been charged to deliver the offensive intimation without delay, left without doing so. Lord Norbury's bullying tactics, however, availed nothing. A few days afterwards he was requested to resign by a letter from the Lord Lieutenant himself. Driven to bay, the Chief Justice asked for time to consult a friend. This indulgence was granted. The friend was in India! This was a twelvemonth gained. The Chief Justice thought so. He deceived himself. Having fallen asleep during a trial for murder, a petition presented to the House of Commons by Daniel O'Connell compelled the Government to require his instaut resignation of the judgment-seat—and Lord Norbury, *alias* John Toler, retired to die at Cabra. His coarse humour did not forsake him in the last hours. He had a neighbour who had been bedridden for years, and was at the point of death. Apprised by his physician that his end was near, inevitable, he, the shock of the announcement over, said to a servant in attendance, "James, go with my compliments to Lord Erne, and tell him it is now a dead heat between him and me." Thus died the bloody-handed Jester-Judge.

THE CHEVALIER D'EON.

The life of this gentleman is one of the still unsolved mysteries of what may be called the occult history of courts and courtesans, royal intrigues, and underplots of bestarred and beribboned flunkeyism. Much has been written upon the subject, but no key has yet been found that will turn the lock of the riddle. I am about to try the effect of my file upon that one which seemed to fit the wards most accurately. It is a subject which requires delicate handling, and I shall so handle it.

Charles Geneviève Louise Auguste D'Eon de Beaumont was born at Tonnerre, France, in the year 1728. It is somewhat curious, considering D'Eon's after-life, that of his four baptismal names two were masculine and two feminine. He was a clever boy—"*mais tant soit peu eccentrique*" (but more or less eccentric). His features being small and delicate, he more than once passed himself off as a girl at rustic fêtes, and could only be induced to abstain from such objectionable license by the serious warnings of a magistrate.

Charles Geneviève Louise Auguste D'Eon de Beaumont's domicile did not harmonise with such sounding titles. The family was poor and proud, and the young man was hugely delighted when he was at last free to seek his fortune in Paris, furnished, it is true, with a light purse, but influential introductions to great people. The old noblesse of France were true to their order, false and tyrannous as they were to the mere people. It was these introductions, and not the wishy-washy pamphlets he wrote and published, which commended him to the notice of the Prince of Conti, and through his princeship to that of the King Louis XV. His handsome presence and pleasing manners secured the favour which princely patronage had initiated. He was appointed equerry to the king, created a knight, thenceforth Chevalier D'Eon, and as if to make a doctor of law and an advocate of the parliament were as easy to the monarch as to manufacture an equerry or a knight, had the dignity of doctor of law and an advocate of parliament conferred upon him.

The sun of good fortune continued to smile. He was appointed to the secretaryship of the French embassy at St. Petersburg, and by his adroitness, spirit of adventurous intrigue, and glozing tongue, so ingratiated himself with the Czarina Elizabeth, one of the most atrocious fiends that ever filled the Satanic throne of Muscovy, that he soon became, to the superseding of the titular ambassador, the medium of communication between the Empress Elizabeth and Louis XV. It is needless to go into the details, so far as they are unreliably known, of the plots, treacheries, massacres, schemes to which D'Eon was privy, and the thread of which web of devilism he held. Enough that both Elizabeth and Louis approved his services. The czarina gave him money, Louis made him a captain of dragoons, and by letters patent granted him a pension of about, in English money, one hundred pounds per annum.

During the chevalier's sojourn in St. Petersburg he was in the habit of frequenting places of amusement, balls, &c., in the guise of a woman. His appearance when so attired was so completely feminine that no one unacquainted with him could have detected the imposture. This was a mania with the chevalier. There was nothing he so delighted in as receiving the amatory compliments of men attracted by the beauty of his countenance, and the artistic make-up of his figure. And yet this man was a brave soldier, and proved that he was in more than one bloody encounter. Verily the contradictions and inconsistencies of human nature are inscrutable, past finding out.

No question that the eccentric chevalier was a very

clever person. There is no more doubt that he was unscrupulous as to the means to be employed for rising in
the world. A young gentleman, moreover, of amazing
fertility of resource, who could conceive and carry out
unheard-of schemes for the replenishment of an exhausted
purse which a less fertile brain would never have dreamt
of. And in this we shall, I think, find the true key to
the unlocking of the D'Eon mystery. The puzzlement—
it scarcely deserves the name of mystery—lies in a nut-
shell. It was simply a novel mode of raising the wind
by the help of unscrupulous intermediaries. It is surprising that Sir Charles Lascelles Wraxall, Mr. Robert
Chambers, and others who have written so largely upon
the subject, should not at a glance have perceived what
a transparent swindle the whole thing was.

The Chevalier D'Eon contrived to obtain the appointment of attaché to the embassy in England, the ambassador being the Duc de Nivernois. In London the
chevalier's restless spirit of intrigue, his audacity of
enterprise in search after political advancement, were as
conspicuous, though not so successful, as at St. Petersburg. He purloined, secreted, whichever may be the
most appropriate word, some important papers, and made
capital of their possession. The Duc de Nivernois returned to France much dissatisfied with D'Eon, who
however continued for some time to fulfil the duties of
Chargé d'Affaires at the English court.

He was at last deprived of his office, and reduced to
subsist upon his pension of one hundred pounds per
aunum—a sorry income for so gay a chevalier. With
the help of gaming, wagering, and other contrivances
familiar to the initiated, he managed to carry on the war
for full fourteen years. By that time he had reached the
length of his tether, and a gaol loomed with dark distinctness in the "illimitable perspective."

This had been for at least six years—much longer,
probably—a foregone conclusion with the chevalier; and
he, if I read his life aright, had prepared for the inevitable catastrophe after a very novel fashion. Doubts of

whether the chevalier was a man or woman were circulated; and Hayes, a surgeon, with whom D'Eon was well acquainted, bet one Jacques, a money-broker and underwriter, a wager, of which the conditions were that Hayes would pay to Jacques fifteen guineas per cent upon the sum of seven hundred pounds till such time as D'Eon was proved to be a woman: whenever that fact should be clearly substantiated, Jacques was to pay over the seven hundred pounds. No secret was made of this wager; scores of persons entered into the speculation, and it was believed that from sixty to seventy thousand pounds were hazarded in France and England upon the result of this strange contention. People said that the chevalier had offended the French court by refusing to publicly acknowledge his sex, and on that account he had been deprived of office.

The chevalier's funds being at a very low ebb indeed, Hayes, his intimate friend, commenced an action in the King's Bench against Jacques for the recovery of the seven hundred pounds. The success of this suit, it was held, would decide the whole of the wagers. The chevalier took care that Hayes should win. It was, of course, in his own power to put the matter beyond dispute. That was not his game. Two willing dupes, or tools, were found—a M. Le Goux, surgeon, and a M. De Morande. The trial, presided over by Chief Justice Mansfield, came off on the 1st of July 1777. Mr. Buller was counsel for the plaintiff, Mr. Mansfield for the defendant. Messieurs Le Goux and De Morande swore positively that to their knowledge the pretended chevalier was a woman. De Morande had jested with her, and something more, upon the subject. He had also been shown her woman's wardrobe.

The fact that D'Eon was a woman could not, it appeared to the defendant's counsel, be disputed, and he relied for the verdict upon the plea that such wagers were illegal, especially as Hayes knew from the positive information of Le Goux and De Morande that the sham chevalier was a woman.

Lord Mansfield was not of that opinion, though he would reserve the point for the decision of the full court. His lordship instanced a case which had come within his own knowledge, when two gentlemen made a wager as to the dimensions of the Venus de Médicis. One of the wagerers said, " Remember, I am sure to win, for I have measured the statue ;" to which the other replied, " Do you think I should be such a fool as to bet if I also had not measured the statue ?" Under his lordship's direction a verdict was returned for the plaintiff for the full amount claimed.

So far Chevalier D'Eon and Co. were successful. Unfortunately for them the full court decided that such wagers were not legally recoverable, and the game was up.

The chevalier escaped to France, and in order, as I believe, to save the credit of his tools and accomplices, assumed female attire, giving out that he was compelled to do so by order of the king. I have seen biographies of D'Eon, the writers of which appear seriously to believe that such was the case !

The next move of this 'eccentric gentleman was an endeavour to put money in his purse by turning author. He wrote and printed twelve volumes of apocryphal history, and equally fictitious anecdotes, entitled *Loisirs du Chevalier D'Eon*—(Leisure Hours of the Chevalier D'Eon)—which netted all they were worth—nothing. He had, however, taken a pretty accurate estimate of Queen Charlotte, of German memory.

The Revolution found D'Eon not at all bettered in circumstances by his artifices. His only and sure friend was M. Elisée, afterwards first surgeon to Louis XVIII. M. Elisée supplied the chevalier with funds, enabling him to reach England, and support himself there, till a sufficient revenue could be obtained from a fencing establishment, which the chevalier set on foot in London, he being a very expert *maître d'armes*. He died in 1810, and the *post-mortem* examination was decisive that the chevalier was a man. The pretence of being a woman was unquestionably a mere swindle, and that of the most obvious kind, though reams of paper have been blotted with the argumentation of writers who persisted that the Chevalier D'Eon was the victim of some mysterious state-policy. The chevalier is not the only whimsical charlatan who has had his foolery exaggerated, though it has seldom been done in so outrageous a fashion as in this case.

JOSEPH BALSAMO.

" BETTER to reign in hell than serve in heaven" is the
expression put by Milton into the mouth of the Prince
of Darkness. I suppose something of the same feeling
influences men who exult in preëminence, and would
pawn their souls to attain it, though it be preëminence
in rascality. A chief amongst this class was Joseph
(Giuseppe) Balsamo, commonly known as Alessandro
Count de Cagliostro.

A very clever fellow, no question, with unbounded
faith in the gullibility of mankind, and amply endowed
with the gifts which enable the possessor to shear the
simpletons of society with effect—voluble plausibility
and impudence—above all, impudence. A sublimer rascal never breathed. There must have been a fatal flaw
in Balsamo's brain, else he could not have failed to discern, before it was too late, that the path upon which he
had entered—turn, twist, double upon it as he might—
must end in ruin, moral and material. Erratic, eccentric
individuals who strike out for themselves new modes of
acquiring wealth, believing, and acting upon the belief,
that they have discovered a short cut to fortune, and
have never pondered the wisdom of the homely proverb
which reminds us that " the longest way round is the
shortest way home"—in fact, all successful charlatans
have been more or less crazed in mind. This is their
excuse, their claim upon the charitable consideration of
mankind.

Giuseppe Balsamo,s on of Pietro and Felicia Balsamo
—the sponsors who gave him that name were not seers
into futurity—was born in Palermo, Sicily, on the 8th of

June 1743. The fat, sturdy little stranger did not open his eyes upon a very promising abode. Pietro Balsamo was a needy, struggling man, and was perfectly resigned, whilst Giuseppe was yet an infant, to let fall the oar with which he had so long and vainly been striving to stem the adverse current of his fortunes, and sink into the silent peace of the tomb. Could Pietro have foreseen the future eminence of his son in the realm of rascaldom, he might perhaps have struggled on till the first beams of its false splendour had dawned upon his darkened life.

The widow had a sore struggle with the world, and but for the assistance of one of her brothers, would have sunk under the burden. Giuseppe, or Beppo, as he was familiarly called, was a most unfortunate urchin, blessed or cursed with a tremendous appetite and strong digestive powers. This, under the circumstances, was a calamity, which became more and more aggravated as the boy increased in years and voracity. It was cruel that one with such gastronomic capacity should be restricted to the scanty fare which irregularly found its way into the dingy Balsamo domicile. There was a world outside full of fat things, and why should not he help himself to a portion thereof by the only means in his power—theft? Beppo decided upon that course, and followed it up so vigorously that a hue and cry was soon raised in the neighbourhood against Beppo Maldetto—who ran off with the good people's sausages, or any other savoury comestible which he could lay hands on.

The uncle must, for his sister's sake, put an end to such a scandal, and Beppo was placed by him in the seminary of St. Roch. The change was utterly distasteful to the voracious, idle young vagabond; and no wonder, the fare for the pupils chiefly consisting of *soupe maigre* —beans, vegetable diet generally, and a scanty allowance of that, whilst flagellation for the most trifling offence was liberally administered. It was not endurable, and the future Count de Cagliostro was constantly running away, only to be driven back to the enjoyment of diminished fare with increase of stripes. Flesh and blood—

Balsamo flesh and blood, at all events—could not stand it. The mother's heart of poor Felicia was melted by her son's sufferings, and she appealed again to the generosity of her moneyed though close-fisted brother. "Well, Beppo," said that gentleman, moved by his sister's tears, "what dost thou propose to do? What career in life dost thou suppose will best suit thee?" Beppo replied that, if he could have his choice, he should decide at once to be a gentleman. "Per Bacco! no doubt of that. But the means, Beppo?" Beppo admitted there was a difficulty in that respect, and finally consented to enter the Church. He was accordingly sent, at the age of thirteen, to the monastery of Cartigione, then in possession of the Benfratelli, or Brothers of Mercy. There Beppo, very early in his novitiate, got into favour with the apothecary of the establishment, and acquired the knowledge of medicine, the properties of certain drugs, &c., which in after-life he turned to such profitable account. The apothecary was an alchemist of small calibre, and was always experimenting in chemical conjurorship with divining-rods, Leyden-jars, acids, phosphorescent compounds, and other aids to the acquirement of proficiency in the science of natural magic—a suggestive school in which to teach the latent Balsamo idea how to shoot.

But though Beppo found favour with the Medicus of the establishment, he was held in great dislike by the Benfratelli generally. They doubted his orthodoxy, and were scandalised by his omnivorous appetite. The reins of corrective discipline were tightened, and, to the infinite disgust of Beppo, it was ultimately resolved to make a strenuous effort to save the soul of the neophyte by mortifying his flesh. They hit upon one very aggravating expedient for carrying out their praiseworthy purpose. On feast-days—every one of which was punctually kept at the Monastery of Cartigione—when the good Brothers of Mercy fared sumptuously, Beppo was condemned to assist at the banquet in the capacity of reader instead of *convive;* that is to say, he, whilst the good

brothers were luxuriously feasting, had to read aloud the
Martyrology of the saints, with the agreeable prospect
that, after dinner and dessert had been consumed, he
(Beppo) might regale himself with dried pulse.

After a while Giuseppe Balsamo determined upon a
singular revenge, one that would inevitably insure his
expulsion from the monastery. The Brothers of Mercy
were seated at the well-furnished table: Beppo was commanded to read the Martyrology. He obeyed, merely
substituting for the names of the saints, as he went on,
those of the most notorious harlots and rogues in Palermo.
At first little heed was given to the reader; the brothers
were absorbed in their dinner. Presently, however, their
attention was aroused, and though scarcely at first believing their ears, it was but a minute before they
realised the blasphemous obscenity in which Beppo
Maldetto was indulging. Rising as one man, they
rushed on the impious wretch, pummelled him to their
hearts' content, and, that done, thrust him out of the
monastery.

The charily-benevolent uncle was again had recourse
to. Well, since the priestly vocation did not suit Beppo,
what was to be done? what other attainable course of
life would he make choice of? Beppo believed, or said
he did, that he was the stuff of which great painters
were made. He should like to try his chance in that
profession. This was agreed to. Palettes, pencils,
colours, were supplied him; and it is said he really
showed some skill in the art. But the results were un-
satisfactory. The labour required was intolerable, and
it would be long, very long, before that labour would
meet with substantial reward, if ever. Meanwhile he,
being expert at imitative writing, might eke out his
scanty income by a judicious use of that skill. Beppo,
in his *coups d'essai* in the line, flew at very small game.
He forged orders of admission to places of public amusement, sold them for a trifle to his scamp acquaintances,
carrying on his very little game with success for a considerable time. His flight as a forger was not, however,

long in soaring to a very dangerous pitch. He was in
the habit of visiting a notary at Palermo, in whose office
he found a will. He determined to substitute a forged
one in its stead; intending to go shares with the community—a religious house—in whose favour the fictitious
will was made. That pretty project fell through, and
though no tangible proof of his guilt could for the time
be obtained, he was strongly suspected to be the forger.
He was besides believed by many persons to have murdered a canon of the church. This accusation appears
to be void of foundation. Be that as it may, Sicilian
soil, especially that of Palermo, was fast becoming too hot
for the soles of his feet. It would be prudent to seek
in other lands the opportunity of mounting the social
ladder which was denied him in the land of his birth,
and with his "usual blubbery impetuosity," to quote
Carlyle's disparaging phrase, he resolved not to defer his
departure. But he had not a feather to fly with. Charily-
benevolent uncle would not assist him; and he finally
hit upon a scheme for bringing a goldsmith of the name
of Marano under contribution. Beppo had already acquired a reputation for skill in chemical divining-rod
conjurorship, and betaking himself to the goldsmith,
who assuredly must have had the organ of credulity
largely developed, persuaded him that he (Beppo) had
discovered, by means of the divining-rod, where a large
sum of money was buried, at some distance from Palermo.
It could not, however, for some cabalistic reason, be secured by the person who made the discovery, though he
(Beppo) might be present and assist at the disinterment
of the treasure. He would conduct Marano to the spot
on two conditions: first, that he should be paid sixty
ounces of gold down, and be afterwards entitled to one
moiety of the discovered treasure, the sixty ounces to be,
of course, deducted from his share. The goldsmith consented: the gold ounces were handed over to Beppo, and
at the time agreed upon—about midnight—he and Marano betook themselves to the indicated spot. Scarcely,
however, had they commenced digging, when they were

set upon by six of Beppo's dissolute acquaintances, transformed into devils by the aid of goat-skins and burnt cork, by whom Marano was severely belaboured and driven off. The goldsmith at once comprehended that he had been duped, and vowed to take signal vengeance on the robber. Beppo would not have been much frightened had Marano merely threatened proceedings at law; but the goldsmith wore a stiletto, and would not, Beppo knew, hesitate to use it should he find or make a fitting opportunity. That was a peril to flee from in all haste, and Beppo forthwith took leave of his native land, omitting in his hurry to hand over to his assistant devils the stipulated price of their services. Beppo subsequently expressed sorrow for the oversight, but it is not said that he paid the money.

Joseph Balsamo visited in succession Naples and Germany. At Westphalia he made the acquaintance of the arch-quack Germain, who declared that he was several hundred years old, a fact due to his possession of the secret of manufacturing the Elixir Vitæ. We next find Joseph Balsamo at Alexandria, Rhodes, Malta—we have at least his word for it that he sojourned for some time at those places—certainly he passed through Venice, and took up his temporary abode at Rome. In the Eternal City he met with Lorenza Feliciano, a Roman donzella of surpassing beauty. She was in a very humble sphere of life, of keen capacity, not encumbered with moral impedimenta, and Beppo, readily appreciating the advantages of possessing such a wife, married her.

Balsamo had supported himself meantime in precarious splendour by the sale of beauty-water, wine of Egypt, and love-philtres: he had acquired a knowledge of the properties of cantharides in the laboratory of the apothecary to the Monastery of Cartigione. His genius soon embraced a wider range. He claimed the power of restoring youth to the aged, and by means of his beauty-water of conferring loveliness upon the plainest of womankind. Hundreds, chiefly of the richer classes, Italian counts and countesses, French envoys, Spanish grandees, believed in Balsamo, and were deservedly well fleeced for their folly.

Beppo now assumed the title of Marquis Pellegrini, and by whatever motive induced, returned to Palermo, was recognised by the vindictive goldsmith, and cast into prison on account of that trifling matter of the sixty ounces of gold. It would have been heart-breaking to have such a future—a future, he himself remarked, "immense, but confused"—compromised by so paltry an incident. His wife, the Countess Seraphina, so rapidly has the lovely Roman servant-girl risen into the highest social regions, procured his liberation. She had fascinated the son of one of the most powerful princes of Sicily, and the enamoured youth, meeting with the advocate of the goldsmith in the hall of the Palace of Justice, so outrageously bullied and beat him, that the President could only rescue the advocate by running to his aid in person. The end was that the prosecution was dropped, and the marquis allowed to leave the prison and Palermo.

The chronology of the life of this eccentric quack—whom M. Alexandre Dumas, with the help of plaster-of-paris, has coarsely modelled into a grotesque likeness of a man of profound science, of wondrous occult knowledge, in direct communication, moreover, with the unseen world of spirits—is obscure and involved. It would seem to be in 1772 that Balsamo paid his first visit to England, and was reduced to such straits as to accept a job from one Dr. Benemio to paint his house. The genius of Balsamo did not lie in that line. He smudged instead of painting the doctor's house, and was refused payment. There is a scandalous anecdote told of Balsamo and the doctor's daughter, an only child; but the whole story may be apocryphal. Balsamo persistently denied that he had been in England previous to 1776. It must have been some other Italian of the name of Balsamo, who undertook to paint the doctor's house, and who corrupted his daughter. Beppo's denial is not, however, of much value. His cool effrontery in challenging the most patent facts was something marvellous.

At all events, his reappearance in Germany with the charming Donna Seraphina is indisputable as his success. Seraphina gives out that she is between sixty and seventy years of age, and that her youthful loveliness has been preserved by the miraculous beauty-water. The sale of that and the Vin d'Egypte goes up amazingly. Count de Cagliostro—Beppo's new and last title—boldly professes to communicate between the living and the dead, and by means of a magic-lantern and phosphorus blue fire, produces effects which leave no doubt upon the minds of thousands that a true miracle-worker, a real prophet, has again visited the earth. It was not only the ignorant, credulous, vulgar, whether rich or needy, whom this audacious quack imposed upon: Lavater—honest, simple-minded Lavater—believed to a certain extent in Cagliostro.

, "Cagliostro," wrote Lavater, "is a great man, a man such as few are, in whom, however, I am not a believer. Oh that he were simple at heart, and humble like a child; that he had feeling for the simplicity of the Gospel and the Majesty of the Lord! Who were then so great as he? Cagliostro often tells what is untrue, and promises what he does not perform; yet do I in nowise hold his promises to be deception, though they are not what he calls them."

O Lavater, prince of physiognomists, once at all events so esteemed, it is passing strange that that broad gross nose, those cunning eyes, blubber lips, and blubber brains, big as the head was, could impose upon you; that one of the most audacious and ignorant quacks that ever breathed could impose himself upon you as a man of divinely-inspired genius!

We may well ask, if Lavater so esteemed Cagliostro, what must the multitude have thought of him? The answer to that query is not doubtful. Cagliostro was literally worshipped, and the offerings of the faithful poured in upon him in such abundance that he rolled in riches; the splendour of his equipages could be scarcely rivalled by reigning princes. If he passed a statue of Christ, the audacious charlatan would dart a recognising glance at the figure and exclaim, as if to himself, "Ah! there you are; we meet again."

The reputation of beauty-water and wine of Egypt was on the wane; it was necessary to invent some new imposture. The scoundrel faculty was still Cagliostro's, and in full vigour. He met with a book, as it is said, written by George Cofton, an Englishman, which professed to detail the mystic ceremonies of Egyptian Masonry. The hint sufficed. The Count de Cagliostro at once gave out that he was a native of Medina, and had been educated at Mecca,—the holy city of the Mahometans, where he was known by the name of Acharat. The prophets Enoch and Elias, who were the true founders of Egyptian Masonry, had visited him in the body, and commanded him to go forth and initiate the western nations into the sublime redeeming mysteries of which they gave him the key, nominating him at the same time Grand Kofti of the order.

But for irrefragable proof of the fact, it would be incredible that so gross an imposture could impose upon a child. Its success was prodigious. Lodge after lodge was established, and the worship of the new Messiah—which he in substance proclaimed himself, and was proclaimed to be—grew in fervency and faith. Disciples would remain for hours together prostrate before Joseph Balsamo, wrapt in contemplative awe and wonder. His wife, the loveliness of whose face the hand of time had begun, though lightly as yet, to lessen, shared in these divine honours. She was the Archpriestess, the female Kofti of the order. The precious pair had discovered a mine of wealth which seemed inexhaustible.

Still the best-laid schemes of mice and men gang aft a-gee. The Grand Kofti's pretensions to miraculous curative powers, his knowledge of the future, the pretence that Egyptian Masonry was a divine institution, were fiercely ridiculed by two exceedingly powerful bodies, the physicians and the priests. The physicians of Strasbourg refused to allow Balsamo to practise in that city. He nevertheless maintained his popularity by distributing gratis amongst the poor medicaments which were very possibly as beneficial in many cases as any to be found in the pharmacopœia of orthodox practitioners. The priests awaited their time.

The first fatal step leading directly to the abyss he was urged to take by Madame La Motte and the Cardinal De Rohan. These two worthies were deeply implicated in the world-known swindle of "The Diamond Necklace." A brief summary of that pretty business must be given in order to follow appreciatively the gyrations of this prince of mountebanks.

Boehmer, a jeweller of Paris, was seized with the ambition to produce the most splendid diamond necklace ever known, and, after infinite trouble, a vast outlay, and the incurrence of a large debt, Boehmer obtained thirty diamonds of the finest water, and all matching in size. The necklace was a *chef-d'œuvre*—that was conceded. The price Boehmer hoped to obtain for it was the enormous sum of 30,000*l*., and even that amount would scarcely clear the cost of the splendid toy. Boehmer had some reason, or pretended he had some reason, for believing the Sultan would purchase the necklace for presentation to his favourite Sultana. The Sultan declined the offer, and Boehmer solicited Marie Antoinette, Queen Consort of Louis XVI., to buy it. Her Majesty peremptorily declined to do so. She remarked, England being then at war with France, "that they had more need of line-of-battle ships than of diamond necklaces." Boehmer was in despair.

Hope shone upon him from an unexpected quarter. There lived at the time in a sort of loose contact with the French Court, one Madame La Motte, or Comtesse de la Motte. She was the Court Milliner, and had apartments in the palace. She claimed to be the descendant in a left-handed way of Henry II., king of France. This lady knew all about the necklace from Madame De Campan, one of the queen's ladies of honour. The apparently wild notion struck her that she might obtain the incomparable necklace for herself. The plan matured in her scheming brain was feasible enough. It might fail, certainly, but the prize was a splendid one. She would try, at any hazard.

The Comtesse de la Motte went to the house of the dejected jeweller, and asked for a private confidential interview. It was eagerly conceded, we may be sure, and Boehmer learned to his intense delight that the queen was desirous, very desirous, of possessing herself of the necklace, but could not venture just then to ask the king for so large a sum of money for such a purpose. Her Majesty would, however, give her acknowledgment for the 30,000*l.*, to be paid as soon as it would suit the queen's convenience to liquidate the debt. Boehmer was overjoyed. With the queen's written acknowledgment of the debt, he would have no difficulty in pacifying his rapacious creditors, for a time at all events. A paper was drawn out, setting forth the purchase by the queen of the necklace for 30,000*l.*, with which Madame La Comtesse left the jeweller's.

She returned the next day with the document, which was subscribed "Bon—Marie Antoinette." Upon receipt thereof, Boehmer handed over the necklace, which, poor dupe, he was never destined to see again.

Boehmer's creditors were satisfied for a time. Still even "Bon—Marie Antoinette" was no available substitute for current coin of the realm, and the bewildered jeweller was again importuned by hungry creditors. Boehmer declared that he must apply directly, personally, to the queen. Madame La Comtesse required time —it was, in fact, indispensable that she should obtain it. On finding Boehmer obstinately resolved upon speaking to the queen, she hit upon another expedient to pacify him till such time as it would no longer signify to her that the gigantic fraud she had perpetrated should be discovered.

The Prince Cardinal De Rohan, a weak, vain man,

was in disfavour at Court. The queen had conceived a dislike for him, and he would do any thing to regain her favour. Upon that foundation our clever Countess set to work. She waited upon the Prince Cardinal, said she was intrusted with a very delicate mission, but the personage who sent her was sure that her confidence in the Prince De Rohan's honour would not be misplaced or abused. "Mission from whom, Madame La Motte?" "From Her Majesty, Queen Marie Antoinette." "The Queen Marie Antoinette!" The Cardinal was lifted off his legs; could not believe that he heard aright.

Madame La Motte explained, ran glibly over the necklace affair, said her Majesty could not at that moment advance so immense a sum, that she feared it would come to the King's ear that she had made so imprudent a purchase, if Boehmer were not satisfied—and that she would feel herself under the greatest obligation if he, the Prince De Rohan, would settle with the jeweller, holding at the same time her written security for repayment.

The gudgeon bit eagerly at the glittering bait. Madame La Motte was to assure her Majesty that his entire fortune was at her disposal, and that she should suffer no annoyance about the matter. Madame La Motte left the Prince, charged with a message to Boehmer, who was to wait upon his Eminence without delay.

The Prince had not a very large sum in cash by him, but his bond, with interest payable at short dates, would no doubt be accepted by the jeweller's voracious creditors. No question of that. The dates of payment are arranged, and the affair appears to be settled.

Yes; but, Ciel! how is this? M. Le Prince Cardinal De Rohan is received as coldly by Marie Antoinette when he presents himself at Court as ever. Not a smile—not the faintest sign of recognition of his devotion in taking upon himself so tremendous a responsibility. Swiftly the months roll away; the time for paying the first instalment—only fifteen thousand pounds—is close at hand.

The Cardinal Prince cannot by possibility raise the money. He communicates the melancholy fact to Boehmer, causing thereby a terrible derangement of the jeweller's system (*dérangement terrible dans ma physique*). Madame La Motte, whose wings are not yet plumed for flight, is sent for. She readily obeys the summons, and having heard all the perplexed prince and jeweller have to say, coolly informs them that if they make any application to the Queen, or speak of the affair so loudly that a rumour may reach the King's ear, her Majesty will deny that she has ever had the necklace, that "Bon—Marie Antoinette" is not her handwriting. At this astonnding announcement the Cardinal and jeweller were seized as with vertigo, dancing, whirling, stamping about the apartment like two madmen, as for the time they probably were.

Madame La Motte succeeded in pacifying them, though with much difficulty. If they would wait for a short time, all would be well.

M. Le Prince Cardinal sullenly acquiesced; but determined to consult the great magician, the inspired prophet, Count de Cagliostro. He had already consulted him by letter, and had received certain cabalistic utterances in return, which afforded him no guidance or comfort whatever. Cagliostro must come to Paris, so that he might be consulted personally. The prophet complied—consultations were held with him by the Prince Cardinal and Madame La Motte; the lady, no doubt, laughing merrily *sous cap*, at the oracular interpretation of his doings and sayings in reference to the diamond necklace, which the soothsayer solemnly enunciates.

The jeweller, who has no faith in Cagliostro, and very little in Madame La Motte, determines to get at once to the bottom of the mystery. To do that it is only necessary to write a plain note to the Queen, and make sure it is delivered into her own hands. He does that, and the astonished Marie Antoinette, carrying it at once to the King, a terrible uproar ensues. M. Le Prince De Rohan is arrested as he enters the palace—*lettres de cachet* are issued against Madame La Motte and the poor Count de Cagliostro, who really had nothing to do with the diamond-necklace swindle. No matter for that, he is seized by command of Chesney, and thrust with Monsieur the Prince Cardinal and Madame La Comtesse La Motte into the Bastille.

In that dismal prison Cagliostro remained during the winter months through which the criminal process instituted by the Procureur du Roi dragged its slow length along. Cagliostro's defence at the final hearing was conclusive, and as it incidentally helped to fix upon Madame La Motte the guilt of the transaction, that lady threw a brass candlestick at the charlatan's head. De Rohan was acquitted, Madame La Motte sentenced to be branded, scourged, and banished the kingdom. Joseph Balsamo was discharged with a caution, and thrust out of the Bastille without a franc in his pockets. Neither the Chevalier de Chesney, by whom he had been arrested, nor De Launay, the Governor of the Bastille, could recollect any thing about the jewels and money he had about him when pounced upon by the King's officers. It was not likely they should.

The imprisonment and trial of Cagliostro did not in the slightest degree lessen him in the estimation of his dupes. It had the reverse effect. Many houses in Paris were illuminated on the night of his liberation, and the following laudatory lines were composed in his honour:

> " De l'ami des hommes reconnoissez les traits :
> Tous ses jours sont marqués de nouveaux bienfaits ;
> Il prolonge la vie, il secourt l'indigence ;
> Le plaisir d'être utile est sa seule récompense."

Escaped from the Bastille, the Count and Countess Cagliostro made the best of their way to England—to London. There they reaped a plentiful harvest for about two years. Then disputes, difficulties innumerable beset them. A number of persons, a Miss Fry amongst them, alleged that the new Messiah had swindled them; and set a pack of hungry attorneys upon the unfortunate Count. Latitats, ne exeats, warrants were showered upon him thick as hail—never had he had such terrible enemies to deal with: all the conjuring in the world was thrown away upon them: the only elixir vitæ which they believed in was the golden elixir which purchases beef and bread. The Count was thrown into the King's Bench prison, but was ultimately liberated by his wife. She was still remarkably handsome.

Some time afterwards Cagliostro published a " Letter to the English people." After depicting himself as one of the most persecuted of human beings, he gave a list of the persons by whom he had been traduced and wronged, showing that he was under the special protection of God, who avenged him of his enemies even during this life:

" The woman Blenay, whom I had loaded with benefits, and who afterwards delivered me into the hands of two scoundrels, is dead.

" The Demoiselle Fry, who unjustly persecuted me, is dead.

" Broad, friend and spy of the Demoiselle Fry, is dead.

" Dunning, the Demoiselle's counsel, is dead.

" Wallace, my counsel, who betrayed his trust, is dead.

" The magistrate at Hammersmith, who issued a warrant against me and my wife, is dead.

" Crisp, Marshal of the King's-Bench prison, who cheated me out of fifty guineas' worth of plate, is dead.

" Villeton, who betrayed my confidence, is dead."

Other parts of the letter are composed of similar rubbish. It produced no effect. Cagliostro's star had long since culminated, and was soon to disappear beneath the horizon. He left England, and by the persuasion of his wife betook himself to Rome. There he was suddenly arrested, whilst engaged in pretended tricks of *diablerie,* by the officers of the Holy Inquisition, and imprisoned in the Castle of Saint Angelo. There was a long tedious trial. Cagliostro was found guilty of being a Freemason and sentenced to death. Pope Pius VI. commuted the sentence to imprisonment for life. He was transferred to the fortress of San Leu, where he died, in 1795. His wife was condemned to pass her life in a convent.

THOMAS, MARQUIS OF WHARTON AND MALMESBURY.

"The Marquis Wharton," wrote Swift, "is a presbyterian in politics, and an atheist in religion. He is a bad liar and a bad dissembler, and yet these are the qualities upon which he chiefly prides himself. He has largely profited by lies, but the ends attained were chiefly to be attributed, it appears to me, to the frequency of them rather than to any art they displayed. . . . . He will go to the castle-chapel and pray on his knees, and will afterwards talk —— and blasphemy at the chapel doors. . . . . He bears the gallantries of his lady with the indifference of a stoic, and thinks them well repaid by a return of children to support his family without the fatigues of being a father. . . . He has been frequently heard to say that he hoped one day to make his mistress —(Swift's is a much coarser expression)—that he hoped to live to see the day when he might make his mistress a bishop."

I should not have dared to transcribe these pages had they not been written by a dignitary of the United Church of England and Ireland. They refer to the time when Lord Wharton filled the office of Viceroy of Ireland. Swift's character of the marquis must be largely discounted, for very cogent reasons. Swift had solicited, in very abject terms, to be appointed chaplain to his excellency; his petition was refused: Lord Somers afterwards endeavoured to persuade the lord-lieutenant to bestow a vacant bishopric upon the choleric dean. "No, no, my lord," was Lord Wharton's reply, "we must not prefer or countenance such fellows. We have not character enough ourselves." Swift avenged the taunt after

his own peculiar fashion. If the marquis had his slan-
derers, he was, on the other hand, amply provided with
pen-champions. His character and administration were
glorified beyond measure by Sir Richard Steele in the
Spectator, some say by Addison. One can hardly decide
which dose must have been the most nauseous, Swift's
coarse abuse, or Steele's adulation—treacle laid on with
a trowel. The treacle, I should think.

This diversely-painted gentleman—a great man in
his time—was the son of Philip, Lord Wharton, who
distinguished himself on the Parliamentary side in the
civil war. Thomas, Lord Wharton, was born in 1640.
He sat in several parliaments during the reigns of Charles
and James, each the second of those inodorous names.

Lord Wharton cared little, I apprehend, whether a
Papist or Protestant filled the throne of England. But
he had a keen eye for the future; he could discern, earlier than most men, indications of the rising sun upon
the political horizon, and devoutly spread his mat and
turned his face thitherward, whilst less clear-sighted men
remained in a state of mental dubiousness as to whether
the sun, spite of those faint pencillings of light, would
rise in that quarter. They might be the indications of a
false dawn! Who knew? Thomas, Lord Wharton, wrote
the draft of an address to the Prince of Orange, praying
him to come over with his army for the deliverance of an
oppressed people; and Thomas, Lord Wharton, was one
of the first to welcome the Dutch deliverer when he
landed at Torbay.

The patriotic keen-sightedness of the noble lord had
its reward. He was made a privy councillor and appointed Controller of the household, by William and
Mary. He had well deserved these preferments if only
for writing the doggrel song of "Lillibullero," which, it
is said, had more effect in exciting the people to stand by
"Protestant ascendency" than all the printed paper issued
during the controversy—more effect than the acquittal
of the seven bishops, and the butcheries of the "bloody
assize" presided over by Judge Jeffreys. It is supposed

to be sung by an Irish papist, the occasion being the appointment, by James II., early in 1688, of General Dick Talbot, created Earl of Tyconnel, to the Lord-Lieutenancy of Ireland. The refrain " Lillibullero, bullen a-la," were the watchwords, it is said, which the Irish Catholics used in 1641, when massacring, in vindication of the divine right of Charles I., the Protestant parliamentarians. There is a rough, telling humour about it:

> " Ho! broder Teague, dost hear de decree,
>   Lillibullero, bullen a-la,
>   Dat we shall have a new Deputie,
>   Lillibullero, bullen a-la,
>   Lero, lero, lillibullero, lero, lero, bullen a-la.
>
> " Ho! by Shaint Tyburn, it is de Talbote,
>   Lillibullero, bullen a-la,
>   And he will cut de Englishman's troate,
>   Lillibullero, bullen a-la.
>
> " Dough, by me shoul, de English do prate,
>   Lillibullero, bullen a-la,
>   De laws on their side, and Christ knows what,
>   Lillibullero, bullen a-la.
>
> " But if a dispense do come from de Pope,
>   Lillibullero, bullen a-la,
>   We'll hang Magna Charta and dem in a rope,
>   Lillibullero, bullen a-la.
>
> " For de good Talbot is made a lord,
>   Lillibullero, bullen a-la,
>   And with brave lads is coming abroad,
>   Lillibullero, bullen a-la.
>
> " Who all in France have taken a sware,
>   Lillibullero, bullen a-la.
>   Dat dey will have no protestant heir,
>   Lillibullero, bullen a-la.
>
> " Arrah: but why does he stay behind?
>   Lillibullero, bullen a-la,
>   Ho, by me shoul, 'tis a protestant wind,
>   Lillibullero, bullen a-la.

> "But see Tyrconnel is now come ashore,
>   Lillibullero, bullen a-la,
> And we shall have commissions galore,
>   Lillibullero, bullen a-la.
>
> "And he dat will not go to de Mass,
>   Lillibullero, bullen a-la,
> Shall be turn out and look like an ass,
>   Lillibullero, bullen a-la.
>
> "Now, now de heretics all go down,
>   Lillibullero, bullen a-la,
> Be Christ and St. Patrick the nation's our own,
>   Lillibullero, bullen a-la.
>
> "Dere was an old prophecy found in a bog,
>   Lillibullero, bullen a-la,
> Ireland shall be ruled by an ass and a dog,
>   Lillibullero, bullen a-la.
>
> "And now dis prophecy is come to pass,
>   Lillibullero, bullen a-la,
> For Talbot's de dog, aud James is de ass,
>   Lillibullero, bullen a-la."

This song became a great favourite with the "Orange Boys," and was for many years the usual musical accompaniment to the glorious, pious, and immortal memory of King William, who saved Ireland from Popery, slavery, brass money, and wooden shoes. There is something in the smack of the song which suggests Thackeray's incomparable Battle of the Shannon; one the production of a cleverish man, the other the creation of caustic genius.

Appointed Lord Lieutenant of Ireland, Lord Wharton entered upon the duties of his high office with much dignity and *éclat*, made an excellent speech to the Parliament, dwelling especially upon the necessity in the interest of vital religion to be united amongst themselves, or the encroachments of Popery could not be successfully withstood. Like George IV., the Marquis Wharton, when before the footlights, could tread the stage with dignity. It was a great relief to him when the hour came to throw off his masquerade robes. It is indisputable that he indulged in low company, disreputable intrigues, and was never happier than when engaged in such *délassements*.   There is much of coarse truth in one of Swift's scathing sentences: " Wharton, by force of a wonderful constitution, though past his grand climacteric, whether he walks, whistles, swears, or talks, acquits himself beyond a Templar of three years' standing."

His Excellency used to delight in playing the part of a sham Haroun Alraschid—this was a favourite pastime of several Irish viceroys—disguised in various ways, and thus made himself familiar with the slang and slander of Dublin.   Like the Dukes of Rutland and Bedford in after years, the Marquis Wharton created more than one knight during his drunken orgies, which it was not always possible to abolish by money gifts, or a good place.   The members of the English aristocracy of those days, of whose inner life casual glimpses have been obtained, cut but a sorry figure; but they are very imposing, magnificent even, in their robes and coronets.

The Marquis Wharton pre-eminently so.   Deprived of his viceroyship by Queen Anne, how grandly he came out as a flaming patriot; with what a noble vehemence did he do battle for the maintenance of the Protestant faith—the Protestant succession!   "Hail, Star of Brunswick!" would be the appropriate tag to his Orange speeches. He declaims well too, and sometimes, in behalf of constitutional freedom, propounds schemes of national polity breathing a brave, clear-visioned spirit.   He was often witty.   That was a capital *mot* of his when Sir Robert Walpole, to swamp a hostile majority in the Lords, created twelve new peers at one batch.   " Pray, may I ask," said Lord Wharton, when the new peers had taken the oaths and their seats,—"pray, may I ask if these noble lords intend to vote singly, *or by their foreman ?*' Yes; Thomas, Marquis of Wharton, has an imposing appearance when seen *en grand tenue;* and who, after all, could brave the ordeal of curious eyes when *en déshabille?*   Very few, I suspect, and certainly not the noble marquis.

He had not only reconciled himself, but had rendered

such efficient services to the Government of the day, that he was created *Duke* of Wharton, an earnest, if the King's patent was to be believed, of greater honours to come. He was not destined to clutch those honours. His only son, Philip, a youth of wonderful promise, in whom all his hopes and projects for the future were centred, contracted an imprudent marriage before he had reached his sixteenth birthday, and gave other indications of a wild, untameable character, which convinced the newly-created duke that the hopes he had indulged in with respect to his son's future career never would be realised. That conviction killed Duke Thomas Wharton. He died within six weeks of the rash marriage of his son. The duchess did not long survive him. Philip, Duke of Wharton, succeeded to the title and estates, worth sixteen thousand pounds a-year. The next paper will relate the sad but instructive story of the young man's life, to whose erratic career the foregoing slight sketch is but preliminary.

PHILIP, DUKE OF WHARTON AND NORTHUMBERLAND.

THE character and career of Philip, the last and most gifted of the Wharton family, was thus epitomised by Pope. I omit some lines which might, in this refined age, offend by their plain-spoken truthfulness:

> " Wharton, the scorn and wonder of our days,
> Whose ruling passion was the lust of praise:
> Born with whate'er could win it from the wise,
> Women and fools must like him, or he dies;
> Though wondering senates hung on all he spoke,
> The club must hail him master of the joke.
>
>   *   *   *   *   *
>
> Thus with each gift of nature and of art,
> And wanting nothing but an honest heart;
> Grown all to all, from no one vice exempt;
> And most contemptible to shun contempt;
> His passion still, to covet general praise,
> His life, to forfeit it a thousand ways;
> A constant bounty which no friend has made;
> An angel-tongue which no man can persuade!
> A fool, with more of wit than half mankind,
> Too rash for thought, for action too refined:
> A tyrant to the wife his heart approves;
> A rebel to the very king he loves;
> He dies, sad outcast of each church and state,
> And, harder still! flagitious, yet not great."

There is *nerve* in these lines, but assuredly they have been much overrated. Pope was a great master of antithesis and rhyme, to the exigencies of which he seldom scrupled to sacrifice truth. The broad, salient outlines of Philip Duke Wharton's character have been hit, in the above quotation, truthfully enough; yet was there an underlying current of goodness in Philip Duke of Wharton, which was constantly welling up from his inner nature, which such a dry-bones formula as Pope could not understand, and much less appreciate at its true value. Alexander Pope was, perhaps, the most melodious rhymer the world has known; he could set off commonplaces in very brilliant colours; but, as I before remarked, no original *thought* of his dwells in the memory of mankind.

There was a soul of goodness in this young, highly-gifted man that shone through all the darkening follies to which he stooped after familiarising himself with the "highest" society, and finding nothing there. I propose to show this by the dry record of his erratic, kaleidoscope career.

Philip Duke Wharton was born in 1699. He early displayed very remarkable powers of both memory and perception. His father caused him to be educated at home. As it was hoped and believed that, in the fulness of time, he would prove himself a stern champion of the Protestant faith, he was sedulously instructed by a French Huguenot in the Genevan Calvinistic creed, by way of a preparative, I must suppose, for a milder religious regimen. The astute intellect of the youth revolted against the doctrines of the murderer of Servetus, and it may be for a time, under the influence of reaction, confounded Christ with Calvin.

Breaking impetuously loose from the ligatures of a false conventionalism, this heir to a dukedom and a revenue of sixteen thousand pounds per annum, having fallen or fancied himself in love with a pretty damsel, and poor as pretty, a daughter of Brevet-General Holmes, married her before he had reached his sixteenth birthday. The nuptial knot was tied by a Fleet parson.

This marriage, blotting out the brilliant future, as they believed, which had been anticipated for him by his father and mother, was, as I have before observed, fatal to both the duke and duchess—a catastrophe which for a short time overwhelmed the impulsive young nobleman with remorseful grief. The unequal union proved to be a most unhappy one, from no fault of the girl-wife, whose personal attractions were enhanced by sweetness of temper, but solely in consequence of the husband's fickleness of temperament. Constancy to one object, one purpose, was foreign to his nature. To this strongly-developed passion for change Philip Duke of Wharton mainly owed the wreck of his life.

The guardians appointed under his father's will endeavoured to carry out the testator's views relative to his son's education. They sent him to a religious establishment at Geneva, and with him his French Huguenot tutor. They could not have taken a more unwise step. Utterly disgusted with the cold, hard formalism which prevailed, the young duke fled to Lyons, in which city the indignant tutor, for whom he had conceived a strong antipathy, joined his rebellious pupil.

The Chevalier Saint George, the Pretender, as he was called, then resided at Avignon. The boy-duke purchased a handsome stone-horse, and sent it, with his respectful duty, to the son of the exiled Stuart. The present was accepted, and he received an invitation to Avignon. He went thither, was very graciously received, and created Duke of Northumberland! He returned to Lyons, but remained there a few days only. He would visit Paris, and shake off the incubus of his hated tutor for ever. His farewell epistle is characteristic. He had some little time previously purchased a bear's cub, which he made a pet of for a while, and on leaving made a present of to the Huguenot, in the following complimentary terms: "Being no longer able to bear with your ill-usage, I think proper to be gone from you. However, that you may not want company, I have left you the bear, as the most suitable companion in the world that could be picked out for you."

Arrived at Paris, Duke Philip further committed himself with the Stuart faction. The queen-dowager was residing at Saint Germains, and there the madcap duke hastened to pay his disloyal respects. He professed unbounded devotion to the banished dynasty, and equally intense abhorrence not only of the Hanoverian Elector, but of his religious creed; he himself being determined, as soon as he attained his majority, and was consequently freed from the yoke of guardians, to embrace the Roman Catholic faith. Meantime, and until he came into possession of his estates, he was cruelly hampered for money. The queen-dowager was delighted at the accession to the ranks of the Pretender's partisans of so considerable a personage as the Duke of Wharton,—one too who, it had been sedulously given out, was destined to be one of the most eloquent champions, as his father had been, of the Protestant succession. Questioning him as to his immediate wants, the gay nobleman said two thousand guineas would be of great service to him just then. The queen-dowager, though startled at the largeness of the sum, promised to oblige him if she could raise the ways and means. Her Majesty endeavoured to borrow the requisite amount of the French king, but it was low-water just then in the Bourbon exchequer; her friends among the French noblesse, who had long bled pretty freely, could not assist her; and her Majesty was at last fain to pawn her jewels. Philip Duke of Wharton had no sooner obtained the money than he plunged into the wildest excesses, and openly proclaimed his devotion to the fallen dynasty of the Stuarts. Earl Stair, the English ambassador, choosing to look upon his conduct as the effervescence of a giddy youth suddenly emancipated from control, remonstrated mildly with him. The earl hoped, nay, he was sure, that he would follow in the steps of his excellent father, that pillar of the Protestant succession. "Thank you, my lord," was the quick-witted retort: "thank you, my lord, for your good advice. You, too, had an excellent father, and I hope you will follow *his* example." This was a home-thrust, Earl Stair having ratted, influenced by not the most creditable motives, from the Jacobite principles of his family.

A very scapegrace was this young duke. Women,

wine, gaming, filled up the measure of his daily, nightly life. The young Bacchanal would never reach middle, much less old age; that was early apparent. Seated at the ambassador's table, he would call a servant, bid him go to the Earl of Stair, and tell him he was about to drink his health as the greatest rogue and traitor in existence. Similar messages were sent to several distinguished guests. No serious notice was taken of them: they were but ebullitions of strong youthful spirits heated by wine, and signifying nothing.

A young English Jacobite medical student studying in Paris, excited by loyalty and liquor, amused himself by smashing the English ambassador's windows, for the sufficient reason that they were not illuminated on the night of the 10th of June. This enthusiastic proceeding brought the student to grief. He was arrested, imprisoned, fined. Duke Wharton resented this conduct on the part of the authorities. The loyal student should have been rewarded, not punished, for his patriotic zeal. He determined to break the ambassador's windows himself; but as the work required to be done quickly, if unpleasant consequences were to be avoided, he asked the help of an Irish colonel in the Pretender's service to assist in the good work. The colonel declined. He was willing to make war upon the Hanoverian usurper, but not after the novel fashion of breaking his ambassador's windows. The young nobleman would not be baulked; he performed the loyal duty himself; was discovered, arrested, and set free at Lord Stair's request. Much must, we all understand, be forgiven a young duke of large intellectual promise, and soon to be in possession of sixteen thousand pounds a-year!

Philip Duke Wharton's adhesion to the Stuart interest was a mere romantic caprice; unsustained by the slightest principle or conviction. Some years subsequently, in consequence of his mad extravagance, he accepted a loan of two thousand guineas—the same amount which he had borrowed of the Queen Dowager—of the Chevalier Saint George. Not long afterwards an English

gentleman remonstrated with him upon the folly, if
nothing worse, of linking his own to the fallen fortunes
of the expelled dynasty. "My dear fellow," said the
duke, "I have pawned my principles to Gordon, the
Pretender's banker, for a considerable sum, and till I
can repay him I must be a Jacobite. When that is done,
I will return to the Whigs."

The two thousand guineas did not last long. His
guardians inexorably refused to forward funds to him
whilst he remained in Paris in connection with the Jacobite faction; and the metropolis of Paris rapidly becoming too hot to hold him, he was fain to leave for
England. It must, however, be remembered that his
money was not all, or nearly all, squandered in debauchery.
The young nobleman never rejected an appeal to his
generosity, his charity; but his gifts, alms-deeds, were
bestowed indiscriminately. The borrower or beggar
might or might not be worthy of relief; Philip Duke of
Wharton and Northumberland recked not of that. It
was this weakness of character to which Pope alludes in
the line:

"A constant bounty which no friend has made:"

a failing, no doubt; a failing, if you will, but one which
leant, if not at a very decided angle, to virtue's side.

The young duke did not remain long in England.
The society of his duchess had no special charm for him,
and he went over to Ireland. His incipient fame—if I
may use such a phrase—had preceded him there. The
fierce Orange peers of Ireland could not have heard of
his backsliding at St. Germains, or they would never
have voted him of age, he being not quite eighteen, and
caused him to be summoned to take his seat in the
House by the titles of Earl of Rathfarnham and Marquis
of Caltheron. The angel-tongue—admitted by Pope to
be an angel-tongue—there first found worthy audience.
His speeches were admirable both in matter and method,
and being untainted in the faintest degree with Jaco-
bitism made him an immense favourite.

Philip Wharton turned his "privilege of Parliament," so to speak, to profitable account. He insisted that the tenants upon his Irish estates should pay him their rents; and when it was objected that he was not of age, he indignantly exclaimed, "How dare you say I am not of age, when the Parliament has declared that I am!" Impudence succeeded, as impudence rarely fails to do, especially when backed by a title—a ducal title too!

Ireland soon became unpleasantly warm, and our young duke left the Emerald Isle for England. Not that his person was in danger; but constant "dunning" is unpleasant, and a too mountainous accumulation of even debts of honour a harassing burden to bear, especially when a fierce Whiskerando—many Whiskerandos —looking pistols or small-swords at your choice, demand practically, highway fashion, your money or your life. Duke Philip was ready enough with his pistol, as he proved upon two occasions; but though he came off unscathed, he could not but reflect that the pitcher which goes often to the well will probably be broken at last, and he wisely banished himself from the land of duelling *par excellence.*

Upon attainment of his majority, the duke took his seat in the English House of Peers. He forthwith plunged into virulent opposition to the Ministry of the day. Not only by speeches in the House that were much admired, the merits of which, as they were very inadequately reported, we must take upon trust; but by pamphlets and speeches at public meetings, he assailed the policy and principles of the Government. His defence of Atterbury, Bishop of Rochester, whom it was proposed to visit with a bill of pains and penalties, was considered a masterpiece of eloquence and argumentation. The vehemence of his opposition was inflamed by practical discomfiture. He strove to stir up the City of London, became himself a citizen wax-chandler, and started a periodical called *The True Briton.* All would not do. The stars in their courses fought against Philip Duke Wharton. Still, so greatly varied were the young noble's powers, that only by his own acts could he suffer irremediable defeat. His wild, extravagant course of life knew no pause or ebb; and finally his creditors appealed to the High Court of Chancery, who appointed a receiver of the rents of his estates, allowing him twelve hundred pounds a-year till his debts were liquidated. There is an anecdote in connection with him and Dean Swift, the rancorous assailant of his father, which is worth transcribing: Wharton was recounting, with excellent glee, the many glorious frolics he had enjoyed. The Dean said, keeping his dignified countenance admirably, " You have had some capital frolics, my lord, and let me recommend one to you. Take a frolic to be virtuous: take my word for it, that one will do you more honour than all the other frolics of your life."

His infant son, the Marquis of Malmesbury, died about this time of small-pox. To him it was a most afflictive visitation. In his rage he attributed the death of his child to the duchess his wife. He left the mother and son in the country, and gave her strict injunctions, as he was leaving for London to attend his parliamentary duties, to remain there with the child. The duchess, for some reason or other, disobeyed his injunction, and followed her husband with their son to London, where small-pox was prevalent. The baby Marquis of Malmesbury sickened and died of that terrible disease. The duke never again spoke with his wife, who died broken-hearted on the 14th of April 1726.

Duke Wharton foiled, baffled in his ambitious projects, mainly, as I have said, by himself, bade adieu to England, for ever as it proved. First he betook himself to Vienna, no doubt as an accredited agent of the Pretender. What may have been the precise nature of the mission intrusted to him is not known. It produced no result. Thence this restless knight-errant proceeded to Spain. His arrival in Madrid caused a great sensation. The Spanish Ministry sent special messengers to the Court of St. James's, with the positive assurance that Duke Wharton was the bearer of no political mission from any prince or power whatever, and that if he were, it would not be listened to. Upon receiving this message, a warrant was issued under the Privy Seal for the arrest of Philip Duke of Wharton, and the bringing him to England.

This act was clearly beyond the power of the English Privy Council. Duke Wharton refused to obey it, and appealed to the Spanish Court for protection. It was granted, and a rupture with England in consequence was with some difficulty avoided—postponed more correctly.

Whatever might have been the volatile young duke's primary purpose in visiting Spain, it was soon eclipsed and set aside by a more potent influence. He fell desperately in love with a Miss O'Byrne, one of the ladies of honour to the Queen of Spain. Miss O'Byrne was the daughter of an Irish colonel in the service of Spain, who had been some years dead; and the widow's sole dependence was a pension bestowed upon her by the Spanish Queen.

Duke Wharton formally proposed marriage to the beautiful maid of honour. The offer was accepted, upon condition that the Queen's consent should be obtained. The Queen peremptorily refused her consent. Such a union, she said, would be one of the maddest acts imaginable; the duke being possessed of a mere pittance of revenue, his rank considered. The duke being this time really in love fell into a deep melancholy, which culminated in a low, lingering fever, that soon threatened a fatal result. The Queen, moved by the lover's sufferings and danger, sent him a message to the effect that he must adopt means of restoring himself to health (the duke had obstinately refused medicine or curative aid of any kind), and she would consider more favourably of his request. Upon receipt of the message the lover rallying what strength he had left, caused himself to be conveyed to the palace, and falling upon his knees before the Queen, implored her to give him leave to marry Miss O'Byrne, "or order him to die." The Queen relented, consented to the marriage, which she persisted they would both bitterly repent of, and Miss O'Byrne became a few weeks afterwards Duchess of Wharton and Northumberland.

The happy pair set out for Rome, where they passed the honeymoon. It was there the Pretender conferred the Blue Ribbon upon the Duke of Northumberland.

The infirmity of human nature is such that bliss, the purest, most ecstatic, soon cloys; and by way of change Duke Wharton decided upon varying the entertainment of life by a little fighting—the substitution of war's alarms for the endearments of marital love. He left Rome for Barcelona. I conclude that writs of "ne exeat" did not issue from the Roman courts, as the duke's departure was unopposed. Privilege of English peer or parliament would not, it may be presumed, have availed in the Eternal City.

Arrived in Spain, the duke lost no time in offering his services to the Iberian king. He was willing to assist in the siege of Gibraltar, war having broken out between England and Spain. The offer was accepted. Philip Duke of Wharton fought in the Spanish ranks, received a severe wound in the foot, and wearied of a service in which neither glory nor gold could be obtained, rejoined his duchess at Rouen, France. There they lived in sumptuous style for a considerable time upon the strength of his ducal title and blue ribbon. His levées at last becoming inconveniently crowded by tailors, butchers, grocers, by milliners and dressmakers to the duchess, the unthrifty lord quitted Rouen in a hurry, leaving his equipages and horses behind to be equally shared amongst his angry creditors. It was at this time, I believe, though some memoir-writers make the date much later, that the duchess applied to be reinstated in her former post of personal attendant upon the Queen of Spain—a request which was graciously complied with. Her Spanish Majesty had a great regard for the poor duchess.

In Paris the conduct of Philip Duke of Wharton and Northumberland was marked by the same *étourderie* as before. I only have space to quote two illustrative incidents. A Portuguese Knight of the Order of Christ, with whom he had casually formed acquaintance, invited him to a high festival to be given in honour of the Founder of the Order. Duke Wharton, whose wardrobe was neither ample nor brilliant, said he should be delighted to accept the invitation, but was ignorant of the *costume* worn upon such occasions. "Oh, a black-velvet suit," said the Portuguese knight; "that would be most appropriate." "Ah, well, yes; but I have no black-velvet suit, nor do I know a tailor in all Paris in whom I could confide to furnish me with one." "That, my dear Duke, is easily arranged. I will send my own tailor to you. He is a very honest fellow, and will fit you admirably." Philip Duke of Wharton and Northumberland consented; the suit of black-velvet was made, sent home, and his grace honoured the festival with his presence. Shortly afterwards the tailor presented his little bill. "What is this for?" asked Duke Wharton. "For the suit of black velvet." "Honest man," said his impudent grace, "you mistake the matter very much. You must carry this bill to the Chevalier R——; for be pleased to understand that whenever I put on another man's livery, my master always pays for the clothes."

Lord M—— (the proper names are only initialed in the memoirs of the eccentric duke), Lord M——, a wealthy, easy-going young Irish Peer, had made the Duke's acquaintance at St. Germains, and, like all who came within his influence, was charmed and delighted with his wit, humour, his conversational powers generally. One night when it was growing late, his grace drove up to the hotel where the Lord M—— was staying, informed his lordship that he was engaged in a very important affair, and begged the loan, for a few hours, of his lordship's coach, coachman, and lackeys. "Certainly." The young Irish Peer was only too happy to be able to oblige his grace. "And now," said the Duke, when it was announced that the coach was in readiness, "I have an additional favour to solicit, which is, that your lordship accompany me." The complaisant lord agreed, and away drove the coach. The first step in the important business was to hire a coach, hunt up seven or eight of the musicians attached to the opera, who were mostly gone to bed, hire their services for the next twelve hours upon liberal terms, seat them in and upon the hired coach, and drive off toward St. Germains. Lord M—— must have been considerably mystified, but all was made clear upon the arrival of the party at the Castle of St. Germains. The musicians were ordered out, and commanded to serenade some young ladies with whom his grace had been flirting. Well, there was a good laugh; perhaps the good-natured Hibernian's laugh was the loudest; and since the musicians were there, it was determined to wake-up a friend of the duke's, one Mr. R——, an English gentleman, who resided near the village of Poissy. The addition of two trumpets and a kettle-drum would make the band complete. These were, with some difficulty, procured, and the jubilant party set out for Poissy, which quiet village was thrown into a state of astonishment and alarm by the visitors with their trumpets and kettle-drums. Mr. R—— was in doubt, when he found the strangers intended honouring him with a visit, whether he had not better bolt at once. Philip Duke of Wharton reassured him—the intruders were liberally regaled, and the affair terminated so far very pleasantly. Yes; but there was the score to pay for the musicians, &c. When it was called for, the sum-total was seen to be something upwards of twenty-five Louis d'or. "My dear Lord M——," said his Grace of Wharton—"My dear Lord, I have not a single franc. Do you pay this time, and if I have ever an opportunity I will requite the favour."

This wretched feverish life grew wearisome, and the Duke's next freak was to enter a monastery near Paris, with the avowed intention of becoming a monk. Writers, favourable to his grace, assert that he entered the monastery not with any intention of becoming a monk—though, before he could marry Miss O'Byrne, he had been obliged formally to embrace the Catholic faith—but for quiet study, especially to finish a translation of Telemachus, which he had begun, but would certainly never finish whilst dwelling amidst the Babel of the world. What a consummate hypocrite—no, not exactly hypocrite—what a consummate actor this gay man must have been! The monks were so struck, so edified by his exemplary devotion, that they attributed it to a direct interposition of Heaven, and the miraculous virtues of the sacred relics which enriched and glorified the monastery. The religious whim is of brief duration,—Telemachus flung aside and forgotten; the wandering Duke betakes him again to Rome, where he has another meeting with the Pretender, who advises him to draw nearer to England, where his services might shortly be required. He accordingly revisits Paris, and having received his half-year's allowance—six hundred pounds—which would go but little way to satisfy the claimants on his purse in that city, he sails down the Seine as far as Rouen. His creditors there had been arranged with, but, as remembrance of the past precluding credit obliged him to pay ready money for all he required, the six hundred pounds dwindled away with alarming rapidity, and he was before long financially out-at-elbows, his ragged servants literally so.

In the meantime a bill of indictment for high treason had been preferred against him, the evidence relied upon in support of which being that he had fought against his sovereign at the siege of Gibraltar.

Neither king nor ministry were disposed to deal hardly with him. An English gentleman of position had an interview with the Duke at Rouen, to urge him to make his peace with the English Government. A letter to the monarch or the minister would suffice, all past offences would be condoned, and he would come into immediate possession of his estate, which now realised, after the interest of mortgages had been paid, 6000l. a-year. Philip Duke of Wharton, though in an almost destitute condition, peremptorily refused to do so. He would starve sooner than make submission to the Elector

of Hanover.   There was sterling metal, after all, in this
Protean man.

Raising, by some means or other, sufficient funds, he
went to Orleans, and thence dropped down the Loire to
Nantz.   There he embarked with his ragged retinue for
Bilboa (they were he said recruits for the King of Spain),
and soon afterwards joined his regiment at Lerida.

His originally fine constitution was fast breaking up.
He was dying in the thirty-second year of his age.
Mineral waters in the mountains of Catalonia effected a
partial rally of his worn-out system—a partial, fleeting
rally.   Becoming worse, he again had recourse to the
mineral waters, was seized with one of his frequent
fainting-fits in an obscure Spanish village, and would
have died utterly destitute of the necessaries of life but
for the compassionate charity of some monks of St. Ber-
nard, who had him conveyed to their convent, where he
died on the 11th of May 1731, uncheered by the presence
of one friend or relative.   He was buried in the monks'
cemetery.   Dying without issue, the title was extinct,
and has not since been revived.   The duchess survived
to a great age.   She died in London, in February 1777,
and was buried in St. Pancras churchyard.   This is the
Duke Wharton's epitaph, as written by Lord Orford:

"He amused the grave and dull by throwing away
the brightest profusion of parts and witty fooleries on
scamps.   With attachment to no party, though with
talents to govern any party, he exchanged the free air of
Westminster for the gloom of the Escurial, the prospect
of King George's blue ribbon for the Pretender's; and
with indifference to all religion, this frantic lord, who
had lampooned the Archbishop of Canterbury, died in the
habit of a Capuchin."

BAMFYLDE MOORE CAREW.

THIS very erratic gentleman, and something more, could boast of quite a distinguished lineage. He was descended from the Carews, an ancient Devonshire family, several members of which had rendered important services to the country. His father was the Rev. Theodore Carew, Rector of Bickley, near Tiverton, and a gentleman of fortune independent of his rectorship.

Bamfylde Moore Carew was born in July 1693. His advent was celebrated with great rejoicings; the baptism which made him a child of God was one of the most expensively got-up affairs—with reference to the quality of the company assembled, and the entertainment provided —that had been known for many years in the west country. The Honourable Major Moore and the Honourable Hugh Bamfylde, the sponsors, who pledged themselves, rash enthusiasts, that their godson should renounce the devil and all his works, the vain pomp and glory of this world, with all covetous desires of the same, contended which of them should have the honour of conferring the first baptismal name upon the boy. The gentlemen tossed for choice. The Honourable Hugh Bamfylde won, and the honoured child was named Bamfylde Moore Carew.

Many years had not passed before the lad was seen to be a youngster of mark and likelihood. He was handsome, lithe, active, brave, and made satisfactory progress at the High School, Tiverton. He acquired the usual smattering of Greek and Latin, and it was hoped by his fond parents that he would prove a shining light in Israel—rise possibly through the gradations of the cleri-

cal hierarchy to the lucrative dignity of a Bishop; the
Carews having considerable Parliamentary interest, which,
if reinforced by respectable talent, might lead to spiritual elevation as great as that.

The youth was clever—that could not be disputed; but,
his juvenile fancy was much more excited by the scarlet
coat of the hunter than the black cassock of the priest.
The High School at Tiverton was, in a provincial sense, a
highly aristocratic establishment. Only young gentlemen,
of rank and (prospective) wealth were admitted. Those
fortunate youths, Carew being of the number, kept a
first-rate pack of hounds. The most eager in the chase
were, Carew, John Martin, Thomas Coleman, and John
Escot. These promising youths were attached to each
other by similarity of taste and sentiment. Genial lads
were they, and if not pleasant in their lives and lovely in
an orthodox sense, were seldom divided in their progress
through this vale of tears and thieves. All four were
" youths of condition."

A sporting farmer, who used to hunt with the High-
School hounds, rode to Tiverton, and gleefully announced
that a fine deer with a collar round its neck, which had,
no doubt, strayed from some neighbouring gentleman's
park, was quietly feeding in a wood no great distance off,
and would afford capital sport. The temptation was irresistible. Carew, Martin, Coleman, and Escot were
quickly in their saddles, and, guided by the sporting farmer, soon found the deer. They had a famous run; none
the less diverting to such madcap youths, that it led
through corn-fields nearly ripe, causing great damage to
the crops. The deer was caught, killed, and generously
offered to the farmer, who declined the gift. The engraved collar proved the animal to be the property of a
Colonel Nutcombe, a gentleman who would pursue to the
ends of the earth any one that stole, shot, or hunted his
deer. The best thing to be done was to send the carcass
to its owner; and a cart coming that way, the driver was
requested to carry the dead deer to Colonel Nutcombe's
house.

This honesty—shall we call it honesty?—did not prove
to be the best policy. The carter knew the young men
by sight and name, though he spoke and behaved himself as if he had never seen one of them before. The successful hunters returned home in high spirits—had a rare
jollification—and, no doubt, slept soundly.

The afternoon's amusement did not, coolly considered,
bear the morning's reflection. The desolated corn-fields
through which they had galloped with such reckless
speed, suggested painful misgivings. And how about
the cantankerous colonel? Supposing he should find
out who it was that killed the deer? The youthful
sportsmen entered upon their morning scholastic duties
with nothing like the alacrity of spirit with which they
had sprung to saddle on the previous afternoon.

Their gloomiest forebodings were realised. Colonel
Nutcombe, accompanied by a number of farmers whose
corn had been trampled down, arrived at Tiverton early
in the day, the treacherous carter identified the culprits,
and the head-master assured the angry complainants
that, notwithstanding the social condition of the offend-
ers, they should be visited with condign punishment directly the duties of the day had terminated.

This was hint enough. Knowing quite well what
condign punishment at the High School meant, the terrified young men—taking brief counsel together—determined to be off, whither precisely they neither knew nor
greatly cared. The world was all before them, Providence their guide.

They did not go far. The first stage on the journey
of independent, vagabond life was a short one—about
two miles only. Being hot and thirsty, and, as I have
said, near harvest-time, the truants concluded to rest and
refresh themselves at a secluded alehouse—Brickhouse
was its designation.

As it chanced, there was high-festival held there that
day by a company of gipsies, male and female, presided
over by their celebrated King, Clause Patch, the venerable father of eighteen children, and of grandchildren,

great grandchildren, past counting. The four truants were invited to partake of the feast, and very heartily they enjoyed the ducks and fowls,—caring nothing that they had not been paid for, except by the trouble and risk of stealing them. There was music and dancing through the night. Some of the Princesses, the old scamp King Clause Patch's daughters and granddaughters, I should suppose, were very pretty—altogether a most delightful party. Carew, Martin, Coleman, and Escot proclaimed their determination to join such a jolly community. The proposition was laughed at. The gipsies could not believe the "house-dwellers" to be in earnest. But when the request was next morning repeated, and with evident earnestness, it was agreed to with some reluctance; and after solemn warning that the bond once signed would be indissoluble, the four truant youths were accepted as members of the Bohemian fraternity, the oaths of implicit obedience to the King or Queen were administered, and they were initiated into the secrets of the confederated vagabonds.

His Majesty Clause Patch addressed them upon their duties to society—*the* society of course. It was a highly philosophic lecture. The community into whose ranks the young men had voluntarily enrolled themselves was very ancient, and dated from time immemorial. Like all other professions, its members lived by the necessities, the passions, and the weaknesses of their fellow-creatures. Vanity, greed, and compassion are the chief characteristics of the human race: these constituted the stock-in-trade of the Bohemian people, and would prove, as long as diligence and fidelity to the rules of their ancient community prevailed amongst them, an unfailing mine of wealth;—with much more to the same effect.

Carew, with whom in this paper I have chiefly to deal, was enchanted. To escape from the plodding pedagogic world into such a free-and-easy society, was a wonderful relief. To be sure, the luxuries of life were, or would be, in his legitimate possession in far greater abundance than could ever be obtained by gipsy wiles, whether of cajolery or theft. But what of that? Was there not the charm of clever cheatery—the romance of robbing by brain-skill—not vulgar violence? and were not stolen pleasures proverbially the sweetest? Besides, had he not sworn fidelity to the laws of the community? Should he break his oath? Not for the wide world! He was a youth of much too tender conscience for that!

A superior education helping young Carew, he soon distinguished himself amongst the fraternity. Travelling through the land, he found many occasions of proving how exactly he fitted the groove, as we should now say, into which Fortune had shunted him. His first *coup d'essai*, on a considerable scale, occurred near Taunton, Somersetshire. A Mrs. Musgrave, residing near that city, was, he heard, possessed of a notion that a large treasure was buried somewhere in her grounds. Carew wrote to the lady stating that if she would grant him an interview, he doubted not that he would be able to point out the exact spot where the treasure could be found. Credulous Mrs. Musgrave would be happy to see the writer, who waited upon her, capitally made-up for the part. Having gravely listened to what she had to say, he required a few days to consult the stars. The time expired, he again waited upon the lady, and informed her that gold and silver in large quantities would be found buried under the laurel-tree, in her garden; but as her fortunate planet would not rule till that day week, and at a particular hour, it would be useless to make the search till then. Mrs. Musgrave was delighted, and gave substantial proof of her gratitude by presenting the astrologer with twenty guineas!

It would seem that Carew had not yet entirely succeeded in casting off old-world prejudices. The grief for his absence of the old folks at home, proved by their constantly advertised offers of reward to any one who would bring them tidings of the lost one, at last so prevailed with him that after about eighteen months' absence he suddenly presented himself at his father's house. He was welcomed with exuberance of joy; not a word of reproach was uttered; the neighbours far and near sympathised with the delight of the worthy rector: the church-bells were rung, both in Bickley and the adjoining villages. Parties of pleasure were got up almost every day for the gratification of the recovered truant; and no means were neglected to wean him from the vagabond career he had madly embraced.

All would not do. He fell ill; not with active malady, but from sheer weariness of spirit. A gipsy girl, who had seen and spoken with him, said in an alehouse, where they were talking of him, that he would not be long with the house-dwellers. "He would either die or go back to the gipsies."

The gipsy girl was right. Carew suddenly left his home without leave-taking, and made his way to the alehouse where he had first joined the Bohemian community. Several persons were there waiting, in expectation of his coming. He was at once conducted, as a prisoner, to head-quarters, where there was sitting a general assembly, on a minor scale, of gipsies, presided over by the queen, the wife of Clause Patch, who could not attend by reason of illness. This was fortunate for Carew, who made a very ingenious defence in excuse of his temporary backsliding; and it was voted that he should be re-admitted, after renewing his oath of allegiance and submitting to the usual penance—a severe one, stripes not a few, and smartly laid on. The queen, however, old Clause Patch's fifth or sixth wife, and a young woman, was so pleased with the culprit's speech, and the manner of its delivery, that she remitted the punishment, reminding him, however, that a second falling away from his sworn duties could not be forgiven, and the penalty, certain to be inflicted, however ingeniously he might try to conceal himself, would be Death! She then sent him "on the forage," remarking that, with his abilities, he might soon make up for lost time by adding largely to the common stock.

Carew may now be looked upon as fully committed to a life of vagabondage. He embraced it boldly; made-up cleverly as a shipwrecked sailor, and in that guise levied contributions. So well did he gloze the melancholy story of his sufferings, on his way to Kingsbridge, Devonshire, that he transmitted a sum to his or her majesty which fully condoned the offence of which he had been guilty in the opinion even of those who thought he had been let off too cheaply.

At Kingsbridge he met with his old schoolfellow Coleman. He too had abandoned the Bohemian fraternity for a time; but soon wearyiug of being penned up in towns and houses, had returned to his allegiance. This was not qnite true. He had been induced by threats and promises—his own wishes inclining him to yield—to rejoin the formidable brotherhood. He had not the luck of Carew, though he reached head-quarters but a day or two after his friend had been dismissed scatheless. He did not find such favour with her majesty as Carew did; he was not so handsome perhaps, nor possessed of such a wheedling, flattering tongue. At all events, he was rudely flagellated, told that he had been most mercifully dealt with, and warned to deserve the mercy which had been extended to him, by diligence and strict fidelity, lest a worse thing befal him. He was then dismissed on the forage, but was not successful, and expected every day to receive a message from Clause Patch, if he were well enough to resume the duties of his kingly office, if not from his brimstone Jezebel of a wife, requiring his presence at head-quarters, to account for the disgraceful paucity of his contributions to the general stock, that is, to the luxurious sustenance, in a gipsy sense, of the king, queen, and royal family—a large number, as we have seen, of voracious mouths to feed. Poor Coleman was quite cast down—disconsolate; cursing, there can be little doubt, the day when the chasing of Colonel Nutcombe's deer led him indirectly into such hopeless captivity. It was pleasant enough, no doubt, to camp out in the fields in fine summer weather, live well and lazily; but there were terrible drawbacks. Gipsy life was one of those things which did not improve upon intimate acquaintance.

Carew condoled with his friend; observed that it was no use to kick against the pricks, and that he would help him from the superfluity of his own gains to make a decent contribution to the royal treasury. With that understanding the young men—once on the first form at Tiverton High School—journeyed on in company, meeting with but poor success, till they reached Totnes. There the dreaded message from the queen was received by the unhappy Coleman. His services were required in another part of the country, where it was hoped and expected he would be more successful. He left with a heavy heart. Carew never saw him again; and heard, not long afterwards, that he had left the Bohemian world for the land where gipsies cease from troubling, and the weary are at rest. How he died, whether by the visitation of God or of man, was a moot-question with Carew. The secrets of the gipsy camp are never spoken of even amongst the fraternity themselves.

Carew, having used up for a time, and in that locality, the shipwrecked-sailor dodge, attired himself in a plain neat rustic suit, and assumed the character of a broken-down honest country farmer, from the island of Sheppey, whose grounds had been overflowed, and his cattle drowned, leaving himself, a wife, and seven helpless children in a state of destitution. The distressed-farmer device was very successful.

I might fill a volume with anecdotes of successful cheating, accomplished mainly by clever personation, by a master in the art; but as there is much to tell more creditable to this eccentric gentleman, and opening a curious leaf in the colonial history of England, which few are familiar with, I can only transcribe a few of the more salient of Carew's exploits.

Justice Hull, of Exmouth, was the terror of gipsies. Like the late Sir Peter Laurie with reference to distressed widows, Justice Hull had determined to put the gipsies down. They were his abomination; and he was especially desirous of getting hold of that disgrace to his family, with some members of which he was well acquainted,—Bamfylde Moore Carew. This was a challenge which Carew determined to accept. He waited upon Mr. Justice Hull,—who had more than once conversed familiarly with him at Bickley Rectory,—in the character of a miller, whose mill and entire substance had been consumed by fire, owing to the carelessness of an apprentice. Carew was severely cross-examined by the justice, but he stood the ordeal well; the magistrate was couvinced he had to do with a very honest straight-forward miller, a myth in popular estimation at that time; but Justice Hull was free of vulgar prejudice, and presented Carew with a guinea, for which he received an acknowledgment in full by the next day's post:

"MY DEAR MR. JUSTICE HULL,—I am afraid that when with you I did not sufficiently express the gratitude I felt and feel for your very liberal donation, yesterday, of a guinea, to the plain, straightforward, honest miller, who had lost his entire substance by a fire, caused by the carelessness of an apprentice; and who had a sick wife and nine children to support. The honest miller now repeats his heartfelt thanks for your generosity to the gipsy,

"BAMFYLDE MOORE CAREW."

Just fancy the rage of Mr. Justice Hull, who was suffering from gout too, upon reading Carew's audacious note!

At a Mr. Portman's, near Blandford, Hants, who was entertaining a large party, he presented himself as an old withered crone, wearing a dirty mob-cap, a high-crowned hat, a ragged kirtle, and carrying a little hump-back child on his back; two others he held, one in each hand. Pinching the hump-back baby, he made it squeal so as to set the dogs barking furiously. A woman servant came out to bid him begone, as the uproar disturbed the ladies. "God bless their ladyships," whined the old woman, "I am the unfortunate grandmother of these poor children, whose dear mother, and all she possessed, was burnt at the dreadful fire at Thirkton." This was reported to their ladyships, who feeling for them, the old woman with her brats were brought into the house, and a plentiful meal was set before them. Some of the gentlemen-guests came into the kitchen. One said, "Where do you come from, old woman?" "From Thirkton." "The devil take Thirkton! There has been more money collected for Thirkton than Thirkton is worth." Nevertheless all the gentlemen and ladies gave bountiful alms-gifts to the old woman from Thirkton. As in the case of Mr. Justice Hull, Mr. Portman received a letter the next day, acknowledging the generous gifts of their ladyships and gentlemanships, signed "B. M. Carew, *alias* an old grandmother from Thirkton."

Carew assumed the character, and made use of the language of Edgar in Lear as "Mad Tom," whom the foul fiend pursues, and so on. This part, cleverly sustained, netted much money.

One Mr. Jones, a very benevolent gentleman of Ashton, near Bristol, hearing from his brother, who was present at Mr. Portman's, how the company were so cleverly bamboozled, declared that he never could be deceived by Carew, whom he knew very well, or more correctly speaking, had known very well by sight. Error, Mr. Jones; Carew pillaged you just three times in one day. First as an unfortunate blacksmith, with sooty face and singed apron, who had lost his little all by a fire. A few hours afterwards, by a poor cripple, paralysed, totally, on one side, and partially on the other, who was desirous of trying the Bath waters, but afraid he should never reach that city for want of charitable assistance. Later in the day, an unfortunate tinner called. He had been disabled by damp and hardships suffered in the mines. Mr. Jones received, in due course of post, the written acknowledgment of B. M. Carew, *alias* the blacksmith, the cripple, and the tinner.

Several times during his predatory rambles, Carew called at the Bickley Rectory, so disguised, so exactly imitative in voice and manner of the character he personated, as to completely deceive his own father and mother. "Avowing myself to be a gipsy, they always questioned me respecting their son: 'Had I seen or heard of him? Was he alive?' I could scarcely restrain my tears whilst with them," said Carew, "and when I left and was unobserved, wept bitterly. But there was no escape from the thraldom to which I had subjected myself,—more than that, I did not really wish to escape."

Carew's cleverness was highly appreciated by the Bohemian brotherhood; and at the annual general assembly for the year, he was honoured with a seat on the right of the king and queen, a distinction which was understood to be the precursor of higher honours to come.

Instinctive love of freedom, independence of action—the consciousness that he was playing the part of a fool and madman—rendered Carew at times very restless under the galling yoke. When in one of these moods, he met, at Dartmouth, John Escot, another of his schoolfellows, whom that gipsy orgie at the Brick House had demoralised, ruined. Escot was wretched, but dared not make the slightest endeavour to emancipate himself. The bare thought of incurring the displeasure of the ubiquitous community in which he had enrolled himself, brought on a fit, or caused him to break out into a cold perspiration.

Carew's bolder spirit infused some courage into his. There was a vessel at Dartmouth, bound for Newfoundland, commanded by a Captain Holdsworth. Why not take passage in her, and if their resolution held to free themselves of, literally, the Egyptian bondage under which they groaned—groaned by fits and starts in the case of Carew—go on to the plantations in America?

They agreed to do this; the berths were engaged; but at the last moment Escot's heart failed him, and Carew sailed without his companion.

Arrived in Newfoundland, Carew diligently explored

the island, studied its commercial and especially its fishing capabilities, and was, it would seem, casting about
for a trade-opening, so to speak, for his restless energies,
when an emissary from the gipsy-king arrived out, with
a summons requiring Carew's immediate return to England. Escot, who, under the influence of some vague
fear that he might be suspected of conniving at the
escape of Carew, though final escape was just impossible,
had informed Clause Patch that Carew had sailed for
Newfoundland, adding that he (Carew) thought he might
reap a rich harvest there for the benefit of the brotherhood. This excuse was unanimously scouted. It was
settled in general council that the field in which the
richest harvest could be reaped by Carew was in England.
Carew was told by the messenger that if he obeyed the
summons, there was nothing to fear, especially as he had
a good friend at court—alluding, no doubt, to the gipsy
queen. Escot was under a cloud and strictly watched.
A charming predicament that hunt of the deer in the
woods and fields about Tiverton had brought the first-
form scholars of the High School of that town into!

Carew obeyed the gipsy chief's mandate, and sailed in
a "fish-schooner" for Hull, where, after a perilous voyage,
he safely landed. It is evident, though the subject is
slightly alluded to, that Carew's peace was soon made.
The queen probably stood his friend. It is certain that
he was quickly despatched on the forage. He was very
successful, his knowledge of Newfoundland standing him
in good stead. His principal prey were just then the
masters of vessels trading to Newfoundland and the ad-
jacent countries. With them he was a master-mariner,
whose ship, of which he was chief owner, had been cast
away, and all hands on board drowned except himself.
Cross-examined, he evinced such a minute knowledge of
the localities, that no doubt was entertained of the truthfulness of his story—so that he had soon money and lots
of it in both pockets. He must have found richer dupes
than sea-captains; and I cannot help thinking have shamefully choused the Bohemian royal family, or he could

ucver have shown out in such splendour as he did shortly after his visit to Newcastle-upon-Tyne—in a new phase. There his constitutional flightiness manifested itself after a novel fashion. He must needs fall in love—serious, not Bohemian love—with a Miss Geary, the daughter of an apothecary long established in the town. The young woman was both beautiful and amiable—superlatively so, looked at through the Claude-Lorraine glasses of Carew's lover-eyes. He made the damsel's acquaintance, wooed her ardently, and knew that he had made a favourable impression, but was quite aware that if he popped the question in the character of a gipsy—a Christian gipsy we will say—his suit would be at once rejected. Carew represented himself to be the master of a trading vessel— an assertion vouched for by Captain Lewis, of Dartmouth, whose friendship he had gained. The young lady coyly yielded to Carew's pressing importunities; eloped with him; and went with him on board Captain Lewis' vessel, which made a swift passage to Dartmouth, where the loving pair were united in the bonds of holy, legitimate —*not* Bohemian matrimony.

Mr. and Mrs. Carew, travelling in quite grand style— no question that the Bohemian royal family must have been awfully swindled—passed a joyous honey-month. I imagine it must have not unfrequently occurred to the bridegroom that the queen might not prove such a zeal- ous protectress as she had been when this marriage with a charming house-dweller became known, and this would be very soon.

Tut! Taste life's glad moments while you may, is sound Epicurean and Bohemian philosophy. Carew and his bride conformed to it, visited Bath, Bristol, and made quite a sensation in those cities, though in what name they travelled I cannot discover. Presently we find them the guests of an uncle, the Rev. Mr. Carew, a dignified clergyman at Porchester, Hants. The reverend relative conjured Bamfylde Moore Carew to abandon his lawless life, and return to the paths of virtue, at the same time promising that virtue should not be its own, that is, its

only reward.   He would provide for him liberally at
once, and make him heir to all he possessed—a tempting
offer, which the young wife was eager to accept.   The
husband was also, we may presume, strongly inclined to
do so.   But there was a lion in the path.   More than
one peremptory message had reached Carew from the
sovereign to whom he had twice sworn allegiance, and
he had no choice but to submit.   The reverend uncle
would not give him a guinea except upon condition that
he withdrew himself at once from the degrading companionship of gipsies; and his own funds were miserably low.   He must even take to the great highway of
life again, and seize such happy chances as may present
themselves thereon.

Carew chose to reappear on the stage upon this occasion as a distressed clergyman, persecuted for conscience-
sake.   He wore a black loose gown, a large white peruke,
and a broad-brimmed hat.   His pace was slow and
solemn.   He appeared overwhelmed with the shame
which worthy, modest men must feel when compelled
to solicit Christian charity.   When questioned, he, with
much reluctance, informed his Christian friends that he
had filled the sacred office of clergyman at Aberystwith,
in Wales.   The change of government had engendered
scruples of conscience which induced him to resign his
living.   The apt introduction of Latin phrases helped
out the imposture, and his attenuated purse began again
to swell into respectable rotundity.

A very fertile brain was Mr. Carew's.   Reading in a
newspaper that a ship bound for Philadelphia, in which
were many Quakers, was lost, he diligently made himself
acquainted with all particulars, the names of the Friends,
and other essential details, and so furnished, presented
himself as one of the shipwrecked Friends at a large
gathering in London.   He had lost all—everything except the clothes on his back.   No doubt was entertained of the truth of his story, and he was generously
relieved.

The few instances I have transcribed depictive of

Carew's career will suffice to guide the reader to a right judgment upon it as a whole. He was a compassionate man. *Real* misery—and who so quick as he at detecting imposture?—he never failed to relieve to the utmost extent, beyond the extent of his ability. He was often known to sell or pawn articles almost indispensable to his own comfort for the relief of starving, perishing wretches.

Carew's reputation amongst the Bohemian brotherhood was at its height when Clause Patch died. He made a pathetic last dying-speech; the most interesting passage in which to his eighteen children was, that he left them one hundred pounds sterling each—not a large sum, the old reprobate observed, " but improveable."

Two or three weeks afterwards there was a grand assembly in London to elect a new king. The voting was by ballot, and there were ten candidates. Carew being one, made a speech, which carried all before it, so resplendent was it with the brilliant rogueries he had perpetrated. He was unanimously elected king. It was a very jolly meeting. The following verses were sung with uproarious applause. It was, and is, the gipsy coronation anthem:

> " Cast your caps and cares away,
> This is gipsies' holiday;
> In the world look out and see,
> Who so happy a king as he.
>
> At the crowning of our king
> Thus we ever dance and sing;
> Where's the nation lives so free
> And so merrily as we?
>
> Be it peace or be it war,
> Here at liberty we are;
> Hang all Harmanbecks, we say,
> We the Cuffins Queer defy.
>
> We enjoy our peace and rest,
> To the field we are not prest;
> When the taxes are increased,
> We are not a farthing cessed.

> Nor will any go to law
> With a gipsy for a straw;
> All which happiness he brags
> Is only owing to his rags."

Harmanbecks and Queer Cuffins was gipsy slang for constables and magistrates.

The new king refused to be a *Roi fainéant,* sitting at home at ease, supported by the contributions of the community, after the fashion of his royal predecessors. The widow of Clause Patch was deputed to carry on the government during his absence, and he himself went on the forage as before. This was imprudent. He should have remembered that Fortune is fickle, and never more likely to desert her favourite than when he is perched on the top of her wheel. He himself, however, attributed the misfortune that befel him to an act of daring impiety. Finding himself at Stoke-Gabriel, near Totnes, and business in his ordinary line slack and unprofitable, the notion came into his head of waiting upon the parson of the parish to request him publicly to offer up the thanksgiving of himself and the reverend gentleman's congregation for the wonderful preservation of himself, James Hawkins, master mariner, when his vessel, the Rose, was struck by lightning, and all on board perished except himself. The Rose, James Hawkins master, hailing from Newcastle, had been struck by lightning a few days previously, off the Devonshire coast. The report in the local newspapers said all hands were supposed to have perished, though there was a rumour that Hawkins, the master, had escaped by swimming. Upon that hint Carew had acted. The credulous parson, who had read the newspaper account, readily believing that the devoutly-grateful applicant was the real James Hawkins, willingly acceded to his request, and preached a pathetic sermon upon the perils and sufferings of those who go down to the sea in ships. A collection was made at the conclusion of the service, and the proceeds handed over to the pious mariner.

A few days only had elapsed when his Majesty came

to grief in a most unexpected, aggravating manner. He rang the outer-gate bell at the house of Justice Lethbridge, near Barnstaple. He had not the slightest fear of being recognised, so carefully was he disguised, although as Carew he was personally known to the Justice, whom he had victimised, and his butler, John Wigan.

A very civil servant, uncommonly civil, answered the bell, promptly unchained the gate, rechained it as soon as the distressed father of a large burnt-out family had passed through, then politely conducted the unfortunate vagrant, who was already struck with a presentiment that he had made a mess of it for once in his life, to the hall. Retreat being impossible, the only chance left was, to boldly play out his part.

"Ha! good morning, Mr. Carew," said John Wigan, the butler, who opened the hall-door, and who had with him two other men-servants—"good morning, Mr. Carew; we have been expecting you would favour your old friends with a visit. The Justice will be glad, very glad to see you; he has stopped at home on purpose. But," added the chuckling butler, "that you may see his worship, it will be as well to pull off the black patch over your right eye." Suiting the action to the word, "the mocking knave" tore it away with his own hand.

His worship was overjoyed, and first indulging in a hearty laugh at the gipsy King's discomfiture and practical deposition from his high office, consigned him to " the care of his myrmidons," with orders to lodge him safely in Exeter gaol. Colonel Browne, of that city, fully committed him, and shortly afterwards he was tried and found guilty, notwithstanding the ingenious pleas of the counsel retained for the defence by his sorrowing subjects.

"You have travelled, I believe?" remarked the facetious chairman at Quarter Sessions.

"Yes," said Carew, "in Denmark, Sweden, France, Spain, Portugal, Newfoundland, Wales, and some parts of Scotland."

"I have heard some story of the kind before. You

will have to visit a hotter climate than either of those
you have mentioned." Sentence was then pronounced.
He was to be transported to Maryland, America, and
there sold into slavery. A terrible downcome this for
his Bohemian Majesty!

Carew was hurried on board the Juliana, Captain
Froade, whose property he with many other prisoners on
board had become. The practice was for the captain of
a ship to pay so much a-head for his convict passengers,
taking the chance of profit or loss upon their sale at the
plantations.

The Juliana cast anchor, all well, in Miles's river,
Maryland, and the sale by public competition of a prime
lot of English handicraftsmen, labourers, and clerks, was
immediately advertised.

The competition by the planters was rather brisk.
One Griffith, a tailor, fetched a thousand pounds' weight
of tobacco. Prices varied. As to Carew, he persisted
that he could do nothing, was not worth buying at any
price, and could not even dig, though to beg he certainly, as his antecedents proved, was not ashamed.
This modest estimate of his own merits was not believed; his thews and sinews were witnesses against him;
his price ran up to a high figure; the punch went merrily round; Captain Froade had made a profitable venture. The competition for Carew was at last confined
to David Hunter, formerly of Lyme, Dorsetshire, and
one Hamilton, a Scotchman. Finally, they agreed, being
near neighbours, to go halves in him, and had just concluded the bargain when it was discovered that Carew
had contrived, during the uproarious jollity, to slip off
unobserved, and was nowhere to be found. He had fled
to the woods.

He managed to evade pursuit during several weeks,
subsisting upon such wild fruits as he could find, and the
product of occasional nocturnal visits to solitary farm-
steads. He was at last apprehended, and not being able
to give a satisfactory account of himself, was lodged in
prison, preparatory, in accordance with the laws of Mary-

land, to being sold by auction, should no one claim him
before the appointed day.

In this pretty predicament he chanced to hear that
the vessels of Captains Harvey and Hopkins, of Bideford,
had cast anchor in Miles's river. He was favourably
known to them as a Devonshire man, of ancient family.
They sympathised with the unfortunate prisoner, who,
in their eyes, had been guilty of no offence calling for
such cruel expiation. Immediately Carew's message
reached them, they sought him out, listened to his story,
returned to their ships, opened a negotiation with Captain Froade, and finally agreed for the price of his freedom.

· Carew, informed of the generous conduct of the Devonshire captains, after taking some time to consider the
matter, refused to avail himself of the generosity of his
friends. The price insisted upon was exorbitant, and he
was not sure of being ever able to repay Captains Harvey
and Hopkins, to whom such an outlay would, he knew,
be a serious matter. He resolutely declined, therefore,
to purchase his freedom at their cost, and to put an end
to all importunity, informed the magistrate by whom he
had been committed that he was the property of Captain
Froade.

This heroic act of self-sacrifice, for such it really was,
met with a scurvy reward. Captain Froade sent for him,
and immediately he had him on board the Juliana,
flogged him without mercy; then sent for a smith, who
riveted an iron collar, called a pothook, round his neck.
He was, however, allowed to walk the ship's deck during
stated hours of morning and evening. This circumstance suggested to the compassionate captains the means
of procuring his release, and punishing Froade through
the pocket for his cruelty. A boat after nightfall was
rowed, as previously arranged between the captive and
the captains, under the Juliana's quarter; Carew slid
quietly down the side, and his escape was accomplished.
Three months afterwards he was in England, not long
before Froade arrived home.

This was a severe lesson, but it failed to cure Carew of his vagabond propensities. Sir Thomas Carew, to whom he paid a visit with his wife and daughter, offered him a handsome income if he would give up all connection with the gipsies. The answer was an emphatic "No, I will not."

His habitual caution must have forsaken him. Walking on the quay of Exeter with his wife one fine afternoon, he was recognised by a convict-merchant, as such men were called, of the name of Davey. This man was co-partner with Captain Froade, and considered himself very much ill-used—robbed, in fact, by Carew's escape from Maryland. "Ha! ha!" said he, seizing Carew with the aid of ruffians by whom he was accompanied—"ha! ha! You came back from America for your own pleasure; now you shall go back for mine." Spite of a frantic resistance, Carew was carried off to the Phillares brig, Symonds master, lying off Powderham Castle, bound to America with convicts, and waiting for a fair wind.

Carew again landed in Maryland, was sold at a high figure, and again made his escape to England. Misfortune, suffering—stern but true teachers—had at last brought home to him an abiding sense of the worse than folly which had flawed his eccentric, wasted life. He gained a large sum of money by speculations in the lotteries of the day, by which means he propitiated Bohemia, and obtained leave to resign the kingly office and cease to be an active member of the community. His influential connections obtained from the Government a kind of ticket-of-leave for him, and retiring to a modest home which he had purchased in Devonshire, he died there in peace, aged sixty years.

MONSIEUR BLAISE.

Jean Louvois Marie Blaise was an invalided French seaman, established for some years as a barber in the Rue du Bac, St. Malo. He was not an old man in 1804, not much more than forty years of age, when the war between Great Britain and France, lulled for a brief period by the truce of Amiens, burst forth again with augmented fury. Monsieur Blaise was delighted. He had never forgiven Messieurs les Anglais for blowing him up almost literally sky-high on the 1st of June 1782 (Lord Howe's victory). He was then serving on board La Sylphide, frigate or corvette, which had been set on fire by the close broadsides of three English frigates. One only really engaged La Sylphide. But Monsieur Blaise, a worthy fellow in his way, had, as we shall see, an inventive genius. La Sylphide, at all events, caught fire, was soon enveloped in flames, which reaching the magazine, up she blew, and Jean Louvois Marie Blaise remembered nothing more till he found himself terribly scorched and shaken on board one of the cursed ships that destroyed La Sylphide. He had been picked up by one of the frigate's boats, and Jean Louvois Marie could not deny that he was treated with skill and a sort of rude kindness—the insular brigands were not all, quite all, bad. "Certainly not," Monsieur Blaise used to say when descanting upon the catastrophe of La Sylphide, a subject of which he never wearied, if his hearers did—"certainly not; but dam! they had made me pay dearly: but for the protection of the Holy Virgin" (here Monsieur Blaise, who was a devout man, always crossed himself and said an Ave)—"but for the protection of the Holy Virgin—nothing less than the price of my soul."

Monsieur Blaise explained. He had been educated in the profession of a barber, and having, when convalescent, happened to mention that circumstance to a "meesheepman"—he had acquired a perfect knowledge of the English language whilst on board the cursed frigate, he candidly admitted having received that advantage,—having, I say, mentioned that he was a barber *par état* to the "meesheepman," he was forthwith pressed into the English service in that capacity, the English shaver on board knowing better how to handle a handspike than razors, scissors, and curling-tongs. "Thunder of God! it was terrible—the temptation, I mean. Imagine yourself to have at your mercy the very captain of the brigands who had blown up La Sylphide, myself with her, holding him by the nose, whilst the sharpest of razors glided over the *gredin's* chin and throat. But that I did not cease to implore the aid of the Holy Virgin throughout the operation, the devil would have had me,—nothing can be more certain than that; but I shall, *plaise à Dieu*, repay Messieurs les Anglais for all their favours yet before I die."

This grievance is strongly insisted on by the patriotic barber in a *brochure* written from his dictation by "a compatriot of genius," and published at St. Malo in 1816, from which *brochure* are derived all the facts—liberally-coloured facts, I suspect—of which this brief narrative is woven. It may be seen in the public library at St. Malo, and is entitled *Faits divers de l'Histoire Navale de la France depuis* 1793 *jusqu'à* 1810. The chapter which dilates in exalted language upon the cruel illegality of being compelled to act as barber on board the English frigate is headed in capital letters:

"TEMPTATION OF JEAN LOUVOIS MARIE BLAISE."

"At last," continues J. L. M. Blaise, *ancien marin*— "at last Providence favoured me — though I hardly thought it a favour at the time—with a chance of escape from the enemies of France and the human race. The brigands projected an expedition intended to burn and destroy the French merchant-ships anchored near the mouth of the Garonne, under the protection of a battery. It was a night-expedition in boats. It was dark as a wolf's mouth, but the English were guided direct to the ships by the lights they showed. This was imprudent. They should either have been extinguished or screened to seaward. I contrived to slip into one of the boats unnoticed, being dressed exactly like one of the English pirates. Ah! that cost me dear. The boats pulled steadily with muffled oars towards the French ships. The boats were not seen. That in which I was, attacked the ship nearest the land. The French crew, completely surprised, could offer no resistance. She was the prize of the pirates. Suddenly a thought, an inspiration seized me. The wind had suddenly veered about several points since we, at a league's distance, left the frigate, and was blowing towards the shore. The English officer commanding the boat had also observed this, and his maledictions were furious, savage. It had been intended to let fall the sails of the merchantmen, and so get them off without the labour of towing. That would be now impossible. A thought, an inspiration, as I have said, flashed upon me. I glided to the bows of the ship, and with an axe severed the cable that held her. Ah! it was delicious to hear the chorus of goddams which arose from the savage Islanders when they found the ship was driving on shore directly towards the battery, the gunners of which had been roused by the firing on board one of the ships of muskets, pistols, &c.; her crew having, with the heroic courage which animates all Frenchmen, attempted a desperate, but, against such odds, unsuccessful resistance. Meantime the Ville de Nantes was driving on shore. Blue lights were continually thrown up from the battery. It was in a certain sense light as day. The French cannoniers directed their fire at the French ships which the English were towing off—not, I regret to say, with success—I mean, the firing of the French cannoniers was not successful. The English sea-wolves carried off their prey. Only the Ville de Nantes escaped their greedy clutch, thanks to me; and charmingly I was rewarded for it. But of that presently. My young friend says I digress too much. *Eh bien!* The English, seeing they could not hope to carry off the ship, took to their boats, the officer shouting through his trumpet to his men to ' bairand,' which is English for *dépêchez-vous*. All but two obeyed. These were below, and already half drunk with some brandy they had found in the captain's cabin. The English sailor *se soule* (gets drunk) whilst you are looking round. He does not drink; he pours brandy down his throat without tasting it. They had been of course left behind with myself.

" The Ville de Nantes beaches without sustaining much injury. We all get on shore;—the captain and crew of the ship are received with effusive cordiality by the commandant of the battery, his officers, and men. They are warmly congratulated upon their escape from the English scoundrels, but I, who was the instrument of that escape, have handcuffs fastened upon my wrists, and am thrust with the two drunken English hogs into a dark hole where we cannot see, and can scarcely breathe. Vainly I have appealed to the commandant — proudly asserted my quality of Frenchman. ' So much the worse for thee, then,' said Monsieur le Capitaine d'Artillerie Hugon; ' for in that case thou must be a traitor; one of the villanous émigrés perhaps?'

" This was charming, as I have said; very much so. I had certainly done a very fine thing for myself. But it had always been so. I had a strange capacity for running my head against stone walls. My excellent father, Pierre Blaise—*ancien marin*, like myself, *perruquier* also—and a superb artist, thousands of the citizens of Saint Malo will testify, for many years kept an establishment at Numéro 14 Rue du Bac, three doors off to the right from the house in which I carry on business at Numéro 11, ou the *right* of Numéro 14, as I have said and repeat, mistakes having occurred. Numéro 14 is now occupied by a *soi-disant* professor of our art. ' Bichon, late Blaise,' is painted over the door. Bichon, which in itself is right, appropriate, in small insignificant characters—Blaise, which in itself is also in good taste, appropriate, in large blue letters. Halte! My esteemed young friend says I am dictating a long parenthesis which has nothing to do with *L'Histoire Navale de la France*. I submit, and resume.

"My excellent father, Pierre Blaise, *ancien marin* like myself, used to say, 'Jean Louvois Marie Blaise, mon garçon, thou art too impulsive—eccentric ; art always getting thyself into trouble.' Believe me, if thou hadst less generous *étourdissement* in thy composition, it would be better for thee. It is not by the indulgence of philanthropic sentiments that one's bread is buttered—in this world at all events: how it may be *là haut* is another question.' From which parental maxim it resulted that I, looking to my own safety, considering the equivocal position in which I was placed, ought not to have cut the cable of the Ville de Nantes, rescued the ship and crew from the English brigands, and have returned quietly to the English frigate. Such reflections certainly crossed my mind during that terrible night passed in the dark hole with the drunken English sailors. But what will you? It is my nature, my destiny to be self-sacrificing. Still I strongly object to the sacrifice being too great, extending to the perdition of one's life, for example:— one must stop somewhere.

"When day dawned through the crevices of the door I awoke the English sailors, who had slept and snored through the night to my intense disgust and irritation. As soon as they had yawned and stretched themselves into a sort of animal consciousness and vitality, and emptied all three pitchers of water to cool their burning throats, I said, 'My friends'—they were not my friends, the brutes—far from that—but it is well to speak civilly to the devil himself, if you want a favour of him—'my friends, you will be asked if I willingly served on board the English frigate. Without doubt you will say I was forced to serve, under penalty of being hanged. Of course you will say that!' The infernal *scélérats* pretended not to comprehend me. It could not be that they did not understand my English, which is known to be perfect. No, they were resolved to betray, to ruin me. I could see that thought twinkle dimly in their blood-shot, ferocious eyes. A cold shiver ran through my veins!

"It was ten o'clock—bread-and-water were supplied to us for breakfast. I could not eat—the least morsel would have choked me—the English ogres ate mine as well as their own. We were taken before the commandant and other officers. An English lieutenant, a marine soldier—and the evil star of my destiny—who had been taken prisoner, and who spoke French very well, excellently for an Englishman, with a certain guttural accent, of course—the organisation of that people is not delicate enough to give pure expression to the refined and noble language of France. They have not, I am informed, a respectable poet. No one could expect that an Englishman could rival the grandeur of our Molières, our Racines. Ah! I am digressing again, and at a most interesting crisis in the narrative. I beg pardon, and resume.

"The affair of the English sailors was soon disposed of. They were to be sent to the interior as prisoners of war. Then came my turn. 'You say you are a Frenchman,' said the Commandant, in a voice rough as gravel, and a face hard as granite. I felt myself to be on the brink of a precipice. A cold perspiration oozed out at my fingers' ends. 'You say you are a Frenchman. What is your name?' 'Jean Louvois Marie Blaise,' said I, rallying, 'native of Saint Malo, Brittany, perruquier *par état*, marin by profession.' 'In what ship have you served?' 'In La Sylphide; blown up at the great battle off Rochefort, so glorious for the French marine, defeated though we were by the tyrants of the sea. The cypress was full as glorious as the laurel.' 'No *bavardage*, if you please, Monsieur le Perruquier,' said Monsieur le Commandant, with a *brusquerie* of tone and manner, which I may be permitted to say was not polite. 'You were picked up, I suppose, by the enemy?' 'Yes, Monsieur le Commandant. I found myself almost as much dead as alive on board the English frigate.' 'And out of gratitude, I suppose, you volunteered into the English service?' 'Pardon me, monsieur; I was compelled, under penalty of being hanged, to take service,—to officiate as barber to the captain, officers, and crew. Ah! it was terrible. The temptation, but for the protection of La Sainte Vierge, would have been irresistible.' '*Farce!*' growled the Commandant; 'the English, brutal as they may be, do not hang prisoners of war. Passing from that, barbers are not usually employed in cutting-out expeditions. Whereas M. Blaise, le perruquier, is found boarding La Ville de Nantes. He is armed to the teeth, and is seen to cut with an axe the cable of the ship. It was essential that the vessel, if it was to become the prize of the English, should be towed quickly out of cannon-fire. Jean Louvois Marie Blaise, perruquier, recognising that important condition, and that time should not be lost in bringing the anchor home, severed, as I have said, the cable with an axe. It is true that, owing to a shift of wind which the renegade was not aware of—' 'Monsieur le Commandant,' said I, interrupting, 'this is a frightful misconception. Permit me to assure you upon the honour of—' 'Upon the honour of a perruquier,' broke in the Commandant with contemptuous anger. 'Holy blue! but that is rich, *impayable!* To finish. You with the others boarded the Ville de Nantes—the Indian weapon, a tomahawk, in hand—you took part in the slight conflict which ensued against your countrymen, and as I have said, to facilitate the capture of the French ship, severed the cable.' 'Excuse me,' I exclaimed again, eagerly interrupting. 'I was by turns cold and hot in every member of my frame; an officer entering having left the door open, through which I perceived a firing-party drawn up, who were, I could not doubt, waiting to bestow their favours upon me, the situation was becoming desperate. Excuse me, Monsieur le Commandant—' 'Hold thy tongue, beast!' thundered the grim old veteran. 'How came it that there were found upon thee twenty-two English guineas? Answer me that!' 'Monsieur le

Commandant,' said I, 'the English officers, to do them justice, are generous—extremely generous as to money—England, it is known, is the country of gold, and I was nearly two years in the infernal frigate. Naturally hoping to get ashore in La belle France, to escape, that is, I placed all the money I possessed in my pocket.' 'Bah!' the Colonel broke in again. 'Let the English sailors be questioned.' The officer of marines interpreted the Commandant's interrogatories. 'What do you know of this man?' 'He is a Frenchman, and *fussraite chinscrapere*,' which is English for 'barber of the highest class.' This I at first thought was generous, chivalric even, as I remembered having more than once gashed the fellow's chin out of spite; he being an impudent rascal, if ever there was one. Ah! I was soon undeceived. 'Did he volunteer into the British service?' 'Yes; and took the bounty. He used to say he hated the *sans-culottes*, and loved the Bourbons.' It was finished with me. I felt that. Nevertheless, I denied the infamous charge with all the energy of my soul. It was useless. I was found guilty of having fought against France. I, that would have shed my life-blood for our glorious *patrie*, and condemned to die the death of a traitor—that is, to be shot forthwith. By that time the room was quite filled with spectators of the beau sexe—several of them girls and women, one the charming daughter of M. le Commandant's wife. *Le beau sexe* is an expression which I take leave to remark is not, according to my experience, strictly accurate, I mean not universally applicable—very far, indeed, from being so. Never mind, the women and girls present, five or six, all counted—the entire female population of the battery—with the exception of Madame, the Commandant's wife, sympathised with me, and when the sentence, *fusillé sur le champ*, to be shot immediately, was pronounced, testified that sympathy by tears and sobs. Several officers interposed, remonstrated —not against the sentence, but its hasty execution. Though unworthy to remain on earth, I might, with a few hours of priestly preparation, be made quite good enough for heaven. Miserable logic that, it seemed to me, but not under the circumstances to be repudiated. Certainly not. Till a man is dead, he lives—that is certain, positive—and whilst he lives there is hope. I prayed—still indignantly protesting my innocence—to be allowed time to avail myself of religious consolation—to receive the viaticum indispensable to a safe passage to the other world, and a benevolent reception there. Monsieur le Commandant smiled grimly, but granted eighteen hours' delay. The firing-party was dismissed, and I led back to the cell. It was solitary now, till the priest came. A famous *gaillard* was the holy man. He had seen so much of death from his youth upwards till he was fifty years of age—he looked, dimly as I saw, much younger than that—in the American war, when France delivered the people of the United States from the oppression of perfidious Albion; during the fever of the Revolution, when the guillotine was in full activity; and since, in the armies of the Republic, that he had at last come to regard shooting a man as quite a natural mode of insisting upon his exit from this world. He assured me it was nothing, positively nothing, when over. 'Good and evil, my son,' said the old reprobate, 'pain and pleasure, are nothing when passed away. Dost thou really wish me to go through the service?' he added, with a guttural accent, which reminded me of the Englishers—blind buzzard that I was—taking out of his pocket an old dog-eared breviary. 'If so, kneel down; but I should advise—as, modestly speaking, I don't think my certificate would count for much *là haut*—I should advise, *par préférence*, that we dispose between us of these two bottles of excellent wine.' I had observed that he had a basket in his hand, and some capital cigars. '*Vogue la galère,*' went on the Père Meulon, 'you will sleep all the sounder, though not, *parbleu,* so sound, my son, as you will to-morrow night.'

"I reflected whilst he was pouring out the wine, the glug-glug of which was pleasant to the ear, that the priest could not be of the least service to me—if I could not get to heaven without his aid, the drunken old sinner, I might as well make up my mind for the other place. *Eh bien*—I could say my prayers when alone—invoke the Holy Mother's protection, which has never failed me. *En attendant,* a few glasses of wine and a cigar would be invigorating, decidedly so. '*Clinquons,*' said the Père Meulon. 'With all my heart,' responded I, affecting a gaiety I did not feel—my heart being just then as heavy as a lump of lead—'with all my heart. *Clinquons.*' We touched each other's glasses, and tossed off the contents. Really excellent wine!

"'Jean Louvois Marie Blaise,' said the Père Meulon, his keen blue eyes glistening in the dark with mirth, much out of place at such a time—'Jean Louvois Marie Blaise, thou art *beau garçon.* I know at least *one* person who thinks so.'

"I did not at first understand what the priest meant; but gradually he enlightened me. 'One Mademoiselle Jaubert, who was present when you were sentenced to death, has taken a fancy to you. She has great influence with Madame, the lady of the Commandant, who is, in fact, *the* Commandant, and can save your life, if she chooses to do so. The condition is *marriage.* I must make you man and wife, here, in this cell,—which I take to be, looking at the situation, genuine priestly consolation!' 'Mademoiselle Jaubert!' I stammered. 'Mademoiselle Jaubert!' My head seemed turning round, and I hardly knew whether I stood upon it or upon my feet. 'Mademoiselle Jaubert!—do you mean the young lady in a blue-silk dress, with a white rose in her black hair?'

"The fellow grinned diabolically, showing his teeth, very white teeth, with disgusting effrontery. 'No,—no, —no. That is an excellent joke, Monsieur le Perruquier! The young lady in the blue-silk dress, with a white rose in her black hair, is Monsieur le Commandant's daughter, *sa fille unique.*' 'Who then, in the devil's name, is Mademoiselle Jaubert? Except that young person, all the other females, as far as my certainly confused recollection goes,—there was, no doubt, a mist before my eyes,—were detestably ugly.' 'That is a matter of taste,' said the Père Meulon, as he called himself. 'The Mademoiselle Jaubert is not probably a Venus, but she is young and sufficiently good-looking. She will make Monsieur Blaise an excellent wife, and, which is the essential thing, save him from the bullets of the firing party. Does M. Blaise consent ?' "

Jean Louvois Marie Blaise, in his prolix narrative, dwells at great length upon the mental *pros* and *cons* which suggested themselves to his mind; the conclusion finally arrived at being, that it was better—varying the precept of St. Paul—that it was better to marry than be shot. He answered in that sense ; and the priest, having settled some minor details, left the cell, promising to return with the lady in some three or four hours, to go through with the interesting ceremony, the means of flight having been previously arranged. M. Blaise and his bride would take wing from the prison-house. Mademoiselle Jaubert would, moreover, the priest said, bring her husband a dowry of six thousand francs!

All this was possible, if we are to accept, without reserve, the version of the story told by Barber Blaise; but he soon discovered a needless mystification played off upon him by the drunken priest, or believed he did. It was Mademoiselle Roland, the Commandant's daughter, who had taken a fancy to the good-looking French seaman. In consequence of her intercession, enforced by Madame's *sic volo, sic jubeo,* it had been conceded, he was presently told, by the Commandant, that the escape of the prisoner should be winked at, facilities even afforded him for getting away.

"The decisive moment approached," continues M. Blaise. "I was trembling from head to foot with excitement. The priest enters; he has a lamp in his hand; behind him steals gently, with softest footfall, a figure— a youthful figure—draped in blue silk. My heart beats violently. Am I awake? Can it be possible? Yes! the bride is the Commandant's daughter. . . . . . The ceremony is over; we indulge in one embrace. The priest—whose face I had not once distinctly seen, it having been almost totally dark when he first came in, and now that he has brought a lamp, his cowl is drawn almost completely over it—the priest gives us his blessing, adding, as he draws the bride away some paces, and in a low voice gives her what I suppose to be confidential pious counsel, '*Ah! le scélérat.*'

"The lady renews the cloak, that of an acolyte; the cowl of a priest concealed her face, as that of the priest did his, and which she had thrown off after entering the cell. The door was closed as the priest hands me a paper, which I read by the light of the lamp. It is a printed form, filled up and signed by the Commandant: —'Let the bearer of this and his companions pass out freely.' We go forth: the sentinels, three of them in all, scrutinise the paper, recognise its validity, and we are presently clear of the battery. A *calèche* is in waiting for us; we take our seats, and are driven off at a gallop. The bride is reserved, draws herself up in one corner of the vehicle, and speaks but in monosyllables. The gravity of the situation, I think to myself, impresses her; placing herself, as she has, in an access of romantic caprice, at the direction of a man whom she had seen but for a few minutes, and of whose character she is necessarily ignorant. Well, she is a charming creature, and will find me a tender husband, a man of strictest honour. I was disquieted somewhat, I must confess, as to the actuality of the six thousand francs; no doubt they were in the *valise* under the seat. Madame Blaise could not, surely, have forgotten to secure that essential item in our contract! Not likely—*cependant.* But it would be indelicate to speak upon such a subject. Besides, Madame Blaise had fallen asleep.

"The *calèche,* after about two hours, stops at a wayside *auberge,* not far, as I perceive by the pale starlight, from the left bank of the Garonne. We do not descend, and as the air is fresh and chill, I willingly accept one, two, three *petits verres,* brought out to me by the obliging conductor of the *calèche*. The *eau-de-vie* is not bad, but has, it seems to me, a peculiar taste. Again *en route*, faster, if possible, than before. Fatigue, the swinging motion of the vehicle, cause a drowsiness which I cannot resist. I fall into profound slumber. . . . . At last I awake, slowly, with effort. I am wide awake. *Grand Dieu!* How is this? Am I mad? Why, a hundred thousand devils! I am again on board of the cruiser Phœbus, English frigate, in my old berth! 'And where is Julie—where is my wife?' I ask frantically of the sailors near by. I am answered with insult, laughter; told to sleep out my drunken fit by the brutal god-dams. What do they know about my wife? I cannot yet believe my senses. Thunder of heaven, I am crushed. It is the end of the world! I jump up, hastily search my pockets. *Nom de Dieu!* I find in them the twenty-two English guineas which had been taken from me—nothing else! A vertigo seizes me, and I swoon outright. . . .

"Recovered somewhat, I seek an interview with the captain. He tells me that a compassionate French fisherman found me lying drunk and speechless on the shore; that a 'Monsieur'—a stranger to him—came up and said I was an English sailor who had escaped from a military prison, and that it would be a charity to place me on board the English frigate standing off and on the coast. The fisherman agreed to do so, and—*me voilà*. I was stunned, and could neither speak nor think connectedly for several days. The mystery was inscrutable."

Not inscrutable, if not of easy solution, even to some who had been behind the scenes when the curious comedy was being acted at the Battery. Poor Blaise was soon made to comprehend the trick which had been played him—partially, at least.

Upon the fourth day subsequent to his being reconsigned to the Phœbus, a boat put off at earliest dawn from the shore, and pulled for the frigate. Restless Jean Louvois Marie Blaise was on deck, and watched with curiosity and interest the approach of the boat, in which females were seated. That curiosity and interest became inflamed, intensified, as soon as he discerned that one of the ladies wore a blue dress. Could it be Julie, his charming wife, who was about to rejoin her husband? Blaise begged the loan of a glass. An officer handed him one. Heavens! the lady was Julie, his beautiful bride. The mystery would be explained, and he should be the happiest of men. No one—not even an Englishman—would have the heart to detain him on board the Phœbus, and deprive him of the society of a newly-wedded wife. Joy! Ecstasy! Jean Louvois Marie Blaise capered about the deck like a maniac, to the great amusement of the captain and lieutenants of the frigate, who were in the secret.

"Julie—adorable Julie!" exclaimed M. Blaise the moment the lady's foot touched the deck, and rushing towards her with extended arms. "Julie—adorable Julie!——" "Go to the devil!" interrupted a gruff voice, accompanied by a violent thrust from a powerful arm, which hurled M. Blaise half across the deck. The assailant was the English lieutenant who interpreted at the court-martial. Malediction!—he—that infernal lieutenant—introduced Julie to the captain of the frigate as "My wife, Madame Seymour." This Monsieur Blaise saw and heard, for the moment doubting the evidence of his ears and eyes. A vertigo must have again seized him, as he was carried below "in a state of insensibility."

The explanation, as given by M. Blaise, is not very clear. It appears that Lieutenant Seymour, who was a prisoner on parole, expecting every day to be exchanged, had found favour with Mademoiselle Julie, daughter of the commandant, and that his secret suit was smiled upon, not only by the desired one herself, but madame her mother. Lieutenant Seymour, besides being a handsome, well-bred man, was the heir of a large fortune and a title—would be a "milord," according to madame's apprehension, and it was certain that his wife would be a "miladi" before many years had passed. That being so, the difference between a peerage and a baronetcy was

inappreciable. But the commandant was a stern hater
of the English. True that madame would ultimately
have coerced her husband into giving his assent to the
marriage, but that would have required time, and time
was not to be had. Now the commandant had never
seriously meant to allow execution to be done upon poor
Blaise, and the expedient hit upon was to obtain the
governor's consent to his escape upon condition that he
married Annette Jaubert, who had really conceived a
liking for the good-looking and unhappy French seaman,
and of which damsel, a great favourite of his wife, Monsieur le Commandant was very anxious, for reasons of
his own, to be rid as soon as might be, or else farewell
the tranquil mind, farewell content on his, the commandant's part, before more than five or six months had
passed away. The drunken old chaplain attached to the
Battery was made an accomplice in the plot. He lent
Seymour his clerical habiliments, and the next morning,
when the flight of Mademoiselle Julie was discovered,
persisted that he had married her to the French seaman,
by the especial order of Monsieur le Commandant. Had
he not said, " A young lady has fallen in love with the
French seaman condemned to death : marry them ; after
which they can both be off. This paper will enable them
to leave without being questioned." It so fell out :
though why Seymour, disguised as the priest, went
through the mock ceremony, is not so clear. One understands that it was essential that Lieutenant Seymour
should be entirely free from suspicion, or the commandant might, till his daughter were restored to him, refuse
—and the military authorities would have sustained such
refusal—to give effect to the exchange which was about
to be carried out. The female who came off in the boat
with Madame Seymour was Mademoiselle Jaubert.

There was some attempt made to bring about a match
between her and Jean Louvois Marie Blaise, but that
persecuted *marin* was too much disgusted with the sex to
listen for one moment to the proposal. It is incidentally
remarked by M. Blaise, towards the end of his pamphlet,

that the commandant became reconciled to his daughter's marriage with the English lieutenant, and that both he and madame speak with a proud complacency of Miladi Seymour. One condition of forgiveness he made, which was that Mademoiselle Jaubert should on no account return to France. He had conceived a violent antipathy to that damsel, who ought to marry and settle in England. "Effectively," adds M. Blaise, "Mademoiselle Jaubert did marry in Albion, and the dishonour which it was thought to fix upon me was reserved for an Englishman. *He* would not care much for that if she brought him a dowry of six thousand francs."

Through the *bons offices* of Lieutenant Seymour, M. Blaise was sent ashore on some part of the coast of France with money in both pockets.

"From that time," says M. Blaise, "I was the irreconcilable foe of the English nation. Like the Carthaginian Hannibal, I shall at a fitting age insist that my two sons, Jean and Philibert, make oath at the altar of God of waging eternal war against that perfidious people by whom I have suffered so much. Meanwhile I volunteered into active service against them. I entered on board the Calypso corvette, and may say, without boasting, that some rays of the glory acquired by that vessel fell upon me. After that I was drafted to the Redoubtable, Capitaine Lucas. That ship was covered with imperishable honours at the fatal, but glorious battle of Trafalgar. I was a capital marksman, and was stationed in the maintop. I saw the famous Nelson on the quarterdeck, pacing to and fro. I aimed at him: my ball took effect, but not that time upon the admiral. No—but one fell! I afterwards, upon reading the bulletins, thought it might have been his secretary. Perhaps: I am not sure. I fired many times, not without effect. At last I had an opportunity of taking steady aim at the English admiral—there was no mistaking *him*. I fired, as did—let me be frank—three or four of my *camarades*, at the same moment, or nearly so. The great admiral—the terror of the French navy—no, not terror; the word is misplaced: terror is unknown to the French heart—I should say the great admiral, who was the most successful commander of the English sea-wolves, fell prone upon the deck, mortally wounded. I cannot positively say—I am not entirely sure that it was by my hand the English admiral fell; but the belief that it was is a balm to my heart!

"In that terrible fight I was wounded in the leg. We made frantic efforts, seeing that the battle was inevitably lost, to avoid an English prison. A dozen of us contrived to let ourselves down into a boat alongside. We rowed towards a Spanish ship, were received on board, and safely landed at Cadiz. Thence, by help of the French consul, I was enabled to reach France—St. Malo. I at once established in the Rue du Bac, married, and have, as I said, two children—boys—devoted to assist in the destruction of England. For myself, I am constantly studying plans for the annihilation of the British Marine whenever the war breaks out again. I incline strongly to the use of balloons. But there are difficulties, which I hope to be able to surmount. My wife is opposed to these enterprises of mine; one reason being, that, by an accidental explosion during an experiment, the roof of the house was blown off, and a woman was killed in the street by the falling of a large piece of timber upon her head. Poor woman! I deplored the accident with a sincere sorrow. But what will you have? Science, like war, has its victims, yet both are glorious! Jeannette also fears that I may neglect my business. That is a vain fear. It is still carried on, as I have said, with vigour and success, at Numéro 11 of the Rue du Bac. Be pleased to notice the number; and I trust, before long, to present my beloved France with terrible engines of destruction, that will enable her to amply avenge Trafalgar, Waterloo, and many other battles, chiefly won by English gold."

These patriotic aspirations were not to be realised.

The enterprising projector blew himself up one fine day, more effectually than did the English off Rochefort. In one of the graveyards of St. Malo there is a rather pretentious monumental stone, upon which is inscribed, " *Ci gît Jean Louvois Marie Blaise, Perruquier, victime de son goût passionné pour le science. His afflicted widow and sons still carry on the business at Numéro 11 Rue du Bac.*" The last two lines must either have been borrowed from an inscription at Père-la-Chaise, or the Paris widow must have copied that at St. Malo.

MADAME LA COMTESSE DE GENLIS.

THIS lady made a great noise in her time, was one of
the self-appointed reformers of the world, and one, too,
who set herself seriously to the task of teaching the nations how to live. The pity of it was that her lessons
had but slight self-applicability. A very clever woman,
no doubt of that, laughingly as we may demur to her
glorifying self-estimate when, writing in her eightieth
year of the magnificent promise of her youth, she says:
"The colossal reputation I have since achieved, and
which, I am bold to predict, time will confirm and ex-
tend, had then scarcely risen above the intellectual
horizon." One may smile at this whilst admitting that
she composed some very pretty papers. The *Palace of
Truth*, for example, might in these publishing revival-
days pay for reprinting. The maiden name of Madame
de Genlis was Stéphanie Félicité Ducret de St. Aubin.
She was born at Champcéry, près d'Autun, early in the
year 1746. That she was destined to distinction was evident to discerning eyes—I am quoting her own *Mémoires
Inédits*—when she was still in her cradle. By a special
Providence only was this future light of the world saved
from extinguishment, at that tender age, by the heavy
blear-eyed mayor of Autun. "The nurse," writes Madame de Genlis, "having much needlework to despatch,
and being careful of my safety, sewed up in a soft pil-
low—my body only, not my head—and placed me in a
large *fauteuil.* I was always a quiet docile child, of remarkable sweetness of disposition. Monsieur le Maire
d'Autun came in; he wished to speak with mamma.
The nurse said she would inform Madame that Mon-

sieur le Maire had called, and wished to see her. 'Thank you,' said the ponderous functionary ; and spreading the tails of his *redingote*, was about to seat himself upon me. Happily the nurse had not left the apartment. Her scream of alarm arrested the movement of Monsieur le Maire, and I was saved. It was not the good nurse who saved me ; no ; it was God himself acting by her instrumentality. He had given me a mission upon earth, which He had decreed should be fulfilled."

The success of that mission was, according to Madame's own account, complete. She thus wrote in the eighty-second year of her age, when her sight needed not the aid of spectacles, and her hearing was as acute as ever ; her memory, intellect brighter, if that could be possible, than ever, and she was preparing to rewrite the *Encyclopédie* with the very laudable purpose of superseding the impious compilation of D'Alembert, Voltaire, and their brother sceptics. "It is I," exclaimed octogenarian Madame la Comtesse, "who will strike down, never to rise again, the monsters of Infidelity and Atheism. To do so will be the fulfilment of my sacred mission. Already have I dealt terrible blows at a false sterile philosophy. And who will deny that I have exercised a supreme and salutary influence upon public and private education, especially as regards the study of living languages, which I have brought into fashion ? The world, moreover, owes to me the total extinction of fairy tales, once permitted to be used in the education of children. To sum up, I have fought victoriously against heresy in all things, especially in literature."

The marquisate and château of St. Aubin had been bought of a bankrupt proprietor by Stéphanie Félicité's father, he thereby acquiring nobility by purchase. "My first title to precedence," writes the De Genlis in those six thick volumes of *Mémoires Inédits*,—"my first title to precedence was derived from a higher source. At seven years of age the Grand Prior of the noble Chapter of Allix, at Lyon—discerning, he has been pleased to say, the *auréole* of moral grandeur, the first rays of which shed light upon my youthful brow—created me a canoness of the illustrious Chapter; a dignity which at once confers the secular title of conntess. If in after years the neophyte chose to complete her profession, to devote herself to a religious life, she could do so, and thereby share in the rich prebends at the disposal of the Grand Prior." Only a Frenchwoman, and a singularly eccentric one, could write thus of herself; and with a *naïve* calmness, too, indicative that her self-laudation was entirely sincere.

Stéphanie Félicité, I should have before stated, was publicly baptised in Paris, whatever public baptism may mean; at which ceremony the precious child wore an iron collar round her neck, "to keep my small Grecian head well set upon my shoulders, and blue goggles on my eyes, to conceal and correct a slight squint, which, if not remedied, would have marred the expression of mild gentle candour which has been held to be my eyes' supremest charm." The Marquise de Bellevue, her godmother, remarking upon the name given her, Félicité, said, "Ah, dear child, felicity will not be hers! she has too much sensibility." "She was right," remarks Madame la Comtesse. "Alas, she was right!"

The reader will understand that I present him with the portrait of Madame de Genlis as painted by herself; I neither attempt to heighten nor subdue its colouring. "I acquired with wonderful facility the elements of education. My brother, who was esteemed a prodigy,—he had learned to read and write perfectly in six weeks,—I distanced with ease. In short, and I have earned the right to say so, before I was fifteen all the mental treasures of the world were familiar to me. Weary at last of poring over the thoughts of others, profoundly imbued with a prophetic instinct, which has not deceived me, that I had faculties, divine gifts, equal to those of the greatest lights in literature; conscious, too, that by force of the harmonies of my being I was a born musician, I determined first to be actress and author. No opposition was offered to the gratification of my wishes.

They were encouraged, stimulated. Private theatricals were extemporised at the château; and it was declared by competent judges that my Zaïre was equal to, if it did not surpass, Clairon's; whilst my Phèdre [Countess Stéphanie being at the time in her sixteenth year] was held to be far superior in passionate force to hers."

Madame de Genlis piously attributes her faculties, her charms, to the all-powerful Being who created her. She seems, when half out of breath in enumerating her perfections, to be always modestly ejaculating with Dogberry, "Gifts that God gives—gifts that God gives!"

The Comtesse Stéphanie, as author or authoress, was from the first eminently successful. "My pen possessed a charm unknown to myself till I was made aware of it by the ardent applause of all classes. One thing I must say in praise of myself. That which distinguished me from all other persons of a romantic imagination was, that I only in my books invented incidents which would afford me opportunity for portraying qualities of the soul which I venerated—patience, courage, presence of mind, firmness. Thus even in the reveries of my infancy there was a foundation of love of glory and virtue, which in a child must be pronounced remarkable."

It was not alone in the field of literature, of poesy, that she could repeat Cæsar's Thrasonian brag, "*Veni, vidi, vici*"—("I came, I saw, I conquered"). Kate Kearney,—Lady Morgan's Kate Kearney's glance could not have been more fatal to the rash gazer than that of the Countess Stéphanie. "I was but eleven years old," she writes, "and small of my age, when I inspired the first passion—at least the first avowed passion—quite unconsciously. I even felt shocked, grieved, when a son of one Pinat, an apothecary, proclaimed a devotion which he could no longer conceal, in verses glowing with a Sappho's fire. If there was no other proof of the distraction of mind, the delirium of love, with which Louis Pinat was afflicted, it would be manifest in the fact that he had overlooked the impassable gulf which must ever separate, as to honourable relations with each other, noblemen and apothecaries." Mademoiselle Stéphanie Félicité loftily rebuked young Pinat's audacity, and advised him, since it was highly improbable he could ever be cured whilst, residing near, he had daily opportunities of seeing her, to leave that part of the country before the mischief already done was irremediable, and betake himself to some part of the world where such fatal facilities would be denied to him. "The young man," says Madame de Genlis, "yielded to my advice, and departed for Paris, where he obtained a situation." When lovers come, it would seem from the young Countess Stéphanie Félicité's experience, they come in crowds. "A Monsieur de Mendorge, the first man," she says, "who gave me the idea of a conversation really agreeable, after hearing me sing one of his own songs, composed in my honour, and feeling, that the disparity in our ages considered, marriage was out of the question, sought safety in flight, rejoined his family—a large one—and ultimately succeeded in banishing my image from his memory." One Louvel, an avocat, was the next victim. He was a young man of great promise in his profession; but coming within the influence of Stéphanie Félicité's "soft spiritual eyes," and meeting with a peremptory refusal, first determined upon suicide, but having been educated by a pious mother, he changed his mind, and emigrated to Saint Domingo.

This irresistible siren did not herself boast of transcendent beauty, with the exception of "the brightest of brown hair, and the sweet candour of soft spiritual eyes." It must, therefore, have been her accomplishments, her wit, her conversational powers—Madame herself inclines to this opinion—which compelled the adoration of mankind. It is true that some snarling objectors—"sceptics of a mean, malignant type"—have asserted that Madame's "conquests," as reported by herself, are stronger proofs of her imaginative powers than all her acknowledged romances put together. But it was ever thus. Envy, we all know, does merit like its shade pursue. If Venus and Minerva were to appear in the flesh, thousands would pronounce one to be plain, the other a fool. So at least says the authoress of the *Palace of Truth* and the *Siege of Rochelle*. She was perhaps right. There are scores of decently-educated men of the present day who will tell you to your face that Thackeray was a sour, pretentious pump; that Dickens is destitute of genuine humour; that Miss Braddon is a mistake. *Que voulez-vous?*

The brightest of brown hair, the sweetest candour of soft spiritual eyes, did not unfortunately avail to pay interest on mortgages, liquidate butchers', bakers', wine-merchants' bills. M. de St. Aubin, after some despairing struggles against adverse fate, sold his marquisate and château to meet the demand of ravening creditors, who insolently persisted in claiming and enforcing their just debts. Finding that but about four huudred per annum remained to him, unmarquised Monsieur de St. Aubin embarked for Saint Domingo, where he met with Louvel the avocat, whose bleeding, broken heart a successful sugar-speculation had staunched and bound up. De St. Aubin himself was not so fortunate, and after a not very lengthened residence in the island, returned to Europe, not to the port of France for which he sailed. The ship in which he embarked was snapped up by the English *loups de mer*, and M. de St. Aubin found himself a prisoner in Launceston castle, Cornwall, instead of with his wife and family at Plassy, France, whither they had betaken themselves when he left St. Aubin, and were still residing.

"It was at Plassy," says Madame de Genlis, "that I myself first became conscious of a faculty bestowed upon me by the Eternal—no question with a special purpose. It was the gift of judging the soul by the face. I possessed that gift in a high degree. I knew, and told Monsieur de la Papalinère, a farmer-general and generous patron of literature, that De Chalons, a neighbour, was a secret assassin. This a subsequent discovery confirmed. And I foretold that the Abbé de la Caste would be hanged. This was not strictly, but substantially correct. The abbé, who was not a clergyman, was condemned to the galleys."

It would have been merciful had the fascinating Countess Stéphanie Félicité published, placarded her inexorable determination, arrived at before she had passed her fourteenth birthday, to marry only a man of quality and attached to the court. It might have saved the life of poor Baron de Zeolachen, Colonel of Swiss Guards, and eighty years of age, who fell so hopelessly in love with the irresistible, fascinating damsel, "that his days," records his destroyer, "were shortened,"—(surely not by many years, he being eighty when he succumbed to the sorceress),—"were shortened by the violence of his emotions. It was better so, perhaps," adds Madame. "There is forgetfulness in the grave."

Mademoiselle Stéphanie Félicité and her mother had meanwhile removed from their dwelling at Plassy to the Convent of Les Filles du Précieux Sang. Whilst there, Mademoiselle wrote a second novel, cured the mother superior and many nuns of seemingly mortal maladies by *sirop de calabash*—a compound of her own invention—and enslaved the Baron d'Audlaw, a gentleman of unblemished descent, who could prove that not one of his long line of ancestors had ever done any thing useful or beneficial to mankind,—built a house or a ship, —written, much less printed, a book,—neither invented nor improved anything. He sent a list of this illustrious ancestry, pedigree so called, to the divine Stéphanie Félicité, accompanied by an offer of marriage. The young lady, upon whose brow the *auréole* of coming glory was daily brightening, declined the honour. "But there was balm in Gilead," she suggested; "could he not transfer his offer and pedigree to her mother?" He did so, it being then supposed that Monsieur de St. Aubin was dead. That supposition was premature; but when, very shortly after, he returned to France, and unmistakably died a prisoner for debt in Fort l'Evêque, Madame de St. Aubin became Baroness d'Audlaw. A Monsieur de Morville, "a youthful widower of large fortune, great accomplishments, and of a noble, romantic style of beauty," vainly struggled to resist the spell which the future Madame de Genlis cast upon him. His suit was rejected, he being neither a man of quality nor attached to the court. Decidedly, if the institution called Committee of Public Safety had been invented in her young days, and the members had known and acted up to their duty, Mademoiselle Stéphanie would have been locked up,—condemned to seclusion for life!

At last we obtain a glimpse of the right man, soon to be in the right place. He is M. le Comte de Genlis, who has served in India, under Lally Tollendal, the crazy, chivalrous Irishman whom the French king beheaded— "murdered," wrote Voltaire, "with the sword of justice," —because he had not beaten the English soldiers commanded by Sir Eyre Coote. The Count de Genlis embarked for France, but, like M. de St. Aubin, was made prisoner by the English sea-wolves, after "a desperate combat," says Madame, "in which twenty-two out of twenty-three French officers were slain, and M. de Genlis, sole survivor, received eight wounds, one of which he kept open till he was married." The last sentence is a puzzling one. It could hardly mean a wound in the heart; wounds in that region, not by soft spiritual eyes, but by a cutlass or pistol-bullet, being generally fatal.

The Count de Genlis was confined in the castle of Launceston with his future father-in-law, M. de St. Aubin. The two became intimate acquaintances, fast friends; and the young gallant captain heard much from the father's lips of the genius and accomplishments of Mademoiselle de St. Aubin, and promised himself the pleasure of seeing her whenever he again set foot upon the soil of la belle France. Both gentlemen were liberated at about the same time, and returned to France ;— M. de St. Aubin to be arrested for debt, and die in Fort l'Evêque; the Count de Genlis to be raised to the rank of Colonel of Grenadiers for his gallantry in the naval action related in the *Mémoires Inédits*, the only record of the fight I have met with. He appears to have been in no hurry to visit the daughter of his deceased friend. Possibly the awkward fact that that friend had died a prisoner for debt had a deterrent effect. He was about to be married, moreover, to a Mademoiselle de la Motte, a lady possessed of forty thousand francs per annum.

At last the Count de Genlis did pay a visit to the convent of Les Filles du Précieux Sang; "saw, conversed with me," says Madame, "and it was immediately evident that I had obtained an irresistible ascendency over him."

So it proved. Mademoiselle de la Motte, with her sixteen hundred pounds a-year, was forgotten, repudiated, and Mademoiselle de St. Aubin was converted by Holy Church into Madame la Comtesse de Genlis.

I rather doubt that the gallant count who had married in such haste thought even earlier than is generally the case that he need scarcely have been in such a hurry. He should have taken more time to consider. He had married a remarkably strong-minded woman—young as she was—when her daughter Caroline was born she was barely twenty; and that particular variety of the female genus does not, with some men, improve upon acquaintance—a deficiency of taste, no doubt, upon their parts. Still one can scarcely help sympathising with a gallant colonel of grenadiers whose wife, being a capital horse-woman, was perpetually scouring the country in quest of interesting people—such as betrayed damsels, neglected geniuses,—indefatigable in her inquiries as to the state and progress of education; and, as if this were not enough, must study phlebotomy under the guidance of one Racine, the village barber, to perfect herself in which science by practice, she paid thirty sous to every peasant or peasantess who would allow him or herself to be bled. M. le Comte complained, and one must admit with some reason, of the frightful expense incurred by such eccentricities. He remonstrates in vain; Madame's mission must be fulfilled.

Soon her aunt, Madame de Montesson, succeeds in inducing the aged imbecile Duc d'Orléans, the father of

Egalité, grandfather of Louis Philippe, to marry her. Great glory that for Madame la Comtesse, who forthwith makes her appearance at court, and soon becomes a great favourite with Egalité and his amiable duchess. The favour of her grace does not long endure, but that of the duke was lasting, permanent. Egalité offered the office of "governor" to his children. M. de Genlis, who had not accompanied his wife to Paris, being informed of the duke's gracious proposition, demurred thereto, and requested his wife to rejoin him in the country. She refused to do so, and they never again saw each other.

Madame de Genlis forthwith entered upon her functions as governor or governess of the Orléans children, at a salary of about five hundred pounds per annum; apartments, board, and a promise of the *cordon bleu*, when her task should be fulfilled.

That task was an onerous one, if the lady governess is to be believed. The children knew nothing—positively nothing. She writes: "The Duc de Valois (afterwards Duc de Chartres d'Orléans—King Louis Philippe), the Duc de Valois, who was eight years old, was totally devoid of application. I began with a few historical lectures. He, not even affecting to listen, stretched himself, yawned, lolled back upon a sofa, and placed his feet upon the table before us." This could not be endured; the young prince was discreetly punished, and thenceforth "he quietly submitted to my firm and reasonable rule."

One of this lady's educational crotchets was that every one, no matter what their station in life, should be instructed in one or more useful trades or professions. The male scions of the Orléans family were in accordance with her theory taught gardening, carpentry, shoemaking, surgery, &c. Madame herself undertook to preside over the pharmaceutical department, which she called instructing her pupils in chemistry. The Duc de Chartres, by diligent practice with the servants of the establishment, could open a vein with tolerable dexterity, and once broke the jaw of a boy-helper in the stables who was suffering from toothache by way of trying his 'prentice hand in dental surgery. It was, however, in carpentry that the future King Louis Philippe best vindicated Madame's educational theory, though his abilities as a bricklayer and builder were far above mediocrity. Madame's success with the Duc de Chartres had but one drawback; he became so violently attached to her as to be quite troublesome. "He attached himself passionately to me," says the Irresistible, who as of right—being as she then was the young prince's senior by more than a quarter of a century—remonstrated with him upon the absurdity of having no eyes, no ears for any one but her overpowering self, putting himself, to use Madame's not very elegant expression, "putting himself always in my pocket." It was useless to attempt moderating the ardour of De Chartres' passionate devotion. It was throwing oil upon flame. Some years subsequently, when a civic crown was awarded to the prince for having saved a man from drowning, he instantly despatched a leaf, not to his mother, sisters, or brothers, but to Madame: "for without you, what should I have been?" That leaf the romantic Comtesse preserved with religious care. It was one of her most precious relics of the heart. The fervid attachment towards her of Egalité Duc d'Orléans, and of De Chartres, caused Madame, who was on an educational tour through France with her grown-up pupils, to exclaim in her very best, most affecting manner, whilst gazing with them upon the sculptured tomb of Diana of Poictiers, "Happy woman! She was beloved alike by father and son."

Madame, who like De Chartres, had at first hailed the Revolution—the Prince, as most of us are aware, joined the Jacobin Club — like him was fortunate enough to evade, and but just in time, its deadly clutch. He escaped to Switzerland, Madame to England, thence passed over to Belgium, and was in Hamburgh, when a message from Napoleon, then First Consul, reached her through Lavalette. The victor of Marengo, "alive to the necessity of attaching to his triumphal chariot-wheels the great intellects of France, invited me to return to Paris. I was to have an allowance of six thousand francs per annum, upon condition that I wrote something every fortnight, whether of politics, literature, morality,—any thing that came into my head.   I eagerly complied, for exile had became insufferable, and Napoleon acknowledged he had made an excellent bargain."   As Madame had previously obtained an annuity of one thousand crowns of Caroline, Queen of Naples, " by her Orphean skill on the harp, and impassioned advocacy of monarchical principles," she was at last quite well off.   The consideration which was stipulated for by Napoleon was a mere bagatelle to a lady who boasted of having written in one short morning an article upon the censorship of the Press, by official order; the first chapter of a new novel; a *feuilleton* called *Frédale the Artist;* and an *Essay upon Sympathy*, at the solicitation of her amiable friends the Misses Byrne.

Madame continued her career of glory to the end; her powers of intellect and fascination remaining as bright,—we have her own word for it, and she ought to know,—" as bright and resplendent at eighty as at eighteen!"

I must not conclude this eccentric life without transcribing an episode which throws a strong revealing light upon it.   Madame shall state her own case; the commentary will be furnished by Thomas Moore, author of *Loves of the Angels*.

In the year 1787 a charming English child was received into Madame de Genlis' family circle, and educated with her princely pupils.   Madame, who was an admirer of Richardson, gave her the name of Pamela. This child grew up to be a beautiful young woman, and was, being very amiable and sensitive, profoundly grateful to her benefactress.   When Madame fled, just in time, from Paris, Pamela accompanied her, remaining with her throughout her continental wanderings, and when at Hamburg, where Madame la Comtesse received the welcome as complimentary message from Napoleon, the charming Pamela attracted the notice and subjugated the heart of Lord Edward Fitzgerald, the unfortunate Irish patriot in Milesian estimation, an audacious rebel in the English vocabulary.

Lord Edward, finding himself hopelessly enthralled by the divine Pamela, formally offered her his hand in marriage. This was a great catch for the young lady, a second edition of *Pamela, or Virtue Rewarded.*

The young lady was quite willing, and her kind, judicious preceptress accepted the homage for her *protégée* of so distinguished a nobleman, upon one condition, that the consent in writing of the Duchess of Leinster to the marriage should be first obtained. This, after some delay, *was* obtained, and the wedding took place in Hamburg. In the marriage-register the bride is called "Citoyenne Anne Caroline Stéphauie Félicité Sims, daughter of William de Brixey." Immediately after the ceremony the happy pair set out for Dublin.

The early history of the interesting Pamela is circumstantially set forth by Madame la Comtesse in one of her books. The pretty story is thus told:

Pamela's father, whose name was Seymour, married in the city of Christchurch, Hampshire, one Mary Sims, with whom he embarked for a place called Fogo, in Newfoundland, where Pamela was born and baptised Anne, after her maternal grandmother. Seymour died, and the widow with her child returned to Christchurch, and there by a happy concatenation of circumstances happened to be M. Forth, an agent of the Duke of Orleans, specially commissioned by his royal highness to procure him a pretty English girl-child. M. Forth was struck with the beauty of the infant Pamela; a negotiation ensued, and Madame Seymour, *née* Sims, parted with her child for a handsome consideration. M. Forth brought her to Paris, and Madame de Genlis, with the tender generosity which distinguished her, agreed to superintend her education. As she advanced in years, beauty, and goodness, she became more and more attached to, and beloved by, Madame la Comtesse, who at last became alarmed lest the mother should reclaim her. "I consulted several eminent jurisconsults," writes Madame, "and was advised that the only mode by which I could legally secure possession of one whom to part with would have been death to both of us, was by inducing the widow 'Sims' (*sic*) to apprentice her daughter to Madame de Genlis, for the whole term of Pamela's or Anne's minority. This was done," says Madame, "in a legal form. The mother was cited before the *grand banc*, then presided over by the *grand juge*, Lord Mansfield; the mother and Lord Mansfield signed the indenture of apprenticeship, and Pamela could no longer be torn from me."

This farrago of absurdities could hardly have been that which imposed upon Lord Edward Fitzgerald and the Duchess of Leinster. Pamela's father, as we have seen, was set down in the marriage-register as William de Brixey,—not Seymour or Sims. The commentary of Thomas Moore in his Life of Lord Edward Fitzgerald, is pithily expressed: " The indisputable truth is, that Pamela was the daughter of Madame de Genlis by the Duc d'Orléans."

Madame la Comtesse continued to live a pleasant life in Paris. She was the adviser and confidante of the successive consular, imperial, royal governments,—"but unhappily," she sadly remarks, " my counsel, the result of profound study of the actual situation—study undisturbed by passion—was not always followed. Hence the catastrophe of Moscow,—the July barricades! Napoleon and Charles X. were wise too late. Had either permitted himself to be implicitly guided by me, all would have been well."

This omniscient, if not exactly immaculate, lady died in her eighty-fourth year, on the 31st of December 1830, a few months only after her distinguished pupil, Louis Philippe, " who without her would have been nothing," leapt from the barricades into the throne vacated by Charles X.

THE LADY-WITCH.

THE curious story of the Lady Morris, once held in Doncaster and the country-side for miles around to be gospel truth, but for the last century pooh-pooh'd even there into oblivion, must have had a strong foundation of truth. Internal and external evidence seem to prove that. The lady, it may be admitted, was a magician, but hers was natural magic—the magic of singular beauty, combined with an astute, unscrupulous intellect; and her moral or immoral husbandry found an exhaustless field for its exercise in the ever-fruitful soil of human weakness and credulity. The success of the Lady-Witch, like that of Joseph Balsamo, is easily enough accounted for without the attribution of supernatural functions. It seems pretty clear that the only mesmeric influence, in which I have any faith—that which flashes from the dark, liquid, penetrative eyes of a beautiful woman, revealing by its dazzling light unfathomable depths—was with her a very potent instrument of power.

Helen Royston was born in a cottage situate in the environs of Doncaster, and distant a few miles only from that city. Her mother died when she was still an infant (1653), and her father, once one of Cromwell's world-famous troopers—" Valiant-for-Truth Royston" was his military *sobriquet*—after the "crowning mercy" at Naseby, where he was severely wounded, settled down for the remainder of his days near his native city; married; had one daughter, Helen; followed his loving and beloved partner to the grave; and thenceforward the stern practical man of war came gradually to be a dreamer of dreams. The near approach of the period when Satan should be bound for a thousand years—which he had once as firmly believed in as that it was his duty to smite the ungodly, hip and thigh, and spare not—faded from the tablet of his creed. He ceased to believe in the Millennium. At all events he ceased to hope that it would dawn upon a sinful world in his own lifetime— that is, if that lifetime could not be indefinitely prolonged. The hazy speculations of the veteran took that direction, and like hundreds of other alchemaic visionaries, he diligently set himself to the study of the science taught by the adepts conversant with the doctrines taught by the brethren of the Rosy Cross. In other words, he devoted himself to the discovery of the Elixir of Life—the manufacture of gold from the basest metals; his dazzling reward, perennial life; inexhaustible riches!

We need not follow John Royston through the mazes of a dream from which he never awoke, dying as he did at the very moment when for the thousandth time he believed that the hour of supreme success was about to strike.

Royston inherited a modest income, partly terminable with his life, more than sufficient for his own and daughter's needs. He had also skill in pharmacy, was acquainted with the qualities of herbs and other simple medicaments. These, in many cases—some pronounced incurable by orthodox practitioners, were administered with great success. His daughter, as she grew up in strength, remarkable intelligence, and rare beauty, took this good Samaritan work into her own hands. She acquired a strange influence over her patients. The most fractious, obstinate, and wayward, were subdued in her presence as by an irresistible spell. Some muttered to themselves or each other that she had "an evil eye," and that though she cured persons for the time, it was only to make them her bond-slaves, and that when the time came they would be made to feel the yoke of slavery to which, by having recourse to her, they had subjected themselves.

No fable was too gross for general acceptance in those days, and, sooth to say, the present day, in many and many a rural district of enlightened England. The old Cromwellian and his beautiful daughter, burrowing in such strange seclusion, were believed by hundreds of men and women, who, in the ordinary affairs of the world had their heads screwed on right, to be wizard and witch; and that, though apparently kind and charitable, their alms-deeds and medicaments were but devils' gifts, which would have to be repaid with hellish usury one day, no one knows how soon. One thing was certain—neither the father nor daughter ever went to church. This would, of course, be the case, orthodox Church-of-England services being alone tolerated. It was not likely that " Valiant-for-Truth" Royston would join a prelatic Church, of which Charles I. was the first martyr, or encourage his daughter to do so.

The old man died dreaming, as I have said, of the immediate realisation of his Rosicrucian visions. Helen shut herself up in strict privacy for a while, during which time her keen, ambitious intellect was casting about to discover the true means by which gold could be extracted from inferior substances.

By and bye it was known that the lady-witch might be again consulted, and it was given out that she not only cured paralytic and otherwise diseased men and women by charms and spells, but that she could tell the future as well as the past of every one's life; and that any one who should incur her enmity was doomed to destruction. Helen Royston had a singularly melodious voice, and would sometimes of a moonlight night betake herself to a sort of arbour not many yards distant from a tiny lake near the cottage, where her father had kept several swans; and, herself concealed, warble forth snatches of delicious song. The singer being invisible, it came to be at last an article of popular faith that on certain moonlight nights Helen Royston assumed the shape of a swan, for some purpose certainly not heavenly, and known only to herself and the Evil One!

Suddenly an epidemic spread amongst the horses about the neighbourhood; scores died; veterinary skill was powerless to arrest the destruction going on, and horse-doctors whispered-solemn hints that the lady-witch was at the bottom of the sad business. Had not old Gaffer Hunsbridge, in whose stables the disease had first broken forth, quarrelled with and, being drunk, cursed her,—otherwise he would no more have durst do so than have taken a lion by the beard,—for allowing or setting on, as he said, the huge savage mastiff, without which animal she never left the cottage, to worry a favourite pup of his? There could be no doubt about it; and was she, because she was a lady-witch,—that is, dressed finely, and was beautiful—a device of the devil that too —to escape the well-merited fate which coarse and ugly witches had righteously undergone?

Certainly not. Still the most furious held back when it was proposed to convert intent into action. At last, the epidemic not ceasing, a professional witch-finder was summoned to the rescue; a kind of minor Hopkins, of the name of Stubbs. He had no scruples; and backed by a mob, the young lady-witch was seized, and spite of the furious resistance of the mastiff, who lost his life in the vain attempt to defend his mistress, would have been subjected to the ordeal by water, in the tiny lake where she had so often appeared in the semblance of a swan, but for the sudden appearance upon the spot of Arthur Morris and a number of college youths, who, like him, were at home for the vacation. Arthur Morris was the youngest son of the lord of the manor, and had been more than once seen sidling along with the lady-witch in her wood-walks. The interference of Arthur Morris and his friends was decisive. Stubbs, "whose heart was well in his work," angrily remonstrated, assuring Arthur Morris and his friends that whoever interfered by force in favour of a witch would certainly pine away and die before the year had passed.

The lady-witch was rescued and restored to her home, and the witch-finder's prophecy was realised so far as regarded Arthur Morris. He was the shadow of Helen Royston whenever she appeared abroad, and made some excuse for not returning to Cambridge, when he should have done so. He was not, however, it seemed, a favourite with the fair witch who held him in thrall; so Arthur Morris gradually pined away and died. At the last hour, or nearly so, of his life, the dying son prevailed upon his father, Sir Richard Morris, to send for the lady-witch, for whom the baronet felt almost as superstitious a repugnance as did the stupidest of the boors upon his estate.

There was no end to the stories related of the mischievous marvels performed by the beguiling lady—her supernatural reputation being no doubt much heightened by the eccentric vagaries in which she delighted to indulge. I have no space to reproduce the many curious anecdotes circulated respecting her.

At last another victim was about to be offered up to the siren's infernal arts. Richard, eldest son of Sir Richard Morris, the brother of Arthur, had fallen under the spell. He, like that unfortunate, might be seen wandering about the woods and meadows with the beautiful witch. Sir Richard was warned. He hastened at once from London, instantly took his infatuated son into strict custody —at his own manor-house, of course—and consulted his brother magistrates as to how a person who habitually conducted herself in such an altogether out-of-the-way fashion, had, it could be proved, ruined the health, destroyed the peace of mind of several very estimable young men, and caused a pestilence amongst the cattle for miles around, should be dealt with.

There were, it would seem, long and grave consultations, without producing any decided result. The stories told of the fair witch—her incantations, her flight across the lake, when, in the shape of a swan, she received a full charge of shot from the gun of a sportsman, screaming as she flew, and that in consequence of the wound she could not appear out for many days—broke down, even in the hazy estimation of the Doncaster Solomons. At last Sir

Richard, it was reported, had determined to take the matter into his own hands, and no doubt justice would be done. The lady had been summoned to the manor-house—that was positive, for several persons had seen her enter therein. Judgment would no doubt be speedily pronounced by Sir Richard. The expectation was verified, and speedily. "It is all settled," said one of Sir Richard's deerkeepers, entering a hostelry one evening. "The lady-witch won't trouble any of us much longer——"

"Hurrah!"

"Won't trouble any of us much longer: 'cause why? She be gwine to be married right out of hand to Sir Richard's eldest son! Talk of witches, I say. Whe-e-w!"

A DESCENDANT OF OWEN GLENDOWER.

I DO not vouch for the authenticity of the genealogy claimed by David Ap Jones Ap Owen, sometime of Glamorganshire, Wales, and now, as reported, a saint of respectable standing, second or third only in authority and distinction to the great Brigham Young himself. Whether David Ap Jones Ap Owen really was, as he asserts, lineally descended from the warlike Welshman, at whose birth the front of heaven was full of fiery shapes, who could call spirits from the vasty deep, but which spirits, if we may believe sceptical Hotspur, did not as a rule come at his call—David Ap Jones was certainly heir-apparent, whilst only six years old, to a pretty estate in the vicinity of Glamorgan, his widowed mother having died soon after her beloved wayward boy had passed his sixth birthday. He moreover inherited shares in coal and iron mines, and was thought to be heir to a nett rental of something like two thousand pounds a-year—not to speak of the accumulations, judiciously invested by his guardians, two highly-respected Welsh notabilities, which he would come into possession of on the day he attained his majority. Blessed moreover with health, strength, fine animal spirits, and a handsome person, David Ap Jones was assuredly, could he have thought so, one of the luckiest fellows upon the face of the earth. The genealogy, reaching up to Glendower, might be, and probably was, moonshine; but the estate and mining shares were substantial verities, in the title to which the most critical and jaundiced antiquary in creation could detect no flaw. Fortunate youth!

Fortunate, do you say? David Ap Jones would have replied, whilst yet but sixteen—" a disputatious lad from

his youth upwards," swore one of his guardians in an
affidavit filed for a certain purpose, to be presently mentioned, in the High Court of Chancery. "Fortunate, do
you say? No, I am a robber, sir. The arrangements of
society are most absurd, and I am one of its absurdest
illustrations. What right, what possible right can I
have to the property which the unsocial law will give
me in a few years? None whatever. A new gospel is
being preached upon the earth, and its apostle is Robert
Owen."

In sober sadness, this descendant of Owen Glendower
—*that* now was a distinction of which he might be legiti-
mately proud—was an enthusiastic adherent at a very
early age to the social theories of amiable, crack-brained
Robert Owen. He was endowed with fine qualities—
brave, unselfish, generous—a heart open as day to melt-
ing charity; but all of which merits, in the eyes of his
matter-of-fact friends and relatives, were marred by his
ridiculous notions of social equality, equally divided pa-
rallelograms, and the like subversive nonsense.

Once, it would seem, in or about 1825-6, his friends
had hopes of him. His fancy was caught by the charms
of a young lady whom he met with at a county ball at
Shrewsbury. A new light dawned upon him as to the
expediency of sharing every thing with every body. He
would have no partnership in the divine Miss ——.
Certainly not. He proposed for the lady's hand—was
conditionally accepted; meaning that he might hope to
lead the enchantress to the hymeneal altar, if, after due
inquiries and wary negotiations, the " settlements" could
be satisfactorily arranged. This, to such a young gentleman as Owen Glendower's Owenised descendant, must
have been altogether distasteful, disgusting. But he
reflected that the peerless divinity herself could have
had no voice in the initiation of such a slave-mart bargain: he would appeal direct to her. Love in a parallelo-
gram would more than suffice for him; and no doubt the
same sublimity of sentiment animated the gentle bosom
of his beloved. Influenced by that conviction or feeling,

David Ap Jones, Esquire, of Glendower Hall, Glamorganshire, penned the following missive, which subsequently
formed one of the grounds of a petition to the Court of
Chancery from his relatives, either to order a commission
de lunatico inquirendo, or at least to issue an injunction
to restrain him from making over a fine property which
had been in the Ap Jones Ap Owen family for thirty
descents, to social swindlers, or dreamers—the petitioners
inclining for choice to the stronger designation. Such
was the malignity of the old immoral world, as seen
through socialist spectacles! In this particular instance,
however, that malignity was foiled by Lord Chancellor
Eldon, who, after much less doubting than he was wont
to indulge in, dismissed the petition *in re* David Ap
Jones Ap Owen. The following is a copy of the letter:

"DEAREST,—The fluttering delight with which I
read your brief, charming though brief, note in answer
to the letter I addressed to you, no words of mine could
express. Angel of my life! every hour of that life shall
be devoted to promote, insure your happiness.

"But, as sometimes happens at the brightest noon
of a summer's day, an envious chilling cloud shadows
and glooms the splendour and warmth of the genial day,
so has a letter from Mr. ——, your esteemed, well-
meaning guardian, obscured, chilled the sunshine of soul
kindled by your smiles. He talks of ' settlements.' I
am to tie up estates, which but a few weeks since I came
into legal possession of, for supposititious heirs: other
conditions are mentioned, the sordid air of which could
only be proposed by a gentleman whose natural goodness of heart has been perverted by the doctrines of a
false immoral civilisation, which doctrines or dogmas, I
feel certain, cannot harmonise with the philanthropic
sentiments of my adored Emily.

"I will, however, to prevent the possibility of mis-
apprehension, be entirely candid with you upon this matter. Candour, openness of speech, is indeed a necessity
of my nature, for which I claim no merit, being, as we all
are, formed by the force of circumstances and education.

"I hold as an indisputable fact that I have no right, no moral right, to a larger portion of the earth or the earth's fruits than an equal share with my fellow-men and women. I intend, consequently, to hold the property which the old immoral law calls mine in strict trust for the general uses of the community, and am now in communication with the venerable apostle of a new gospel of peace and harmony, Robert Owen, as to how the property at my disposal may be best invested in order to contribute, as far as it goes, to the general benefit of the human race—the community dwelling in this principality to be first considered.

"This declaration of a fixed principle, which nothing can shake or weaken, may, I fear, shock in some degree, I trust in a very slight degree, the natural prejudices which an erroneous system of moral polity may, by education, have engendered in your mind. I shall not therefore object—and I am certain that the Gamaliel without guile, whose reverent disciple I am proud to avow myself, would approve of the proposal—to settle upon you for our exclusive use, so long as you may deem it right to avail yourself thereof, three hundred pounds per annum. Beyond this my conscience would not permit me to go. Waiting with ardent impatience for a reassuring word from you, I am, with my whole heart,

Your devoted lover,
DAVID AP JONES AP OWEN."

In the Chancery proceedings the young lady's reply is not set forth. She was, there can be little question, alike mystified, angry, and indignant. Three hundred a year! Preposterous! She, too, who might, by a smile, bring Sir ——, one of the wealthiest magnates of Wales, to her feet. Not, perhaps, so handsome—certainly not so young, as David Ap Jones Ap Owen; but having an uncracked brain at all events, and a clear rental of twice the amount of that which David Ap Jones was going to toss to a lot of Bedlamites to scramble for. Three hundred a year! Absurd! It would scarcely do more than find her in gloves.

I take the foregoing to be a pretty accurate guess at beloved Emily's soliloquy, basing that guess upon the fact that the lady's guardian promptly replied on behalf of his ward as well as himself to the "preposterous" letter of the eccentric descendant of Owen Glendower, respectfully declining an alliance with a gentleman infected by such levelling, outrageous principles.

David Ap Jones forthwith fled from his ancestral demesne, spite of the dissuasion of his best friends, amongst them a well-known M.P. for a Welsh county, betook himself to London, where he consorted, in all innocence of heart, with the chiefs of the Socialist fraternity, and was seen, so his relatives alleged, engaged as a salesman in a bazaar at or near King's Cross, opened under the auspices of Robert Owen, of Lanark, and closed under an execution for rent.

David Ap Jones was far from being cured by that catastrophe of his "old corrupt world-despising" opinions. His vagaries, however, did not run in a straight line,—I suppose vagaries seldom do,—and he diverged from King's Cross to some amateur theatrical concern, carried on in what is now Wellington Street, Covent Garden; played Romeo, Hamlet, and all the topping characters; but had not, it seemed, hit upon his true vocation. Certainly he had the gift of genius, inventive genius, if it be true that he wrote a fictitious narrative, which attracted much attention at the time, purporting to be the actual experiences of a young man from the country, who had been buried alive by the falling in of the roof of the Brunswick Theatre.

It was written, unquestionably, with much graphic power, and I am inclined to believe that the damsel therein mentioned was no mythic personage, but the Rosina Kendall, a pretty and amiable milliner-girl, ambitious of stage distinction, whom the heir of Owen Glendower ultimately married, and with whom he lived in tamed-down contentment somewhere in Devonshire. His wife died—whether she was Rosina Kendall or not, but there is very little doubt about that,—and three children, all they had, followed her in quick succession to the grave.

David Ap Jones Ap Owen had not yet made away with the bulk of his patrimony, and appears to have contemplated returning to the old corrupt world, in accordance with the advice of the M.P. before spoken of, who had never lost sight of him. There was blood-relationship between them, and blood, we all know, is thicker than water; especially so in Wales, and amongst all Celtic nations.

Unfortunately, judging from my own standing-point, some Mormon itinerants made the acquaintance of Owen Glendower's lineal descendant. Their theories seemed to harmonise with those which had been the dreams of his youth. Joe Smith and his golden book were swallowed by the neophyte, and in defiance of the reasoning and efforts of his friendly relatives, who again vainly essayed to invoke the restraining power of the law, David Ap Jones Ap Owen, the descendant of an ancient family, if not of the half-mythic Glendower, sold his paternal estate, and, on the 21st of September 1846, embarked at Liverpool, in the Baltimore liner, for New York, with the avowed intention of joining the community of Mormons. He realised that purpose,—became, and still, it is said, remains the confidential friend and adviser of Brigham Young. He sustained the hardships of the exodus with the people he had joined, till they found at least a temporary resting-place for the soles of their feet at Utah, on the Salt Lake, and, as previously stated, is there, says report, second only in authority to the arch-impostor, Brigham Young. A melancholy catastrophe for such a man, who, no one can deny, was possessed of gifts, both mental and physical, which, under proper guidance and discipline, might have assured him a high social position in his native land.

THE END.

LONDON:

WHITING AND CO., 30 & 32, SARDINIA STREET, LINCOLN'S-INN-FIELDS.